THE FATE UNFOLLOWED

The Dark Ocean Saga – Book One

Phillip J. Peterson

For my mother.

Chapter 1

Daemon Pramoore was as close to being a god as anyone could be in a world without heavens, in a city without sky.

Even in a dead world, people will still look up. Their eyes will seek out the highest point and they will plead for direction. They'll beg for subjugation. In the city of Mallis Two, that highest point was Daemon Pramoore, standing stoic at the window wall of his office on the eightieth floor of Pramoore Tower, a ziggurat of black steel and mirrored glass.

Beneath his feet, the city spanned for miles in every direction. It was a glittering tarp of shadows, moving lights, and capitalist ads. Mallis was a tightly packed metropolis that seemed desperate to burst and sprawl outward forever, but it was restrained inside a monolithic wall that encircled its borders. Like muddy water crashing against shoreline rocks, when the city could grow no wider, it grew higher. It was a bundle of bricks and steeples that were bound together in the middle of a derelict world, and beyond the wall there was nothing.

Mallis Two was the only city in the world, the last city, built atop the ruins of a forgotten age that was now boiled down to the bare and embellished tales of mythology. Outside its mighty wall was the gray and umber barrens, a world of cracked deserts and brittle mountains. The sparse trees that had survived the planet's final days were huddled in tangled charcoal forests. Their gnarled roots wound deep beneath the dry and crumbling crust into the subterranean layers of silt and clay. Across the arid land, red dust twisted in sour trails of wind, and the only things that moved through the biting haze were the unnatural beasts of the badlands. They were larger than horses and weighed as much as two. They bristled with large, black scales and lumbered on four thick legs, with clawed, reptilian feet that raked the desert floor.

Above it all, above the barren desert, the black forests, and the bound city, there was the endless storm. Dark, torrential clouds filled the sky and encased the world in a shell of leaden dust. It made the nights as black as tar and smothered the days in eternal dusk. It was a fierce storm that covered the world and reached back further than any surviving record or living memory. Jagged arcs of lightning leapt between the sky's churning plumes and cracked whips of white fire down to the surface, marring the desert with scars of burnt glass, and shattering any structure that dared to rise too high.

Pramoore Tower was one such brazen building, as were the four towering obelisks that Daemon's ancestors had constructed at the corners of the border wall. They were built to defy the storm, to make a statement. The towers were there to prove to the population of twenty million souls that the Pramoores were beyond reproach. For as much as it mattered, the statement worked. Throughout a century of lording over the city, no Pramoore had ever been defied or denied. Their regal lineage had gifted the people with safety and security in an otherwise deadly world. But comfort grants people time to reflect, and the citizens of Mallis Two were beginning to think back and think ahead. They were beginning to reconsider the power they'd given to Daemon. They were beginning to want it back.

Frenzied light built in the clouds above the city and with an eruption of thunder like crashing boulders, it spit out a lash of lightning against Pramoore Tower. The brilliant light crackled at its peak and was immediately channeled into blue lines of speeding light that raced like ancient and magical runes down its face. They lit up around Daemon's office window, humming an electric hiss of defiance and coloring him in a pale-blue halo before fading into shadow a half-hundred stories below.

Daemon was an unflinching oil slick of a man with porcelain skin, black eyes, and black hair. His expression was hardened and stern, as though he had been sculpted as an angel of death and judgment. His face would have been right at home beneath a dark cloak with a sickle in his hands, but he instead wore a black three-piece suit with a purple silk shirt underneath. Every fold, every thread was perfectly fitted and perfectly pressed. He tolerated nothing less.

"How many will we have?" he asked with a deep and silken voice.

"Twelve," a man answered from the sofa across the room. Valen Kirsch was a finely tuned sample of posture and silver poise. He was long into his sixties with high cheekbones, a pointed nose, and beady eyes, giving him the appearance of a tall and wiry eagle. Even his soft wisp of snowy hair looked like thinning, feathery down.

"Twelve?" Daemon repeated as he turned from the window and leveled a predatory gaze at the old man. "You promised me twice that."

"That was more than a week ago, sir." Valen lifted his arm and tapped at the silver disk wrapped like a watch around his wrist. The face of the disk lit up and projected a series of holographic images into the air. They were medical scans of hulking silhouettes, plotting out bone structures, nervous systems, and cerebral maps. "One of the creatures is ready now, but brain activity in the others has yet to fully develop. These new energy restrictions have slowed our progress more than we had anticipated."

Daemon moved to a mirrored wall and examined the square shoulders of his suit then craned his neck against its snug collar. "The Energy Distribution Act," he groused. "The law hasn't even been enacted yet and it's already a thorn in my side."

"It's unlikely to improve. Even with the new restrictions, there are rolling blackouts in sectors three and five. With their re-election coming up, the sector lords are getting desperate. Each time they convene they seem to tighten their grip that much more."

Daemon straightened his posture and smoothed the lapels of his jacket. "Sector lords," he spat the title like poison sucked from a wound, "nothing more than hand puppets with imagined power."

He turned to cross the room to his desk, his mirror-polished shoes passing over a broad pattern stamped into the carpet; a square and a diamond, intertwined to form an eight-pointed star against a crimson field. It was the proud and perfect logo of Pramoore Industries, Daemon's inherited empire amidst the gray wastes. "Between the towers and our mining operations, I supply nearly eighty percent of the power to this ungrateful city, and those enfeebled politicians think they can tell me how to use it?"

Valen finally lowered his arm, allowing the bio-scans to sputter and vanish from view. "You control the electricity, Mr. Pramoore, but they control the people. Until that changes, we must still tread lightly."

Daemon waved off the advice. "How many of the lords do we currently own?"

"Four," he replied, "though it appears that Aldan Pharos is set to win Sector Six this year."

"Pharos," Daemon paused to contemplate the name. "Is that the excitable youth, always rolling up his sleeves like a commoner?"

"That's the one. If he were to win Six, that would leave you with only three of the eight lords. Pharos is hardly a supporter."

"Tell me, Mr. Kirsch, where is all my power going?"

"The hydroponic farms and medical grids I believe."

"Farms and hospitals," Daemon simplified with spite. "Of course." He retrieved a crystal decanter from the bar behind his desk and filled a tumbler two fingers deep with bourbon. "These cancerous people breed beyond control and then demand more power. And what do they do with it? They use it to live longer and breed more." He replaced the stopper on the bourbon and rounded his tall, leather chair. Smoothing his slacks with one hand while suspending his glass in the other, he sat and turned placidly towards the desk. "And now they seek to put restraints on me? They don't need power; they need a lesson in self-control."

Valen rose from the sofa and strolled with long strides across the room, choosing to not indulge Daemon's frustrations. He stopped to examine a framed painting that was hung beside a tall wooden bookshelf. The art piece was simple, overly so for his taste. It was a black ring on a white canvas, nothing more.

"This is new," he noted, forcing a right angle into their conversation.

"Yes," Daemon acknowledged with only half a glance.

"Rather simplistic, isn't it?"

"It's perfect."

Valen shrugged. "I suppose all art is subjective."

"It's not art," Daemon clarified. "It's perfect." He raised his glass to the painting as he sucked on a sip of bourbon. "That canvas is flawless white, the paint is absolute black, and the ring, down to the smallest measurement, is a perfect circle.

Perfection, Mr. Kirsch," he continued between sips. "It strikes the senses differently, don't you think? We can feel it when we look at it, satisfying some primal need inside of us. To seek it out is the only truly noble pursuit in life."

Valen rubbed the soft skin of his fingertips together in front of his chest, reluctantly noticing the tiny imperfections in their texture. He turned away from the painting and walked to the front of the desk, running his imperfect fingers across its glossy wood. "I see your new desk has arrived," he said in an overly diplomatic tone. "Ebony ash?"

Daemon leaned back in his chair and sipped again at the bourbon. "Directly from the Black Forest."

"You redirected the calibrite miners to the forest. That's a rather dangerous area for a vanity project, isn't it?"

"Is it?" he responded callously.

"Sir, each time a worker is killed in the desert we risk losing an entire shipment, to say nothing of our public image."

"Our public image? That's the opinion of roaches. Their misery doesn't grant them the right to deprive me of every little pleasure, now does it?"

"Of course not, sir. Their opinion of you is moot, but it is my job to shape their view of this company. Every time a calibrite miner is killed, there are press releases. Cameras are pointed at our work. Auditors and over-zealous reporters come snooping about."

"Don't be so dramatic, Mr. Kirsch," he replied. "It was over a month ago, and any casualties we incurred were well within the expected scope of a normal run." His black eyes sliced up at Valen, motioning with an amber slosh of his drink. "Don't forget, you were once one of these side projects yourself."

Valen's steely eyes stared through the desk as though he were crunching numbers in his mind and balancing a mental spreadsheet. When he seemed to have finished, he tapped two fingers with finality against the polished top. "Of course, sir. Will there be anything else?"

Daemon nodded and swallowed another mouthful from the glass. "Reduce output to the clinics in Sector Four by ten percent. That should be enough to put us back on schedule."

Valen raised his arm and tapped at his wrist, summoning back the holograms. "And when the auditors do come asking?" he inquired while swiping through the orange text displays. "Rumors have already begun to spread."

"Rumors?"

"Of course. People have begun speculating as to where all this power is going," he replied. "Even your own agents have started asking questions. There are whispers of secret laboratories hidden throughout the city, mad scientists conducting illegal experiments and sucking up all the electricity. That sort of thing."

"And where would they be getting ideas like that?"

"Well, they are agents, sir. You can hardly recruit an army of psychics without expecting a few of your own secrets to slip through the cracks."

"No, I suppose not," Daemon replied with a feline smile. He imagined the halls of his security force filling with those clouds of psychic whispers. He pictured them slipping from mouth to ear, blurring in a mixture of conspiracy, hearsay, and truth.

"The auditors, Mr. Pramoore?" Valen broke in, his finger hovering near his holographic notes.

"Power is an unpredictable thing, Mr. Kirsch. Lie."

"Very good, sir," he replied before swiping away the data and moving for the door.

"Mr. Kirsch," Daemon said, stopping him at the exit, "I'd like to meet with Aldan Pharos. Tonight."

"I'll have Ms. Weiss arrange it," he replied with a courteous bow.

Daemon called out behind him, "And raise the price of calibrite by four percent for the next quarter."

# # #

From street level, and without the benefits of elevated social stature, Mallis Two was a very different place. Under a sky of electricity and dust, the buildings were looming shadows with eyes made of colored light, and wicked grins shaped in glass. It was a bombardment of flashing adverts that were stitched together beneath crisscrossing skybridges and the roar of the elevated train. Sleek cars, covered in the desert chalk that had blown over the wall moved in a clogged formation through crowded streets. They pulsed between intersections like a bloodstream of brake lights, beating around the central, black heart of Pramoore Tower.

Hovering transports slid through the air above the highways. The light-laced, floating blocks, each as wide as a four-lane street, slipped above and below each other as they crossed paths. The ferries moved high above the congested traffic, allowing for rapid and reliable schedules. It made them ideal for industrial freight and public transit, but they never rose above forty feet. Anything that might ascend too high would be quickly struck down by a vengeful whip of lightning. In Mallis Two, anything too tall or too audacious, anything that stood up too proud was destroyed by the ceaseless rage of the storm.

The city was the sole survivor of the end of the world, huddled against the dark and cold, hopeless and helpless, waiting for its final light to fade. It was an end that would never come. Despite the howling winds and clawed beasts that battered at its walls, and the lightning that lashed at its peaks, Mallis Two labored on. Day after day the city survived because even in the ravenous dark, there will always be a light that is waiting to be found.

While the populace sulked and hobbled along, masked in upturned collars, there were still those untouched by shadow. They walked through darkness like someone walking on water, unaware of peril, shining with a light of their own. These beacons were rare and difficult to spot. Their glow wasn't that of a candle in the dark, but a camera flash of light, and only with patient eyes could they be seen.

The evening crowd of Deidre's Diner was a patchwork of oily hair and tattered clothes. Their regular patrons were the sheltered homeless, the swelling average of Sector Six. They made up the working class who had earned the right to live, but those lives were worn down to the nub. They were people with roofs over their heads, but the cost of that roof swallowed up all they could earn in an overstuffed work week. They weren't dying, they weren't living, nor were they walking a tightrope between the two. Whatever social safety nets that Sector Lord Kaddler had installed were just enough to ensure that the people didn't care whether they'd succeed or not. They survived just well enough to not lay down and die. They were the face of the weary masses, now gray and running like a masterpiece splashed in turpentine.

The small crowd filled the row of booths that formed an 'L' and hooked around the front of the diner. The remaining regulars and stragglers took up stools at the front counter. Overhead lamps hung above the tables, dimly lit bars of light that were dangling from metal strings. The tinkling clatter of tin on plates added texture to the muted murmur of casual conversation.

Deidre's was considered a staple of Sector Six, a landmark for the locals. The food was lab-grown, and the floor was sticky, but the portions were cheap and served on clean plates and with authentic smiles. That was what cinched Marianne Price's decision to work there. When she'd first moved to Six, she'd stopped in for a cup of coffee between job interviews. The generic brew was bitter but hot, and the woman who poured it, a bubbly woman named Dee, talked Marianne's ear off for the better part of an hour. Marianne had been desperate for the company, and Dee poured it out with every refill, always smiling, always genuinely excited to hear about the successes and hardships of her customers.

Marianne had later learned that Dee was short for Deidre Kane, and that it was her name scrawled in neon pink above the door outside. She was a big, mocha-skinned woman, brimming with stories and sass. She was a pile of smiling, chocolate marshmallows who seemed to know everyone in the city by their nickname. As Marianne had been paying her bill, she'd asked if the diner was hiring. Without missing a beat, Deidre slapped her hands together and asked when she could start. She also went into a tumbling rant about the weekend coming up and how she needed off to see some 'sexy stack of beef' at a comedy club. Marianne was happy to take the shift.

The two of them became fast friends as Marianne picked up the slack at the diner and Dee guided her through the pitfalls of life in Six. She helped Marianne find an apartment, a cozy one-bedroom on the outer edge of the sector, a neighborhood they called the Squall, just inside the shadow of the wall. She talked her out of buying a car, a fruitless notion that would only add to the overcrowded streets and would have her spending thirty minutes to travel a distance she could have walked in five.

The only choice that she didn't sign off on was Marianne's love life. Dee held her tongue when her fresh-faced prodigy had met Akara Krosse, the handsome stranger who had rushed in from the street. Deidre watched from the kitchen like a mother hen as the two of them tripped over their words at the door, apparently unaware of the goofy smiles that had taken over both their faces. She stared with her face buttoned up as the budding couple had made plans to meet again. Deidre never intervened, and Marianne knew it was eating her up inside.

Marianne was a young beauty, a weightless ghost of golden hair and soft white skin that could somehow walk through a room, untouched by its soil and cynicism. Dee had thought that, after a few weeks, the wide-eyed optimism of Sector Four would have worn off and been replaced by the gritty weight of Six, but it never was. Marianne was a cool breeze at the top of every stuffy morning. Plenty of patrons flirted with her. They were always finding excuses to touch her arm or talk themselves up. There was a new phone number scribbled on a napkin every day, but she was more than a little discerning when it came to men. Still, it was only a matter of time before one of them caught her eye, and this Akara fellow, Dee had decided, was as good a man as any to be found in Six.

He was young, handsome, and apparently funny based on all the giggling coming from Marianne. He was an accountant or some such thing, a respectable man of means. If Marianne had to date someone from Six, she supposed this Akara Krosse would do.

"Dee," Marianne called as she backed through the kitchen door, her arms loaded up with stacked plates and table scraps. She rounded the tiled walls and maneuvered between steel prep tables. The steam from the grill and the mist of the dishwasher wrapped her face in muggy moisture. "Dee," she called again, "do you mind if I take off a little early tonight?"

Deidre's head popped out from behind a shelf of well-seasoned and rickety pans, her black hair woven into coils that were clipped behind her head. She turned an eye to the clock then back to Marianne. "Early? You only got ten minutes left."

"Right," she replied with a nod as she lowered the plates to the wet steel beside the sink. "So can I leave now?"

"Sure, honey. I got this." Dee poked a curious finger toward her. "Hot date tonight?"

"Uh, a date, yes," she replied, knowing the conversation that was brewing as she pulled at the knot in her apron.

"Is it with Mr. Silky Milk?"

Marianne paused and turned to face Dee's big round eyes. "I don't know what that means."

"Don't play with me," Dee said. "You know exactly what that means."

"Akara, yes, we have a date," she admitted with a smile and a bobbing nod. "I'm meeting him on the Square, and I wanted to stop home to change."

"What's wrong with what you got on?" Dee waved a finger at Marianne's black skirt and white blouse, decorated in orange stains from the soup-of-the-day.

It didn't warrant a response, and Marianne just laughed, her eyes sparkling blue atop a wide smile as she hung her apron on the wall.

"Oh, sweetie," Dee called across the kitchen, "I almost forgot." She wiped a sleeve of soap bubbles from her arms and wrung them dry on her smock before heading towards her office in the back. Marianne followed her, slipping her arms into a thick coat with a furred hood as she went.

The office was smaller than their cooler, and only a little bigger than the broom closet. Dee kept animated holograms of her favorite dates on the wall. Some were handsome suitors with rugged smiles, leveling their smoldering eyes at the camera. Most however, were needle-nosed men that appeared to be drowning in confusion. Dee loved them all. The single life was her buffet. The centerpiece of it all though was a square-jawed black man with a sculpted smile. 'He was the one that got away,' she'd always say. He was also the one who bought her a jade succulent that was now a lump of brown mulch in a very expensive, ceramic pot on her desk.

"I saw this last night," Dee said, flipping through a series of displays on a small, rectangular datapad. Each screen of text was decorated with animated pictures and company logos, all of which Dee ignored until she found the article she was looking for. "Available immediately," she began to read.

Marianne's head dropped to the side. "Come on, Dee."

"Research Assistant at Clairmont Pharmaceutical Labs," she continued, speaking louder on the words that sounded most impressive. "Applicant will be responsible for monitoring pheno... typing... array something," her voice shrunk as she muttered through the words. "I don't know what that is," she finally admitted and swiped the article away, "but I bet you do."

"Dee, I like it here. I'm not looking for another job. Besides, I worked with plants in Sector Four, not drugs."

"Drugs come from plants, don't they?" she argued. "You're so much better than all this, sweetie. You were a scientist. A *scientist*. You went to college. You helped people."

"I still help people," Marianne said, then pointed a finger at the dining room. "I just cut Mr. Hurley's fillet for him. His arthritis is getting worse."

"That's exactly what I'm talkin' about," Dee said. "Pattin' folks on the back, cuttin' up their meats for 'em. You're makin' these people happy. You're goin' around givin' 'em hope. It's not healthy. And it's not good for business."

Marianne laughed. "What's wrong with hope?"

"This is Sector Six, honey. Hopelessness is all these folk have got left. If you start puttin' ideas in their heads like 'a better tomorrow', they might start to believe it."

"So?"

Dee's voice went soft and serious. "So, what happens when it never comes, sugar?"

Marianne paused and dialed back her jubilation. She tried to match the somber tone, but her smile was fixed with gentle adoration. "Well maybe if enough of them believe in it, it might."

"There's just no gettin' through to you." Dee sighed with feigned disappointment and surrender.

"I know, I'm the worst." She tapped at the clock beside the door. "And I'm late." Marianne planted a quick peck on Dee's rounded cheek then slipped out the door. "I'll give Akara your love."

"Give him your own love!" she yelled back before grumbling on about the value of her particular brand of love.

Periphery Boulevard was the four-lane artery of Mallis Two. It carved out a ring inside the city, dividing each of the eight sectors in half. On the outside of the ring, low-income and makeshift housing was tucked in at the base of the wall. From crumbling apartments to aluminum cubes that were bolted together and stacked ten high, more than half of the city's population was crammed together in a weave of back alleys and repurposed garbage.

Inside Periphery's circle, however, was the vibrant tangle of life and light that gave Mallis Two its purpose. Each sector had a theme that seemed most prominent along the inside arc of the highway as it cleaved through each pie-sliced borough. Sector One, the theater district, was a deep stretch of radiant fonts and scrolling marquees. Its sidewalks were always adorned in silk fashion and black ties discussing the latest performance. In Sector Four, the garden district, the curve of Periphery was lined with slotted, ivory towers. Dozens of stark silos huddled together, each of their layers filled with the slim selection of grains and lab-grown fruit that fed the hungry populace. Natural vegetation was a rarity reserved for the rich, but even in the slums, a couple could treat themselves to a weekend of synthetic steak and green leaves.

Sector Six was the outlier of the city with no distinction on either side of the road. It was a gaudy flare of nightlife. Its stacked hovels spilled from the crux of the wall, across the boulevard, and mingled into spaces between the multi-story bars, seedy arcades, and strip clubs. Six was the forgotten middle child of the city. The laws were lax and overlooked. The buildings were old and veined with cracks, pocketed with secret, bygone rooms. The hunched and huddled people were ignored and, for the most part, that's exactly how they liked it.

In Sector Six, even the homeless had homes if you were willing to stretch the definition thin enough. Sandwiched between every column of rundown apartments were alleyways draped in colored awnings and hanging lights. Unkempt shopkeepers peddled polished junk and served up steaming plates of meat that always tasted better when you didn't ask too many questions. It was a perfect bustling beehive of neon and nihilism for someone to disappear inside.

Akara Krosse was nobody in the swarming crowds of Six. He was another twenty-something face, shadowed beneath the downturned brim of a black fedora, with his body wrapped in a long leather coat. Snaking down from under the hat, his hair was tied back in a silken tail, held by a knot of silver behind his neck. The street vendor hawking mid-grade jewelry on the side of the road never asked him for his name. Akara was just a young man with money to spend and a woman to impress, so he handed him the loose pair of sapphire earrings and they parted ways.

The jeweled facets gleamed in Akara's open hand. They would nearly match Marianne's eyes; a shade of deep blue that had no business shining in a world gone gray. It was their five-month anniversary. He imagined five months was a trifling span for most, but for Akara, every milestone mattered. He'd never had a relationship before. He'd never even spoken to a human until he'd met Marianne.

Of course, he could never tell her that. He could never tell her the truth. His secrets didn't belong to him. They were the secrets of his father and of their people. All Akara could do was buy her pretty gifts. He could piece together poetry and cherish every night until the world might choose to change. He could spend his evenings beside her, reminding her of how she made him feel, then he would disappear from the world once more, to count the hours through another torpid day until he could see her again.

"Akara," her voice carried on the breeze across the street. It was smooth and melodic, like a three-note song she was born to sing. That was Akara's favorite sound, her voice speaking his name.

He stuffed the earrings into his pocket then turned toward the music. He found her immediately. Despite the dusky gloom and dense crowds, he could always find her. She stood apart, unmarred by the grainy streets and growling skies. Where others wore gray coats and huddled against the wind, she wore a blue silk dress and a sheer and glittering shawl. Where others were weighted by unwashed mats of hair, hers was a crown of vibrant gold that poured across her bare shoulders. Most noticeable though, what caught his eye every time and clipped her out from the prosaic world like a paper doll was her smile. Marianne was always smiling. It shone like a halo for anyone who bothered to look up. She was a light within a sea of despondent strangers.

Akara smiled back and raised his hand above the masses. Marianne broke from the sidewalk and crossed between the slow crawl of vehicles that jammed up the streets, then she hopped up the curb to greet him.

"There you are," she said, grabbing and hugging his arm. "I thought I'd lost you."

"Sorry, I lost track of time."

"Distracted again?" she asked while scanning the collection of booths and wares.

"Distracted? No, not at all." He followed her glance and shooed away the jeweler's attention with a flicking nod. The vendor's eyes popped open. He smiled knowingly at the couple then turned an exaggerated and innocent look to the sky. Satisfied, Akara turned back to Marianne. "You just usually run a little late when you're at work."

"Sometimes, maybe, but tonight's special. It's our five-month anniversary."

# # #

In dark worlds and in dark times, avenues of escapism are squeezed out of us by the pressures of simply being alive. They are veins that burst open the seams of our weakest traits. For some, these bleeding paths of clemency are violence, or drugs, or sordid entertainment. We instinctively struggle to reel in these floodgates, often through sheer force of will, but many excise these pressures by seeking out release. This is the birthplace of art; untempered emotion spilling onto canvas in the form of music, paint, and poetry. People will search for something deeper and larger than themselves, an assurance that there is more than the prison cell inside their minds.

In Mallis Two, when the streets seemed too thick or the storm hung too low, the people would 'walk the wall'. Large, open-platform lifts could carry ten at a time to the walkways atop the great barrier that surrounded the city. A hundred feet above the streets, the citizens would gather and stroll its elevated rim. Though it was wide enough for a car, the pathway hosted only peddlers and pedestrians, too dispirited to endure the cumber of the streets. They'd gaze out across the desert and watch lightning stab at the horizon. They'd gather into cliques to discuss any opinion they could pluck from the bouquet of their daily grinds. They'd do anything to pretend for a moment that they were anywhere else but trapped inside their lives.

One of these crestfallen orphans was a young girl named Bwrynn Lucane. She sat with her back to the desert, ducked down behind the brick railing of the wall. Her soft face, midway into its teens, was hidden beneath a thick mess of black curls, and her small frame was wrapped in a heavy cloak. With her knees tucked up against her, she held her hand open towards her face, the holographic text of another book swiping by in her palm.

The people passing by gave a wide berth to the little pile of a girl. The umbral cloak that she wore like an armored shell was adorned with silver markings along its edges. They were cryptic sigils that few understood, but everyone knew what they meant. The quiet creature sitting alone at the top of the wall, lost in the glow of her text, was an agent of the Dark Ocean Legacy, Daemon Pramoore's psychic police force.

Bwrynn understood every symbol embroidered in the cloth. She could even translate them from their ancient Caern script, the language of the previous world from which they stemmed. Her life, from her earliest memories to her latest bookmark, was a tunnel that burrowed through books, collecting tiny pearls of science and secrets along the way. Locked behind her deep and flicking eyes, she'd amassed countless anthologies and mountains of ideas that others had thrown away.

No one would ever ask about her cherished secrets. No one ever had before, and joining the Legacy, wrapping herself in that cabalistic cloak ensured that no one would ever dare speak to her again; nothing beyond official business anyway. It was just as well. Even before her initiation, Bwrynn had never been very good at conversation. Not to say she hadn't tried. Oftentimes, before she could realize, she'd be banter-deep in small talk with cooing strangers who cared too much about a girl too quiet. Then she'd glean a recessed thought from their minds and try to relate where it wasn't wanted. She'd under-share and over-share and stumble over pleasantries. Eventually she'd always mess up and then give up. She'd shoo them away and stare back into her books, pretending to read while cursing herself for every fumbled phrase.

The cloak protected her from all of that. It kept people away and it kept her focused. The tomes of the Legacy library were her drug, her respite from the cluttered world. She sifted through the latest finds, re-reading each sentence when her attention slipped. Her mind continued to teeter between the depths of written history and the uncertainty of the present. There was just one man with which her words had become effortless, a wise and smiling old man whose eyes had likely seen more than Bwrynn could ever hope to read in her books. He was the man who found her, and the only one who understood her.

Jaga Demain had been her master in the Legacy since the day she'd crossed its marbled threshold. His thoughts had always come honestly across her budding psychic mind, and his voice was the only one capable of leveling the peaks and valleys of her nervous progress. Jaga had been more of a father to her than anyone, more than her real parents for sure, and more than the passing tourists who sought to fix her. He was her mentor in its purest sense, and now he was in danger.

She tried to focus on her book, but her attention trailed off to the desert at her back. Her mind sketched out an image of him wounded and bleeding in the dirt, the calibrite miners battling desert hounds all around him. Bwrynn shook off the idea. She gathered up fragments of her training, sorting psychic vision from imagination, but fear and doubt prodded at her. She squeezed her eyes shut and ground her teeth. Something dark was twisting at the base of her skull as Jaga's imagined screams punched inside her thoughts. 'He's fine,' she'd reassure herself. 'Of course he's fine. He's Jaga.'

"I thought I'd sensed a troubled mind," an old man's voice poked at her attention.

Bwrynn's eyes jumped open, and her head sprung up. Jaga was standing over her. He was very real and very alive. His white hair was brushed aside in thick, snowy waves, and his short, sculpted beard was shifted up into a smile that deepened the familiar wrinkles around his eyes. He had already removed the heavy armor of the caravan and had changed into his more comfortable smoky suit and cornflower tie.

"Jaga, you're back," she yelled, flipping away the holographic book and leaping into a hug that nearly toppled the old man.

"Yes, child, I'm back," he replied with a voice chopped up in laughter. He embraced her and leaned his face into her wild curls, allowing his mind to move past the previous week and be wholly present for her. "I had half expected to find you at the Legacy Hall, pacing trenches in the floor."

"I was," she said, "all day, but I couldn't handle another second of Bryce, and besides, you were late." She spoke the last part as though she were scolding him for disobedience.

"I am sorry about that," he said. "We had a few delays."

Bwrynn took a step back, her expression going soft. "Was the caravan attacked?"

"A minor scuffle with some hounds," he answered dismissively. "They were very small, and the soldiers made short work of them."

"Was anyone killed?" she asked after a long and thoughtful pause.

"Young Bwrynn, you shouldn't trouble your mind with such things."

"I don't like you going out there, Jaga."

"I know you don't, but that's part of our job."

"Our job is to protect the city, not cross the desert with gun-toting calibrite miners."

"Those miners are citizens too," he said, lowering his head and raising his brow. "They also supply us with calibrite which is used to power this city. Would you have them risk their lives for you without the favor of your gratitude?"

Her chin slumped to her chest and her hair fell back across her eyes. "No, sir."

Jaga rested a hand on her shoulder and turned up a closed-mouth smile. "I know you wouldn't. You're one of the most thoughtful and gracious people I've ever known. But don't let your concern for an old man like me cloud who you are."

"Yes, sir."

"Come," he ordered, straightening his slim stature, and wrapping an arm across her shoulders. "In my haste, I've forgotten to check in at the loading docks."

"Oh, your haste?" she perked up. "Were you clouded by your concern for me?"

He hummed thoughtfully and squeezed her into his side. "Who's the master here?"

Chapter 2

Most of the dives and diners in Sector Six were carved out hollows with empty, metal floors that echoed as you walked in. Food was typically labeled with little more than adjectives, and unless the patrons were hiding from something else, they would only stay long enough to refuel their bellies and wash away the flavor with sour beer. The tables would be thick with dust that had been partially brushed away by bare hands, their marks still visible as trails in the murk left behind.

That isn't to say there was no fine dining in Mallis Two. Most of the northern and eastern sectors were sculpted from white stone and bathed in soft lights. They hosted countless restaurants adorned in glittering crystal, red plush carpets, and mirror-shined silver. In the more regal blocks, even the static taste of calibrite could be overpowered by the scent of fresh greens and sugared bakeries.

The Castellar in Sector Six was ranked squarely in the middle. The flatware was matching and always clean, and the food was natural enough if you ordered from the right menu. It had the kind of ambiance that demanded proper silence but allowed soft conversation to whisper up and mingle with the light melody of a piano and the polite tapping of silver on ceramic.

The upper-class wouldn't dine at the Castellar unless they were avoiding the press or had gotten lost and stranded in Six, but it was the nicest place Akara could afford without drawing too much attention. He urged Marianne to order whatever she'd like while choosing a dark-grained pasta for himself. It was cheap enough to hide in his expenses, but pricey enough that she wouldn't think he was counting cost.

Their conversation, for the most part, was just as low key as his expenses. They volleyed topics back and forth with an occasional spike of wit and shared laughter. The moments that were strung across appetizers, entrees, and wine were paced by the occasional rumble of thunder from outside. It caused the lights to fade and flicker, leaving the room candlelit for stretches of slow moments. The dining room would go quiet, and the candles would dance shadows across silent smiles, then the lights would return and carry the murmured volume back with them.

Akara would steal each faded moment to look at Marianne the way he wanted to in the light, to study the curves of her cheek and the sharp, ruby angles of her lips. He would imagine himself plunged into a dream, the world having gone quiet all around him and only the two of them existed. Nothing was forbidden in those moments, and he could look at her forever if he wanted.

It was between a sip of wine and a serving of cake that his dream would end. A flare of lightning lit up the urban diorama outside before dipping the restaurant into shadows once more. This time though, Akara couldn't look at Marianne. His eyes had caught something else across the street in the burst of light, a slender silhouette of man.

It was little more than a shadow in a trenchcoat with a tangled mop of long, black hair. There were plenty of ominous figures in the city, but this one stood out. It wasn't for his mannerisms. The shadow man wasn't moving. Nor was it for his stature because, although he was tall, the man was thin and tucked away inside an alley. What made him stand out was just how invisible he was. While others outside walked or talked or even swayed in the crowds, the man was standing motionless and apart, as if he were made of stone. He was masked in darkness and his shape could only be carved out in the half-second, polaroid flashes of the storm. What stood out most however, was the glint of violet light where his eyes would be, and that they were piercing through the crowds. The man was staring across the street, and into the restaurant's window. He was staring at them.

Akara propped up a practiced smile as he took his eyes from the figure and settled them back on Marianne. "You have the time?" he asked.

She had just slipped a corner of cake into her mouth and flicked a hand towards his arm. "Check your wrist thingy."

"My wrist thingy? You mean my comm?" He held up his hand with the silver band clasped around it.

"Yeah, that," she replied, smiling with chocolate between her teeth.

"You're wearing a watch," Akara pointed out while motioning to the scratched chrome and sapphire face on her wrist.

Marianne glanced down at the watch and shrugged one shoulder while carving off another bite of cake. "It doesn't work."

"What do you mean, it doesn't work?"

"It doesn't work," she repeated. "It's never worked."

"Never? Then why do you wear it?"

She cupped a defensive hand across the face of the silver and sapphire band. "I like it."

The sentiment pulled up a genuine smile on his face, a smile that would have been harmless on its own. But Akara was already wearing a false expression, a feigned happiness that cracked in the presence of true emotion. Marianne noticed.

"Is something wrong?" she asked.

The question caught him off guard, but his surprise only lent credibility to his denial. "Hmm? No. Why?" he stammered while rebuilding his composure. His eyebrows lifted, his face stretched out, and his poise was reset.

She lowered and tilted her head as though she were preparing to attack from a different angle. "You can flash that smile all you like, but it's your eyes that give you away."

"My eyes?" The response seemed to jump without permission from his lips.

"Mhm, your eyes tell me everything."

"They do, huh?" Akara hadn't noticed that those eyes had grown wider as she questioned him.

Marianne took a proud and defiant bite of her cake then leaned forward on the table. "So, what is it? You got somewhere to be?"

"I do actually," he replied, grateful for the excuse, even if it wasn't true. "My father, he's got this thing and he needs me to do a little late-night bookkeeping."

"You have to work? Tonight?"

"I know, I'm sorry. I completely forgot."

She waved off the apology and sipped at her wine. "No, no, it's fine," she said. "I'm just glad we could spend a little time together. When do you have to be back?"

Akara tapped at his comm and pretended to read the display, his mind still hanging on the shadow man lurking outside. "Pretty soon," he lied, "but you can finish your dessert."

Their evening began to wind down. Their conversation was lighter and superficial as they finished their food and lobbed ideas on when to meet again. After the bill was paid and they were gathering up their coats, the storm flared outside and lit up the street once more. Akara tilted half his attention to the window. The alley was empty. The shadow man was gone.

# # #

When the world had ended it came as a fire from the sky. A meteor had punched a hole in the land beyond the wall. It carved out canyons, splintered mountains, and burned the world to ash. It had shattered and buried the original city of Mallis and extinguished all but the brightest flames of life. It was that destruction, they say, which summoned the endless storm and cast the surviving world into darkness. But this harbinger from the skies had brought not only death, it brought life as well. A strange radiation from the fractured crater had begun to transform the land. Most of the world became mutated and toxic, but one stone in particular had changed into something else: calibrite.

It was the ancestors of Daemon Pramoore who had first discovered the secret of the desert stone. They taught the other survivors that, when activated, calibrite would not only absorb contaminants from the air and water, but it would generate a fair amount of heat as well. A single, yellow brick could be recycled several times, purifying hundreds of gallons of water, and powering a dozen generators for a week.

Since those early days, the Pramoore family has controlled the flow of calibrite. The inconspicuous stone had become their generation's discovery of fire, and for more than two hundred years, they used its power to rebuild the great walled city. Once each year, then twice, then soon every month, for as far back as memory could reach, the Pramoore's caravans would venture beyond the wall and out to the desert. Miners and soldiers would brave the elements and the desert hounds, skirting the edge of radiation to harvest the waxy stone and bring it back to the furnaces in the heart of Mallis Two.

The most recent excursion had just returned, and two large tankers had already been backed into place, latched into the loading dock at the base of a refinery. Their heavy treads were still caked with the gray soil of the desert and their armor plating was marred by chipped paint and long-forgotten scratches. Gunnery cages rattled empty along the sides of the trucks while workers scrambled to unbolt the remnants of another that had been torn apart. Its steel mesh was broken and hanging, with pieces of its last occupant still wedged and dripping inside the grill.

Bulky men and women dressed in battered and dusty armor moved back and forth along the entrance to the loading bay. They pressed their thumbprints onto data screens and mingled with their regular handlers, occasionally readjusting the weight of heavy rifles that were slung across their backs. To them the guns weren't weapons.

They were tools of their trade, dirty and damaged, their barrels still hot and steaming against the midnight air.

Four scouting buggies, encased in roll cages and flanked by fat tires, had already been parked further inside where masked workers were hosing them down. The high-pressure water scraped off the night's debris and dumped a pool of deep red water onto the floor. It washed against their thick-soled boots and gurgled down large drains in the center of the room.

Flushing tubes had been attached to the wide sockets along the sides of the tankers. Pumps hissed and rumbled to life, growling against the bustling night shift. Their chemical mixture kicked up a bitter scent that quickly overtook the usual oily flavor of the docks. The trucks had both returned full. Despite ammo cost and missing soldiers, the mission would be entered as a success in the monthly logs.

A slender figure passed through the docks, clacking out slow, high-heeled steps on the cement floor. Faedra Weiss stood out in any crowd. She was tall, slim, and fierce. Her pale skin was a white backdrop that highlighted her crimson lips and striking, emerald eyes. She had graceful, predatory movements and a head of thick and fiery hair. Everything about her gave the impression that she was a living flame, beautiful, brilliant, someone to be approached with wise and wary caution. In the clumsy sea of jumpsuits, hardhats, and armor, Faedra prowled the scene dressed in a black, low-cut dress with violet trim that left her shoulders bare.

She moved like a queen among her subjects, paying little consideration to the workers that zig-zagged and slipped by underfoot. Faedra would grant a look to the tankers. She would occasionally glance across digital reports, but her demeanor was spread out across the docks as though it were a being unto itself. It was a large, growling, and profitable beast and she was its keeper. So long as the parasitic workers kept moving, they warranted no attention themselves, and they always kept moving.

After another slow lap around the tankers, Faedra's attention finally zeroed in and hardened like a tempered blade on a single man. "Mr. Bathor," she said, her voice tightened with poise and practice.

Lumbering a full head taller than the scuttling peasants of the docks, Kaelus Bathor was a broad and hulking man. His face was chiseled into hard, square lines and his scalp was glossy and shaved bare. For all the pretense his imposing build could portray; a boxer, a brute, a blacksmith, he chose instead to dress in a cobalt shirt beneath a black vest and black tie. The clothing would have appeared to strain against his muscled form, but he wrapped it all in a long, navy coat that flicked at the edges in the bustle of the docks.

At the sound of his name Kaelus turned, slow and robotic to face her, his eyes hidden behind narrow, red sunglasses. "Faedra," he replied in a chilled baritone that was already bored of her.

"Three dead and five wounded," she said, double-checking the numbers of an orange projection above her wrist. "That must be a new record." The shadows around her eyes deepened, and her irises began to sparkle with green light. When she spoke again, her voice echoed inside his mind. "Explain yourself."

Kaelus narrowed his gaze at her. "Mind control? Really?" he sneered, his mouth shifting sideways into a square smile. "Your tricks don't work on me, you shifty witch." He tossed a nod toward the tankers. "The trucks are full."

"I don't have to control your mind for you to obey," she replied. Her eyes cleared, though her devilish intent remained. "I speak directly for Mr. Pramoore. My words are his words."

He stared her down without a word, asserting with size and silence instead, but she didn't flinch. Faedra Weiss recoiled at nothing. Growing bored of her again, Kaelus finally spoke instead with a curt and biting tone. "What brings you down from the tower, Ms. Weiss?"

"A call came in from Six," she answered with a tap at her comm. She flicked the information at him, summoning a buzz and orange glow from under his sleeve. "There's a rogue psychic and Daemon wants him brought in."

Kaelus glanced down at his comm then turned away from the entire encounter. "I'll send someone over."

# # #

Daemon was leaning back into the leather of his chair behind his broad, black desk when the office door opened. Valen bowed his head and announced, "Mr. Aldan Pharos, sir." He slid a knife-hand forward, directing the young politician inside.

Aldan's tie had already been loosened for the day and the top button of his powder blue shirt had been undone. He was a man clipped from a magazine, with thick, styled hair, a perfected politician's smile, and a strong jaw with just enough stubble to make him hard-working and relatable. His tie was a darker blue that matched his slacks as well as the jacket he had hooked on a finger over his shoulder.

"Mr. Pramoore," he greeted with an excited pace and outstretched hand toward the desk. "It's a pleasure to finally meet you."

Daemon didn't meet the handshake. He sat and studied the grinning man, from his pearly smile to his professionally scuffed shoes. "I'm sure it is."

"It's a lucky thing your people caught me," he said, finally giving up on the handshake and giving a gesture to Valen at the door. "I was just on my way home. My wife whipped up a roast and, as you can imagine, I don't get home for dinner much these days."

Daemon clicked his tongue and sat up straight. "Yes, it appears you've been quite busy. If the polls are any indicator however, it seems that your work is paying off."

Aldan feigned humility and turned up his smile. "Well, I don't put much stock in predictions, but I'm happy to give the people a voice."

Daemon hummed an indifferent agreement. "And what is that voice?" he asked, rotating his glass of bourbon on the desk. "What is it saying?"

"Well, I don't have my notes on hand," Aldan replied with a gentle laugh, "but I believe it's a simple message. People want transparency and equality. They want to know that we're all in this together, from the single mother in the Squall to proud magnates like yourself."

"Mhm," Daemon mumbled, then nodded out the word, "Equals."

"Of course. Take away our money and our fancy suits, and none of us are all that different, right?" He patted at his tie to make himself an example. "We just want to be happy. We want our families and neighbors taken care of."

Daemon didn't bother to stifle his chortle. "You're quite the idealist. I can see why the people admire you."

"Well, I appreciate that, Mr. Pramoore. Coming from you, that means a lot. If you don't mind my asking though, why am I here exactly?"

Daemon's black eyes narrowed and sized him up once more. "I do a lot of work with the sector lords," he said, then nodded towards Valen at the door. "My associates seem to think you'll be taking over Mr. Kaddler's seat in Sector Six."

"Well, I welcome the optimism, but the election is still a few days off and I don't have to tell you how quickly things can change."

"Certainly not. I am curious, however," Daemon added with a raised finger, "what is your stance on this Energy Distribution Act."

Although his smile remained propped up, a bit of the polished charm bled out of Aldan's eyes. "Well," he began then cleared his throat and stammered a bit, "it's a complicated bill, but I think it has promise."

"I see. Kaddler believed it was a bit of an overreach. You don't agree?"

Aldan shrugged with one shoulder. "There are some parts that could still be negotiated."

Daemon gestured wide to the room. "My family built this company, Mr. Pharos. It was a Pramoore who built the towers around the border wall that now protect the people from the storm. It was a Pramoore who rooted out and destroyed the tsesh while they were hiding in plain sight amongst you. Wouldn't you agree that Pramoore Industries has proven itself capable of making its own decisions for the greater good?"

"I'm familiar with your family's contributions to the city, Mr. Pramoore, but this isn't about me. If I may be frank, the people already don't trust you, living up in this tower with seemingly unlimited and unregulated power." He let the sentiment burrow into Daemon's steel demeanor, hoping it would dull its edge and reveal a man hidden somewhere underneath. It didn't. Daemon was a deity, an image made of shadow, painted on some cathedral wall, undaunted by the opinions of men. "You spent most of your early life in this tower, didn't you?" Daemon didn't respond. "You ate here, you slept here, you were taught by private tutors inside these very walls. Heck, no one in the city even caught a glimpse of you until you were what, seventeen?" He tried to lob the last bit with a laugh and a smile, but Daemon remained stoic and unfazed. "Even your own son—"

"My son?" Daemon finally responded.

Aldan bobbed his head. "Yes, he must be approaching his teen years now, right? Yet no one's ever seen him outside this tower. You never talk about him. I mean, even you have to admit that's unusual."

"There's a difference between secrecy and privacy, Mr. Pharos."

Aldan peddled back from the topic. He shook his head clear and refreshed his smile. "My intention isn't to meddle in your day-to-day affairs. As you said, you've got things well in hand. My goal is to simply pull back the curtain a bit, give the people a peek at the real you."

Daemon appeared to mull the idea, staring down his outstretched arm while he sloshed the bourbon in its glass. "I imagine you see that as some kind of reassurance."

Aldan hesitated, his expression teetering on the pointed peak of the wrong answer. "Right up until I said it, yes."

The lower lid of Daemon's eye twitched as though a smile were slithering beneath its black and murky surface. "We'll have to speak at length on the matter once you've been elected."

"If I'm elected."

"Of course," he conceded. "If."

Daemon's eyes shifted up from his glass and into the young politician, examining him as if he were a hanging slab of fatty beef. A grueling silence crept across the room like a panther on the prowl. It shook the pit of Aldan's guts, but he suspected Daemon was enjoying it, a quiet and trembling struggle for power in his own private pantheon. He seemed to be waiting for Aldan to break, and finally he did.

"Is there anything else, Mr. Pramoore?"

Satisfied, Daemon popped open his mouth and sprung his hands up. "For the moment, I suppose there's not. Ms. Weiss will show you out. Enjoy your roast, Mr. Pharos, and give your wife my best."

Aldan approved with an unsettled nod. He took two steps backwards, his feet eager to leave, but his eyes were fixed on Daemon, working to decipher the intent of his words. Daemon's cold gaze and stone demeanor though made it impossible to pierce his façade. Finally, Aldan turned and moved for the door. As he passed by Valen, he kept a cautious eye on the skeletal old man as if he were a statue that might suddenly spring to life.

When Pharos finally reached the hallway, Valen pressed the panel beside the door and sealed him out. "He's going to be a problem," he noted.

"They're all problems," Daemon replied. "That one is just forthcoming about it. I respect that." His mind was working like iron gears behind his eyes, stepping through and sorting out imagined plans. "Still, I can't have him getting the people riled up, can I?"

"It could prove troublesome."

"You said one of my bio-wraiths is ready now?"

Valen didn't mean to pause, but he did. His mind had already heard and played out the sum of Daemon's plan. It was grim and gruesome, and it peeled a wide grin across the old man's face. The very notion was the release of a long-held breath, and it took a moment for him to recognize his own silence. "Yes, sir," he finally managed. "Shall I make the call?"

Pramoore's eyes were focused like lasers on the door. He shook his head, subtle and slow. "Tonight is too quiet, too delicate. I want there to be witnesses. Let him enjoy his home-cooked meal. Tomorrow he'll be making headlines."

# # #

Despite his previous urgency, Akara and Marianne took their time walking back to her apartment. They talked about their days apart and laughed at each other's quips while she smiled and swung herself around on his arm. The streets were damp and sparkled black against the pale streetlamps that perforated the sidewalk shadows with oblong puddles of light.

Marianne's posture would shift each time they'd pass one of the rundown slums. She'd trace her fingers through the cracks in the buildings as though she might heal them with her touch. Akara would watch her and pretend he was living that life. He'd try to imagine they were going home together, that his world wasn't dark and somewhere else. He'd try to forget the shadowed man whose footsteps matched his pace at their back. For all his effort though, he could never forget.

Akara held out a gentlemanly hand, waving a path ahead of Marianne as they climbed the chipped and chalky steps to her apartment building. It was a rundown block of tan bricks stacked ten stories high with strips of window bulging out on every floor like glass ribbing. The front door was thick metal, traced in a yellow band of light, secure enough for a building in the Squall.

"Thank you for the lovely dinner," she said, swaying her golden hair as she turned to face him on the steps. "I'm sorry you couldn't stay out longer."

"Yeah, me too." Akara's head bobbed a few quick nods.

She reached behind her back and pressed a thumb into the panel beside the door. The light around it switched to green and the dull thunk of a heavy lock punched through Akara's distracted mind.

"Oh hey," he stammered while fishing through his pocket. "I got you something."

"A present?"

He snorted through a smile and shrugged. "Well, it is our five-month anniversary." He opened his hand in front of her, revealing the sapphire earrings he'd bought off the street vendor. They rolled to the center of his palm and a flicker from the storm gleamed against their edges. "They're nothing fancy," he defended, "I just thought—"

Marianne's fingers hovered in front of her parted lips. "They're beautiful." She clamped one hand over his and pushed the door open with the other. "I want to show you something," she said, pulling him inside.

Akara stumbled over his own boots, sputtering out confused sounds all the way to the elevator. Inside, Marianne just seesawed on her heels and turned an occasional smile towards him while waiting for the speaker to chime at the eighth floor. When it did, and the door rattled open, she clutched his hand again, and towed him to her door halfway down the hall.

It was warm inside the apartment. More than just the air, the rooms were small, and the close-together walls were bathed in a gentle, yellow light. The front door opened into a tiny kitchen that surrounded an oval-shaped island. In front of them was a simple living room. It was minimalistic, with a loveseat adjacent to the black mirrored wall of her television display. The far wall was a low shelf topped with a window that bowed outward and overlooked the street. Stacked and scattered along the floor were plastic totes, some left open and half-emptied. Despite the months that had passed since she moved to Six, she was still partially living out of boxes. She always defended the clutter by claiming she'd put things in their place as she needed them. Apparently, she needed less than she thought.

Marianne maneuvered around the kitchen island and pulled Akara down the hall, giggling like a child with a secret. Her bedroom was small and lit by a single red light in the corner. The bed took up most of the floor and had a pile of thick blankets bunched up on top of it like the cream topping on a pie. It was, without question, Akara's favorite place to spend their afternoons when they had them. There were two large pillows, one at the head of the bed where you'd expect a pillow to be, and the other lying sideways beside it, squished in the middle like a teddy bear hugged through a storm.

Like the living room, the back wall was a wide strip of concave glass with her bed slid right up beneath it. Akara had spent hours in that bed, staring up at the storm with Marianne sleeping beside him. For a flicker of a thought, he wondered if the swirling clouds soothed her to sleep at night or if the lightning spikes drove her in the morning. Neither would have surprised him.

Marianne ignored the dirty laundry on the floor and the dresser that had become overwhelmed by knickknacks and pulled him around the bed to the corner with the little red light. Her face was consumed by a smile by then, pinching up her cheeks and squeezing sparkles from her squinted eyes. She hummed an excited tone and nodded her nose at a small glass box beneath the lamp.

Akara contracted a bit of her excitement and stifled a laugh as he followed her eyes. The floor of the little cube was filled with dirt. Aside from that there was nothing but a single, narrow twig reaching up from the middle of the soil. It was crooked and looked tired, and it had a green-tinted bulb bulging out at its top.

"It's a..." Akara was smiling and nodding while sifting through embellished or flattering nouns. "It's a stick."

She jabbed at his ribs, her smile holding firm. "It's a flower."

"It's a flower," he repeated with slightly less conviction. Then his eyes and mouth scrunched up. "Is it though?"

"Yes," she replied with exaggerated gall and animation. "Well, it will be. I mean, it hasn't blossomed yet, but it's going to be beautiful."

"Wow," Akara worked out. He bobbed another nod and pretended to admire the twig. "That is really great."

"Nope," she popped the word out like a champagne cork.

"Nope?"

"No. You don't get to do that."

"Do what?"

"Patronize me."

"Wha— I'm not," he defended. "I'm sorry, it's just..." Akara shrugged and found himself searching for words again. He finally broke down and offered up an honest thought. "It takes teams of scientists to keep a plant alive, even under the most ideal conditions."

She nodded, flattening and puckering out her lips. "I see," she mocked with thoughtful concession while standing and wrapping her arms around him, "and do you happen to know any of these brilliant scientists?"

"I'm not doubting your skills," he assured her, "but you aren't working in the farms anymore. This is Sector Six. Nothing grows out here."

"Well then, it's a good thing I moved here. It sounds like you need me."

He rested his forehead on hers and smiled.

"Besides," she continued softly, "we have something they don't."

"Do we?"

"Mhm," she hummed out happily.

"A secret gardening tip?"

"A little bit of soil, a little bit of light, and a whole lot of love." Marianne let her thoughts sink into his as they embraced. She laid her head against his chest and turned her eyes back to the would-be flower. "It's going to be beautiful."

Akara squeezed her and looked into the little glass box. "You're beautiful."

She breathed in the scent of leather and midnight air from his clothes for a quiet minute before daring to ask, "Are you sure you can't stay a little longer?"

The question flung Akara's thoughts back to the streets and the shadowed man from outside the restaurant. He released a deflating breath and pulled back, keeping his hands on her shoulders. "Believe me, I wish I could."

She pouted and bumped her forehead against his chest. "Okay."

"How about tomorrow afternoon?" he offered. "You've got the day off, right? I can sneak out early and we can spend some real time together. We can catch a movie, walk the wall, whatever you want."

"I'm running a few errands in the morning," she said, "but afterwards, yeah. You want to pick me up from the hospital?"

"The hospital?" he asked. "Sure. Is everything okay?"

"Yeah, fine," she replied. "It's just a checkup. Booster shots and stuff. You can pick me up a little after noon."

He agreed and placed a celebratory kiss on her forehead. "So, I'll see you tomorrow then."

She looked up at him and hummed through a smile. "Bye."

Akara stared into her glittering eyes and said goodbye, but he didn't move any closer to the door.

After the quiet moment grew out long and unwieldy, a quick laugh slipped from Marianne. "You're not leaving," she said barely above a whisper.

"I'm not?"

She pressed her lips together and shook her head. "No."

"You caught that, huh?"

Sucking in her laugh with a deep breath, Marianne straightened herself up. "Perhaps 'goodbye' is just too final," she offered. "Maybe we should say something else."

"Okay? Like what?" he asked. "See you around?"

Her face scrunched up as though the words had landed sharp and bitter on her tongue.

"Too casual?" he asked, mirroring her expression.

"Very non-committal," she confirmed. Marianne wrapped her arms around him again and pulled herself in close. "Let's just say... goodnight."

"Goodnight?"

"Mhm," she hummed and hugged him, pressing her ear against his heartbeat. "It's not even a valediction, really. It's more like wishing you well until tomorrow."

He squeezed her with both arms and rested his chin on top of her head. "Goodnight," he repeated as though he were trying it on for size. He kissed her head and breathed her in. "It's better. I like it."

"I'm glad you approve," she mumbled against him.

"Well then, until tomorrow," he said, stepping back to perform a shallow bow. "Goodnight, Marianne."

She approved with a satisfied nod and bow of her own. "Goodnight, Akara."

He finally left and stepped into the hallway, watching her face for as long as he could until the door slid shut. After it clicked into place, the world hardened like armor around him. He left his smile with her and tightened his coat around his chest as he made his way back to the lift and down to the front door. The lightning and thunder welcomed him back outside, and the cold air swept away the warmth of the apartment. The street had even less color than before, mottled by flares of red and blue from passing cars. He stared through them all and quickly found the shadowed man across the way.

Akara didn't look for traffic. He crossed the boundary of pavement and cut a straight line to the darkened alley. The tall man in the shadows stood still and waited for him. His violet eyes were gone, swallowed by the shadows beneath his long, wild hair. He towered nearly a foot taller than Akara, but his smooth skin and shaded eyes matched him in age and complexion.

"Malehk," Akara said.

"Akara," he greeted with a deep voice and a shallow nod.

"What are you doing here?"

"So, you work for your father now?" Malehk asked, ignoring the question.

"You were listening?"

"As what, like a bookkeeper?"

Akara's jawline flexed, and he chewed at the answer. "An accountant."

Malehk stared down at him, his eyes grim and serious. Then his mouth opened and stretched into a wide and toothy grin before breaking open with a belly's worth of laughter. The tall, lanky man doubled over as the crowing fit shook his body and he braced a heavy hand on Akara's shoulder.

"Shut up," Akara said, looking away at nothing.

"I'm sorry," Malehk eked out between snorts. "I'm just— I'm just trying to picture you as... an accountant." The word spun up another round of wheezing cackles.

"Yeah, it's hilarious."

"For your dad!" Malehk cried. As his bellowing waned, he gulped at the air and hoisted himself back to his full height. He wiped the tears from his eyes, his laughter settling into snickering aftershocks. "Oh man," he managed to get out, "that's good stuff."

"Why are you here?" Akara pounded out the question like hot iron on an anvil.

Malehk hissed a breath through his nose and cocked his head. "Okay, fine. Your father sent me."

A hint of fearful confusion tinkered across Akara's brow. "My father? Why?"

"He knows you've been coming to the surface, Akara. He sent me to make sure you're not consorting with the humans."

Panic gripped Akara's stomach, forcing him to swallow dry air.

Malehk eased him down with an open-palmed gesture. "Relax," he said, "I'm not gonna tell him about your lady friend." He didn't seem to care what the reassurance did for Akara's tension, looking past him and up to Marianne's window. "If," he stipulated firmly before returning to look his friend in the eye, "you join me for a drink."

Akara shook a cockeyed expression at him. "A drink?"

"Yeah, come on, it'll be fun," he said, slapping a hand on Akara's back. "Besides, you owe me. I've been following you around all night, and you didn't even have the decency to take your lady to a pub."

"How thoughtless of me," Akara quipped as they turned and disappeared into the shadows.

"I am thirsty," Malehk said, bouncing the words playfully against the gray brick walls of the alley.

CHAPTER 3

If you were to ask someone to imagine a bar in Sector Six, they would picture the Under Point in perfect detail. From its dim, overhead lights to its round tables and tacky plastic floors. There was a long stretch of bar to greet you at the door, deep brown and glossy, and edged with brass pipe. Rough brick pillars and archways loosely divided the pub into separate rooms. The front held the bulk of the tables and a crowd of patrons, all compressed together up to the bar. The middle section was open with only slightly improved lighting, and housed the older crowd, clacking through games of hologram pool and laughing through loud, nostalgic tales of better times that never happened. The final portion of the pub was dark and sliced up with laser lights. It boomed with the bass beat of muddled music and heaved with smoke machine fog and the body heat of dancing youth.

Malehk led Akara to one of the tall, round tables at the back of the first room. It was shadowed and out of the way, but still in view of the bar. It was a quiet cul-de-sac nestled along the last stop of the waitress' rounds. A swirling haze of pale smoke lingered roughly between the tops of their heads and overhead lights and though the sweet tang of the fog machines couldn't reach the corner, the air was heavy with the scent of sugary vapor and bitter booze.

"This certainly seems like your kind of place," Akara said, hoisting himself into one of the stools at the table.

"Does it?" Malehk feigned a curious look around the room before catching the eye of a waitress.

"Hey, Malehk," she greeted as she approached the table, "haven't seen you in a few days. Can I get ya a whiskey?" The question was obviously rhetorical as she placed a glass tumbler in front of him, half full of alcoholic amber. She was a cute girl with two whips of blonde hair tied at the back of her head. She had a pointed chin and thin lips. Her eyes were synthetic and brushed with a wide stroke of dark makeup. The irises were bright pink shutters that routinely spun and dilated as her attention shifted from one customer to the next.

"Two actually," Malehk replied, raising the glass and gesturing to Akara.

She lifted a bottle from her tray, hovering it above a second tumbler, and squeezed the metal handle at its top. A splash of liquor swished and gurgled into the glass, climbing just as full as Malehk's.

"No, thank you," Akara responded with a raised hand.

She hummed through a fake pout and held the glass out to him. "Sorry, I already poured it. Bar policy."

"It's bar policy," Malehk repeated, shrugging helplessly with his drink.

Akara angled an upward look at the girl and took the glass from her hand.

"I'll be back later," she squeaked with a wide grin before continuing to the next occupied table.

Akara watched Malehk's eyes trail hungrily after the girl, focused mainly on the shifting pink leather of her skirt. When the crowd had swallowed her up, he turned a smile to Akara and wagged his eyebrows.

"Really?" Akara asked plainly.

"What?" he pleaded. "She's an old friend."

"She's not that old." Akara placed his glass on the table and shook his head. "So, this is what you do with your time here? Drink booze? Flirt with pretty girls?"

"You're one to talk," Malehk fired back.

Akara coughed up a laugh. "Fair enough."

"How are things going with her anyway?"

"Marianne?" he asked, shifting up his brow and nodding. "Good. Real good. She uh... she planted a flower."

Malehk's face cocked and waited a beat for clarification. "Good," he finally replied. "Flowers are... umm... a flower?"

Akara shook his head and waved away his friend's confusion. "She was a botanist. She likes flowers."

"Okay," he said with a shrug. "And I'm assuming she doesn't— " he let the question draw out and trail off.

"Doesn't?" Akara tried to usher the broken question along.

"She doesn't know that you're—" the words stretched out again.

"What, a tsesh?" he whispered. "Are you crazy? Of course not."

"Of course not," Malehk repeated back, shaking his head and spitting out a breath as though the notion itself were preposterous. "Although, telling a girl you're a prince could have its perks."

Akara spat a tired breath. "Prince," he said, twisting the word into mockery. "Prince of what? Rubble and shadows? Prince of strict rules and oppressive laws? We're roaches in hiding, Malehk, so what does that word even mean anymore?"

"Same thing its always meant," Malehk replied simply. "When your father's gone, you'll be responsible for all of us." He gave a wide and careless shrug with his long arms. "Besides, those outdated laws are from our parents' war. Maybe when you're king you can loosen some of em up, eh?"

"Yeah, right. And why? What would be the point? As far as the world is concerned, we're all dead, and they like it that way. Face it, Malehk, I'm inheriting nothing. It's a stupid title."

Malehk sipped at his drink and rolled his eyes before dropping the glass to the table. "Will you stop with that?"

"Stop what?"

He turned up an accusing finger at the prince. "Do you believe in the Sasha Kel?"

"Huh?" Akara asked as though he'd missed some lynch pin step in the conversation.

"The Sasha Kel, the Dragon Child prophecy," he clarified before tumbling his hand in the air while listing off its bullet points. "One day a child will be born, he'll save the world, restore the tsesh, all that?"

"I guess," Akara answered. "We were all raised on the story."

"Well, there ya go," Malehk concluded.

Akara was sure he'd missed another step. His eyes narrowed and he shook his head, searching for a bridge between the topics.

Malehk leaned in and chopped a hand on the table as though he were sorting pills while he spoke. "It's written down for us, Akara. The Dragon Child will be born, he'll fix everything, and we'll be able to return to the surface."

"Well, that's just stupid," Akara replied. "You think we can just do whatever we want, and some magical kid is gonna come along and clean up the mess?"

"It's in the prophecy." Malehk emphasized each word separately as though Akara had simply misheard him. "And as stubborn as you are, I don't think even you can stop destiny."

"And what if the prophecy is wrong? What if it's just a story?"

Malehk chirped a laugh into his glass. "The tsesh can literally see the waves of fate, Akara. If anyone can nail a prophecy, it's us." He tossed back half of his drink then pointed a long finger at him. "You, my friend, should have more faith in your faith."

"We've been wrong before."

He shrugged and smacked his lips at another swallow of booze. "So what?"

"So what," Akara scoffed back. "Is that like a motto?"

"Kinda," he admitted thoughtfully then shrugged. "If we're wrong then it's all chaos and nothing matters anyway, right? You, my dear prince, are too uptight." He nudged Akara's glass an inch closer. "Drink this. You'll feel better."

Akara gave a slow blink then slid a bored gaze from Malehk to the cup. "What is it?"

"It's poison," he answered, tossing the last of his shot into the back of his mouth, "and it's delicious."

#

Jaga had barely checked in at the docks when Kaelus Bathor approached them with an assignment. He'd hoped for a brief interlude of peace before being called back to duty. His mind already had him sipping tea with Bwrynn and rediscovering the rhythm of her studies, but Kaelus needed an agent, and they had the bad luck of being in front of him when he did.

The encounter had conjured a storm of emotion in Bwrynn's belly. Kaelus was an intimidating hulk of man, and he was one of the very few people in the city that psychics couldn't read. Dwarfed inside his shadow, she felt as though he were an angry mountain come to life, cold and lifeless, yet simultaneously furious and imposing. She hated him, and she hated herself for fearing him.

Resentment grumbled inside Bwrynn's belly like a jagged diamond that was forming beneath the weight of her own submissiveness. Jaga had only just returned from the desert, risking his sanity and his life against its terrors for the sake of the city and Daemon Pramoore's bottom line. How dare they ask another thing of him before the night's end? Even a young psychic needed to draw long breaths between assignments. Jaga was exhausted and his airy blue eyes, the pools in which Bwrynn often found her own respite, were wilting at the edges.

Beyond all those feelings however, she was laced with a guilty excitement. By serendipitous or mundane luck, this would be her first venture into the field. She'd reviewed countless recordings and watched every live feed of every arrest the instructors at the Legacy would let her sit in on, but she'd never been on the ground herself. She'd never had the chance to scan a real room for real rogues. The fact that she'd be aiding her own mentor her first time out bubbled up a smile that was difficult to mask.

Her nerves were buzzing, and her heart was hammering inside her chest as though it were begging for a peek at what all the excitement was about. Jaga had accepted the mission with grace and Bwrynn bounced back toward the car behind him. Every mile of the drive into

Six had her rocking in her seat and patting out nervous rhythms on her lap. Bwrynn was anxious to burst out of the car right up until they pulled in beneath the cement awning outside the Under Point Bar.

All of those emotions that had been pummeling in her ribs, fidgeting at her limbs, and cranking up her smile, they suddenly retreated into her stomach like startled rabbits. They were cold and heavy, as though she'd swallowed a rock. Staring at the foggy windows, humming with neon ads, Bwrynn's smile went stale and slumped. She mashed her tongue around inside her mouth and tried to swallow the dry lump that had become lodged in her throat.

Jaga felt the abrupt shift in her mind and allowed a bit of time to roll over them while they still had the quiet safety of the car. Its engine had gone silent, leaving only the occasional rustling of their cloaks against the leather seats and the muffled beat and clamor from the bar when its door would slide open.

"Nerves," he said. "Quite the bothersome bunch, aren't they?"

"Yeah," she replied with a shaky voice posing as laughter.

"Tell me, what emotions are you feeling."

"My emotions? Uh, nervousness," she said, kneading her hands together. "A little fear, I guess?"

"Fear?" he asked as though the word had caught him off guard. "Describe it to me."

Bwrynn turned a curious look at him. Her muscles were tightening, and she was shrinking into her shoulders.

"Indulge me, please," he pressed with a smile that folded up curves in his rough beard.

Her voice came out trembling and unfamiliar as she began to catalog the feelings. "Umm, well my hands are shaking," she began with a quick glance from her balled fists to the front face of the bar outside. "My mouth is dry, and I can't seem to catch my breath. Everything feels tight in the back of my head."

Jaga was nodding in silence like a doctor forming his prognosis. "Is that all?"

She replied with a hopeful and tight-lipped, staccato nod. "Yeah, I think so."

"I see. And who told you that was fear?"

Bwrynn stopped fidgeting for a moment and a wave of tension strummed across her chest. She gave Jaga a quizzical stare, not understanding the question.

"Dear child, fear is a thief. It's paralyzing and debilitating, but it's also surprisingly rare." He motioned out the windshield. "We don't know what to expect in there, do we?

She shook her head.

"So how could we possibly know to fear it? No, what you're feeling is power. Strength and awareness are pouring into you. They are arming you for any possible scenario." He leaned back and shook his head. "Fear," he said at the edge of laughter. "Can you imagine? My student, Bwrynn Lucane, the most stubborn and unstoppable girl I've ever known, afraid."

"I'm not?" she asked.

"The very notion is absurd," he answered. "It's insulting to the woman you've battled to become, to say nothing of my own tutelage."

Bwrynn looked down at her hands as she slid them apart. She found herself marveling at the vibration in her fingertips. She imagined electricity firing through her veins, and she welcomed the rushing sound in her ears. "This isn't fear," she whispered and reaffirmed to herself.

"It can be a bit jarring, of course," Jaga added, "but when you think you've got a handle on it, we'll go in, okay?"

She licked her lips and nodded, studying her hands as they hovered above her lap. "Okay."

#

The Under Point had just reached its stride. The line along the counter had doubled its density, even squeezing out a few of the quieter customers, leaving them to hover sheepishly behind the crowd. A bald and pot-bellied bartender was rushing between customers and taps, lingering long enough for courteous banter before sliding away to the next waving hand. The arm he used to volley the mugs was artificial, and he hadn't paid extra to hide it. It was a cluster of pivoting joints and pistons that flicked and hissed inside their bare, metal casing.

The pool tables had filled up and there were dotted lines of players waiting to take on each winner. They recycled compliments and trash-talk for every shot and raised their glasses to toast each game. One of the wider tables nearby had settled into a card game with modest stakes. Bets and antes were being tallied up on a hologram above the dealer's wrist and the players tapped at the table to indicate their wagers. Some laughed and applauded their fortune while others scowled and cursed their luck.

A hodgepodge of ever-changing music jerked the mood and tempo of the room back and forth. The crowds would dance and stomp their feet, then they'd sit and sing along with sour renditions. The few empty tables that had provided Akara with a social buffer from the bar had been filled up with loud and chortling drunks. Their howls and laughter and slamming bottles mixed with the rising volume of the room. Alone at the table with Malehk though, it was solitude enough, hiding in plain sight. The tables sat four and they were only two, leaving a spacious patch of land that was theirs and theirs alone.

Each time the door opened, a cold rush of midnight air would spill in between the rabble and draw the attention of everyone left sober enough to notice. The first half of Akara's drink was burning on his tongue and, despite mixing with the warmth of his wine from dinner, he still felt the icy draft. It wasn't the first of the night, but this one was different. The commotion of the bar sank as if the floor had dropped out from under them and a wave of tentative silence poured out beneath the music. It was reason enough for Akara to look up.

Two figures had walked in, an old man with a powdery beard and a young girl, masked beneath dark curls of hair. They stood like statuesque sentries at the door as it chimed and clicked shut behind them. Their age and build were opposites, but their stance and clothing were identical. Their backs were straight, their eyes were forward, and they were both clad in the long black cloaks of the Dark Ocean Legacy. They were psychic agents, members of the same consortium that, only a decade before, had hunted down and slaughtered the tsesh.

"Shen," Akara blurted out in ancient tsesh. He ducked down and leaned across the table. "Malehk," he whispered, nudging his chin at the door, "agents just walked in."

"What?" Malehk looked over his shoulder then recoiled back and joined Akara at the tabletop. "Shen. That's Jaga Demain."

"Who?"

"Jaga Demain," Malehk hissed. "He's hunted down and killed more tsesh than any two agents combined."

"What do we do?" Akara asked in a panic. "That's the only way out."

"Okay, okay," he offered after a moment of thought, "psychics navigate by emotion, right?"

Akara's eyes went wide when he realized what Malehk was about to suggest. "No. No way. No way." He was barking the words as loud as a whisper would allow.

"What?" Malehk defended. "We just shed our emotions and walk right past them. We'll basically be invisible to them."

"And what about our eyes when we do that? You think people won't realize what we are when they see our eyes?"

Malehk smiled and retrieved two pairs of sunglasses from his pocket. Akara twisted an incredulous look at the foolish and patchwork solution. His heart was beating cold and hard inside his chest and his breathing had fallen short and shallow. Past Malehk's shoulder, he saw the eyes of the agents glaze over and shimmer with ghostly blue power as they began scanning the room with their minds. They were out of time.

He growled and snatched the glasses from Malehk's hand. "Fine, let's do it."

Akara filled his lungs with a long, deliberate breath and relaxed his thoughts, allowing them to fall aside like beaded water. The skin beneath his eyes stiffened and shaped itself into several rows of black scales that cupped his eyes just above his cheekbones. His dark irises lightened into gold and began to shine with internal light, and their pupils sliced downward to form glowing, serpentine eyes. Anxiety and fear faded to darkness in his mind, leaving behind the skeleton and bare gears of calculated thought.

Malehk followed suit, his eyes shifting to deep and luminous purple, underlined by a strip of silver scales. They slid the sunglasses into place to mask their tsesh appearance and rose from the table together. Through unbiased eyes, the heaving waves and smoky wisps of fate became visible to them. Golden drifts of lights swirled around the room, twisting from the mouths of those who dared to speak and pulsing outward from their thoughts. Sharp needles of light spat from the agents to the tsesh. Akara watched casually as they passed through him while he made his way towards the door.

By the time they'd reached the agents, it was obvious what was about to happen. The amber smoke was rushing from their feet and biting at the hands and face of one of the card players at the wide table. They weren't there for the tsesh, they were there for one of the gamblers.

Without pause, the two tsesh turned and slid past the psychics. They were nearly out the door when Akara's coat lapped at the young girl's hand. Golden light erupted all around them, twisting like a dragon that had been awoken from its slumber. Akara's eyes shot down at the agent's hand and followed the swarm of fate into the air, lashing out blindly for its prey. The young girl turned her head and furrowed her brow as if she were straining to hear a distant sound.

Malehk's hand clamped around Akara's wrist and jerked him through the exit. When it rattled shut behind them, the girl's focus blazed awake and burned against the door. There was no one there, and the two snake-eyed tsesh were already diving into the deep shadows of a frigid night.

#

Agents of the Legacy are a people of two minds, each one blind to the other. Their forward mind is the familiar mind. It can see lights and colors, shapes, and faces. It's a mind they share with common people witnessing common things. It sees only what the physical world offers up and nothing more.

Their other mind, the psychic mind, lies further back in the candle-lit and secret corners of their brains. It's cut off from the forward mind, immune to its typical lies and misconceptions. It views reality instead through a crystal-blue lens which blurs the illusory edges of the living world. Through it they can see only energy, presence, and intention. Emotions rise from people like smoke. They breathe each other in. They breathe themselves out. They pour their attention into those who demand it and flock like scavengers around those who have it.

The concrete and metal walls of the city would all but vanish, save for the blue and white wisps of awareness that would creep across their surfaces. All that would remain was the truth of the living world, a vision far deeper and broader than the forward mind would have one think.

It wasn't uncommon for the smoky attention of onlookers to swell and heave toward the Legacy agents when they stepped into a room. That was the very purpose of their cloaks and posture, and their uniformed presence. An attentive and startled mind would leave itself exposed. Suspects would crack open and spill their secrets before realizing what had happened. This occasion was no different. The moment the door latched shut behind them, a heavy haze of thought tumbled toward Bwrynn and Jaga. The gray fog pooled at their feet and twisted up the embroidered symbols of their cloaks, coiling around each arcane shape.

Jaga had begun his scan of the room and he felt Bwrynn do the same at his side. Her focus was strong and well-trained, though it would stutter when moving from one target to the next. She was allowing her mind to process their emotion rather than letting it pass through her. It was a common trait for new agents and not a terrible sin, though he made a mental note to bring it up to her later.

The thoughts along the bar were tightly woven. People bumped and shoved, then apologized and scoffed. Most of their intentions were tangled up into tight and private auras. The crowded space, the brushing and mingling would fire up new strands between knots of people though the alcohol in their blood would quickly water down any sensation more than a few seconds old.

The bartender was a long brushstroke of wispy consciousness that spanned the length of the bar. He was a spiderweb of concentration with ropes lapping at the beer taps and bottles in one direction and a half dozen patrons in the other. His glow was bright though, happier than Jaga would have expected. Maybe there was a woman. Maybe he was just a man who loved his job.

In the middle of the tavern floor, drunkards of every age were shooting pool and playing cards. Their focuses were sharp and dense, and the winners were drinking in their opponents' moods just as much as they were raking in their money. There was one figure, however, that caught Jaga's attention, a card player with his back to the room. His mind was radiant and blazed like a halo of tentacles that would stab into his peers and gulp at their thoughts. He was a psychic, and he was the reason they were there.

Jaga had only just begun to analyze the man when Bwrynn burst into a flurry of panic beside him. Her attention flared up and out and spiraled toward the door at their back. Her concentration shattered and her power fizzled away. It wasn't uncommon for a rookie, and certainly not enough to shake Jaga, but it was clumsier than he'd come to expect from his star pupil.

Without a word or thought, he reached a subtle hand aside and grabbed her wrist. With a prodding tap of his thumb, he regrouped her thoughts, and she gathered her focus back up. Rather than have her restart her survey of the room, he ushered Bwrynn's mind to the psychic rogue at the table. He saw her intentions envelope him, but streaks of her own thoughts continued to jab toward the door. Her attention was shaken and split. He squeezed her arm and let go of the psychic vision. The dingy pub blurred into focus, full of electronic music and sweaty drunks.

Bwrynn's eyes had faded dark and deep again, and she titled her head up to read Jaga's face. A sense of concern played through his eyes, but he didn't linger on it, motioning instead toward the card table. She nodded an understanding then turned one last look to the door before crossing the room with her master.

The rogue hadn't sensed them, despite the other gamblers going stiff as the agents approached the table and stood behind him. He was too busy counting his latest winnings to notice the area grow cold and quiet. He was a fat man, stretching out the seams of a new tan suit. His hair was gray and balding on top, and a long and frazzled beard hung like wires from his face to his belly.

He'd been laughing and jeering his friends, but the laughter slowed and soon he fell as quiet as the others. Bwrynn sucked in a breath, straightened her shoulders, and braced herself for the encounter.

Jaga placed a gentle hand on the man's shoulder. "Pardon me, sir."

The gesture punched through the man's drunken shell and spun him in his chair. His gaze was met by black robes and silver sigils. He kicked back and toppled against the table. Cards and cups spilled to the floor. A half-empty bottle shattered and cut the man's hand, mixing blood and whiskey over the plastic tiles. He hissed a breath, his eyes scowling beneath thick eyebrows and jumping between Jaga and Bwrynn.

"Easy," Jaga said, patting an open hand toward the man's flailing form.

The rogue locked on Bwrynn. She felt his thoughts lash at hers like languid ropes beating against a wall. He was powerful but untrained and his telepathic parlor tricks were just a tantrum, pounding at her skull.

Her mind flipped from confusion to surprise then settled down quickly to the muddy banks of anger. 'How dare he challenge her?' Bwrynn's dark eyes blazed with ghastly power, and she gripped the man's clumsy thoughts. Her fury sliced down the belly of the telepathic rope as though she were dissecting a worm then lunged into the man's brain. He coughed and choked on the bile rising from his belly and his thick brows bunched together.

"Please, calm down," Jaga pleaded, but the man had already wrapped his bloodied hand around the neck of the broken bottle.

Bwrynn saw the drunk's thoughts spreading out like a devil's wings. They beat forward and wrapped around Jaga. The fallen man lunged at him, leading with drunken rage and blades of jagged glass.

"No!" Bwrynn shouted as she snapped back to rigid awareness and dove to protect her mentor. She stretched out her arms just as the man thrust his attack. The glass shards punched into her hand and carved down the back of her wrist. Her skin tore and what felt like wet fire began dripping down her arm.

Bwrynn's legs buckled, but Jaga was quick to catch her. She landed heavily in his arms and tugged him down to his knees. He saw the blood pouring over her delicate skin and overflowing the grout between the tiles on the floor. Jaga pulled her against his chest then turned a stern glare on the rogue. Wisps of blue light cracked across his eyes just as the man reared back for another attack.

"Enough!" Jaga boomed. His voice had changed to something unnatural. It was loud and full of rage and roared like furious thunder. All eyes turned to him. The full attention of the room swallowed him up in a whirlwind of smoke and light. Filled with the trembling minds of dozens, Jaga bore down on the fat psychic. "You are finished," he commanded, unloading a heavy emphasis onto the words to leave no question as to whom he was speaking. The storm of attention poured out from Jaga and plunged into the drunken man. It was more than his crapulent mind could manage. His eyes rolled back, and the bottle fell from his hands. His legs waggled beneath his weight until he finally collapsed into the wet and shattered debris of the fight.

Bwrynn was clenching the folds of Jaga's cloak with her bloody and trembling hands. "I'm sorry," she whimpered over and over against his chest. "I'm so sorry."

"It's okay, child," he said, wrapping her up in both his arms. "It's over now. You're safe."

Chapter 4

"That was really stupid," Akara said, clawing the sunglasses from his face. His eyes had shifted back to their human guise. The black scales were gone, and his irises were dark. Anxiety and panic smoldered and swelled then blazed awake in his mind like paper resting on a hot ember.

"Relax," Malehk replied, stuffing his own shades into his pocket, "they weren't even there for us."

"But they could have seen us, Malehk. They could have seen our thoughts, our memories of the others. You think my father is crazy now, can you imagine what he would do if Pramoore knew the tsesh were still alive? If his own son exposed us?"

"Umm, yeah," he answered after some thought. "He would kill me to teach you a lesson."

Akara shook his head, his pulse kicking up its pace with each passing thought. "We have to get back. And this night never happened."

They crossed the road to a single-story, concrete cube of a building. It had one door and one window, both facing an unlit side street. The window was small and covered in dust and cracks. The door was simple and featureless metal with a fingerprint lock they'd bypassed years ago. Taking up the entire wall beside the door, the numbers '6-4' were stenciled in chipped and fading yellow paint.

The tiny buildings were a common sight throughout the city, identical to each other save for their numbered markings and varying states of neglect. They called them drop parks, though they were little more than abandoned elevators and outdated software once used to monitor the water conditions and airflow beneath Mallis Two. Their vacant lots were overlooked and long forgotten, now unofficially used as long-term parking.

Malehk scanned his comm against the biometric lock. The door grumbled a lazy buzz and clicked open. They were greeted inside by a room that was circled in obsolete tech, mostly covered in tarps like burial shrouds in a mausoleum. Against the center of the back wall was a large mesh cage with an iron lattice gate guarding its face. For anyone left that remembered them, it was nothing more than a freight elevator that once lowered workers like coal miners into the depths below the city. For the tsesh however, it was a gateway between worlds. The simple lift was a portal between their subterranean isolation and the open air and dazzling lights of the city. When they stepped out on the surface, they were stepping into a realm of myth and wonder. Then, at the end of the day, when they entered that cage again, they would disappear, erased from the world as though they were never born.

Akara had typically found it to be a somber moment, as they left behind the city of lightning and lights to vanish once more inside the shadows. Some nights it felt like falling asleep, descending the elevator shaft, and fading away from the world. On other nights, particularly when he'd meet with Marianne, the elevator felt more like waking up, leaving behind the dazzle of dreams, and returning to a cold and rigid truth.

That night though, he couldn't wait to hear the rattle of the gate, the clack of the lock, and the howl of hydraulics as they sank beneath the floor. His eyes held fast to the front door while Malehk slammed the lattice shut and pulled back on a rusted lever. The lift moved slower than he'd remembered, and he expected the door to burst open at any moment and fill the room with shouting agents. His heartbeat counted down the seconds until they'd descended into the unlit crust of the world.

Inside the tight black walls, lingering between two worlds, the rattling cage went quiet. The tsesh were in the dark and silence, the metal box filling up with memories, and the smell of oil and whiskey-scented breath. The howling machines that lowered them beneath the city were reduced to a steady and muffled hum. It was seven seconds in the dark, then another eleven to the ground. Eighteen in total from one world to the next. In the sluggish moments to and from the surface, Akara had timed the trip a hundred times. Seven seconds to himself, to recall an entire night. Eleven seconds to imagine what might happen next and to craft an alibi for his father.

After seven seconds, musty air and wide-open echoes flooded the lift. They'd passed beneath the streets, beneath the maintenance machines and sewer pipes and emerged from the ceiling above Old Mallis, the abandoned city of an ancient world. Sliding down the elevator track, hundreds of feet in the air, they could see the wreckage of the forgotten city that sprawled out for miles in every direction. There were two distinct areas within the ruins. The center of Old Mallis was an island that was little more than two miles across and separated from the rest of the city by a thousand-foot moat of placid, rusty water.

The rest of the city was a thick ring of broken buildings and shattered streets, surrounded by a wall of packed dirt and stone. Centuries ago, Old Mallis may have been the jewel of the world, but now it was a potter's field, half buried in a ten-mile crater. The natural barrier around the city stopped just inside the great wall around Mallis Two above them. Large metal doors were embedded into the dirt walls, housing narrow roads that burrowed out deeper and ended beneath the towers. They existed for maintenance, though none had been needed for decades.

The ring was the best place in the world to hide. Though many of its archaic slums had been replaced by new machines that now roared and recycled water and air for the sparkling city above, Old Mallis still held countless blocks of labyrinthine alleys and hollowed out shelters. Enormous buildings, many of which were largely intact, littered the broad plots of the ruined metropolis. A few sticks of old furniture and a door left on its hinges could oftentimes even cast the illusion of a normal life beneath the world.

That was where the tsesh existed, in misquoted myth and forgotten squalls beneath the world. They lurked in the black ring of a lost world. Even the tsesh though, rarely ventured across the river to the core of the ancient city. There were only two surviving bridges and a single tunnel that reached the center island, but they were almost never used. The tallest ruins filled the middle of the distant city-center, still brittle and raining down bricks every day. They stood apart, not huddled together in blocks like the buildings in the ring. The core was a span of broken towers and wide, sinking streets.

For all its hazards though, crumbling architecture wasn't the reason the tsesh avoided the island. Above the ruins of Old Mallis was the underbelly of the new world, a steel framework of service tunnels, thick girders, and iron plates that held up Mallis Two. Slow blinking lights bathed the underworld in red and yellow light and cast long shadows across their metal sky. Thick pillars of concrete and steel braced the surface world, and basement-level pockets hung down from the city like braille letters overhead. None of them hung as low however as the sub-levels of Pramoore Tower. The inverted steeple stabbed downward at the ruins and pierced the island at its core. It was a tapered blade of black metal and racing, yellow lights, droning out an electric tone like an angry idol at the center of their world.

The black spire was enclosed. There were no windows, no doors or hatches. No one could see in or out, but the tsesh didn't dare draw near. The horror of the apocalypse had even blanketed Old Mallis in a fog of emotion that Daemon's own psychic agents couldn't pierce, but the tsesh were never sure of the full power of Daemon Pramoore or his acolytes. They didn't know what might be seen or gleaned if they got too close. Even their bravest and most foolhardy soldiers, even Malehk Knight erred on the side of caution and avoided the island core.

The elevator sunk below the nearest buildings, sketching up a new horizon of looming walls and crumbling bricks. Another second later, it hammered into place on the ground. Malehk flipped up the latch on the door and pushed the gate aside. The old wheels shook in their tracks and kicked up a taste of dirt and rust.

"Home, sweet home," Malehk said as he stepped from the lift. He moved to a nearby pedestal of controls and, when Akara was clear of the cage, he cranked a dial and pressed a thumb into its buttons. Both their heads angled up, watching as the elevator rumbled along its track and ascended back up to the sky. When they were sure it was well on its way, they moved into the street and began heading to the outskirts of the world.

#

There was no day or night in Old Mallis. Even in the city above, the clouds would lighten and darken to herald the passing days, but deep underground, the world was a steady, dull dusk of maintenance lights. The streets were slightly brighter around the edges where the beams sloped down, and the lights shone closer. That was where the tsesh had made their home, scattered amongst the broken walls of an abandoned college campus. A collection of dorms to the north acted as their private rooms. A gymnasium had been repurposed into their training grounds, and lecture halls had been converted into meeting rooms for the royal family and its council.

The two young tsesh hadn't yet passed beneath the yellow stone archway that led into the courtyard, when Akara sensed that something was wrong. The air was always still beneath the world, but in a realm of deprivation, you learn to pick up on subtlety. There was a placidity hanging over the campus like a curtain deliberately hung to blot out the light. The typical tension that's born from a society in hiding was gone, but it hadn't been removed, nor had it left behind an air of ease or freedom. It had been covered up, camouflaged in stoic reverence, like an apathetic mob boss inviting you to stand on a sheet of plastic.

When they passed through the arch, they found six of the elder tsesh standing in the middle of the dirt courtyard, circled by stone walkways and chiseled benches. Lord Rhago, Akara's father was among them. He was a stocky, square man with an equally square head that's edges accented the deep widow's peak in his long white hair. He was clean and primped, dressed in his white suit and navy tie, pacing the ground in front of the others. Kneeling at his feet were three young men that Akara didn't recognize. They were lined up before the king and their hands were bound behind their backs.

"Ah, crap," Malehk muttered after taking in the scene.

Akara's pace quickened, crossing the yard to the elders. Rhago had spotted them but gave no notice. It was Kade Whitlock, the king's advisor who stepped forward to greet the young prince with an open hand to halt him. Kade was dark-skinned and chubby for a tsesh, but he was tall for one too. Akara had come to view him as a jolly heap of a man, his bare cheekbones always curved up in a smile atop a coarse beard of dark and peppered hair. As he approached though, he wasn't smiling. His head was cocked, and his small eyes were slanted down with apologetic concern.

"Akara," he began with his guttural voice as they met a few meters before the small crowd.

"What's going on?" Akara asked.

"It's nothin' that needs your concern."

"On the contrary," Rhago called out behind him, "this concerns my son very much." His eyes were sweeping across the young men in the dirt. "Very much indeed."

Akara huffed out a breath and stepped around Kade. Malehk took his place, smiling and shifting up his eyebrows at the large man.

"Father?" Akara greeted, walking to his side, and turning a glance to the bound men. They were all in their teens, with young eyes that looked brighter behind faces muddled by dirt and tears. They would have been mislabeled as homeless were it not for their relatively newer clothes, now torn and as soiled as their skin. Akara shook his head and gestured to them. "What is this?"

"Meddling eyes from the surface," Rhago explained. "Clumsy and loud, they were caught pilfering our supplies."

"We weren't stealing, I swear," one of them offered up in a panic. "We were just looking around. We didn't know anyone lived down here."

"Your intentions do not forgive your actions," Rhago said, "and ignorance does not grant you additional rights."

Akara turned a sympathetic look to his father and mumbled under his breath, "All right, fine, but they're just some stupid kids."

"Inquisition has no age," Rhago hissed back. "They are vectors. Their world is stitched together by a web of whispers. A single word from their lips can pluck a strand and shake the whole."

Akara looked over his shoulder at Malehk who had been watching the exchange. His remorseful eyes locked on Akara's and tried to convey some message. He looked as though he were extending some sense of consolation, but Akara couldn't read it.

"Father, this is stupid," Akara said, turning back to the king. "You've frightened them, now cut them loose. What harm could they do us?"

"We won't say anything," another teen promised.

"You're still young," Rhago answered back to his son, "and though it is senseless, if you must shed your emotions for this, you may."

His mind had been cemented and Akara may as well have been talking to a stone. He hissed a breath through his teeth and bowed his head with his back to the young men. "Father, please," he pleaded one last time, but Rhago wasn't listening. The king drew a long, straight blade from under his coat with a slow and ritualistic motion. Akara bit down hard, then released his mind. His eyes hardened into their serpentine shape and his horror was sucked from his mind like a soul being excised from a body. Without emotion, he turned back to face the young men with cold, golden eyes.

"Y— you're— you're tsesh?" one of them blurted in a child-like squeak.

"No, no, no," another said. "They can't be. The tsesh are all dead. They're dead!"

Rhago held the sword at a downward angle away from his body and spoke like a priest to his congregation. "How does a tsesh dodge bullets?"

"By being where the bullets are not," the other tsesh recited back. Akara chanted with them.

At the end of the answer, Rhago struck like a cobra, slicing the sword across the first captive's throat, nearly severing his head. He gasped and gurgled and slumped aside. He thrashed in the dust and gravel, his blood pouring out a deep and dirty red toward Rhago's polished shoes. The other teens screamed. They howled and kicked their feet in the dirt, falling backwards and away from their convulsing friend.

Rhago continued his sermon. "How does a tsesh see the light of fate?"

"By standing silent in the shadows," they answered.

He plunged the tip of his blade into the second kid's chest, pinning him to the ground and twisting a crimson burst from his quivering mouth. His eyes were bulging and pouring out tears. He died staring at the belly of the city, with a violent swarm of questions fading from his eyes.

By then the third prisoner had scrambled to his feet and was sprinting with rigid strides toward the archway, his hands still locked behind his back.

Rhago leveled his eyes on him and drew a gun from his coat. He flicked a switch at his thumb and the pistol hummed to life, a streak of blue light sliding down the length of the barrel. "How does a tsesh cheat death?" he asked coldly.

"By living an unseen life," they answered as though it were an order.

The pistol boomed and a line of metallic dust sliced through the air. Akara saw the dark spray against the yellow stone as the teen dropped in a puff of dirt at the exit. Rhago had not shed his emotion for the execution. The look in his gray eyes was that of putrid satisfaction and disdain for all life. He hated them, and he was proud of the blow he'd struck against their world.

When the last echo of the gunshot bounced away, the king switched off and lowered his gun then turned a stern glare at his son. "You're dismissed."

Akara gave a subordinate nod and headed for the dorms. Malehk walked with slow, defeated steps after him.

"Malehk," Rhago commanded, "do you have anything to report?"

Malehk turned a dead look at the king. He consciously stopped short of answering with defiance. "No, sir."

# # #

Jaga's office was quiet, even with the two of them sitting within it's warm, wooden walls. Bwrynn was curled up on a thick sofa with a wall of books at her back. Jaga was sitting in a chair opposite her, wrapping a length of gauze around her hand. The wound had already bled through the first two layers, and he patted at her wrist as gently as he could, making another pass with the bandage.

Bwrynn was watching his hands work, unable to look him in the eye. "I'm sorry, Jaga," she finally whispered, barely breaking the silence.

His eyes remained on his task, and he answered simply, "I know."

"That man was going to attack you."

"That man," he replied, punctuating her blasé description, "was only defending himself."

"And what, that justifies his actions?"

"Yes, it does," he answered sternly, pausing mid-pass with the gauze. "For as much as actions require it."

"Well, don't they?"

"Don't they what? Require your permission?"

"No," she said. "I mean, there's right and there's wrong, and what he did was wrong, wasn't it?"

"He did nothing. What you saw was the reaction of a frightened man. Surely you felt that."

"I didn't really feel anything," she admitted. "He tried to attack my mind. I—I thought I was defending myself."

"Then you were reacting as well." Jaga secured the tail end of the bandage to the back of her wrist and squeezed her hand in his own. "Young Bwrynn, we are all made up of mind and body. Our flesh can be protective and even selfish, while our minds can be passive and forgiving if we let them. Both are necessary to make us who we are. It is that dynamic which gives us life. It's what drives us forward and forces us to evolve." He brushed a soothing hand down her cheek and cupped her chin in his fingers. "It isn't our place to judge others on this path."

Bwrynn had closed her eyes, breathing in the warm scent of the room and the calming wisdom in his voice. She nodded in his hand. "I understand."

"Besides, he's with us now," Jaga said, finally rising to his feet. "The Legacy will help to strengthen his mind and, as he grows, he will come to judge himself as we all do. And trust me child, that judgment will be far harsher than anything we might have done to him in that bar."

Bwrynn pressed her lips together, forming a straight line with her mouth as she nodded again. "Yes, sir."

"So," Jaga continued as he circled around his desk. He tapped at the screen on its dark surface and began drumming his report into the computer. "What happened?"

"What happened?"

"Your actions were rather rash," he clarified without looking up. "That's not like you. So, what happened?"

"Oh," her voice went soft and remorseful. "I guess I was just distracted."

"Mhm, I sensed that, but distracted by what?"

"I'm not sure. Do you remember those men at the back of the room when we entered? The two in long, dark coats?"

"I can't say that I do."

"Well, it's just that," she paused and pieced together her thoughts into a shape that might pass for an explanation. "They weren't there later. I don't know where they went."

"That's hardly cause for alarm," he said, looking up and offering an academic shrug with his hands. "People's individual lives aren't our concern, Bwrynn. We had a job to do." His old, blue eyes narrowed as he watched her fumble with her thoughts. "Did you sense anything unusual from these two men?"

"Well, no, that's just it," she said, "I didn't get a chance to read them. Before I could try, they were gone. One moment they were there, then they were just gone. It was like the room went empty where they were."

Jaga had gone perfectly still. Even the subtle movements; fidgeting fingers, shifting lips, every idling motion had disappeared. Despite his stiff posture Bwrynn could feel her master's mind spin up at a frenzied pace. "Empty?" he asked more calmly than his thoughts would suggest.

She replied with a slow and cautious nod as though even she was doubting her memories of the night. "Yes?"

He gave a pensive nod in return. "Did you see their eyes?"

"Their eyes?" Bwrynn attempted to recall the encounter as best as her doubting mind allowed. "No, I don't think so. I think they were wearing glasses."

"I see," he responded thoughtfully.

"Why?" she finally asked. "Master, what's this all about?"

He twisted his lips and swiped a hand through his beard before standing up from the desk. "You've had a difficult night. You should get some rest."

"Rest?" she repeated, reluctantly rising to her feet, and moving away as he ushered her toward the door. "Jaga, please, what's going on?"

"It's nothing you need to worry about," he reassured her while mustering a smile and guiding her into the hall. "You did well tonight. We'll talk again in the morning."

With that farewell he tapped at the door's controls, sliding it shut and closing her out to stand alone in the hall. Bwrynn's eyes were twisted and twinkling with confusion. 'Their eyes?' she thought. What could have him so concerned? A myriad of explanations swam through her brain with youthful vigor, blinking away one by one under mild scrutiny until only one remained. The lone possibility perched on the forefront of her mind. It silenced all other thoughts and chilled her skin.

Bwrynn's wound burned to life beneath its dressing, and her expression went cold. Her eyes leapt back up to the door. "Tsesh." She whispered the thought aloud. She'd heard the stories from other agents, but they'd been nothing more than that, stories. The tsesh were a faded mythos in the world she'd grown up in, old yarns of war from old and boastful agents.

As the notion filled her mind, her pulse began to quicken and throb beneath the gauze. She sped from the door and raced down the winding, amber halls of the Legacy, her feet pounding the red carpet and her black cloak spiraling in her wake.

CHAPTER 5

The night had stretched out thin. Malehk had seemed desperate to talk, but Akara locked himself in his room and ignored the sympathetic rap of his friend's knuckles at the door. It would have been the same conversation they'd exhausted over the years. Malehk would ask him why he stood by and allowed his father to commit such atrocities. Akara would remind him that no one allowed Lord Rhago to do anything. The king's word was law, and his actions were a force of nature. It would be like accusing him of allowing the rain to fall or lightning to strike.

Akara had kept his emotions at bay with a snake-eyed stare into the tattered gray carpet of his dorm. The amber pools of fate were always faint underground, trembling like puddles at his feet. Each time he eased back his obsidian scales, daring to summon back emotion, the twisted and bloodied shapes of the three teenage boys came screaming back to his mind's eye. It was like testing your weight on a broken leg, only to feel it crack beneath you. He'd push the image away and his eyes would flare back up with golden light, slamming the lid on a box of horrors.

It's only emotion that makes the mind weary, the thoughtful process of gathering up a day's events and sorting them one by one into compartments built from experience. At night these collections form our dreams, abstract pictures of moving memory. They speak to our souls in a foreign tongue and, while we're not looking, they shape us into who we are when we wake.

Akara didn't sleep. He regarded the passing night with clockwork gears instead, turning and ticking across the span of hours. The lights had gone out, leaving him alone with the shimmering plash of stagnant fate around his boots. He thought it best to leave the previous day in the past, to not take it with him into sleep and to try again tomorrow.

He hadn't slept, but the slow hours had somehow gotten away from him anyway. It was the distant sound of generators spinning up that finally reeled in his attention. A lazy hum and erratic clicking prickled in from the hallway past his door, like insects tapping against glowing bulbs outside. The night was over and the tsesh compound was lumbering back to life.

Akara released his serpentine vision and allowed his emotions to pour back in like muddy water through a broken dam. He was grateful to find that the murdered teens weren't among them. The night had stitched the wound shut, dulling it to a muted ache and storing the memory like stacked bodies tossed on a basement pyre.

He heard Malehk's footsteps trotting down the hall. They were full of light and sprightly vigor. Malehk had once told him that the secret to an efficient day was pairing the proper beverage to the hour. It was apparently ten minutes past coffee o'clock.

"Akara," Malehk's voice garbled behind the door, punctuated by the lively jackhammer of his fist.

The prince was slow to respond, drawing a measured breath and pinching his thumb and finger into his all-too-human eyes.

"C'mon," Malehk continued, "let's get up and get moving."

He was always so excited to shoot from the dorms at the first sign of morning and plunge headlong into the day. Akara couldn't blame him. The night crawls by reluctantly underground, and ever since their first venture to the surface, the two young tsesh had learned to savor their waking moments. Time away was what they lived for, sneaking out and sneaking up to breathe in the open air and shoulder through thick crowds unseen.

After rattling the loose cylinder of the lock, Akara pulled his door open to find his friend's predictably smiling face. His eyes looked fresh and white, and the black burst of his hair had been tied back into the thick bushel of a ponytail.

"You good?" Malehk asked.

Akara tensed his lips and nodded. "Yeah."

"Great," Malehk cheered, ignoring Akara's obviously contradictory tone. "Grab your gear."

"My gear? Where are we going?"

"It's midweek... I think," he said with a curious look around the room. "Time for training."

# # #

The tsesh training arena was an abandoned gymnasium with broken and skewed bleacher seats and thick cinder block walls, painted white and chipping to gray. The ceiling was a weave of rusty beams and hanging lights that were more than twenty feet above the floor, and small windows dotted the upper half of the walls, peering out to the dusty landscape of the buried city. The tsesh had polished the floor as best they could, resurrecting some semblance of veneer to the broad sea of wood.

In place of the stenciled goal and point lines from sporting events of the past, they'd painted a series of interlocking rings, each feeding into the next before joining the largest circle at the center of the court. It was ten feet across and used by fledgling tsesh to get a sense of movement in typical combat. Tracing the rings with sidestep motions, they'd initiate a dance of ranged attack and counterattack, moving ever closer to each other.

It would be impossible for Akara to recall the number of times he'd entered that arena. He was no more than five years old and barely able to lift a boka training sword when he was first paired up against Malehk Knight. Their fight had been drawn out and clumsy, two fumbling children struggling to remember every parry and attack they'd learned, swinging wildly and without awareness. Malehk had knocked himself flat with the recoil from his training pistol. The soft bullet had shot wide, missing Akara by several feet, but the sound had been enough to startle him to the ground. His father had been furious. He ripped the pistols from their hands and shot them both in the chest.

It took a week for the bruises to fade, but after five or six of those lessons, Akara was no longer afraid of gunfire.

All tsesh were expected to train whenever time allowed, and beyond managerial affairs and scavenging of resources, time was one thing they had in abundance. Still, training wasn't officially a law. There were no schedules to abide by, but sometime in their teens, Malehk had deemed midweek as their allotted shift. It wasn't long before the others took note, and the arena was always empty now when they'd arrive, a vacancy set aside for the prince and his retainer.

"No kalesh," Akara ordered as he walked to his preferred starting position along the ring. He was wearing jointed plates of plastic armor across his chest, and his ponytail swished against the leather straps that were buckled down his spine. His training pistol was secured at his back, and he was spinning a wooden boka sword in his hand, testing its weight and adjusting his grip.

"I wasn't gonna," Malehk defended.

"Guns and swords only," Akara reiterated pointing at him with the boka.

A few weeks back, they'd chosen to spar in the Hollows, a mile-long stretch of gutted buildings, filled with partial cover and broken terrain. Kalesh, the manipulation of energy, was an ability that all tsesh shared, though its uses were limited in a dead zone like Old Mallis. That's what Akara had thought anyway, which was why he hadn't bothered to make the stipulation before. The fight had lasted only a few minutes and was as near to a draw as the two had ever been. Then Malehk used kalesh, channeling his own kinetic energy into his gun. It made the bullet powerful enough to blast through a wooden wall and crack three of Akara's ribs.

The prince rolled his shoulder and stretched out his side, recalling the sharp pain of the wound.

Malehk smiled and snickered across the ring. While Akara was tensing his muscles and aligning his stance, Malehk's limbs swung loose and casual, his sword dangling like a pendulum in his hand. "So, tell me, about this girl," he said. "Marianne."

"Marianne? Why? What do you want to know?" Hearing her name had caught him off guard. He wasn't used to the sound of it beyond the voice inside his head. She didn't exist in Old Mallis. The Akara that Marianne knew didn't exist there either. They were separate lives being lived by separate people.

"Anything," Malehk shrugged. "What's she like? What do you guys do?"

Akara's eyes narrowed to suspicious slits. "Why the sudden interest?"

"What? Nothing. Neither of us have ever had a real relationship. I'm just curious. I wanna know more about this girl that's got your head all twisted. Or maybe it's because, if your father finds out, he'll bury me in a hole right next to you." He wagged his sword in the air at him. "Come on, spill."

Akara hummed out a few thoughtful sounds and his eyes began to drift and scan the floor. "I don't know. What should I say? She's smart, she's beautiful, she's incredibly kind— to everyone," he added the last note as though he had just remembered. "She's nicer than I knew anyone could be."

Malehk's eyes and head rolled back together. "Yeah, yeah. She's not like all the others," he griped out the cliche.

"No," Akara said, "that's just it. She is like the others, she's just the best of them. I see pieces of who she is in everything. It's like she showed me what people could be."

"When they're not hunting us."

Akara conceded with a raised brow and tilted head.

"So, what's your long-term goal with all this?" Malehk continued.

"What do you mean?"

"Well, you can't exactly invite her to meet the folks, can you?"

Akara lowered his head and pretended to examine the boka in his hand. "I don't know. It's not really like that."

"Not for you maybe, but you already know the score."

"The score?"

"Come on, man. She thinks you're human. You don't think she's already fantasizing about a life together?"

"We have a life together."

"You have half of a life together," he corrected. "She'll never get to meet your friends, assuming you had any friends. You can't invite her over. You can't have kids. She doesn't even know what you are."

"What I am." The phrase tasted like dust and bile on Akara's tongue.

"Yes," Malehk said plainly. "You're tsesh. She's human."

"What's your point?"

"My point," he replied, jutting his arms to the side. His body loosened and he began strutting along the rim of the circle. "My point is that when your father is gone," the words slipped out carefully and quietly from the side of his mouth, "you're going to have the power to do something about that, right? No more hiding underground? No more running from the psychics."

"Technically, yeah," Akara replied with slow hesitation. "But not right away. We'd have to be careful about it. The humans won't exactly welcome us back with open arms."

"So, we'll be careful," Malehk agreed then pointed his sword at him. "At least we got one on our side."

Akara smiled to himself. There was a comfort in Malehk's celebration of Marianne. His two lives had seeped together, however so slight, and the world hadn't come to an end. There'd been no great catastrophe. Life went on and he was allowed his happiness. "Yeah," he muttered through a fearless smile.

"Good," Malehk said, though the word was buried beneath the loud pop of his pistol.

The training bullet punched Akara in the chest and toppled him to the floor in a puff of red dust. Through the haze he saw Malehk's wide grin, laughing behind his smoking gun.

"Ready?" Malehk quipped.

Akara groaned and worked himself up from the floor. "No." He snatched his own pistol from his back and fired a round across the circle. Malehk ducked and leaned out of the way, his smile still fully intact while the bullet whizzed by and popped against the distant wall.

He allowed Akara time to stand and return to his position at the ring. They both stood motionless and predatory, each squeezing the pistol and sword grips in their hands. Their eyes challenged each other and skipped along the telling muscles that might telegraph the other's next move. Malehk was the first to act. He lunged to his knees and spun into the circle, firing two more rounds. Akara slid aside to dodge and fired two shots back of his own.

It was like they'd pricked a hole in the rising tension and a flurry of gunfire and motion had exploded out. After another three shots and fluid evasion, they met in the middle of the ring with a loud crack as their boka swords slammed together. Akara ground his teeth. Malehk grinned with his. They pushed into each other for a second then shoved themselves away, spinning the weapons and hammering them back together. Each attack was met with a parry and a clack of wood.

Malehk struck low against Akara's sword then moved in close and pushed the weapon from his hand. Akara's boka rattled to the floor and slid out of range. He immediately ducked the follow-up attack and slid back on one hand, raising his pistol with the other. As Malehk swung his sword down like an ax, Akara fired. The shot exploded against Malehk's knuckles, launching the boka from his hands and wrapping his face in red smoke. Akara seized the opportunity and kicked at his chest.

The attack pushed the two apart again. Akara stopped in a runner's stance with his pistol at his side. Malehk leveled his own footing while swiping and rubbing at the red powder in his eyes.

"Ugh, that tastes gross," Malehk whined, spitting the bitter tang from his mouth. He'd barely finished the sentence when he swiped his pistol up and fired back at the prince.

A half-beat later they were locked together at the center of the ring. They blocked and landed punches and fired their guns when an opening appeared. Each shot was dodged and slapped away, the bullets pounding red bursts along the high ceiling and distant walls. Gunfire filled up the expansive space, echoing together into a roar of thunder while the red talc rained down around them.

With a final shot, the two tsesh spun an arm's reach away and leveled their guns on each other, the barrels smoking side by side. The heavy echoes faded away, leaving only heavy breaths as they stared each other down.

Malehk nudged his chin at Akara's gun. "You're out."

He puffed a laugh through his nose and tapped his pistol against Malehk's. "So are you."

His big grin stretched back across his face and Malehk raised his hands in surrender. "A draw then."

Akara's body relaxed, and he was quickly back to standing casual before his friend. "I think I hit you more."

"Not if you count that first shot."

"I don't," he said, already working to loosen the straps on his armor.

Malehk huffed out a few more breaths then motioned at him. "You in a hurry to get somewhere?"

"Yeah, I've got a date."

"A date? But you just had one."

"And now I have another," he replied with a deep nod. Akara pulled the armor from his chest and brushed the scarlet dust from its battered plates. "She's got the day off, so we're gonna go for a walk on the wall."

"Oh, okay," Malehk answered in a wounded voice. "I guess I'll just go lie to your dad again."

"Thanks," he answered, clapping a hand on Malehk's shoulder before heading for the door.

Malehk watched his friend disappear into the halls and tugged at the armor that had been biting beneath his arm. When he was sure the prince was gone, he aimed his pistol at the far wall and squeezed the trigger. A final shot burst from the gun and coughed a ring of smoke against the bricks.

# # #

The morning drifted upwards to noon and the deep clouds above the city were bleeding out to a smoky gray. Life inside the Dark Ocean Legacy had awoken early. The windows of their headquarters blinked to life and cloaked agents had already been crossing the broad curve of marble steps outside for hours. The building was a twenty-story tabernacle, nestled at the foot of Pramoore Tower. Although smaller streets wound between the two, the major highways and long skybridges held Legacy buckled against the tower. Pramoore Tower was more than a building, it was a neighborhood at the heart of Mallis Two, and Legacy HQ was one of its better-known landmarks.

The words, 'Dark Ocean Legacy' were carved simply into the stone above the line of glass doors at its front. Just above the lettering, a six-foot ring of black marble was mounted to the building's face. It was filled with dark and rippling, holographic water that stared out across the piazza like a watchful eye. Around the rippling ring, concrete walls stretched up for two hundred feet. They were plain and flat with tall grooves of inset windows carving stripes down the full length of the building. The building's silhouette curved outward near the top, each floor stretching wider than the last and lined with their own rings of glass.

Silence is the sign of minds at work, and inside the Legacy, chatter never rose above a whisper. There was often the rustling of cloaks and the soft plodding of hard soles on the lush and crimson carpets, but never a ruckus or a scene. The agents could feel the ebb and flow of each other's thoughts, and the rolling fluid of emotion that filled every room. There was no call for small talk or pleasantries. If something needed to be said, it was said. If a question needed an answer, it was asked.

It was long believed that there were no secrets within the Legacy, that the agents could hide nothing from one another, and so they never tried. But secrets are like shadows, stretching long and late behind us all, driving us forward and away. For every light you shine on them, another shade is formed, and the ones not found on the surface are the ones that run the deepest and the darkest.

Bwrynn wasn't in her room when Jaga went to fetch her, but he had a good idea of where to look next. The outer hallway of the headquarters was a corkscrew of glass-plate railings that were capped by black oak banisters. The winding path spiraled all the way to the upper floors, with every inch overlooking the marbled lobby far below. A grand, crystal chandelier hung eighty feet above the center of it all, suspended just below the uppermost floors. There were countless doors along the way to the top, some were steel, some were wood, and each one led to the offices, training halls, and dormitories that filled the outer bulk of the building.

The top five floors were isolated from the rest. Only those with special permission could access the upper tiers by way of elevator, and Jaga had long forgotten the days before he was granted entry. Reaching back, he couldn't recall his first ride up the lift, but he could remember the feeling that it had stirred up in his belly. A boil of snakes had swirled in his guts and the brief climb had stretched out to a slow and cruel span.

He had ignored the first two stories, the meeting halls, the strategizing rooms, and the executive offices. His interest, much like Bwrynn's, had been on the top three floors. They were the meditation chambers, the fire lit dens for quiet reading, and of course, the great library of the Dark Ocean Legacy. It took up the breadth of the building's eastern cap, with interweaving stairwells climbing and descending between its deep layers.

The library was the largest in the city and contained every known book to have survived the apocalypse. Many were torn and missing pages. Very few were unscathed by the city's long and tumultuous history. Some of the books were mindless fairy tales, whimsical nonsense fit only for children, but priceless nonetheless. Others were cryptic tomes, stamped in a forgotten language and studied by every proud and arrogant scholar to have ever passed through the famous atheneum.

The library was filled with tall shelves that were lined up in long rows, and squat chairs that were tucked into corners. Rare plants of every species stretched up from large pots on the floor and small ones on the tables. The only hollow space in the library was at its center. In place of bookshelves, it was populated with long tables, each topped with green-shaded lamps casting pools of amber light across the varnished wood. The ceiling loomed high above the center space and was decorated with golden bars and eight-pointed stars. The area was big and empty, leaving room for ideas to linger above quieted minds.

The upper levels of the library formed a 'U' that was cupped around the center floor. They were two layers of carpet and bookshelves, and rich wooden banisters. There was only one wall that stretched up the full height of the room. The eastern wall was tall and wide, and filled with a large arched window that looked out toward the city.

Oftentimes, new initiates would forget the books around them and stare out at the furious sky above the world. The overwhelming window offered a generous view of the city, and the students couldn't help but be reminded of how small they were, how small everyone was. Jaga had always approved of the distraction. He liked to remind them that, regardless of their power, they were no greater than anyone else. The library was a place for learning, and not all answers would be found in books.

That was where he would find her. That was where he always found her. Bwrynn was asleep at one of the tables, a small pile of dark hair atop folded arms and an open book.

Jaga approached with a coffee mug in each hand. He turned sideways and sat on the table, placing one of the cups beside her head, allowing it to land heavily on the thick wood.

"Something wrong with your bed?" he asked as her eyes fluttered awake, hidden beneath her wild curls.

She groaned and rubbed a firm hand across her face. "What time is it?"

"Very nearly midday." He pulled a tiny cube from his pocket and dropped it into her coffee. It sizzled and dissolved, releasing a fog of steam and earthy aroma into the air. He slid it closer to her waking face, his eyes glancing down at the book beside her. "You've been busy."

"Just a little studying," she replied. Bwrynn closed the cover and cupped her hands around the mug, pressing out the chill of her sleepy pulse while the scent chased grogginess from her mind.

"I see that," he said, nudging the thick tome and glancing at its spine.

Bwrynn took a drink from the cup and focused on the warmth while a silence settled in around them. She had to ask, and he knew that she would. "They were tsesh, weren't they?"

Jaga seemed to swallow a single sip of coffee two or three times while staring toward the window.

"The men from the bar last night," she pressed. "You asked me if I saw their eyes. One of the articles I found said that when the tsesh activate their abilities, they shed their emotions. It makes them invisible to psychic detection. It said that when they do that, their eyes change to snake eyes, and that's why we called them serpents."

He didn't answer. Jaga only chewed on the inside of his lip, his head nodding imperceptibly.

"I couldn't actually find much information," Bwrynn confessed as if she were working on a school report, "just some news feeds and editorials."

"No, of course not," Jaga said, his attention easing back. He waved his coffee toward the long alleyways of shelves. "These books are centuries old. Most of them even predate the destruction that ended the world."

"So what, the tsesh didn't exist back then?" she asked. The remark was only half serious.

"Possibly," he shrugged. "Or they may have just been hiding. The most accepted belief however, the one that we've been taught, is that they are a product of that destruction, that they were mutated by its radiation; a tribe of people who stood too close when the fire fell."

"So, what do you believe?"

The lines around Jaga's eyes went deep and his true age crept across his face. His mind filled with the bitter taste of a man exhausted. "It doesn't matter what I believe," he answered, "the tsesh are all dead. We killed them."

"But what if they're not?" she insisted. "What if they just went back into hiding? What if they've been out there this whole time?"

"Young Bwrynn," he said, "do you know why we hunted the tsesh?"

She shifted in her chair and didn't speak, suddenly feeling foolish for not knowing the answer to such an elementary question.

"Purity," he answered simply. The word was curt and soured by disdain. Jaga took a moment to work its flavor from his mouth before he continued. "The last Pramoore had made the case that, inside the walls of this city, we survive on limited resources, and that every life has a cost. He suggested that this cost must be weighed against our value." His voice was emphatic and sarcastic, as though he were reading the script of wartime propaganda. "He even pointed to the evolution of our psychic abilities as evidence of that; carefully plotted families lead to more valuable children."

For a moment it seemed as though Jaga had forgotten he'd been speaking. He lost himself in memory and thought. His eyes stared through the floor with the softness of regret shaping their edges. "But you see," he began again then paused to take a long breath, "the tsesh can't bear children with humans. They are genetically incompatible. They couldn't evolve with us, and so they couldn't give anything back." Jaga raised his mug and made a mock toast to the air before taking another drink, then concluded as mildly as he'd begun. "Our fear of them turned into tension. That tension turned into war."

"But if that war isn't over, shouldn't we tell someone?"

"It is over," Jaga answered sharper than he'd intended. He paused for the length of a slow breath and studied his coffee. "Bwrynn, I'd like you to leave this alone."

"Leave it alone? Jaga, the Legacy spent years hunting these creatures down. They were the reason the agency was formed in the first place." She swept a hand to the city beyond the window. "They've only just finished rebuilding the boardwalk after the last of those things blew it up."

"And killing himself in the process," Jaga added, staring at the window as though he could still see the explosion from years back.

"He killed himself?" she asked, her voice retreating to passivity. "I didn't read that anywhere."

"No, I suppose you wouldn't." His thoughts were coming like building blocks, placed and balanced with careful precision. "It's a defense mechanism that all tsesh have. When cornered, they can choose to purge their power all at once." He motioned back to the imagined bomb in the distant streets. "The result is a large explosion."

Bwrynn's face had gone slack. She narrowed her eyes at the floor as she processed the information. "They would kill themselves?"

"And they'd take a city block with them."

"But why?"

His chest heaved then slowly deflated, pressing out a steady breath. "Nothing was ever confirmed, but there were plenty of rumors; theories about what they would do to the tsesh we had captured." He rubbed his thumb along the edge of his cup and shrugged. The gesture made him appear almost childlike, even to Bwrynn's young eyes. "Apparently death was the better option." Then all at once, his composure returned, and he looked her straight in the eye. His mind shrugged off the weight of his memories and he became her master again. "The truth is, we don't know what you saw in that bar, and officially, there's no such thing as tsesh anymore."

Jaga flipped his nose toward the book on the table. "Now, put that back and drink your coffee. We have lessons to get to."

"Lessons?"

"After last night?" he said. "Yes, my dear, we need to work on your focus."

CHAPTER 6

Bwrynn and Jaga approached the railing at the edge of the spiraling hall. They'd descended by a few laps around the corridor, their eyes now just below the hanging crystals of the oversized chandelier. The lobby was still more than fifty feet down. The eight-pointed star shaped into the marble floor was large enough to be seen from any height, but the people were little more than cloak-covered dots, swishing back and forth across its face.

Bwrynn's posture was that of a rigid sentry that was standing at attention. Her spine was stiff and straight, and she was holding her mug in both hands as though it were a candle at a vigil. Her eyes closed like a stage curtain, and she measured out her breathing, almost counting the appropriate breadth of seconds for each inhale before allowing herself to exhale and repeat.

Jaga was precisely and lazily her opposite, leaning an elbow on the black-topped railing and casting a sideways look down the corkscrew pit to the lobby floor. "You can't read their minds, so don't try," he said while casually scanning the crowds up the winding stretch of the hall.

Her posture broke slightly, but her eyes remained shut. "So, I'm practicing not trying?"

Jaga slid his coffee mug along the banister and held it beneath her face. Bwrynn's nose twitched as the rising steam dampened her chin and played across her senses.

"Do you smell that?" he asked.

Bwrynn counted out another breath then answered. "Mhm."

"Because you're trying?"

"People don't practice smelling, master."

"Of course not," he replied, looking down at the cup as if to make sure it was placed evenly beneath her. "But tell me, what do you smell?"

"I smell your coffee."

"Very good. Can you tell me the flavor?"

She immediately knew but drew another breath to be sure. "Red chaga?"

"Exactly right." He withdrew the cup and sniffed at it himself. "And honey," he added before taking a silent sip. "With a bit more practice, you might have picked up on that."

"Very funny," she said, finally opening her eyes. She shrunk an inch when she relaxed and took a drink from her own mug.

"People are the same way." He gestured to the masses that were winding around beneath them. "Their emotions drift outward like aroma, but the very nature of thought is abstract. They are a puzzle box of sensations and the individual's mind is the cipher. Only they can translate their ideas into real language. You don't have their mind, so there's very little sense in wasting your time trying to decode them."

"So, what am I supposed to do?" she asked, feeling like a novice all over again.

"Just feel their intentions," he said with a single-handed sweeping motion toward the halls. "Allow their feelings to pass over you as if they were gusts of wind. Soon enough, you'll begin to notice patterns. Only then can you make a judgment on what they might be thinking."

Bwrynn fidgeted with her lips and hissed a breath from her nose.

"Try them," Jaga suggested, pointing his cup toward three agents gathered against the wall across the gap. There was an older man with thinning, silver hair and a dark-haired boy, barely into his twenties at his side. From their posture and spacing Jaga already knew that the boy was the man's pupil. He was standing apart and proud but hovering close enough to hide behind his master's cloak if need be.

The third in the group was a woman in the early half of her fifties. She had a stocky build and a round and wrinkled face that was topped by a bushel of auburn curls. Her eyes were soft chestnuts, deep and knowing yet curious and wonderful.

Bwrynn realigned herself to face the trio and rocked on her feet until she was level. She reset her body with a fresh lungful of air, letting it whisper out over slightly parted lips. Her eyes flickered with a subtle blue light just before she shut them and opened her mind. She saw her perception pour over the railing like a waterfall, a tapestry of spectral smoke, whipping and flicking in the current of life. Gradually, her stream of thoughts began to catch the minds of the agents, slurping them up like droplets of water running down a spattered window.

The vague pressings of average lives formed a blase sense of repetition. The minds were flavored by flutters of bold ambition, but there was something else as well. Bwrynn felt it most in the woman. It was a trembling pressure, a forced restraint. It was the feeling of large thoughts trying to be small.

Bwrynn resisted the immediate urge to open her eyes. She let the impulse slip away and carve out a path for other sensations to follow. There was a pattern, just as Jaga had said. The background noise of their superficial thoughts was nearly identical. They were practiced and rehearsed, a false front for something else. Bwrynn ignored the vibrating murmur of their cover and opened herself to the thoughts they were hiding underneath. She opened the tap of her mind, slow and cautious, approaching the trio like an eavesdropper sidestepping toward a private door.

The secrets crawled up one by one, each from a different angle, each with a different rhythm. Once they wove together, their collective sensation began to paint a picture behind Bwrynn's eyes. She knew what they were hiding beneath their molded guise. She saw Pramoore Tower, painted darker than the sky, with blue flames burning at the tip of every peak. It was wrapped in smoke and tendrils that slithered out across the city until they reached the four towers along its brim. The spires burst into the same blue flames and shook Bwrynn's body as though someone had reached inside her and throttled her by the spine.

She gasped a breath and her eyes leapt open. The black tower and blue flames were gone, replaced once more by the three agents standing across the way. They were engaged in seemingly casual banter, a cool shell around their dark secrets. Bwrynn's heart was pounding furious inside her, screaming at the invisible nightmare that surrounded them. She could feel the air shaking in her throat and swallowed at it twice until the trembling slowed.

"Jaga," she said when the world finally became more solid and mundane.

"Better?" he asked.

"Huh? Oh yeah," she replied then nodded toward the agents. "But I think there's something going on between them."

"Something going on?"

Bwrynn turned her back to the railing and the trio and spoke softly with a lowered head. "They're filled with paranoia and suspicion. They have really dark feelings for Mr. Pramoore and the company."

Jaga glanced once to the agents then turned back and gave a dismissive smile. "That's not surprising. Pramoore is a secretive man. The people who have been here longest tend to build up their own ideas about him. I expect there's a different conspiracy about him for every mind in this building."

"No, this was different," she rasped. "There was a solidity to their thoughts. It felt like intention." Bwrynn's eyes jittered side-to-side then returned to her master. "I think they're planning something."

Jaga's eyes widened, and his smile became more patronizing. "That's a broad jump. You shouldn't let your imagination fill in the gaps of other people's thoughts."

"I'm not."

"Come," he said, wrapping a warm arm across her shoulders, "that's enough practice for today. Let's get you some real breakfast."

Bwrynn held a serious look on him for as long as she could hold a breath. Eventually, she relaxed into his embrace and bowed her head. "Okay."

As the two of them moved away from the railing, Jaga turned another look to the agents. His eyes narrowed into slits and his jaw twitched beneath his ears. Her inexperience didn't mean Bwrynn was wrong. Even the innocent have secrets. Jaga knew that more than most.

The Akrin General Hospital was more than the best in the sector, it was one of the best in the city. This title made it shine above the uneven seas of commonality, even more so in the unremarkable ebb of Six. Akrin had become a talking point for Lord Kaddler at every funding review, and for all the good it did, he'd praised its reputation more than once during his election debates with Aldan Pharos.

The hospital was made up of three conjoined buildings rising up from a wide base of waiting rooms and offices. Each high-rise portion was a different height, all nestled together like a crown on the hospital. They were built of pale steel and lined in arching lines of white light. The reception floor at the front was glass and pillars and pallor-gray stone. Two large ferns in heavy planters sprawled out beside the door, and two more encircled the desk, sitting front and center inside. The administrator had once made the argument that the expensive plant life aided in relaxation and recovery. Each time Kaddler won them a grant, they'd buy another fancy fern to accompany their latest tech. Anything to polish the single glint of prestige in Six.

Marianne's visits were still technically covered by the hydroponic labs in Sector Four. She'd made a point of getting in every check-up and minor procedure before her coverage ran out. Her visits had become so frequent that she'd become rather well acquainted with much of the staff. Tira at the front desk had just gone through a complicated breakup, and Marianne never minded her venting rants. Caden was a squat little man that worked the counter of the visitor's cafe. Marianne was pretty sure he had a crush on her, but managed to keep things polite and airy whenever she came in. She never turned down the free brownies though.

Of course, there was Dr. Hal Fineda, a middle-aged stock-photo of peppered hair and sterile smiles, and Marianne's primary care physician. He always had a medical tablet in his hand, even when there was nothing to jot down or diagnose. Marianne would imagine him having breakfast with his wife, that pearly grin on his face, the white coat over his pajamas, and the tablet at his side, just in case he wanted to check the nutritional value of his egg whites mid-meal.

Hal was going to miss her visits. He'd told her as much as they wrapped up her latest vaccinations. In the few short months that she'd been seeing him, he'd come to think of her as more than another patient. She was a friend. He even offered to have them over for dinner; Marianne and this Akara person who had so quickly stolen her heart. She thanked him but avoided giving an answer. Not for her sake of course, but for Akara's. He was always nervous around strangers, and she didn't want to ambush him with an awkward date.

Akara had been waiting in a corner beside the check-in desk on the third floor when he caught sight of Malehk in the hall, who made no attempt to hide. He simply curved up his half-smile and tipped an imaginary hat when he realized he'd been spotted.

"Again?" Akara asked as he stepped out to meet him.

Malehk shrugged. "What do you want me to do? I'm under orders."

"Since when have you been so diligent?"

"I'm duty-bound," Malehk corrected snidely.

"You're bored." Akara's eyes darted up and down the hall and his voice cinched to a whispered growl. "Just go find something else to do. We can meet up later."

Malehk's eyes rolled, and his shoulders slumped. "Fine."

"I'll call you later," Akara assured him as Malehk turned and walked back toward the elevators.

Marianne stepped out from the doors behind the back desk, catching Akara's eye. He shook off his thoughts of Malehk and the proximity he'd brought between his underground life and Marianne. He smiled at her in view of the open room just like a human would. He waved at her with large and unafraid motion just like a human would. He hushed away the ghosts in the back of his mind and convinced himself that, in her presence, he wasn't a tsesh at all.

"Hey," she greeted him with a hug at the center of the room, "how long have you been waiting?"

"Just a few minutes," he said. "Everything good?"

"It was just a couple of shots," she said, noting the small bandage on her upper arm. "I'm the picture of health."

"I never had a doubt," he joked, sliding an arm around her, and leading them toward the hall.

CHAPTER 7

Malehk was taking his time leaving the hospital, moving in slow steps, and sliding his fingers along the textured walls. Akara wasn't wrong, he was bored. Venturing to the surface was supposed to be exciting for them, two adventurous and kindred souls exploring the forbidden bustle together. They were supposed to be getting drunk on their wines and mingling with an oblivious population. Instead Malehk found himself stalking the prince's shadow and drinking alone in unlit corners of lonely bars. His life was spent on the dulled edge of a never-ending cusp, always a second away from something great. The stale anticipation was wearing him thin.

His eyes had been skipping from light sconce to painting then on to the next fixture as he strolled toward the collection of elevators. It was a distinctive voice that finally pulled him out of his own head. It was a low and raspy voice, speaking sentences that were broken into unusual and off-putting fragments as though the person were always out of breath, or overthinking the articulation of every word as it came. It was a voice Malehk had heard before, in thirty-second news clips framed by interviews of Daemon Pramoore. It was the voice of Caul Cerrone, Daemon's head of research.

"I understand. You had a patient. Come in. Only. A moment ago," Caul asked a receptionist around the corner. "An industrial. Accident."

Malehk couldn't hear the response but slid against the wall and edged his way toward the lobby.

"Mr. Pramoore. Has asked that I. Check. On his. Condition."

Peering around the corner, Malehk saw the nurse at the desk pointing in his direction. Caul was standing in front of her, hunched over and nodding. He was dressed in brown shoes, and a brown suit with a matching bow tie hanging crooked under his chin. He was short, if only from his stooped posture, and held a leather briefcase in one pale and withered hand. The contents of the bag seemed to pull him down with its weight, leaning him forward and to the side. He had a small, round head with thinning blond hair that was futilely groomed, and round glasses over his uneven eyes. One was wide and wild, the other drooping and tired. All his movements, even the simple nod he offered to the nurse, were that of an insect playing the role of a man, irregular, exaggerated, and uncomfortable.

As the tottering scientist turned toward him, Malehk pressed himself back against the wall. His eyes took stock of his surroundings, searching for a corner or cove, someplace to disappear. With limited options, he slipped toward an open door. He rolled around the frame and into one of the rooms. The tsesh stood packed into the corner like a living coat rack, unmoving as Dr. Cerrone scuffled by.

Malehk's dark, suspicious eyes leaned into the door and followed the hobbling man. Caul was scanning the room numbers that were glowing against black plates beside the doors. When he finally found the one he was looking for, he nodded and mumbled to himself before stepping inside.

Confident that the way was clear, Malehk slipped out of his hiding place and crept after him. His footsteps moved between casual and cautious, trying to appear natural, but making sure each step landed quietly. When he reached the room that Caul had entered, he leaned against the wall outside and crossed his arms. He appeared relaxed to the occasional passing staff, but his senses were hooked around the corner, listening to the hissing scientist as he spoke to the patient inside.

"Mister. Hagen. I presume," he said alongside a rustling of fabric and buckles. "My name is. Doctor Caul. Cerrone. I work. For Mister. Pramoore."

Malehk couldn't hear any response from the patient, and the silence stirred up his curiosity. With a smooth and muted motion, he leaned toward the door and peered inside. It was a large room, neatly organized with small desks, short stools, and the signature potted ferns. There were three steel beds, broadly spaced, though only one was occupied. The patient was a dark-haired man lying shirtless under a thin sheet with a breathing tube down his throat. It was impossible to guess his age. His face was swollen and criss-crossed with crimson gashes. One eye was wrapped in bandages that he'd already bled through, but the other was awake and following Caul as he approached.

"My expertise. On paper. Is research. And. Development," he said. "That is of course. A diluted. Interpretation. My true calling. Is in. The essence. Of life. Itself."

He lowered an open hand to the patient's chest, his fingertips barely brushing the thin sheet. Mr. Hagen's face furled with nervous curiosity as he watched the disconcerting man, helpless to recoil or respond.

"I can sense. Your essence. Beneath. This form," Caul continued, retracting his hand and moving to the foot of the bed. "Your soul. As some. Like to call it. As your body. Begins to die. It rises. To the surface. Like smoke. From an extinguished. Fire."

He placed his leather bag near the man's feet then paused and squinted at his face as if he were deciphering a code behind his one good eye. When the moment passed and Caul seemed satisfied with his thought, or at least, no longer puzzled by it, he unfastened the buckles on the briefcase and flipped the top open.

"It is. Of course. Unfortunate. What happened to you," he said, turning his attention back to the man. "But accidents. Happen. And as a scientist. I prefer to think of them. As. Opportunities. Wouldn't you. Agree?"

Again, the man didn't answer. It was more than having his mouth plugged by the breathing tube. He didn't moan or groan or make any of the vowel sounds someone might make. He didn't shake or nod his head. His only movements remained in his one good eye, jumping wide between Caul's face and the bag beside him. Malehk could see that the man was frightened; more than frightened, he was paralyzed by terror. It was only another second before he understood why.

Caul reached into the briefcase and retrieved a smoky white crystal. It was the size of a fist and edged with dozens of smooth and oddly shaped facets. When the patient saw it, he finally tried to make a sound. It was a low and whimpering moan, choked by gurgling noises as he tried to speak and swallow at the tube. His gaping eye leapt around the room for help and found Malehk.

The man howled over his tube and tears slipped from the corner of his eye, tracing the bloodied lines in his face. He tried over and over to form some kind of word, pleading with his eyes to the dark stranger watching from the door.

There was nothing Malehk could do. He could only watch with horrified fascination as the crystal began to hum and glow. Caul started muttering strange words beneath the buzz of the crystal, and small tongues of smoke flicked out from its surface. The man in the bed began to seize, and the same kind of smoke began rising from his body. The wisps thickened and grew, lashing and swirling around the bed.

Malehk swore he saw a face in the whirlwind of clouds. It was the horrified face of the gurgling man, looking back at his own spasming body before being sucked into the furious glow of the crystal. The ferns inside the room withered, their broad and tapered clusters wavering and falling flaccid against their blackened soil. As they died, so did the man in the bed. As if a final breath had been sucked out of him, his body slumped back against the mattress. His arms went limp, and his tear-filled eye was glossy and gray.

The room was quiet again and the smoke was gone, having been vacuumed into the crystal, still glowing with its summoned light. Caul lowered the jewel back into his bag. His demeanor was unnaturally calm, as though he were politely excusing himself from a dinner table.

"Thank you. For your. Contribution. Mister Hagen," he whispered to the gaunt body before tapping at a switch beside the bed.

The room filled with the noise of panicked alarms, matching pace with a flashing red light on the wall. The sudden burst of commotion slapped Malehk's attention back into his mind. He jerked away from the door and flattened himself against the wall. After a quick breath, he turned and headed for the reception desk as nurses and doctors sped by, rushing into the clamorous room.

# # #

It was just past midday when Malehk stepped out of the hospital doors. The thick and rolling sky had faded out to light gray, muting the whips of lightning, making it appear as though the silver clouds themselves were sputtering with internal glow.

The lot was busy. All manner of people, wrapped in overcoats and scarves, were either shuffling towards the clinic or back out to their cars. Malehk did neither. He leaned his weight against a steel pillar and pulled a silver flask from one of his deep pockets. His appearance was casual again, as casual as he could make it. He was just another man, bundled against the cool breeze and waiting for someone on their daily errands.

As he tipped back the flask and gulped a modest mouthful of whiskey however, his mind was reeling and playing back what he'd seen inside. He was struggling to make sense of it, and his eyes were hungry for something solid, something plain and knowable. He scanned the lot, following random passersby, reveling in their firm steps and their ordinary clothes. They were nothing more than people living nothing more than lives. Malehk was desperate to find his way back to that.

What had he just witnessed? Was it magic? Had he just seen a human soul? Did Caul Cerrone pull that man's lifeforce from his body and imprison it in a crystal? Enigma piled on top of enigma, building up a pressure in his mind that he tried to quell with every swig of booze. The answers wouldn't come, and he knew it; not right away anyhow. He allowed the maddening thoughts to fill up his imagination, examining each question as if it were an alien insect with too many legs to count.

Perhaps it was the horror and revelation of what he'd seen, or perhaps such a mundane thought had gotten lost in the shuffle, but Malehk suddenly realized that there was at least one puzzle he could solve: 'why'. Letting go of the vaporous questions regarding how Caul had done what he'd done, or even what he had done, why did he do it? What was the purpose, and what was he going to do next with that crystal? There was an answer, and Malehk was certain he could find it inside the very real walls of a very real city. He'd just have to start asking questions and pulling at threads, and the first thread was about to walk out the door.

Caul was cradling his briefcase under one arm as he pushed through the hospital door. His head was sunk low, and his steps were short and irregular. At first Malehk assumed the mad doctor was mumbling to himself again, but then he saw the twitching glow of a comm on Caul's wrist.

"Yes," he mumbled. "I have just finished. My work here. I am. On my way. To the southwest. Tower. Now."

Malehk pretended not to watch him maneuver through the parking lot and slip into the back of a black-tinted, luxury car. He began his way into the lot as the car rolled smoothly from its space. There was no need to hurry. Malehk knew where he was going, and he knew who he was meeting. A man like Caul Cerrone would never check in with his subordinates. He would only ever report to a superior, and he had only one superior. Daemon Pramoore.

After a smooth and silent cab ride across Six, Malehk tapped at his comm to pay the driver and stepped out of the car. It hummed as it drove away, leaving him standing on the sidewalk that ran alongside a wire mesh fence. Beyond the fence was a large and vacant field of dirt, dotted with metal boxes and transformers. They stood like sentries around the field, as if they were guarding their king, the dizzying height of the southwest tower.

The tower was merged against the border wall, reaching up nearly a thousand feet higher, scratching at the belly of the sky. Black metal was wrapped around the body of the spire, like armor bolted at varying heights, exposing only a zig-zag shape of the core underneath. At its very peak, the nucleus of the tower outgrew its plating and stretched the final height with upward reaching antennae and iron barbs. Lightning spat from the clouds like a petulant child, swatting at the tower and causing its grooves and edges to glow with deep, azure light.

The sidewalk was mostly empty, save for the occasional hobo or hurried pedestrian. No one stopped to gawk at the tower, not through a fence and a hundred feet of barren field. It was a magnificent sight, but there were better places for that kind of tourism. Most would be gathered atop the wall, where they could touch the tower, and run their hands down its armored sides. The black plates that hugged it were insulated underneath, but it was always warm to the touch, and conjured up smiles and wonder for every first timer.

Caul's car was parked a half-block away with the driver drumming away the time against the steering wheel, but the doctor was nowhere to be seen. There was only one conclusion as there was only one place Caul and Pramoore could both have gone, a place only they could go. Isolated from the city, locked away and insulated by silence. They were inside the southwest tower.

There was a lot of ground to cover between the tower's base and the sidewalk, and Malehk had no way of knowing when they'd come back out. He would also have to avoid the eyes of the driver, though the man seemed too involved in whatever music he had playing to be of much concern. With the risk and stakes concerned and the area mostly clear, Malehk was quick to make his decision.

He reached into his pocket and pulled out an oval-shaped, metal disk. It was black and filled his palm, with narrow vents making up its surface. He placed it over his mouth and nose and clicked a button with his thumb. Steel plates slid out from the oval, wrapping up the contours of Malehk's cheeks and jawline. They hugged his face and locked into place, securing themselves into the shape of a mask that covered the lower half of his face.

Once the mask was in place, he shed his emotions and allowed the silver scales to form beneath his eyes, gleaming above the vented rim of the mask. His eyes blazed violet and hardened into slits, and the golden smoke of fate appeared in the field all around him. Malehk's attention panned slow and cold around the field, gathering potential threats and viable paths to follow.

There was a small guardhouse beside the gate. The gray light of computer monitors highlighted two cut-out shapes of men in the windows. They were barely moving inside the metal shed. A head would turn, a coffee cup would tip back, but not much else. It was just enough to know they were awake, though their attention was likely occupied by a video, a phone call, or a casual hobby they'd picked up to fill the long hours of an uneventful shift.

After his quick assessment, Malehk leapt into the air, clearing the six-foot fence with only a gloved-hand tap at its top as he slipped across. The moment his boots punched the dirt field, the tsesh moved like a speeding wraith toward the tower, low to the ground with his black coat snapping at the wind behind him. In seconds, he had disappeared inside the shadows of the corner where the tower met the wall, only his purple eyes peering out like pin pricks in the night.

The door leading inside the tower was just around the corner, but he didn't dare approach. He knew that Daemon and Caul stood just beyond it, and he saw the writhing coils of fate twisting around themselves outside. A powerful event was brewing inside the southwest tower, and Daemon Pramoore, the scourge of the tsesh, was deeply embedded in its birth.

Malehk slipped off a single glove and placed his hand against the wall of the cold metal surface of the outside wall. His head bowed and his eyes began to glow beyond the seams of his closed lids. He felt the subtle vibrations of the steel plating and allowed it to shudder through his body. He amplified the trembling patterns until he could hear the muffled voices, gently brushing the surface of the interior.

# # #

"The towers are nearly at capacity," Dameon said as Caul retrieved the latest crystal from his bag. It was still glowing and warm from his recent catch.

"I am aware. Of the tower's. Limitations," he replied, balancing the gem in both hands as if it were a delicate egg. "But Mister Hagen's. Willpower. Was incredible. I'd hate to see it. Go to. Waste."

The inside of the great tower was hollow all the way to its peak, its interior walls encircled by metal catwalks and grated stairs. A single pillar rose up through the center, each of its four sides occupied by tall, glass tanks, stacked atop one another along its full height. Each glass vessel was filled with a bubbling, orange gel and was large enough to fit an over-sized adult. Most of them contained precisely that.

Nearly every tank in the center column contained a large, slumbering beast that still vaguely resembled a human being. Some had snouts and long, twisting horns, others were covered in bone armor plating and far too muscular to be man or beast. They slept in static silence as small bubbles gurgled up around their faces.

Small monitors attached to the glass fed wires through the gel and into the bodies of the sleeping beasts. The digital screens charted and displayed the vitals of the creature contained within. Each readout was headlined by a name, the human name of who the monster used to be.

Caul rapped a command across a nearby console, and the center column rotated and shifted. Some tanks slid aside and hissed before climbing further up the shaft on motorized tracks, while others locked in place above them and descended the pillar towards them. The vessel that finally arrived at the ground floor was empty. There was no orange gel or occupant, only a robotic, six-fingered hand mounted inside, extending outward at chest height.

Daemon's black eyes followed the tanks as they moved around within the tower, taking mental note of each of the creatures inside. "How many of them are there?" he asked.

The doctor was waddling toward the empty cylinder with the crystal still perched in his hands like a treasure box. "More than. One hundred subjects. In this tower. Alone," he answered. Caul reached up and pressed the glowing shard into the robotic hand. It gripped it and hummed before sliding back and locking into place inside the compartment.

The small display scrolled out the name, 'Hagen', and began reporting a stream of flatline data.

Daemon stepped forward and brushed a gingerly hand down the face of the one of the tanks, admiring the barbed beast inside. He nodded to the fresh container that Caul was sealing shut. "And how long before that one becomes viable?"

"Each of them. Are unique. Of course," he replied, returning to the computer and going back to work at the controls. With a quick thump against another button, the tank began to fill up with the same orange gel as the others, quickly swallowing the crystal that contained Mr. Hagen's soul. "A few jolts. From the storm. Is all that it will. Take. To form an. Embryo."

A sinister smile crawled up Caul's face as he returned to the container, the bubbling gel and glowing gem reflecting against the surface of his glasses. The bare wires that hung from the machines drifted upward in the gel and began reaching for the crystal, like hungry hands. "After that. The essence. Of the person. Inside. Must.

Take over." His eyes turned upward, and he gestured with elderly rigidity to the bubbling compartments above them. "The enzymes. In the fluid. Read the information. Inside. Each. Shard. It then. Creates a body. To best. Represent. The subject's. True. Nature."

Caul tapped at the capsule in front of him. Lumps of the orange sludge had already begun to coagulate around the glowing crystal inside, thickening into red blobs along its surface and swallowing the gem. "Take Mister. Hagen. For instance. In life he was. A driven man. Full of. Intention. And. Motivation. I imagine. As a bio-wraith. He will have. Similar. Traits. Perhaps he will have. Wings. Or multiple. Legs. To always carry him. Forward." He looked back to Mr. Pramoore and smiled excitedly beside his gurgling creation. "Only time. Will tell.

None of these. Of course. Have the nuance. Of the subjects. I tend to. Myself. Back in my. Lab. But what they lack. In subtlety. They make up for. In. Raw. Power."

"And the bio-wraith for this afternoon?" Daemon asked. "Where is that one?"

Caul hoisted a finger to the nearby tank that Daemon had forgotten he was touching. "That is it. In front of you."

"This one?" Daemon asked, his eyes returning to the creature inside. It was humanoid but top-heavy and hunched, with gray skin and tusks. The muscled flesh along its shoulders was covered in black spines that looked like large fangs protruding from its skin. "I thought it'd be bigger."

"It will be," Caul assured him. "Normally. When the subject. Has reached. Such a state. We would. Transfer them. To my lab. To refine. Their appearance. And their. Abilities. As we have. With the others. But as you wanted. This new batch. To be. Expedited. When the time comes. The beast. Will be flushed. Into tanks. Beneath us." He gestured to the floor, sliding a finger at the seams between the panels. "The compounds there. Are much more. Volatile. And will quickly. Apply. The finishing. Touches." He smiled again, as though he were delivering a presentation at a science fair. "I assure you. You will be. Pleasantly. Surprised."

"I'd better be," Daemon said, turning a suspicious eye to the wretched man. "The world was easier when we had our own enemies." He gave a disapproving sneer at the sleeping beast. "We didn't have to grow our own."

Outside, Malehk removed his hand from the black walls of the tower. His mind worked behind his violet eyes, considering the horrors he'd just heard. Bio-wraiths. He thought. This afternoon.

Chapter 8

The winds at the top of the wall were warmer than Akara had expected, and though they were fresh, they were flavored with the taste of desert dust. The pale gray light of the midday storm, he was told, was the perfect time to view the desert. It felt bigger than he'd expected or, perhaps more accurately, it made him feel smaller than he'd expected.

The ashen plains stretched out forever. There was no break between the horizon and the sky, they simply merged into darkness somewhere beyond where his eyes could see. Having grown up between the walls and beneath the city, Akara's mind had never dared explore a thought so large. Standing beside Marianne, staring out at the boundless landscape, it was all that he could do to maintain his composure. He tried to focus on the mountains to the west. They were closer than the flicker void of the horizon. They had shape and structure he could understand. He'd occasionally look at the stone beneath his feet, allowing his boots to fall more heavily, testing the firm sound they made.

Most of all though, Akara would stare at Marianne. She was right there beside him, more tangible than the storm or any imagined world beyond the barrens. He could reach out and touch her if he'd wanted, and he did more often than not. But even something as slight as holding her hand was larger than he was used to. The world above his childhood cave was massive, and atop the wall, holding onto her was all that he could do to keep himself from being swallowed up by it.

"You never told me why you moved to Six." Akara said. He loved small talk. It was easy to navigate, and the rhetoric fringe was far away from his secrets.

"Yes, I did," she replied.

"Well, you told me you weren't satisfied with your job in the farms, but you never really told me why."

Marianne shrugged absently then turned toward the deep sprawl of Mallis Two. "It's such a big city," she said with a hint of wonder in her voice. "If you were to dream up any possible action, odds are, at least one person is doing it right now."

Akara nodded in agreement. "Like someone, somewhere, right now, is changing the subject," he quipped.

"I'm not changing the subject," she defended, then nodded out to the city. "Somewhere in the city, someone is being born. Somewhere else, someone is being killed." Her voice went soft and remorseful, as though she hadn't expected to say what she had. "Someone is scared. Someone is hungry."

Akara's humor dissolved. They'd stopped walking and he simply stood and watched as sadness glossed her eyes. "Okay?" he added helplessly.

Marianne tried to compose herself with a well-forged smile, though her sapphire eyes still glistened at their corners. "It's just one of those things that always haunted my mind," she said. "No matter how well I did my job, no matter how many crops we could harvest, there would still be people out there who were hungry."

"Yeah, but there were also a lot more who weren't."

"I know," she conceded. "Maybe it's selfish, but I just wanted to be somewhere that I could see their faces, ya know? Like working at the diner, when I bring someone their food, I know that they're fed. I can see them enjoying their meal, and I know that, at least for that night, they're going home happy." She shrugged and looked down at her feet as though she were embarrassed by the sentiment. "It's stupid, but I somehow feel like I'm making a bigger difference here."

Akara watched her head hang and sway, and he felt a big, stupid smile climb up on his face. He'd never known someone to be so powerful and so timid all at once. More than anything, he wished that she could see herself as he saw her in that moment. "It's not stupid," he said, reaching up to stroke her hair and rest his hand on her shoulder. "You're... amazing." He immediately regretted such a trivial platitude, but he could think of nothing else to say.

She smiled at her feet and huffed a short laugh then looked back up to his eyes. They were dark and tender and beaming with love. "So, what about you?" she asked, her voice jumping up in volume to clear away the tension like a wind clearing smoke.

"Me?"

"Yeah, what goes on in that brain of yours? Are there any thoughts haunting you?"

He huffed a laugh and smiled, his face stalling for time while his mind scrambled to hide away his secrets. "I don't know," he said, searching for mundane scraps to offer up. "It's basically the same with, um—" He quickly recovered the lie that he'd given her. "-accounting."

"It is?" She asked with bunched-up look of surprise.

He sucked in a breath to respond. He held it while hoping the words would come. They didn't. The breath puffed from his mouth, and he lowered his head. "No, it's not," he admitted. "It's nothing like that."

Marianne laughed and nudged his arm. "Am I making you uncomfortable?"

Akara lied and shook his head.

"I'm just curious," she prodded, poking at his temple. "I wanna know what goes on up there."

Akara's muscles relaxed when he looked at her, as if he'd just remembered where he was and who he was with. Secrets or not, there was no need to hide behind guarded thoughts. She didn't know where he was from, but she knew who he was. He couldn't tell her the truth, but not everything had to be a lie. Suddenly, the answer slipped from his lips without permission. "This."

"This?" she asked.

"This is what haunts me," he added. "Being with you. It scares me."

Marianne's head slipped back, and her expression twisted up. "It scares you? What do you mean?"

"It just feels like…" He sighed and tried to piece together words to match his thoughts. "You're just so perfect and being with you feels like I'm living someone else's life; someone better than me. Every day I wake up and I wonder if that will be the day that the truth catches up to me, that you'll figure out I'm not the man you deserve. That this was all just a dream. I guess I'm afraid of waking up."

It was only when she laughed that Akara realized she'd been crying. Marianne cupped his face in both her hands and smiled, the tears filling her eyes with sparkling light. "I'm always worried you'll think that of me," she confessed through another blend of weeping laughter.

Akara snorted. He kissed her forehead and pulled her close, wrapping his arms around her completely. He laughed into her hair and shook his head. "That's so stupid."

"You're stupid," she replied, muffled against chest.

# # #

Malehk had waited for Daemon and Caul to leave and for the black car to vanish around a corner before emerging from his hiding place in the shadows. His eyes had eased back to their human shape, and he tapped at the face mask, retracting its sides in a whisper of rapid clicks before dropping it back into his pocket. It was a long way to Pramoore Tower, deep in the heart of the city, and even with his powers he couldn't go unseen the full distance.

He had no need to match pace with the two men. His plan wasn't to follow them anyway. It was simply an inconvenience that they were all headed to the same destination. There was nothing more he could learn from them. Malehk's intention was now focused on Pramoore

Tower itself. Caul had been using the souls of the dead to craft these monstrous bio-wraiths, and Malehk was hoping that something in the mad doctor's lab would explain why.

Finding a cab on the outskirts of Six proved to be more difficult than he'd hoped. By the time he saw one, he'd already walked five blocks. It was another two before he managed to flag one down. When asked for his destination, Malehk picked a pub that he knew was a few miles east of Periphery, The Smoke and Mirror. He didn't want to be dropped on Daemon's doorstep, and it would only be a five-minute jog from the bar to the tower.

By the time he'd ran the distance, it was mid-afternoon. The tower would be crowded, but Malehk was hoping the staff would be too busy with their work to be pacing the halls. He reached the wide, open gate before the courtyard and realized that security was busy with their work too. Two of the guards, dressed in their black uniforms and silver badges, were walking slow laps around the stone fountain in the middle of the yard. He saw another walking toward him along the side of the main building and he assumed a fourth would be tracing the opposite side as well.

There was more than a hundred feet of open terrain between Malehk and the door, and he counted four cameras covering every inch. A casual approach, strolling in as though he belonged might work, but he'd still be recorded and logged in their servers. It was a risk he couldn't afford. He had to get in without being tagged by security or their cameras. He had to find the blind spots and shadows that would lead him inside.

The main central building of the tower, the place where Caul's labs would surely be found, was guarded by an eight-foot wall, with breaks in only two locations: the main entrance, wide and well-guarded, and the parking garage. The ramp leading down to the garage housed only a single guard, but the gate remained closed unless someone was passing through. Vehicles were checked for permits. They were scanned and tagged as they came and went. But

Malehk wasn't driving a car, and he had no intention of rolling through the gate.

Assumption always gives way to an overlooked weakness. Pedestrians were assumed to pass through the front and vehicles through the back. This meant there would be gaps in their perception, too small for a car perhaps, but plenty wide for a lone tsesh.

He approached the guard house from the rear. The road and ramp were empty, and the officer inside the glass booth was relaxed, idling through his shift with some puzzle game on his comm. Malehk retrieved his mask and clicked the controls once again, wrapping its metal plates around his face and masking all but his eyes, now slipping back to their violet and serpentine glow.

A shallow and faded river of shimmering fate rolled down the ramp, nothing of immediate consequence. The tower itself however, looming overhead and beyond the security wall, was wrapped in the golden light. It coiled like fiery serpents around the black tower, striking toothless against its shell. Malehk noted the size and speed of the phenomenon while keeping half of his attention on the guard house.

The amber flow moved around him, heaving in time with his pulse and pumping up the wall to merge with the coiling serpents. In the lull between beats he crouched, then leapt with the rhythm of fate, spiraling his body over the wall. Malehk landed with a wide stance on the other side, the slithering light around his feet snaking away and up to Daemon's blackened palace.

A few dozen feet away was the long and covered corridor that ran the length of the building. It was perforated by gaps and pillars, forming an exposed hallway along the southern base of Pramoore Tower. The security guard was strolling casually under the concrete awning, giving an occasional rap at the windows, and looking inside to wave at a familiar face.

Malehk was watching with cold and violet eyes, his breathing paced out evenly beneath his mask. He moved with the belief that it was not his destiny to be arrested or killed that day, and so he allowed fate to be his guide. The patrolman was drawing nearer, each gap between the pillars providing a clearer view of the tsesh that was crouched inside the wall. It would be eight more steps from the sauntering guard before Malehk would be fully exposed. Two more gaps and two more pillars. By the third, all he'd have to do is turn his head and they'd be face to face.

Malehk watched the lines of fate. The guard disappeared behind one pillar, but the golden strands remained dim, and the guard emerged again. His footfalls were heavy and hollow along the concrete walk. He disappeared behind the second pillar, but still, there was no signal from the fates and the guard appeared again in the second gap. When he stepped behind the next column, the light of rushing fate surged at Malehk's feet and urged him toward the building.

His footsteps were fast and quiet in the dirt. The only sound was Malehk's coat flicking in the wind that was whispering in his ears. He approached the archway in which the guard would appear at any moment. As he neared, he saw the guard facing the tinted windows, his back to the approaching tsesh. It was a fractured second that Malehk had to his advantage, and he took it.

With a planted foot in the dirt, Malehk sprung upwards, sailing silent up the guard's back. The tail of his coat brushed the officer's black cap as Malehk grabbed the steel beams in the awning overhead and rooted himself there. The officer turned and looked out at the empty dirt field, narrowing his eyes and adjusting his cap. The tsesh was planted in the framework above him, his steadied breath echoing inside his mask.

After the ambling patrol had passed by and rounded the corner, Malehk dropped down and moved to one of the doors leading inside. He peered through the glass and down the hall. It appeared to be a rarely used exit, dark and seemingly abandoned, likely reserved for lunch breaks and fire drills. Vacant offices acted as its shoulders and at the end was a reception desk. The desk was a half-circle planted in the corner of an intersection and brightly lit. A young, black-haired man with bulging eyes sat behind it, typing someone else's agenda into his computer.

Malehk pulled open the door and deftly slid inside and moved to the shadows in a corner. He stood motionless, making sure there was nothing of the outside light to reveal his silhouette. The door itself was quick and quiet, but the taste of outside air soon reached the young receptionist and drew his eyes that way. There was nothing to see. It was the same quiet hall he'd stared down day after day, and soon he was back to his work.

Once inside, there was nothing dark or still about the passageway in Malehk's eyes. The stream of fate was thick and glowing, heavier than anything he'd ever seen in Old Mallis. It poured into the intersection and curved with a curious intelligence around the corner, knowing precisely where it meant to be. There was no other path left to him, no doubting where he needed to go, and no chance of being unseen.

He began his walk towards the light, allowing his weight to land heavy and loud with each step. The resonant clop of his boots drummed out a steady tempo, like a heartbeat emerging from the darkness. It took only three steps to recapture the receptionist's attention, even fewer to bleed out the color of his cheeks. His large eyes rounded out and his mouth went slack at the sight of the slender shadow carving itself out of the darkness. Its breathing was heavy and echoed beneath a mask. Its eyes were purple and burning brightly against the umbral hall.

The young man was frozen in Malehk's approach. When the tsesh stepped into the light, it did nothing to alleviate his fear. Malehk's hair was wild, his breathing hissed through the vented mask, and his serpentine eyes bore down on the man as though he were little more than a rat in the path of a snake.

He tapped at his comm and tried to stutter something, but Malehk spoke first, his voice hissing out in a monotone whisper. "You dropped something."

The receptionist's eyes relaxed and glossed over as though he were suddenly looking past the looming intruder and into another world. Malehk reached across the desk and plucked the security badge from the man's shirt pocket. He flipped it over in his hands, studying its text and pictures. 'Dana Lester, Clerical, Security Clearance One.' Almost useless. Then Malehk turned to see where it was that fate had led him. The glowing tendrils on the floor had curved to meet an elevator door, slipping under and between its seams. With a final look to the hypnotized clerk, Malehk moved to the lift and slid the badge through the scanner on the wall. After the doors chimed and opened, he tossed the plastic badge to the floor at Dana Lester's feet. By the time he'd come out of his trance, Malehk had shut himself in, behind the elevator doors.

"Dana," a voice called to the man through his comm. "Is that you? What is it?"

The receptionist wet his lips and blinked his eyes. He looked around while stammering back into the comm. His eyes finally settled on the badge at his feet. "I um— I just—" he stuttered while stooping to pick it up. He examined the badge as though it were unfamiliar to him. "I dropped something."

###

Deidre's Diner was a bustle of activity in the afternoon, a clamor of flatware and midday conversation, pierced only by the clang of the entry bell as Marianne and Akara walked through the door. They were immediately greeted by the welcoming scent of barbecued meat, hot coffee, and kitchen grease. They were also greeted by Dee.

"Ooh, Marianne," she excitedly called out like someone about to slurp the crown of whipped cream from a milkshake. Dee was waddling quickly toward them, her arms together in front of her and her fingers wiggling outward, hungry to join hands with anyone who would have them.

Marianne obliged, taking Dee's chubby hands in her own, if only to calm them down. "Yes, Dee, hi. What is it?"

She hardly had to ask. There was a cluster of activity around a single table in the corner. People were gathering around and standing on seats to look over the crowd while cameras flashed at whoever lay hidden inside the mob.

"Aldan Pharos," Dee explained. "He's here. He's right over there."

"He is?"

"Aldan Pharos?" Akara broke in. "Aldan Pharos, the councilman?"

"Soon to be Sector Lord Elect," Dee answered before turning back to Marianne. "Go on over and say hi."

"No. No, we couldn't do that," she replied, tilting her head toward the crowd. "It looks like he's being bothered enough as it is."

"She's right," Akara added, "maybe we should just go somewhere else, leave the man be."

Dee fired a look at him as though he'd affronted her very soul. The truth was that the cameras and the eyes behind them made Akara nervous. A dense throng of paparazzi was even worse. The last thing he needed was his face in the backdrop of some surface world publication for his father to see.

"That's ridiculous," Marianne said. "We'll just have a seat and order." She gestured deliberately to the quieter half of the diner. "If things calm down, maybe we can go over to meet him."

Dee snorted a breath through her nose and scrunched up her face, cocking a look to the empty and lonely table at the back. Akara suspected she was blaming him for Marianne's reluctance. She was.

"Fine," Dee finally conceded, then jutted up a single finger, "but I'm tellin' him you're here."

Marianne agreed and wrapped her open hands around Dee's broad shoulders, beaming her a grateful smile. Akara followed her to the empty table, pausing for a second to meet Dee's wide and accusing eyes as he passed by. He offered up a diffusing and submissive grin then slinked away.

"She really likes this guy, huh?" Akara noted as he sat down in the vinyl-wrapped seat.

"We all do," Marianne confirmed. "It was before my time, but I guess Aldan used to be a regular here. People like Dee were there supporting him when he became a member of the council. When he announced his candidacy for Sector Lord, it was kind of a big deal around here."

"You like him?"

"From what I know, yeah," she answered. "Why, you don't?"

Akara gave half of a shrug and half of a look to the crowded table. "I don't really know much about him," he admitted.

"Really?" she replied with a giggle. "He's been all anyone's talked about for the last few months."

"I don't really follow politics."

Marianne tapped at the glass panel near the corner of the table and began swiping through the menu while she talked. "Well, he seems like a really good guy. He respects his roots, and he really works to help people."

"They all seem like that," Akara replied, his mind spitting venom at thoughts of his father.

Marianne only angled up a look at him, casually and quietly regarding his cynical tone.

"There's only one reason someone would want a ruling position," he continued, "and that's to rule." He was speaking more to defend himself than convince her of anything.

She replied with a smile, shaking her head while her eyes scrolled over the appetizers. "It's a limited and elected position, Akara. Sector Lords are public servants."

"That's just a paint job to keep people complacent," he argued. "They make their own rules for the elections. It's nothing more than a show they put on."

She repeated her glance at him, this time with less light behind her eyes. "You feel like fried curds?" she asked.

Akara bit down and closed his mouth. "I'm sorry," he finally said, his voice silkened by sincerity. "Like I said, I don't follow politics, and I don't know anything about Pharos." He waited for her to accept the apology, but she continued to tap thoughtfully at the curds. "I'm a jerk," he continued.

"You can be," she replied with a brief glance up.

Akara looked over his shoulder, trying to catch a glimpse of the young councilman through the crowd. "You understand people a lot better than I do, and if you like him, then he must be a good guy, right?"

She shrugged. "Maybe not. I seem to like jerks."

CHAPTER 9

The panel of lights inside the elevator was larger and more detailed than Malehk had expected. It was a full computer interface, capable of searching and sorting all the various floors and departments in Pramoore Tower. His hooked finger hovered in front of the screen, his violet eyes scanning and rescanning every option. Even filtering out accounting, housing, and countless others, there were still chemical labs, research departments, bio-medical floors, and no listing whatsoever for Dr. Caul Cerrone.

Reaching up to sort the list for a third time, Malehk's attention was suddenly pulled away by the shimmer of fate. It pooled and pulsed around his ankles, swirling like water down a drain at his feet. He checked the display a final time before disregarding it entirely. Whatever significance the tower held in the city's future, it wasn't programmed into some list. Fate lay beneath his feet, in the sublevels that pierced the skin of Mallis Two and spanned the distance between the old world and the new.

There was no listing for basement levels and the floor was solid, each panel welded in place. Malehk slid his hands along each seam, following smooth lines along the walls until he finally looked to the ceiling. It was a series of interlocked plates with rounded edges, each bolted into an overhead frame. Off to one side was an access hatch and an inset lever. Malehk climbed onto the railing around the elevator's walls and braced himself like a wedge in the corner. He reached up, cranked the lever, and pushed the hatch open with a clack and metal gong as it dropped open on the roof.

Gripping the edges, he lifted his head out of the hatch and studied the hollow shaft with piercing violet eyes. It was six feet around and stretched up to a pin pricked vanishing point above him, with a core of thick cables wound into the elevator's roof. The air had the smell of an undisturbed and forgotten cave, shut out of the world, and filled with the tang of oil and steel. As he expected, there was no room to crawl down or around the lift. The only space it didn't completely fill up was the dotted line of tall recesses in the wall. They were cavities in the shaft, like shallow compartments stacked atop each other, each one barely large enough for a tall and slender tsesh to hide inside.

He dropped back into the lift and tapped at the controls once more. Malehk glanced up to the open hatch to reaffirm his plan and work out the timing and the angles, then thumped a finger at two of the panel's buttons in succession. One to open the door, one to send the elevator up ten stories. It would buy him a three-second window between the doors rolling shut and the lift beginning its ascent. Three seconds to climb up and out the hatch and then to tuck himself inside one of the man-sized cavities in the wall.

The doors slid open, easy and smooth. Malehk was sure Dana Lester would be out of his trance and would likely notice the movement of the doors. He couldn't give the twitchy receptionist a chance to see inside, so before the doors had finished moving, Malehk leapt up and gripped the edges of the hatch. He hoisted himself quickly enough that Dana never saw the black boots or long coat as they slurped up into the ceiling. By the time Dana's attention had turned to the elevator in the hall, it was quiet and empty. He stared at it the full three seconds, waiting for someone to emerge, but no one ever did, and soon the doors were rolling shut again.

Three seconds. They began ticking down in Malehk's mind the moment he pushed the button. Two had already passed by the time his feet were on the roof. Hesitation would surely kill him. His snake eyes locked on his chosen compartment, and he heard the doors settle shut beneath him. The metal roof and its motor began to hum. He dove for the wall, his gloved hand slapping at oil-slicked metal as he pulled himself against the wall and stretched his body thin to fit inside the hollow. The elevator groaned then blasted upward, its outside walls tearing up Malehk's shoulder. His mechanical mind acknowledged the jarring tug and the whips of pain that sliced through his coat and raked against his arm, biting through the flesh. He didn't flinch. A half-second later the lift was gone, gliding to the random floor above and leaving the tsesh on a narrow ledge, overlooking the deep chasm of the tower's bottomless depths.

He pulled his damaged arm forward, studying the bloodied skin as best he could beneath the shredded leather. The wound was superficial, easily cured with salve and a bandage. Until then, he knew that he could still rely on the muscles and that he'd only lost minimal mobility in the limb. He assigned the pain to a secondary block in the back of his mind and turned his attention back to the elevator shaft.

Fate was still pouring down the pit, hugging the walls then spiraling into a drill hundreds of feet below. Malehk's eyes slid up and down the oiled cables that ran its length, considering for half of a second their width and texture. Then he fell. Leaning forward, the tsesh rolled off the ledge and plunged headlong into the abyss.

Three seconds more. He counted them out in his mind, keeping his eyes open but thinned against the rush of bitter wind that pulled across his face and whistled over his mask. When the moment drew near, he pressed the palm of his glove against the steel cables that were racing past. The heat and friction were instantaneous. He felt it glow and burn through the leather. Malehk's eyes blazed bright again, his steely mind going to work reshaping the fire that was building in his hand. The heat, the speed of his descent, and even the pain he'd stored in his mind slowly began to change. The power grew heavy in his hand, sapping his speed and wrapping a weighted grip on the braided steel.

Sparks burst out from between his fingers as he squeezed down on the metal ropes. His hand suddenly stopped like a leather-wrapped vice that had clamped down on the cable. His body dropped and swung violently beneath him, the sudden jolt punching out an angry groan from inside his mask.

He'd arrived, hanging inside the golden clouds of fate that coiled around him before slipping away, sneaking through the cracks of another door. It was an unmarked stop in the shaft, absent from any controls or directories. Malehk calculated his depth, imagining himself a third way down the black spire that hung inverted above the center island of Old Mallis.

He'd always pictured its innards to be little more than tightly packed pipes and motors. Maybe he'd believed there would be a machine or boiler room, but this was something else. This was a secret, redacted from public record and kept hidden from even Daemon's own staff. This was a traveled room that was built with purpose.

A mechanical cough echoed down the pit. The elevator was alive again, traveling up or down he couldn't tell. Malehk fixed his eyes on the door and leaned forward, pressing the fingertips of his free hand into its center seam. He twisted and pushed until the doors lurched and slid open, allowing the ribbons of fate to pour inside like rushing water.

# # #

"Pharos is in a cheap diner off the boulevard," Kaelus announced as he entered the control room on the 75th floor. "Near the 108." His voice was confident and heavy, pouring over the conference table where Dr. Cerrone was seated and filling up the back corner where Daemon was standing stoic beside the feline curves of Faedra.

"Will that be enough?" Daemon asked, turning to meet the intensity of Faedra's stare.

"I'll find him," she replied. She went to work, tying the thick curls of her fiery hair back into a tail, then called over to the doctor at the table. "Is it ready?"

Caul turned toward them as though he'd been caught sleeping. "Of course," he answered, strumming quick jabs at his comm, and tapping at the resulting projections. "You will have. Difficulty. Tracking the beast. Under. Ground," he said. "Be sure to. Have a lock. Before. I initiate."

Faedra glanced at Daemon then nodded to Caul, blowing out a long wisp of breath before allowing her eyes to lose focus. Her pupils dilated and the irises shimmered to emerald rings of glitter, radiating out from the shadows that seemed to creep in around them. Her thoughts expanded outward, surging like a sphere in all directions until it touched every corner of the city. The voices of the world were noise and static, like a box of rats all pressed together and clawing at the walls. She pushed them aside, dropping the floor of her mind and focusing only on the spikes of power that rose above the rest. Like a length of string riding the wind, her thoughts sought out a single mind in particular, a mind that was slumbering inside the southwest tower. She moved past the tower's shell and found her quarry, the sleeping beast of flesh and fire, locked and bound inside its glass chamber.

"I've got it," she said.

Caul tapped at his comm and the projection above his wrist jumped to life. It became a holographic animation of turning gears and yawning hatches. Overlaid across it all was a single word; "Release".

Beneath the tumbling roar of thunder, the southwest tower howled out a noise. It was the sound of lumbering machines echoing inside its core and blaring out like a thousand trumpets on the air. It snared the attention of those passing by, but the roar was everywhere, filling the sky and pouring down on the city. As the single, harbinger note began to fade, a creature awoke inside the tower. The hulk of a man, covered in blackened barbs opened his eyes, his attention drifting side to side in the bubbling gel around him. With a final click, the floor snapped open beneath his feet and he was flushed into unlit tubes that dove down beneath the city.

Lightning stabbed at the spire's tip as though the storm itself had grown furious with the tower's audacity. Blue cables surged to white as electricity raced down the structure's edges, drawing lines and angles to its base.

Far below, in the bubbling dark of an underground basin, the barbed man twisted and writhed. His muffled screams gurgled out in thick bubbles that slid up his stretched cheeks. His flesh grew thick, and his bones grew heavy. He felt his jaw break from its hinge and sinew racing to stitch it back into place. His shoulders hunched forward and heaved up, and his muscles stretched long, like piano wire beneath his hide. The beast's fingers and toes all twisted beyond its control. Claws punched through their tips and scraped at the metal inside the flooded tomb. His screams became a roar, a pained and furious bellow of rage.

Then light poured in. A square of yellow light snapped into being and the viscous gel poured out of the basin, carrying the twisted monster with it. It dumped with a wet slap onto a metal floor, the embryonic fluid of its birth spattering all around it. There was nothing left of the creature now that might have once been a man. It was an enormous beast of muscle and spined flesh, eight feet tall if it were capable of standing upright. The creature's own mass pulled it forward, hunched forward on long arms and propped up on balled fists.

There was a sensation inside its thoughts, not quite a voice, but a motivation that took the place of instinct. The feeling was a half-step louder than its pain, and it gave the creature direction. It called for him to climb. It called for him to kill.

"It's out," Faedra said without inflection while staring blankly with glowing eyes across the control room inside Pramoore Tower.

"You have control of it?" Daemon asked.

"Yes."

"Then you know what to do."

Caul rose from the table and tapped at his comm, clicking away the holographic images. "I believe. I am finished. Here," he said. "If you will. Excuse me. Mr. Pramoore. I would like to. Study this data. Back. In my lab."

Daemon answered with a nod and a dismissive wave of his hand. The doctor retrieved his leather bag from beneath the table and hobbled across the room, pausing only for a moment to study Kaelus at the door, as if to size him up or measure him for a casket. Kaelus stared back, offering no expression, but finally stepping aside.

#

Malehk stepped cautiously down the short hall, his breath hissing steady beneath his mask. Long rows of fluorescent lighting led the way overhead, glinting off his silver scales and washing out the details of the room. There was nothing in the hallway, no benches or tables, no hanging artwork or ostentatious plants. It was a ceramic floor and stark walls. It was the kind of white that robs you of perspective and fools you into thinking the world had disappeared.

Even the silence of it all was alien to his senses. In the streets above there were all the sounds of a city, rumbling engines, blaring car horns, and the abstract roll of conversation that emanated from every large crowd, like a colorless aura. Then, of course, there was the storm. Endless and relentless bursts of light, jagged and stuttering lines of electricity, always followed by a tumbling roar or furious clap of thunder. Even in Old Mallis, in the secret rooms of the tsesh, there was the nonstop hum of machines and the far-off echoes of a heavy city shifting about above them. But in that hallway, suspended somewhere between those two worlds, it was deathly quiet, as if time itself had forgotten about that tiny stretch of blanched walls.

Malehk might have found it all unsettling had he the human mind to care about such things, but he had the calculating mind of a serpent, and fate was guiding his path. Its trickling streams were thin and cautious inside the hall, but it showed him where the corners were and it crept to the left ahead of him, revealing an open door.

More than the emptiness of the hall though, what he found around that corner was what finally gave him pause. It was a laboratory, a madman's playhouse filled with beakers and machines. Shelves along the walls were filled with jars containing every imagined body part, they may have been grown in that very lab, or possibly carved from a hapless subject in one of the curtained and unlit rooms that extended off the back.

A divider wall cut the room in half, effectively shaping it into a squared 'U'. At the widest section of floor, in the bowl of that 'U', there was a steel table, polished and reflective beneath a large, hanging disk of light. It was large enough to support a body and it was disturbingly empty, as if waiting for its next occupant to arrive at any moment.

Aside from the table and various oddities on the shelves, the lab was empty. The quiet of the room worked to amplify his footsteps and the hum of electricity that seemed to emanate from the walls. There was another noise though, hiding inside the silence of it all. It was a bubbling sound, muted and faint, but constant and distinct.

Malehk crossed the floor with slow steps, the hollow echo of each footfall calling out to the empty room as if to summon the source of the bubbling sound. It took only three of his long-legged strides to pass the divider and reach the steel table. It was there that a shadow caught the corner of his eye. Amidst the white and chrome of the lab, there was something dark around the corner, tall and metal, and growling out a bubbling sound.

On the other side of the divider wall was a large alcove, packed wall to wall with giant cylinders made of glass and deep-gray metal. Shallow grooves, hanging wires and control panels decorated the metal sides. Inside the glass face of each tube, however, was a blurry, humanoid form, suspended in an orange gel with slow bubbles rising and bursting at the surface.

Curiosity crept up in Malehk's mind. He allowed his eyes to relax and his scales to retreat. The drifting glow of fate dissolved away, leaving him alone with the sleeping and gurgling shadows. He counted nine of the bubbling sarcophagi, three standing shoulder-to-shoulder along each wall. Reaching under his coat, he tugged a pistol from its holster. He switched it on, listening to its electronic hum join the quiet babble of the room as he stepped closer.

"Hello," Malehk muttered absently to the obscured beings inside the tubes. He stopped in front of the closest and squinted at the murky form inside. It looked human enough. She was a slender figure with a halo of long, weightless hair, drifting in the fluid around her face. Her eyes were closed, and she appeared to be naked, save for the plastic mask that covered her nose and mouth. It hissed out a repeating pulse of small bubbles, the slow beat of slumbering breath.

Turning his attention to the cylinder itself, Malehk saw a series of displays and technical data. They may as well have been gibberish and shapes. Beyond simplistic heart rate and temperature readings, they meant nothing to him. The label at the top of each screen, however, bore a single word; 'Trace'.

Malehk repeated the word to himself then looked to the sleeping woman as if she might know what it meant. His attention moved to the other containers. Each held a sleeping form, varying only in the same simple way that one shadow varies from another. As far as he could tell, the technical displays all looked alike as well. The only differences were the labels. Malehk panned his head, reading each in turn and whispering them aloud. "Kane, Rieger, Bale... Pramoore."

His eyes jumped quickly to the murky form inside the canister. "Pramoore?"

Chapter 10

"The creature has reached the surface," Faedra said to no one in particular, her eyes still glowing and distant. The vision of her mind was bound to the barbed and lumbering bio-wraith, now clawing its way through concrete and steel as it rose up and into the city.

Daemon's posture straightened with a twinge of anticipation beside her. "Where?"

"A storehouse on 110."

It was closer than he'd expected, and his heart matched pace with his accelerating plan. Daemon's mind sliced through each of its stages, imagining and re-imagining every detail of what might come in the next few minutes. He turned his attention quickly to Kaelus who remained standing near the door like a sentry. "Are there agents in the area?"

Kaelus nodded, slow and obedient. "I have two units on patrol near the diner."

"Good. Allow the beast to carry out its task, but once the job is finished, I need them there to subdue it quickly."

Kaelus nudged his squared chin at Faedra. "Can't she just tell the thing to roll over and play dead once it's done?"

"I do not command them," she said, once again speaking more to the air in the room than Kaelus himself. Her words came slow and perfectly sculpted, like someone diffusing a bomb. "I only direct their intentions."

"Just make sure they're ready," Daemon repeated the order back to Kaelus. "This isn't just about eliminating Pharos. It's about reminding this city of the strength of our own agents."

He nodded again. "They'll be ready."

#

Malehk moved faster than he had before, stepping quickly to the controls of the center tube inside Caul's lab. He read its label again to assure himself of what he'd seen. "Pramoore." His eyes moved up the glass and struggled to peer through the bubbling gel. It was like looking through your hand against a bright light, seeing only the silhouette of vague shapes, knowingly only by instinct what you were seeing. Whatever was inside was human, but too small to be Daemon. The sleeping shadow was no larger than a young teen, barely filling the bottom half of the tube.

He rubbed his leather sleeve against the glass as if it might help. It didn't. He reexamined the numbers and scrolling lines on the console's display, hoping to decipher some sense of them. He couldn't. Questions begged desperately for answers, swirling like a boil of snakes inside his mind. On the other side of that single pane of glass was the key, a key which he was sure would change everything.

His hand hovered above the controls, his fingertips rubbing anxiously together while he considered which button to push. Which button would reveal, in plain language, the contents of the tube? Or, if nothing else, which button would open it and show him? He settled on a green one, rectangular with rounded corners and no label. Green was a safe color, better than red or even yellow. Nothing bad happens when you push a green button.

Before he could ultimately convince himself, another sound, a mechanical sound, bellowed into the room. It was the sound of the elevator stopping outside the door, followed by a chime to announce its arrival.

"Shen," Malehk growled out in a whisper. He slipped quickly away from the room of tubes and stole his way to one of the shadowed rooms in the back. He slipped around the curtain that covered the door, and his feet landed more loudly than he'd hoped, banging against a hollow metal grate rather than ceramic tile. Behind him, he heard the subtle roll of the elevator doors sliding open. He didn't have time to check, but the scraping sound of scuffled feet told him it was

Dr. Cerrone. "Shen, shen, shen," he whispered, darting his eyes around the unlit space.

The room was small, no bigger than the alcove had been. It was more of a storage closet than a room. No wall was more than an arm's reach away and there were no windows, nor was there another way out. The darkness would have been as thick as tar were it not for the light that spilled in from under the curtain and the faint blue of glowing orbs that dotted the walls.

Malehk approached one of the orbs. They were subtle and dim, each one the size of his fist. As he drew closer, he knew immediately what they were. They were the same glowing crystals that Caul had produced from his bag at the hospital. None of them were shining even half as bright as the one he'd captured that poor bastard's soul in, but Malehk couldn't help but wonder if each of them contained another life. He looked around the room, giving up on counting them after twenty.

A digital buzz from a computer inside the lab yanked his focus back. He heard another swish and clop from the doctor's scuttling shoes as he hobbled around the room. Malehk moved to sink further into the shadows and cursed himself as his boots rapped again against the hollow floor.

'The hollow floor?' His attention shot to the grating beneath his feet. It was a large vent that ran atop a wide duct, likely used to circulate air into and out of the subterranean lab. Malehk crouched and, with a quick look to the door, he tugged the grate up and out of place. It made more noise than he'd liked, but he had no choice.

At the center of the laboratory, Caul stopped. His hands hung above a computer keyboard while his head lurched around the room. He tried to separate the sound that he'd just heard from the bubbling and hum that filled the air around him. It was a quiet sound, but it was out of place. Whatever it was, it was something that didn't belong inside his lab.

The doctor lowered his bag to the floor and retrieved his hat from the steel table. He used slow, predatory movements, as if he were laying a trap for the noise's return. Creeping across the floor, his head turned toward the alcove with his sleeping subjects. There was nothing there but the bubbling gel and silhouette bodies. He then looked to the doors at the back. There was no one there, nor was there any sound, but one of the curtains was moving. It was a subtle wave in the fabric and may have simply been touched by the breeze of his own movements.

Nevertheless, Caul ambled for the door. His glassy eyes flicked between the doors, seeking out any other clues, but he continued toward the shifting fabric. He gripped its face with bony knuckles, paused, then jerked the curtain aside. It hissed a loud scraping noise along its rails and light from the main room shot in. There was no one there. Caul stabbed at the switch on the wall, turning on the overhead light, but still there was nothing.

Everything was as he'd left it. Stacks of shelves circled the room, and his precious crystals were lined up and spaced out evenly along them. He began mumbling under his breath as he stepped to each of the shards in turn. He'd clamp his fingertips around them and turn them slightly in place before moving on to the next. Even as he crouched to reach the lower shelf however, he never once looked down.

Malehk was lying flat on his back inside the duct, his arms straightened down his sides. He was rigid and unblinking, staring up at the soles of Caul's shoes as they shuffled and stamped at the grating above his face. The unsteady footsteps rang inside the duct, which echoed back the howling sound of emptiness. Malehk tried to shrink, to hold his breath, but that only seemed to amplify the noise of his pounding heart. He heard it hammering inside his ears and he was certain that Caul could hear it too.

The doctor moved away from the grate, inspecting the crystals that were placed deeper inside the room. A moment later his brown soles returned, their clanging and scraping on the vent twisting up Malehk's belly with every step. Caul found nothing to explain the out-of-place sound, and nothing in the storage closet had been disturbed. He turned a full circle on his heels, his glasses catching and reflecting sheets of light. Then he stopped and his foot tapped at the floor. It may have been nothing, just a hunched man adjusting his stance. Then he tapped again.

Akara was working through a mouthful of synthetic meat. It was a bit tougher than some of the other places he'd dined, but the flavor was good, and the price was better than anywhere else in the sector. The funds the tsesh skimmed off the city were technically limitless, but he tried to keep his expenses to a minimum so as to not alert his father.

As he sunk his fork into another bit of steak, Marianne slurped a quick sip of tea and placed the cup back on the table. The motion was abrupt and decisive, as though she'd finally settled a debate in her mind that Akara hadn't been aware of.

"Okay," she said, "I'm gonna do it. I'm gonna go talk to him."

Akara chewed slowly at the meat then looked across the diner. "Pharos?"

She nodded a reply. "I'm just gonna go over and say hi," she explained. "I'll tell him that he has my vote... if it comes up."

He stifled a laugh around a cheek full of steak. "Okay."

She threw a look over her shoulder then turned back. "The crowd's thinned out around him, right? I could just pop over for a quick 'hello'."

Akara looked back to Pharos and was about to respond, but Marianne cut him off.

"Of course, they could just be leaving him alone because he wants to eat in peace. It'd be rude to interrupt his dinner, wouldn't it?"

"Just go over and talk to him," Akara said, a half-step louder than necessary. He smoothed out his voice. "You just want to say hello. I'm sure he won't mind."

She nodded again and thumped her napkin on the table. "Okay," she finalized, rising from the booth. "I'll be right back."

Akara snickered and shook his head, turning his attention back to his plate. "I love you."

"Love you," she replied with a quick turn, biting off the words before heading across the room. She walked cautiously and thoughtfully, as though she were crossing a tightrope or stalking a prey.

Akara's eyes followed her, turned up in a smile and filled with amusement and adoration. When she'd made it halfway, he went back to work, sawing at the slab on his plate. As his knife cut through and scraped the porcelain, there was another sound that accompanied it, a distant boom that came from outside. It sounded like a car accident, and as Akara stabbed at the next cube of steak he turned to see what it was.

He expected to see two cars banged up on opposite ends. He expected to see two drivers bickering over blame. Expectation draws lines in our minds, it sets the baseline for our reaction and response to the world. What Akara saw outside the window punched deep beneath that line and hollowed out his belly. It was the kind of sight that plunges so far past expectation that you have to blink to reset your eyes, to be sure that it was real.

An enormous beast, as tall as a bus and nearly as wide was barreling down the centerline of the street. It charged forward, punching craters in the pavement with tight fists and shouldering cars aside to bulldoze a path. The monster was covered in taut, gray flesh and black spikes that flickered and flashed with arcs of electricity. Its large mouth was stretched painfully wide and filled with row behind row of wet, pointed teeth and a flicking purple tongue.

It was stampeding toward them, showing no sign of slowing down or changing course. Akara had only enough time to rise from the booth and call out half of Marianne's name. The monster crashed like a truck through the diner's front wall, sending shattered glass and concrete dust exploding into the room. The sound was deafening, and all but swallowed the trailing screams and raining glass. Smoke and the powder of cement billowed into the air, filling Akara's throat with a bitter tang and biting at his eyes. The haze washed away any detail in the room, leaving only vague shapes and silhouettes scrambling in a mad panic away from the hulking beast.

Akara was shoved backwards to the floor, and as his spine caught the corner of a table, he saw the looming, gray body stumble and smash through the front counter. He watched as Deidre turned to face the monster moments before she was crushed between the rubble and the wall. The room spun and twisted Akara's mind. His ears rang and the surrounding screams were muffled, as if they were underwater.

It was the roar that spun the world back into focus. The beast bellowed with furious rage, and Akara zeroed in on the sound. He kicked away debris and scrambled to his knees. Through the chaos and smoke, he found Marianne. Rather, he saw a head of blonde curls that had barely the time to flinch at the attack. She had just reached Pharos' table and now the gray beast shook and raged between her and Akara. He could only watch as the monster gripped a section of the shattered countertop and hurled it across the room. Marianne turned the moment it left the creature's hand, and the jagged stone slab cracked against the side of her face.

Through the smoke Akara saw blood, Marianne's blood. It sprayed against the window and poured out over her golden hair as she dropped to the floor, disappearing into the white and lingering fog. His mind filled up with a thousand thoughts, a thousand words, and a thousand memories. His head became so full that the pressure made him truly deaf. He forgot the taste of dust on his tongue, and he could see nothing but her body, crumpled and bloody beside the booth.

He meant to scream. He meant to rush forward and scoop her up. He meant to do all the things men imagine they'd do when it mattered. But Akara wasn't just a man. He was tsesh.

He pulled his steel mask from deep inside his pocket and clicked it into place across his nose and mouth. His mind went cold and flushed out the panic and fury. His thoughts hardened and clicked forward like iron gears washed clean. His eyes went serpentine and gold, glowing atop a line of rigid, black scales. A flood of yellow ribbons filled his vision like water rushing into the room. Akara had never seen the glow of fate so thick. Drawing his sword and pistol from beneath his coat, he knew it was there for him.

Akara rose like death itself, a cloaked figure of whipping shadows and glowing eyes amidst the smoke and bedlam that filled the room. The blue lights of his pistol sliced a line through the fog as it powered up. The monster at the center of it all howled again, spraying thick saliva at the people who were scrambling all around it. It reared back, about to move, about to lunge forward and finish its bloody work. Then a gunshot exploded through the noise.

The bullet tore through the creature's jaw and shattered a row of fangs as it punched out its mouth. The blast commanded silence and, for a moment, the room obeyed. It was a brief pause in the chaos, like a police whistle blaring through the din of a crowded room or a single drop of oil dropped into a pool of murky water. Everything was pushed aside in its wake; smoke, screams, even fear, but only for a moment.

Akara fired three more shots, whipping up the frenzy once more. One shot pierced the creature's side, the other two seemed to glance off the electricity that was whipping between the barbs along its back. It was enough to redirect the monster's attention.

Akara hesitated, reassessing his attack as the creature turned to face him. He was turned sideways, with his gun hand locked forward, smoke from the barrel mixing with the dust that was hanging in the air. His other arm was straightened low behind him, the tip of his blade grazing the floor. He fired two more rounds, center mass. One drew barely a drop of blood and the other ricocheted again.

The monster's jawed stretched open and its tongue flailed ahead of a raging shriek. It hammered its fists into the floor and shook its head, fanning out a stream of bloody spit before charging toward the tsesh. Akara dove under its thrashing arm, slicing his sword across its thigh and turning to fire a point-blank round into the back of its knee.

Blood and meat popped out around his pistol and splattered up Akara's sleeve. The creature buckled sideways and roared, toppling against another wall. Two more shots rang out. This time, both bullets were deflected. Electricity lunged at the would-be points of impact, drawing crackling spiderwebs across the monster's back.

The onlookers of the room had stopped and pinned themselves against the walls. To them, it appeared as though the masked stranger was winning. In truth, he simply wasn't dead yet. The attacks were futile and Akara knew it. The electricity that it was producing seemed to act as a magnetic shell around the beast, dispersing or diverting most of his attacks. Akara bared his teeth, his serpentine eyes jumping around the room and surging ever brighter. Finally, he locked on a space above the toppled creature, a small cylinder peeking out of the ceiling; the fire-suppression system.

Before the hulk could turn for another attack, Akara raised his gun and fired at the ceiling. It sparked and shattered the metal, releasing a torrent of watery foam that rained down and drenched the scrambling monster. Its web of electricity lashed erratically across its back and up its shoulders, leaping out at everything wet or conductive. The smell of burning meat rose up in the smoke from the creature's flesh. It howled again and punched a crater into the wall, launching itself into a hammering sprint at its attacker.

Akara stepped backward, firing round after round, each landing with a satisfying and meaty thunk in its belly. It stopped just short of him and raised both of its boulder-like fists into the air. Akara felt the heat from its roaring breath and searing flesh. In a flash, he flicked his sword up, severing an artery beneath the monster's thick arm. His snake eyes glowed brightly, channeling the heat into his blade. He leapt and spun in the air, landing two strikes along the creature's throat. The first split it open wide, the second removed its ugly head entirely.

The body and its parts landed with wet and heavy sounds on the floor. Akara stood over the mound of red blood and gray muscle, his jacket heaving with his breath and his sword still glowing and spitting electricity to the floor.

The sudden calm and quiet only served to highlight the sound of car doors outside. Akara counted three, followed by the stomping of boots and rustling of cloaks. It was the Legacy, three agents drawn to the scene by noise and smoke.

'That was quick,' Akara thought, his eyes shifting toward their approach, his breath huffing through the vented mask.

The agents rushed in through the hole where the door used to be. The first thing they found was the body that used to be sweet Deidre, now a bloody mass running thin beneath the spray of water. Next, they saw the creature, lifeless, headless, and twisted on the floor. Then they saw the tsesh, an amber-eyed devil with a stained sword and smoking gun.

The first thing Akara saw were their weapons, thick pistols clutched and ready in their hands. Two of the agents were clearly veterans, grizzled and serious, their middle-aged eyes scanning the room. The third was a young boy in his late teens with a mess of blond spikes on his head and a black, pointed sigil tattooed over his left eye; a cocky young rook desperate to prove himself.

One of the veterans opened his mouth, but Akara spoke first.

"Stop," he hissed out. His eyes remained narrow but flared with yellow light. The order filled the room and muted every other thought. The agents and the people around them did exactly as he commanded. They stopped, their arms and jaws going slack.

He had only a few seconds, just enough time to gather up Marianne and leap through one of the broken windows. Her hair was red and sticky, but she was still breathing, and her eyelids fluttered with his movements. Akara let a sense of relief lead his emotions back to his mind as he raced into an alley. By the time the agents in the diner had come to their senses, the mysterious tsesh was gone, swallowed up by the shadows of the city.

# # #

Malehk held his breath and crept a hand to his back where the pistol waited inside its holster. Caul tapped at the grate above his face once more. Malehk touched the weapon's switch, knowing he'd only have time for a single round once he activated the gun. His mind slipped back to the hospital where Caul had stolen that man's soul and imprisoned it. He wondered if Caul might do the same to him and, for a second, he wondered what it would feel like if he did.

There was no time for those thoughts. He pushed them aside and eased his finger inside the trigger guard of his gun. He could feel his chest pounding like a war drum, beating ripples into the breath that was trapped inside his lungs. His thumb pressed up against the weapon's switch.

Two quick and electronic notes chirped into the room, catching both Caul and Malehk off guard. It was the doctor's comm, alerting him of a call. He swatted a fingertip at its face and answered in a frustrated tone that was muted by his raspy voice. "Yes?"

Malehk couldn't make out what was being said. The voice on the other end was male and angry, perhaps excited.

"I am. On my way," Caul answered back. His next few motions were fast and hasty. He switched off the comm and ambled away as hurriedly as he could, then snatched up his bag and scuffled toward the elevator door.

Malehk pursed his lips and eased out the breath that he'd been holding, quickly enough to relieve his cramping lungs, but slow enough to make only the slightest whisper of sound. He waited for the elevator to open then close again before he moved. Once he was sure the doctor had gone, he pushed the grate up and out of its setting, then sat up, his head and shoulders peeking from the floor. He blew out another breath, this one loud and heavy with relief.

The curtain had been thrown open and he could see that, save for the bubbling tanks, the lab was empty again. Reaching into his coat, Malehk retrieved his silver flask and twisted off the cap. He took three long gulps of burning whiskey then huffed another breath.

"I hate this place," he muttered to no one. No sooner had the words left his mouth than a new sound boomed in the room, a loud groan of twisting metal. Malehk fired a look in every direction, but then felt the aluminum shift beneath him. His eyes closed and a curse was halfway across his lips when the duct broke loose. It dropped out from under him, transforming the shaft into a steep slide and sending the tsesh flailing headlong down its slope.

He bounced against the thin and rumbling walls, filling the duct with grunts and echoes as he struggled to regain control. His hands swatted at every surface, grasping for a handhold, but the tube was smooth and sheer, and he only slid faster and faster. The tunnel turned a few times, granting him a handful of seconds to slow his fall, but there would be no stopping. Wherever the duct emptied out, that's where he was going.

After more than a hundred feet and a half dozen fresh bruises, Malehk saw light. It was dim and smoky red, but it was definitely an opening, and it was coming up fast. He tried to press his arms and legs into the walls, slicing out a long shriek against the smooth surface. The opening was covered by a vent. If he could slow himself enough, he hoped it might support his weight. He couldn't, and it didn't.

Malehk punched through the vent and shot out of the opening. His feet kicked up and his head dropped down. Before he could think, his hand shot back and caught the swinging vent. His body jolted then swung in long pendulum arcs beneath its groaning hinges. Looking around his strained arms, he saw the familiar ruins of Old Mallis a thousand feet below. He was hanging from the downward spire high above the center of the subterranean world. He grunted and gasped and worked to readjust his grip on the dangling metal.

Another sound then began bouncing down the shaft. It was hard and hollow and tumbling fast. Malehk's silver flask spun from the opening. He stretched out desperately to catch it. The flask danced along his frantic fingertips before tipping away and spiraling out of reach. He watched it vanish to the streets and shadows far below, then, defeated, returned his free hand to grip the hanging vent.

"I hate this place!" he shouted loud for all of Mallis to hear.

Chapter 11

Akara took an irregular path back to Marianne's, ducking in and out of crooks and pausing at every corner. It was late afternoon, and the traffic was picking up in the Squall. He used every sidestep and zigzag he could across the span of city to avoid anyone seeing them. Even if the Legacy hadn't been at his back, he wouldn't know how to explain himself carrying a bleeding and unconscious woman through the slums.

He reached her front stoop, gratefully vacant, and lifted her hand to press a valid fingerprint against the scanner. It left a bloody smudge on the panel but lit up an obedient green and he heard the thick locks drop open. Akara shot a few glances around the street, reassuring himself that no one was near enough to raise any questions.

Halfway down the hall, before he could reach the elevator door, he heard it chime out its welcoming note. Someone was coming. Akara turned away and cursed the end of his luck, huddling over Marianne's body that was hanging limp in his arms. Over his shoulder, the elevator doors rolled open. There was the sound of a few hurried steps that slowed dramatically as they drew near.

"Uh," a male voice stretched out cautiously behind Akara's back. "Is everything okay?" the man finally asked.

Akara spun to face him, his eyes now blazing, golden slits. "Shh," he hissed abruptly.

The man standing there was a middle-aged nobody with dark hair and a day's worth of scruff painting his jaw. Everything about him was generic, even more so as Akara's command drained the color from his face and forced his expression to go limp.

Akara hoisted Marianne back up to his arms and shoved past the generic man. He stepped quickly into the open elevator and pressed the button for Marianne's floor. The serpentine daggers in his eyes relaxed but held fast to the dazed man in the hall until the doors rattled shut.

Marianne was already stirring in his arms when he reached her door. Her shifting body and meek breath flushed the aching tension from Akara's chest. He immediately spoke soft words of comfort in her ear as he rushed her to the bedroom and laid her down. He brushed the stained mats of hair from her face and smiled at her fluttering eyelids before darting back to the kitchen to fetch a bowl of water and damp cloth.

Moments later he was at her side, wiping away the blood and wringing pink water back into the bowl. He was careful to avoid touching the cut that sliced up from her forehead and into her hairline. He was even more careful to maintain his smile and caress her cheek whenever signs of worry began to appear on her perfect face.

"What happened?" she asked, her thoughts and eyes still foggy.

"You don't remember?"

Her gaze drifted aside, searching the murk of her mind for an answer. "We were at the diner..."

"There was an attack," Akara said, filling in the simple blanks.

Her eyes swept back up to his and winced against the pain in her brow. "An attack?"

He nodded. "Some kind of creature broke through the wall. You were hit by the debris."

"Deidre," she said, her eyes going wide. She almost made a move to sit up, but the pain forced her to reconsider.

Akara tensed up his muscles and clamped his teeth shut. Behind the veil of his collected expression, he could see the twisted remains of Deidre, broken and unrecognizable beneath the shattered countertop. He pushed the image away and focused on Marianne. "Don't worry about any of that right now," he said as vaguely as he could. "You need to relax and let me clean this cut."

Marianne finally reached up and discreetly tapped her fingers at the cut. The pain spat out like spiderwebs down her skull and cinched up her face. While lowering her hand, she paused at her ear and rubbed the lobe. "I lost one of my earrings," she said, looking to Akara with a growing face of worry.

He only smiled and shook his head. "It's okay. Look." He jutted his head towards the glass box across the room. Inside the hollow cube, sprouting up from the dark soil, their flower had begun to bloom. Where once there was a small and pale-green bulb, there now were bright, ruby pedals that were just beginning to reach outward at the world. They were streaked with hairline strokes of black and edged in faded pink that blended down and into the stem.

"It blossomed," Marianne said, her voice whispering with wonder.

"I told you you could do it."

She coughed out a laugh and jabbed at his chest. "You're a jerk."

He laughed and nodded. "I am a jerk."

"Oh, Akara," she said, turning a loving gaze back at the flower, "That makes me so happy."

He wiped away another patch of blood and paused to take in her smile. The blood and dirt, and her stained and matted hair drew a sharp contrast against her smooth skin and those vibrant, sapphire eyes. Framing her features in the mud of the world only made them stand out. It made her that much more beautiful. For half a beat, his mind went back to the diner. He saw Marianne struck down by the beast, and his belly sunk into thoughts of what might have happened had he not been there to stop it.

He shook off the haunted thoughts and looked instead to the solace in her eyes. "I love you," he whispered simply.

Marianne brushed a weakened hand down his cheek and smiled against the pounding in her head. "I love you too," she replied before lifting herself to kiss him.

Thunder roared outside and an afternoon rain began to patter against the window. The twinkling of the city painted watercolor lights on the walls and somewhere in the distance, sirens were blaring out in search of the tsesh. Akara knew he should have left. He should have hid. He should have fled underground, told his father what had happened, and begged for his forgiveness. By revealing himself to the world, war would be inevitable and close behind.

He was surprised to find that he didn't care; not tonight. If those would be his final hours of peace, he wanted them to be with her, hidden away from the predatory world, laying among thick blankets, warm lights, and blooming flowers, burying himself in her skin and scent. War was coming, but the world hadn't ended. Not tonight.

By the time Caul had returned to the control room, the others had already retired around the long table. Daemon sat at the head with Faedra at his side. Kaelus was sitting back with casual posture in a seat at the far end nearest the door. Valen Kirsch had also joined them, seated in the perfect center of the table's long edge. All but Kaelus turned toward him as the doctor entered the room.

"A meeting?" Caul noted aloud. "So soon." He shuffled towards an open seat across from Valen. "This is very. Counter. Productive," he muttered almost to himself before sitting down, planting his bag on the floor beside him. "I really must have time. To analyze. My. Data."

"Something's come up," Daemon responded plainly.

Caul's good eye went wide behind his glasses, and he turned a quizzical look to each of the others in turn.

It was Faedra who finally addressed him. "Your bio-wraith was killed before it could finish the job."

Caul continued looking around at the others as if searching for confirmation. "That is. Highly. Unlikely," he defended. "Perhaps you. Simply. Lost control."

"It was a tsesh," Kaelus boomed in baritone from the side, snatching up Caul's full attention.

"A tsesh?" Caul looked to Daemon. "But that is. Impossible. The tsesh. Are all—"

"Dead," Daemon finished for him. "Yes, we thought so too." He leveled an accusing look on Valen.

Valen didn't respond or even care. He sat up straight and stoic in his chair, offering only half of a glance to Dr. Cerrone.

The long and pointed silence left Caul wondering about the purpose of the meeting. Were they blaming him for the failure? "It was. An unforeseen. Variable," he finally said. "I can. Divert. More power. To the others. They will—"

"No," Daemon cut him off. He bowed and shook his head while repeating the word as if it were a giggle. "No, no, no." When he finally looked up, a smile had crept across his lips and the overhead lights were glinting off the black marbles of his eyes that pierced with sinister intent at the doctor. "This is a rare opportunity, and like all things rare, it has value."

Their eyes all jumped around at each other across the table, all but Faedra who sat like a fiery statue beside her master.

"New information demands a new course of action," Daemon continued.

"What do you suggest?" Valen finally spoke up from his center seat.

"You," Daemon answered with a sharp tone. "You are going to pay a visit to Lord Kaddler. Tonight."

"Kaddler?" Valen questioned. "You mean Pharos."

"No, I mean Kaddler."

"But sir, Lord Kaddler is one of your staunchest supporters. We need him on the—"

"I don't need any of them." Daemon's black eyes stabbed at Valen and froze the moment in stone. "Kaddler is an aging fool who is losing his seat to an ideological child. He's used up. But perhaps he can serve us one last time."

"As you wish," Valen conceded after a thoughtful pause.

"You'll be going with him," Daemon added with a stabbing finger at Kaelus.

The bald and pale flesh of Kaelus' head cinched up. "Me? Why? I'm no assassin. My work is on the front lines. Send me after these tsesh."

"In due time," Daemon said, patting down his argument with an open hand. "Kaddler will be an unnatural and high-profile case. It will appear suspicious if we don't have the Legacy investigate, but we can't have those psychic pests tracing anything back to us. You are going with Mr. Kirsch to ensure there is no psychic trail for them to follow."

"It will still raise suspicion," Faedra said. "There are whispers of conspiracy in the Legacy halls, and the agents are no fools."

"How many?" Daemon asked.

Faedra shrugged. "Maybe ten percent of the agents."

"That's nothing," Kaelus argued.

"Two weeks ago, it was five," she fired back. "We can't risk stoking those flames. We have to stop these conspirators before they become untenable."

"Agreed," Daemon replied. "Do what you can to gather a list of their names. Have it on my desk by tomorrow."

"And what of. My work?" Caul hissed from the side.

"Your work continues as planned," Daemon ordered. "Have as many bio-wraiths ready as you can before the election." He turned an almost gleeful look to the rest of the table. "You see gentlemen? Opportunity. Perhaps this tsesh can rid us of all our problems with one artful stroke."

#

Bwrynn had taken a late lunch. Jaga's call for extra training had shaken her and filled up more thoughts in her mind and hours in her day than usual. He had approached the subject with his usual grace and patience, but she knew that he'd been more than a little disappointed. She was only eight years old when they met, and not a day had passed since then that he hadn't praised her strength. Recently however, that praise has felt gaunt and shallow, like water from a tap that was slowly closing up. Had she not been advancing as quickly as he'd expected? Was she growing weaker? She felt as though his expectations were a bottomless cup that she could never hope to fill.

Whatever it was that lingered in his mind, it lingered in hers as well. It became a cycle of distraction in her day, rusted gears grinding out dust in the back of her mind. She'd try to focus on her training, only to have her thoughts become haunted by Jaga's disapproval. With every failed attempt, Bwrynn would curse her feeble mind and mirror her master's frustration.

She finally decided to take a break and grab lunch in the Legacy cafeteria. She wouldn't try to read anyone. She wouldn't extend her mind or scan the thoughts of others. She was simply going to eat a sandwich and drink some tea. Maybe she would watch the other agents as people do, observing their normal interactions, not caring what their thoughts might be.

It was a good and simple plan, and she was halfway through a chicken sandwich when it all went off the rails. Bwrynn's chewing slowed then stopped entirely as a familiar figure walked into the cafeteria and sat down two tables away. It was the stocky, auburn-haired woman from that morning, the casual smile masking a mind of black towers and blue flames.

She wasn't with the other two, the old master and his pupil. She was alone, and Bwrynn knew that she'd never be able to unlock the woman's mind as it was. Without distraction, a trained agent can bury secrets so deep that they themselves might not know they exist. If Bwrynn wanted to find out what the woman was hiding, she'd have to catch her off guard. But this woman was a veteran with decades of training circling her mind like growth rings in an ancient tree. How could an initiate like Bwrynn rattle someone made of iron?

As other agents filtered between the tables, toting trays of food and making casual conversation, Bwrynn's eyes flicked between them. In an instant, she knew what to do, her good and simple plan. Legacy agents were trained to fight and defend with the power of their minds, but they were still just people. Everyone in that room was a simple human being, each capable of distraction, of frustration, and of tripping over their words.

Bwrynn finally swallowed her bite of sandwich and stood from the table, her plastic platter of food hoisted up and tucked in against her chest. She maneuvered through a clique of agents and made her way to a seat two tables down. She planted her tray across from the auburn-haired woman, rattling it against the false wood a bit louder than she'd intended, and certainly louder than necessary.

The sudden approach and commotion didn't seem to bother the older woman, who was lifting a dainty portion of potato to her mouth. She chewed happily at the bite and turned her smile to the young and very serious agent that had decided to join her.

"Hello," the woman said before motioning to a chair with her fork. "Please, join me."

Bwrynn was suddenly unsure of herself. Standing there, in front of this all-too-pleasant woman, she realized that she had no idea what to say. She really had no plan at all. Her mouth had gone dry, but she managed to work out a slow and mindless, "Um." 'Something casual,' she thought. 'Say something normal people say.'

"My name's Thisa," the woman said, beating her to the punch, "Thisa Rosewood." She punctuated with another gesture to the chair.

An introduction. Why hadn't she thought of that? "Bwrynn Lucane," she answered back, lowering into the seat.

"Master Jaga's rising young star," Thisa replied. "Yes, I know."

"You know?"

The old woman laughed quietly and bobbed her head, still chewing at the dollop of mashed potato. "Of course. I dare say everyone knows of you. Youngest initiate in the Legacy. A pretty good one too, if the rumors are to be believed."

"Rumors?" she asked, suddenly uncomfortable in her seat. "What rumors?"

"Oh, nothing of a secret," Thisa reassured her. "People just talk. You know, tall tales and third-party accounts. You just brought in a rogue, didn't you?"

Bwrynn's expression sunk. "You heard about that?"

Realizing that she'd struck some kind of chord within the young girl, Thisa straightened up her posture. Her face changed from friendly old lady to something more akin to a consoling mother. "It didn't go quite as you'd expected, huh?"

Bwrynn was hesitant to reply. She was supposed to be throwing this woman off her guard. She was supposed to be prodding around inside her hidden secrets. Yet here she was, tumbling through her own mind, rattled within seconds of sitting down. Jaga would have been so disappointed. "No, I guess not," she finally answered.

Thisa snorted out a laugh and went back to being a smiling old woman, busy with her potatoes. "It never does."

"But he was still brought in," she defended.

"That is true."

"It was a minor incident, really."

Thisa's narrow mouth turned up on one side, deepening the tiny cracks and wrinkles around her lips. She looked thoughtfully at the young psychic with her cocked smile for a long, friendly second. "We all miss things when we're young."

The motherly glow of the woman's smile made Bwrynn feel small again, forever the student, forever the child. The master agents always made her feel welcome, but it was a patronizing swaddle that she'd grown tired of. Her teeth bit down behind tense lips, threatening to break the mask of gratitude she wore on her face. "I saw you in the halls this morning." Bwrynn hoped the jarring change of pace would rattle the old woman's mind and show some break in her defenses.

"I saw you too," Thisa replied before taking a sip of tea.

The response spat Bwrynn's tactic back in her face. She felt her thoughts break from their rails and kick up panicked dust inside her mind. She punched her tongue around inside her mouth, trying to make way for words to come. "You saw me?"

Thisa's smile turned coy and playful, her eyes twinkling over her steaming mug. "It's a difficult lesson to learn," she said, "to never lose track of yourself."

Bwrynn's cheeks had gone flush. Her mouth was a pursed beak, tiny and quiet on a flustered face.

"Thoughts are everywhere," Thisa continued, pretending not to notice the girl's bewilderment. "They're always coming and going, creeping about, this way and that." She paused as if to weigh her thoughts, then smiled a mischievous and knowing smile. "When we open our minds, it's a bit like sneaking out a window. You know? To meet up with some boy or to see that movie we were told we couldn't see."

She furled her brow and sank back in her chair. Thisa had clearly lived a much wilier childhood than her. Bwrynn was less than ten years old when she'd been recruited by the Legacy. Her first dorm had been on the twentieth floor and the window didn't open. Any movies she wanted to see, Jaga would watch with her. And boys? A boy's mind was always a jumbled mess of sharp edges that she simply didn't have the patience for.

"The problem is," Thisa added with her sly and sideways smile, "we have to leave the window open if we're going to sneak back in, right?"

Bwrynn's eyes were twisted in bare confusion. "Okay?"

Thisa shrugged. "So, what's to stop someone from walking right in while we're away?"

"Were you in my mind?"

Thisa offered another smile, not warm and maternal, but devious and snide. "Never lose track of yourself," she repeated before taking a bite of a sandwich; a sandwich she didn't have before. Bwrynn's eyes jumped down to her empty tray. It was her sandwich!

Bwrynn was about to bark a protest, but something in the air had changed. There was a buzzing in their minds, like a swarm of bees beneath a tarp. It was a growing surge of urgency cascading through the room that flushed away all simple banter, replacing it with trained reaction. Both her and Thisa turned their eyes across the room. Agents were racing through the halls outside, and others were piling up around the cafeteria door, pushing past each other to join them. Thisa and Bwrynn left their food and moved toward the crowd.

The mass of black cloaks and shoving hands was pouring out the sound of excited chatter. It was a mess of broken syllables smashing together and Bwrynn struggled to isolate any single word.

"What's happening?" she shouted into the crowd, the futile question only adding to the chaos.

Finally, her ears picked out a single voice that spoke a single word. It was buried beneath the noise, and she may have misheard it, but she swore she heard them say, "Tsesh!" Then another voice on the edge of all the panic repeated and confirmed, "There's a tsesh in Sector Six!"

Thisa noticed when Bwrynn didn't push herself into the crowd with the others. She noticed the young initiate step back and whisper to herself, "They're real."

# # #

The pale gray of the sky was finally settling to choppy black. The spikes of lightning had recessed back to a fluttering strobe, giving way to the pattering rain that was now painting the cement of the city two shades darker and washing the metal with glossy veneer. The day had been long, full of rumor and hearsay. It was Lord Kaddler's job to hear them all out, but he hated vague opinions and mismatched stories. He wanted concrete answers, not panicked stories of monsters.

Kaddler had asked sector security, slowly and in turn if they'd seen a tsesh. Some simply said 'no'. Others prattled on about suspicious characters that may or may not have been the serpentine devils in disguise. Both responses were useless. He may as well have been asking his five-year-old nephew. The Legacy agents weren't talking, and anyone who might have been at the diner during the attack had been taken into custody. Pramoore was overstepping his authority again, but it didn't matter. If the polls were true, Kaddler would be out of a job within the week, and if Daemon wanted the headache, he could have it.

The sector lord's house was big, though not as big as he'd wanted. He had a swimming pool, but Lord Kinney's in Sector Two was larger. He had five acres of land, but Lord Aurich in Sector Seven had just as much as well as a fountain in his backyard. Lord Pandril in Sector Four had less space, but his lawn was covered, front to back, in real grass, soft, green, and worth a small fortune. Kaddler's house would have to do. It was three stories of red brick and cream-colored trim. Five modest bedrooms were spread out between the top two floors. The main floor was filled out by a kitchen and dining room, his enclosed pool, and of course, his den.

The warm, wooden room was his favorite place in the entire house. It had a wall of real paper books that he had no intention of ever reading. The maid was never allowed in the study and the dust, he felt, added to the authenticity of his collected tomes. Another wall was taken up by a stone fireplace that he kept lit, even on the warm nights. In the corner of the room, he kept a stocked bar, ornamented by every shade of amber-filled bottles. Tucked away in that room, amidst the earthy-wooden smells, the deep-brown walls, and the red carpet with golden edges, he hadn't a care in the world. No one could ask him for anything and there were no scandals creeping around the corner. When he was in his den, sitting in the padded throne behind his important-looking desk, Sector Six could burn for all he cared, and he was anxious to retire there tonight of all nights.

He crossed the marble floor of his lobby and pressed a thumb against the panel beside the door. While the electronics buzzed beneath the surface, Kaddler blew out a held breath, a sour breath, tainted by pleasantries, empty promises and falsified smiles. Finally, a familiar click sounded out from inside the dark mahogany and the door opened. The fireplace in his den had already been lit. Its warm flames were flicking shadows that danced around the unlit room like puppets on strings. It would have appeared welcoming had it been a casual encounter, but Kaddler immediately wanted to know who had been in his study, and who had lit his fire.

A pale man, tall and thin, was sitting at his desk, his long fingers forming a steeple in front of his face. The firelight painted the edges of the man's gray suit and snowy hair but cast his eyes into deep shadows around his pointed cheeks and pointed nose.

"Lights," Kaddler called out to the room, his voice laced with irritation.

The overhead lights faded into life. They finalized the edges of the man at the desk but failed to reach the dark shadows of his eyes. He didn't flinch at the change in the room or the sector lord's approach.

"Valen Kirsch," Kaddler realized aloud. "What are you doing in my house?"

"I just realized," Valen said, panning his head along the width of the room as though he'd only just now seen it, "I've never actually been inside your home before. It's quite nice."

Kaddler followed his attention, his expression growing ever more puzzled. "Thank you," he responded out of reflex. "Why are you here?"

Valen's stone stature finally broke, and he sat forward in the chair, pointing a slender finger at him. "The polls suggest that you're about to lose your seat."

"Some of them, yes."

"That presents a problem for Mr. Pramoore."

Kaddler looked around the room once more, as if searching the shadows for Daemon himself. "Well, uh, you can tell Mr. Pramoore that I apologize for the inconvenience."

"Inconvenient?" Valen repeated, rising from the large chair. "This is more than a simple... inconvenience. Daemon Pramoore has poured more hours into his work than you and your campaign dogs could ever possibly imagine. So much so that it dwarfs you into insignificance."

Kaddler stepped back and steadied his stance. He felt his legs quivering inside his expensive, silken slacks. "Well, what does he want me to do?" he stammered. "I've dug into Pharos. I've tapped every resource, employed every strategy."

"You're old," Valen responded simply, his steps still creeping closer to the trembling lord. "You're losing to a child because you can no longer relate to people. They don't like you because they don't trust you." He gestured over his shoulder to the window and the bursts of lightning above the city. "Those people out there love Aldan Pharos. They love him because they trust him."

Kaddler shook his head. "So, what am I supposed to do about that?"

"You?" Valen wagged a finger and clicked his tongue at him. "No, not you. That is why I am here, to disarm Aldan Pharos. To take away his adoration. To take away his trust."

Kaddler's head was jutting around the room, faster with every step that Valen took towards him. His breath was shortened into useless gasps, barely enough to fill a single word at a time. "I s-see. And, um. How, uh. How will you be doing that?"

Valen stopped. His head lowered and his eyes went dark. "Tragedy," he said, his voice seeming to rise from a blackened pit. He turned his black eyes up with predatory intent. "You see, Aldan Pharos had you killed tonight."

Kaddler broke from the door and rushed around Valen. He was sprinting on clumsy legs toward his desk, toward the pistol he kept locked inside. He hadn't crossed even half the gold and crimson carpet when he felt the skeletal hand clamp down on his shoulder. Valen's grip was robotic, heavy, and oblivious to its own strength. Kaddler heard a snap as his collarbone buckled and pain stabbed upward into his eyes, blinding him.

He wasn't sure how, but Valen lifted him from the ground with that single, demonic hand and hurled him toward the fireplace. His spine cracked against the expensive, decorative stones. He felt the heat from the flames by his hand and heard the evenly paced steps of Valen drawing near. As Kaddler's vision began to clear, he could make out the tall, wraith-like form of his attacker stooping towards him.

"You can scream if you'd like. We're alone here," Valen offered as consolation. He raised a shadowy hand in front of Kaddler's wide and teary eyes. "This will not be quick."

Thunder exploded in the skies above the modest manor. Lightning flared overhead, splashing blue and white hues across the large yard. There was more than two hundred feet of manicured lawn between the window and the street, much too far for anyone to hear the screams of a dying politician.

Chapter 12

The morning bled in slow and lazy, though still too fast for Akara's liking. He'd hoped he wouldn't sleep. He wanted to keep his human eyes open, to draw out the hours with long thoughts and make the night last forever. He only lasted an hour past Marianne. Exhaustion from the night before had made his mind heavy, and the thick blanket bundled up all the heat of Marianne's naked body beside him and eventually buried his thoughts in dream.

Were they dreams? He couldn't remember a single one. He couldn't remember falling asleep either, or even waking up. He simply had become aware that he was awake, so it stood to reason that he had slept. Even awake though, he didn't move. He allowed his eyes to trace peacefully along the curves of Marianne's sleeping form, the rise and fall from hip to waist to shoulder. Her hair poured down the lines of her back, still accented by streaks of dried blood.

Akara knew, somewhere in a bitter corner of his mind, that he may never see her again. People had seen him. Agents had seen him. He'd exposed his kind to the public eye. War was coming, and no matter the route he plotted through his scheming thoughts, Akara couldn't find a way past it and back to her.

'One more hour,' he thought, looking at the digital clock sitting amidst a clutter of knick-knacks on the bedside table. If he had just one more hour he could memorize the moment, he could make it whole and lasting. It would become a beacon for fate, shining on this real world he'd built so that he could find his way back. He swore in silence that he would ask for nothing else. He promised to obey his father. He promised to lead the tsesh in battle. He promised a lot of things that he knew would count for nothing. His dream was coming apart, and the more he tried to stay asleep, the faster reality would tear it all down.

Marianne's breathing changed, going from a quiet, level hiss to the deep inhale of morning air. A satisfied and waking moan hummed between her lips as she rolled over to smile at Akara sitting propped up beside her. "Good morning," she greeted with sparkling eyes.

Akara saw the details in her face twitch as the smile tugged at the red line of pain just above her brow. He reached up and brushed a mess of hair from her cheek. "Morning."

"How long have you been up?"

"Only a minute," he lied.

"You want some breakfast?"

Akara's mouth cinched up in a smile on one side. "Let me cook you something."

"No, no," she replied, straining the words as she stretched out her slender body along the length of the bed. "You saved me last night, remember? You deserve a hero's breakfast."

"A hero's breakfast?"

"Yep."

"And what is a hero's breakfast?"

"I will have to check," she admitted slowly while realizing she'd forgotten the kitchen's inventory.

He propped his head up on his hand and answered with a smile and nod. "Okay."

"Okay," she repeated back before pecking a quick kiss on his lips and slipping away from the bed. Akara marveled at her nude form for as long as he could before she wrapped herself in a thick and pale-pink robe. While tying the plush band around her waist, Marianne took a step toward the crimson flower that was now beginning to bloom on her nightstand. Conversations from the night before poured through her thoughts and a proud, little hum slid from her lips as she brushed her fingers down the face of the glass box. With one last smile over her shoulder, she disappeared through the door, leaving Akara in a warm pile of memories and blankets.

He folded his arms behind his head and fell back into the pillows. There was a flicker of a moment in which he'd forgotten who he was. He'd forgotten the Legacy and his father's war. He was nothing but a man in the bed of a loving woman. He was happy, and life was no more complicated than that. As the simple imagining lingered on his thoughts, his eyes drifted down to the flower in the box. It really was beautiful, with wide, scarlet petals, textured by faint veins. Even the stem was a deep green with two broad leaves that shrugged upward at the blossom.

'Just one more hour,' he thought again. One tiny slice of time to hold onto through all the horrors to come. The clock on the bedside table ticked away another minute and Akara closed his eyes to hide his tears.

# # #

The bars of light that traced the upper corners of Bwrynn's dorm switched on, drawing a trail of white around the room until every surface was saturated in fluorescent glow. Bwrynn's eyes squinted shut before she rolled her face into the thick pillow on her narrow bed. She groaned a muffled and discontented sound into the bunched and beaten stuffing.

It had taken her half the night to fall asleep, her mind swirling with history and snakes. The thought of tsesh living amongst them in the city had kept her mind racing and frustratingly alert. She'd replayed every encounter she could remember, every casual conversation with every introverted stranger. How many times had she passed a tsesh? Had she spoken to any directly? It was impossible to know the truth, but surprisingly simple to lose sleep over the question.

Before her mind and eyes could adapt to the wake of morning, Jaga's voice filled up the room. "Get up," he said, "we have work to do."

Work. The simple word had hooked in her ears. He didn't say practice or training, he didn't even say breakfast. He said work. She rolled her face away from the pillow. A tangle of black curls clung to her face and sprouted up all around her head. The bright lights still glared against her waking eyes, and she could only make out a Jaga-shaped blur standing in her doorway.

"Get dressed," he added with the same authoritative tone. "I'll meet you in the garage in fifteen minutes."

A long night of sticky film had filled her mouth, preventing any kind of verbal answer. Bwrynn worked at it with her tongue while settling for a groggy nod and half-hearted wave.

Bwrynn was excited, though the early morning haze had clouded her brain and kept her exhilaration smothered. She dressed in sluggish haste, slipping into black jeans and a white button-down shirt, all strapped together by a pair of black suspenders. They weren't necessary, her clothes fit fine, but the monochromatic garb was a traditional uniform for an agent in the field. Few ever adhered to the look anymore, and she'd probably draw snide glances just for wearing it, but Bwrynn reveled in the outfit. She had grown up watching agents patrol the streets in their black cars and symmetrical fashions. It was a powerful and proud appearance.

It hadn't even been ten minutes when she hurried out to the hall. She shoved her arms into a black cloak and did her best to tie back her wild hair while making her way to the elevator. By the time she'd reached the car park behind the building she'd forced herself alert and mostly presentable. Jaga was already there and waiting.

There were more than a hundred vehicles in the Legacy fleet, and the car park was wide enough to house them all. It was a broad expanse of cement with evenly spaced pillars that gave it the appearance of a synthetic, urban forest. Twenty feet underground, the garage was naturally dark, and the dawn hadn't yet crept down the steep ramps that angled up to the street. In place of natural light, the cold and grease-slicked forest was bathed in sickly yellow lights that all but eliminated any kind of shadow against the rigid walls and structures.

The garage was full of cars but empty of agents, save for her and Jaga. Her footsteps echoed all around her and fell off into distant darkness as she approached Jaga's car. It was a glossy-black, four-door Runcourte, the staple of the Legacy fleet, every pair of agents was assigned one. The windows were tinted, though Bwrynn could still make out Jaga's well-dressed and patient form inside.

He glanced at the time on his comm as she slipped into the car. "Impressive," he said.

"Yeah," Bwrynn agreed absently as she tapped at the dashboard computer and logged her code into the car. "Where are we going first?" she asked. "The diner?"

"The diner?"

"Yeah, to scan the scene, interview witnesses..."

"You mean from the tsesh sighting."

Bwrynn's expression went slack, and she slowly leaned back into her seat, her eyes fixed on Jaga. When Jaga woke her so early, she'd assumed it was connected to the tsesh. Between her excitement and the morning haze, she'd never considered anything else. In her mind, there wasn't anything else. "Yes?" she replied with the tail end of enfeebled hope.

"I'm sorry, Bwrynn," he replied, shaking his head, "we weren't assigned to that case."

Her breath shortened and puffed from her nose. She didn't want to come off as impetuous and tried to quell her frustration before responding. At first, all she could muster was, "but...". She worked through a dozen objections before gathering up her thoughts. 'Don't whine,' she thought, 'Take the job you're given and do it well.' "So, what are we doing?" It was a simple and neutral question that still stung with a bite of dissatisfaction.

Jaga's face softened and shifted up into a parental smile. He didn't have to be psychic to know his young pupil was disappointed. She was a gifted student, but headstrong and eager. No amount of his training could iron out those traits. Only age can make someone appreciate time. Looking ahead, a year can seem like an eternity. Even to an old man like Jaga, a year still sounded far away. But looking back on a lived life, one stacked with so many of those long years that half of them fade away against the twilight horizon of memory, a person eventually comes to accept that years pass by quicker than we think.

One day Bwrynn would wake up old and wonder where the time had gone. She'd wonder if she'd wasted it. Jaga's job, one that he took on with considerable pride, was to make sure that, on that day, she'd be certain that not a moment had been wasted.

"Political assignment," Jaga said, tapping at the dashboard controls. A digital file spun up on the screen in front of Bwrynn and Jaga pressed another button to start the car.

The young psychic staved off the urge to roll her eyes, allowing them to shift slowly from Jaga to the monitor instead. 'Political assignment,' was code for 'security detail', which was another code for babysitting semi-significant officials. It was a pointless job meant to offer up the illusion of security to feed into the illusion of importance.

'Murder.' It was the first word she read when she finally focused on the screen. It's one of those words that catches the eye, an arrangement of letters we're conditioned to notice. It's like the hissing sound of the letter 'S' in a noisy room. We hear it first because it's a threatening sound, drummed up in our primordial minds, telling us to take notice, to run away.

Bwrynn quickly scanned the report then turned to Jaga. His eyes were focused on the road as the Runcourte left the garage. "Lord Kaddler is dead?" she asked.

Jaga's eyes turned halfway to the display in front of her. "It would seem so."

Her eyes went back to the text, though her own thoughts were playing out behind them, giving little notice to the details of the case. "Less than a week before the election."

This time, Jaga turned his full attention to the young psychic. She was swimming around inside her mind, grasping, stitching together theories and seedy conspiracies. "We're not there yet," he said. There was a sternness to his voice that seemed to slam shut the doors of her mind and shove her back in the seat. "All we know is that he's dead. Our job is to collect information, that's all. Polluting your head with vague suspicion before you know anything will only hinder your abilities."

Bwrynn nodded. He was right and she knew it. "Yes, sir," she lied.

#

Akara had been slow to eat his hero's breakfast, and slower still to leave Marianne, but halfway into morning he had no choice. His father and the elders would be awake, and even Malehk was likely wondering where he was. They said their playful "goodnights" despite the early hour, and before her last embrace could cool from his skin, Akara was back in the gray landscape of Sector Six. His belly was full of fried potatoes and synthetic meat, his clothes still smelled of perfume and warm air, but it all felt like a paltry shell around a pit of dread that had been growing in his stomach.

The walk home seemed to stretch out for miles, though they passed by in seconds. It was the kind of journey that starts out daunting then ends in a blink, leaving you wondering where the time had gone. Most of Akara's thoughts and all his heart remained back at Marianne's, and as he boarded the service elevator to the underground ruins, he wondered if he'd ever see that part of himself again.

He deliberately counted out the eighteen second descent as he'd done so many times before, hoping his awareness of the time would somehow slow it down. He found himself uncomfortably aware of the food in his belly, and the muscles along his shoulders tensed and tingled as the elevator landed in the dust below.

"Eighteen," he whispered the last second away and pulled open the gate.

With Malehk's goading, Akara had built his childhood on defying the king, but it had never been anything like this. What could he even begin to say in his defense, that he'd exposed the tsesh to protect someone? That in itself was an offense, let alone an acceptable excuse to his father. There was no wordplay or evasive explanation that could justify his presence on the surface.

He could lie, and for a long walk across the wastes he considered it. But what kind of lie would it be? Something stubborn and outlandish? Maybe it wasn't actually him they'd seen in that diner? Perhaps it was a psychic trick of the Legacy, and the witnesses had all been entranced. Akara shook his head at the thought; too far-fetched.

Something dutiful and self-serving? He could tell his father that he'd been studying with the scavengers, learning to siphon money and supplies from the surface when a Legacy patrol had scanned them and given chase. His teeth clenched and his eyes rolled behind their lids. Flimsy at best.

By the time he'd turned the last corner and the front gate was in sight, Akara had decided to tell a beveled version of the truth. He'd stand before the king and tell him that he'd acted in self-defense. He'd proclaim that the oppressive laws of the tsesh no longer served them, and that it was time they took a stand as a people. He'd act bold and certain, and maybe, if his father was in an uncharacteristic mood, Akara's confidence would pierce the surface of Rhago's glacial mind.

He reworked the speech a dozen times before he'd crossed the courtyard, and a handful more before descending the stairwell inside. By the time he'd reached the musky hall to his father's den, Akara had worked up a respectable swell of conviction. It all melted away however, the moment his hand touched the icy brass of the doorknob to the study. His heart withered inside his chest, leaving him hollow and quaking. He bit back a reconsideration of his potential lies and pushed the door open with a slow, taunting creak that drew out longer than he'd liked.

One wall making up the back corner was lined with wooden shelves, each packed with thick and dusty books. The other wall was bare cement, awash with deep and gnarled shadows being cast by a single lamp that sat atop a lone desk. Rhago's aging features cast shadows of their own behind the lamp, softened only by the glow of a pale-blue monitor. Akara couldn't tell if the scowling lines across his father's face were deeper than usual, but his pale eyes were fixed on the silent newsfeed playing out on the screen.

"Father?" he eked out, immediately cursing himself for the feeble tone. It was flat, weak, and devoid of any of the conviction that he'd promised himself. It was so weak, it seemed, that Rhago didn't even look up from the screen. Rather than risk another meek attempt, Akara began his way across the room. Still, Rhago didn't react, his eyes furious with thought, deep in the story on his screen.

Akara stopped at the front corner of the desk, subconsciously just outside of striking distance. "You've seen the news?"

Rhago's eyes tilted up then gave one last look to the monitor before he reached forward and switched it off.

The room plunged into a deeper, darker, more chasmic tone, and Akara's stomach churned as though he'd leaned over the edge of a cliff. The contrast between lamp and shadow sharpened, cutting thick outlines around every movement. He felt his knees weaken and nearly buckle beneath his weight. It was all he could do to remain standing and mask the momentary wobble with a readjustment of his stance.

"I've seen it," Rhago answered with a husky whisper as he rose from the desk. His snowy hair was drifting loose around his face and his smoky eyes, like his voice, were cold and unfeeling. Despite their human form, they offered up nothing, no sign of anger or disappointment. He was a walking and whispering statue.

The slow approach of the king's demeanor made his left hook all the more surprising. Rhago's fist punched like stone against Akara's face, and it took more time for him to realize what had happened than it did for him to hit the floor. His elbow cracked on the cement, and he could immediately feel the itching crawl of blood across his cheek against the cold swelling of the skin. He kicked and palmed his way along the floor and away from the desk but stopped short of rising to his feet. Through blurred and watering eyes, he could see Rhago standing above him, his broad chest heaving and his eyes flaring with rage.

"You stupid, spoiled child!" he raged, his voice filling the room before spilling back on itself. "Do you have any idea what you've done?"

"Yes." The answer squeezed from Akara's lips before he knew it was there. He pushed himself further back, rubbing the haze from his eyes before raising a defensive hand in front of his face.

"Do you?" Rhago maintained a slow approach, allowing his son to grovel and slither back until he reached the stone and shadow of the far wall. "All that we've endured, all that we've sacrificed," he emphasized the last word with a forceful kick at Akara's arm and his voice dipped down into something personal. "All for nothing. All because you wanted to play on the surface, to play with some human whore."

Something instinctual fired up from Akara's chest and took control of his body. The cowering boy was swept aside, and years of training took control. He deflected the next kick, shoving his father's foot away and rising quickly to hammer both palms into the old man's chest. It wasn't an attack; it wasn't meant to hurt the king. The blow was meant to create distance. Possibly it was a dare for his father to try again, or more simply a line in the sand. It was a decisive divide between everything the young prince could endure and everything else.

"Stop," the prince commanded to the surprise of them both.

Rhago glared at his son, his eyes churning with muddled anger, but he didn't make another move.

The pause was more than Akara had expected, and, for a slow moment, they simply stared each other down, both waiting for whatever Akara had intended to say next. He imagined it to be something forceful and retaliatory, but the reactionary burst had already begun to fade, leaving him uncomfortably aware of his own breath and the chill air of the room. He slowed his breathing and partially relaxed his stance.

"You don't know anything about her," he finally replied, only in that moment realizing that his father was aware of Marianne.

"She's a human," he spat back, "and she's dulled your mind." Rhago lowered his arms and rose back up to his stoic form, signaling that the physical confrontation was over. The old king turned his back on his son and began back toward the desk, but his words continued to pierce like poisoned daggers. "She's twisted your values and now we will all pay for it."

"How did you know about her?"

Rhago cocked his head over his shoulder then turned away again. The question was an insult in itself. "I am your father and your king," he said, his voice like grinding gravel. "Hiding from me is a juvenile waste of time. Do you think Malehk is the only tsesh I had keeping tabs on you?"

Akara's eyes drifted away as all the memories of his foolish sneaking around washed over him like cold water.

"He's as irresponsible as you," Rhago continued, "but I thought his presence would at least keep your impulses in check." He slumped back down in his chair and looked through the glow of the lamp to his befuddled son. "But you're even less mature than I'd thought."

Despite the insult, the tension in the room had begun to break and Akara's focus snapped back, hoping to inject perspective into the forming cracks. "Father, we can still salvage this. Let me—"

"No," Rhago snapped, biting off the coming plea. He let his scowl burn any remaining objections from Akara's mind before speaking again. "This will be salvaged, but it will be done as I say. You've already proven that you can't be trusted, and I won't allow you to make a fool of me again." The words would have sounded hopeful had they not come from a fuming king and disappointed father.

"What can I do?" Akara conceded.

"The only thing you will do is end this foolishness with that human girl."

"Father—"

"If Pramoore discovers your connection to her he will use it to draw you out. That endangers us all. We cannot be safe until you sever your emotional ties with the surface."

"But we can—"

"Akara!" The air shook beneath the booming word and echoed back and forth until the room was left once more in dark and quiet. The king's next statement came calm and measured. "The lives of our people weigh more heavily than yours alone. You will remove your personal feelings from this. You will act like a prince, not a child. You will do as I say, or I will have you executed for the good of all tsesh."

The young tsesh was deflated and defeated. His arms dropped to his sides, and he bowed his head. The king wasn't one to make idle threats, but worse than that, Akara knew he was right. "Yes, father."

#

Akara was nearly back to his room, his head dropped low and his thoughts running like roaches fleeing the light of what must be done. He needed a moment to breath and a moment to think, or more aptly, a moment to accept what he knew was coming next. Leave Marianne. The idea was a foreign invader in his mind. It was a black figure emerging from the corners of his subconscious, one that had always been there, but he had just been too blinded to see it. This was always only going to end one way. This was his dream and finally, he was waking up.

"Akara," Malehk's voice spiraled down the hallway after him. He was excited and out of breath.

On any other day, the tone may have piqued Akara's curiosity or, at the very least, rattled his belly with concern. But this wasn't any other day. His excitable whimsy lay dead in his throat and his heart's cage had been sealed shut. Malehk's vibrance only tapped at him like pebbles against a locked window, feeble ticks on a thick pane and there was no one inside to answer. The best Akara could muster was an upward glance at his bounding friend.

"Akara," Malehk repeated, the volume of his voice dropping to match the closing distance and his panting breath. He stopped at the prince's side, buckling forward, and bracing his hands on his knees. "I found something."

"Why are you out of breath?"

"I spent the night climbing," Malehk said, turning a look and weak-handed gesture toward the center of the city.

Akara responded with barely a glance and continued toward his room.

"I found something," Malehk said again, "something... crazy." He struggled before finally settling on the simple yet befitting word.

Rubbing at the growing pain between his eyes, Akara let out a slow breath from his nose before engaging. "What is it?"

"What's the matter with you?" Malehk asked, his expression cinching up.

"It's nothing. What'd you find?"

"It's Pramoore," he said, "I think he's growing these... things in his basement?" When the weak description landed on a blank expression, Malehk tried again. "There's these big containers in a secret lab. I think they have creatures inside."

"You think?"

"Well, I couldn't see. They might have been people."

Akara mixed up his dead stare with a shift in his jaw while huffing out another breath.

"No, no, no," Malehk stammered, "there's definitely something growing inside them."

After a long pause, Akara was sure that his panicked friend had finished. "That's it?"

"I think there's more in the towers too," Malehk added, working frantically to piece together what he knew into a coherent discovery.

"Just let it go, Malehk," Akara said, waving off his friend and walking away.

"But there is something down there."

"Forget it. It's over."

Malehk's eyes skipped around the empty hall. "What's over?" he called after him.

"Everything. We're finished."

Chapter 13

Legacy Headquarters was filled with classrooms, wide squares sprouting off from the center stairwell in every direction on every floor. Although there were hundreds of students, instructors, and field agents housed inside the grand tower at any given moment, many of the countless rooms remained vacant for weeks and months at a time. The specialized rooms with specific purpose were often darkened shells, sitting silent and hollow. They were ideal sanctuaries for when students wanted to hide away, and the library was too crowded, or their rooms were too obvious. They were also the perfect, secluded cells for a Pramoore executive to lure and trap a wayward student for discreet questioning.

Faedra was circling around the back of one such student, who'd been fidgeting nervously in a center desk for the past half hour. He'd been summoned to the room at an early hour and told it was for evaluation. It was a loose interpretation of the truth. Faedra had begun evaluating him the moment he slid open the door and found the classroom dim and empty, save for the fiery hair and feline silhouette of Ms. Weiss. She'd gestured to the chair at the front and center of the room, and her huntress eyes tracked his nervous and obedient steps until he was seated.

She was on her fifth or sixth pass around his back and hadn't yet gotten to the meat of their meeting. "Are you nervous, Alexander?" she asked like a cat batting at its prey.

The young agent straightened up his posture to an absurd and rigid extent, looking straight ahead down the ridge of his nose with his chin jutting out. "Yes, ma'am."

Faedra leaned in close as she rounded his shoulder and stepped into his line of sight. "And why is that?"

Alexander cleared his throat in that quick and quiet way that people do when their hoping that no one will notice. When he spoke it was with the armor of militant certainty which guarded genuine timidity. "It's early, ma'am," he answered. "I wasn't expecting a review today. I feel unprepared."

"Unprepared?" She passed by in front of him and, once more, moved to his peripheral vision. "And what would you have done to prepare?"

His lips puckered and squeezed together, and he swallowed a lump of tension down his throat. "Just, um, I guess I would have cleared my mind a bit."

"Cleared it of what?" she asked in a silken voice that was just above a whisper and just across his shoulder. "Savage secrets? Dark perversions?"

Alexander's eyes widened as her hot breath snaked over his neck. "No ma'am," he answered too quickly. "Just daily distractions. Daily chores and the like."

Faedra's green eyes narrowed, and her lips curved up in a devilish smirk. She let out a sharp snicker then held her glance to consider the tension of the young man. "Relax, agent, this isn't a review, it's an evaluation."

Alexander's eyes jittered back and forth, and his brow furled. "Ma'am?"

"We're not here to discuss your performance," she clarified with a slow, disinterested tone. "This is a private meeting, off-book."

Alexander stirred in his seat. The metal chair suddenly felt even less comfortable than it had during long lectures and those suffocatingly silent meditation sessions. "Regarding what?" he managed to squeak out as she passed by in front of him again.

"Uniformity is what gives this agency its strength," she continued from his flank. "Common procedure, common goals," Faedra lifted both her palms and gave a subtle bow with her head, "a fixed point."

The young agent didn't dare turn to follow her pacing, but when she rounded his shoulder and stepped into view, he turned a shy eye up at her. "Yes, ma'am."

"That being said however, we can't deny that you are still individuals. You have your thoughts and your lives, things that pull your minds one way or another."

"I suppose that's true."

"This isn't a crime, of course, but too much of it can sometimes be distracting to the whole. Do you understand what I'm saying?"

As Faedra moved to his back again, Alexander allowed a look of confusion to twist up on his face. "I'm not sure that I do, ma'am."

"Rumors," she answered plainly and pointedly, planting a firm hand on the back of his chair. "Unfounded, unproductive rumors. Distractions, you might call them, swimming around inside this place."

Alexander's belly went cold, and a prickling shiver fluttered and tapped up his back. Of course he knew what she meant. It was the biggest, unspoken story inside the Legacy; hidden labs, secret experiments. Most agents shrugged it off as wild conspiracy, but for those who lingered on the thought too long, the questions became an endless thread of a black and unraveling veil.

"Rumors, ma'am?" he finally said, fearing that his knee-jerk reaction had already tipped his conscience on the floor at her feet.

She circled around to his front again, her narrow eyes gathering up the wiry bundle of nervous agent. "I'd prefer we skip this part," she said in a tired voice, "your ill-prepared and fumbling lies."

Alexander's eyes and expression were frozen on her accusing gaze.

"I know about these stories, as does Mr. Pramoore," she told him. "Dark experiments performed beneath Pramoore Tower, hidden from the Legacy by the psychic fog of the old world. We even know the names of a few of the perpetuators of these rumors, which is of course why we're talking."

"It is?"

"There's no need for your defenses, Alexander" Faedra said. Her tone was that of a spider enticing a fly, amused and patronizing, erasing any comfort that the statement itself might have offered. Her focus seemed to slide across the young man, analyzing every twitch and curve in his trembling features. "Do you know what my gift is?"

Alexander swallowed and shook a quick nod. "They say you hijack people's minds; take control of them."

Half of her expression curved up in amusement while the other remained serious and annoyed. "That's a rather crude depiction." Faedra slipped a smooth hand up the agents arm and gripped his shoulder with sharp and painted nails. "I simply borrow your abilities. If I'm feeling particularly generous, I can even show you their true potential."

An unsteady chuckle broke from Alexander's lips. It was a clumsy and deliberate laugh, a noise that someone makes to fill in gaps of time while they rush to pile more dirt atop their buried secrets. "I'm afraid my abilities won't be much use to someone like you, ma'am," he said in a thin attempt at flattery. "I'm near the bottom of my division. Years away from making field agent... so they say."

"Yes, I know," she replied with a whip of irritation in her voice. "But I'm not interested in your abilities. I'm interested in the memories that you hide beneath them."

"Memories?" he puffed out, his hands now visibly trembling against the arms of the chair. "I'm not hiding anything from—"

The agent's voice faded out along with the light around Faedra's eyes. Darkness crept in around her face until she wore a mask of shadows, with only her burning emerald eyes and crimson lips to lend her definition. "You're going to show me who you've been talking to."

# # #

Loose gravel ground and cracked beneath the wide tires of the four-door Runcourte. Jaga had to park to the side of the main drive of Kaddler's mansion. Every space along the curve out front was occupied by sector security patrol cars. Bwrynn counted six cars in total, all white and electric blue, muddled by desert dust. Red laser lines swept back and forth along the light bar that capped their windshields and the identifier 'SS6' was glowing on the side panel of every door. There were plenty of officers on the scene, some talking to each other while others were taking statements. The 'witnesses' they'd managed to wrangle were likely the closest thing Kaddler had to neighbors.

There was also another Runcourte parked dead center at the crest of the driveway. A Legacy team had gotten there before them. Bwrynn knew that others would be arriving soon and throughout the day. Their roles would be to monitor scene integrity and witness memory, but the report was clear in placing Jaga Demain as the lead agent. As his pupil and now a certified field agent herself, Bwrynn wasn't sure if she fell under the umbrella of the title.

The reality was, this would be little more than another training exercise. She had minimal experience on patrols and had only briefly assisted in murder cases from the safety of Legacy Headquarters. This would be something new, another medal on her chest and a new page in her sluggishly growing list of accomplishments. At any other time, a high-profile murder would clench an agent's career and quickly raise them to the upper echelon of the Legacy. Now however, with the resurfacing of the tsesh, Kaddler's death would be all but overlooked. The old politician would be a subtitle in a newsfeed chyron while the city buzzed of serpents in their midst.

"So, who got it?" Bwrynn asked as she rounded the car and met Jaga at the front.

"Got what?" he asked, carving off a slice of attention for her while he studied the large house.

"The tsesh case?" she clarified. "Who's handling the diner?"

His pale eyes turned and narrowed at her and his lips pressed shut. "Bellest," he answered with a hint of reluctance. He dropped the name like a scrap of food for her to pick up before heading for the house.

"Niram Bellest?" she said, doubling her steps until she caught up.

Jaga nodded without looking back.

"And I suppose Bryce is assisting?"

"He is his student. Besides, Bryce was the first one on the scene."

"Bryce?" she gawked. "Bryce Bishop saw the tsesh?"

"That's what they say."

Bwrynn paused to let her mind work without having to worry about her steps. As Jaga walked ahead, she pieced together a handful of scenarios in which Bryce might have encountered a tsesh, then shook her head free of all of them. "No way," she concluded, jogging to Jaga's side. "There's no way Bryce saw a tsesh. He's making it up."

"There were other witnesses, Bwrynn."

"And he survived?" The phrase came out as more of an accusation than a question.

Jaga snorted and smiled ahead of her. "You know, Bryce was once the young and rising star of the agency before you came along. He has his own set of skills."

"Sure, but a tsesh? They would have killed him for sure."

"And what makes you say that?"

"He's an agent," she proclaimed directly.

"There are lots of agents, young Bwrynn," he replied, "and the tsesh seem to have gotten along without killing them for the past fifteen years. Why would they start now?"

"That's what I'd like to ask if we were given the case."

"Yes, but we weren't," he responded as they crossed the last few slabs of the concrete walk and approached the large double doors at the front of the house. "We were given this case, so let's focus on that, shall we?"

Bwrynn chomped at the inside of her mouth and gave a sideways glance and frustrated nod. "Yes, sir."

Jaga waved off the dotted line of officers as he and Bwrynn passed through the foyer and into the den.

The house was even larger than Bwrynn had expected from her view outside. The walls were made of dark-stained wood and the floors were gray marble. Two sets of stairs ascended from the foyer, bowing outward before joining the wood-banister walkway above them. Tucked beneath the stairs was a glass wall, and beyond it was a large, indoor pool. The room was dark, lit only by white strips of light rippling beneath the crystalline water.

Jaga seemed to know his way around, or perhaps he'd simply been through enough crime scenes to know where he was going. He and the security were like ants, following each other along an invisible trail to the left and down the hall. Jaga led them into a study at the back of the house. It was a smaller room, though still the size of an average classroom at the Legacy. There was a large bay window at the back that looked out to the side yard of the house. The concrete walks and brushed dirt outside were fading into an umber gold beneath the morning gray.

Had it not been for the bustle of police and the hum of cameras, the study would have been rather cozy. It was the kind of room that Bwrynn could spend a week inside without ever missing a single person. The crimson carpet was soft, there was a stone fireplace that was large enough to warm the room in minutes, and an impressive collection of paper books, all bound in red and black leather.

Her first two steps into the room, Bwrynn wondered what would become of the house now that Kaddler was dead. More specifically, she wondered what would become of that room, the perfect little sanctum of wood and books. Those questions and wonder evaporated the moment she saw the body. Her mind flushed empty and filled back up with nothing but the twisted, gray horror on the floor. At first, she wasn't sure what she was looking at. It didn't look like a dead body. A dead body is just a lifeless person. Maybe there would be blood or some upsetting wounds, but it's still just a person. The thing on the floor near the fireplace looked more like a sculpture, like a gruesome expression of torment, squeezed out of clay by a morbid artist.

Bwrynn's hand jumped to her lips to mask a startled gasp. Her dark eyes went wide and glittered in the overhead light as she leaned in cautiously toward the corpse. "Is that him?" she asked foolishly.

"It was," one of the officers replied.

Kaddler's remains were clenched in the fetal position and surrounded by flaking ash. The skin was dark and dry, shriveled gaunt over his skeleton. What little remained of his hair was white and thin, and the face was stretched out long as though he'd screamed so loud it broke his jaw. Bulging eyes, now dead and milky, were barely set into the skull, hanging wide towards the floor. The only thing untouched was his suit, an expensive, silk three-piece, draped over the body as an ironic shroud.

"What happened to him?" Bwrynn asked anyone who could answer.

The officer cocked his brow at the corpse. "Got me," he said. "I imagine that's why you're here."

'That's right,' Bwrynn thought. She was a field agent of the Legacy, a powerful psychic and the youngest ever to join the agency. Horrors like this were why she was there. The people looked to her for answers, and she had to pull herself together and find them. "Of course," she finally answered aloud, before turning her most professional expression back to Jaga.

"Witnesses?" Jaga asked the cop.

"Nothing reliable," he answered, "and security shows no one in or out besides Kaddler himself."

Jaga offered a thoughtful nod, then crouched down beside the body. The bones cracked as he turned the head and pulled aside cuffs and collars to examine the skin. "He struggled," he noted after a minute of study, "and he suffered."

"Didn't figure it was natural causes," the cop snickered before reconsidering the remark. Bwrynn cast him a subtle scowl and Jaga turned a slow look over his shoulder.

"But why?" Jaga asked as though the answer should be obvious.

The officer shook his head and shrugged. "Lots of reasons to kill a sector lord," he said, "money, politics."

"Yes, but why make it slow? Why make him suffer?"

The cop's lips puckered, and he shrugged again. "Torture? Maybe the killer was looking for something."

"Uh huh," Jaga said absently. He turned his eyes upward and panned around the room. "Or they were making a statement."

"A statement?" he asked. "A statement for who?"

"Mhm." Jaga gave up pretending to answer the officer. "Have the other agents scanned the room?"

"Yeah," he replied. "They said there was nothing."

"Nothing?" Bwrynn chopped in as though the answer itself was absurd and off-putting.

"They said it just like that too," he said, pointing a finger at her confusion.

Jaga rose to his tall and slender height, an easy half-foot above the cop. "Agents don't find nothing," he said. "We sometimes find confusion, sometimes we find nothing useful, but never nothing."

"Well, that's what they said," the officer defended.

"I'll scan the room," Bwrynn said before Jaga could draw another breath.

He turned his attention back to her and smiled as though he'd forgotten she was there. "Do that," he said, giving his young and eager pupil a smooth nod. "I'll have a look around."

Bwrynn's eyes twinkled atop a smile as Jaga broke away and headed for the broad desk near the window. She squared her shoulders and fixed her stance. Her eyes began to dance with blue veins of light before she drew in a deep breath and let them fall shut. Her thoughts snuck away from her, testing the room at first, touching and tapping at the walls. The officer in front of her was a smooth twist of light, doling itself out in even doses to everyone in the room. For the moment, his focus reached out and was patting at Bwrynn's face, but he quickly grew bored and turned his attention elsewhere.

The warm room was alive with energy. There was a swell of curiosity and a healthy dose of caution. Despite the investigation, most of the officers in the room worked to ignore the corpse. Its presence pulled at their thoughts, but they purposely lassoed other tasks to keep themselves distracted. No one wanted to acknowledge the shriveled horror on the floor, frozen in a silent scream.

The body even tugged at Bwrynn's psychic mind. It teased her curious nature, but beyond its shocking presence it had nothing to offer. It shimmered with the thoughtful glow of the others in the room, but it had no light of its own. It was a centerpiece that kept everyone talking but provided nothing more.

Bwrynn's mind filled the room with curious blue light. Her thoughts traced every corner, memorized the hard curves of the desk, and permeated the wide shelf of old and beautiful books. She lapped consideration at every nook until she was as familiar with the place as Kaddler himself had surely been. She lived there in her mind. It was her space to sprawl and to retreat. The study had become as comfortable to her as a childhood bedroom, filled with far away memories, despite feeling strange and foreign.

When she was satisfied with her standing in the room, Bwrynn tensed the muscles in her brow and tried to remember what had happened there the night before. Her eyelids struggled to squint and the blue light snapping from within her pupils spun and sputtered. She thought back to what had happened in that perfect room. She remembered coming home. The door to the study slid open. Then there was nothing, no light, no dark, no heat or cold. There was nothing. The room itself didn't exist last night. Kaddler had stepped into oblivion and simply disappeared, as if those memories had been wiped away.

Bwrynn's eyes jumped open and darted around the room. "Nothing." She repeated the simple and looming word to herself. Her eyebrows dropped down to a quizzical frown and mulled over the notion of nothingness. It's an impossible thing; nothing. Everything is something. The deepest chasms in the northern mountains are devoid of many things, but they're always filled with something else, air and shadows, cold and wonder. A place or time of nothingness just can't exist.

She cocked her head to Jaga who was busy rifling through the desk. It would be one thing to confirm the assessment of the other agents, but did she want this to be her report? Her first big case and Jaga's prize student found 'nothing'? No, there had to be more. There had to be a flicker of thought, some hint of recognition or remembrance. Bwrynn had to find something that the others had overlooked.

She shut her eyes again and drew in an even deeper breath than before. It hissed out slow between her pursed lips as her thoughts returned once more to the night before. Kaddler had come home. The door slid open. He stepped inside... Nothing. Kaddler ceased to be and time itself vanished from the room.

A psychic's mind can only reach back so far, a day at the most, before memories begin to fade into obscurity. They become watered down brushstrokes of vague ideas. Bwrynn urged her mind back as far as it could manage, but anything before the void was muddled and useless. Whatever had happened in that room had happened in that missing moment, and Bwrynn was going to find it.

She allowed herself to exist in the emptiness, in the hollow dearth of everything. Her thoughts tipped around like a top-heavy drunk with no bar rail to guide them. She stumbled in her mind throughout the space where the room had been, searching for an edge of the vacuum. There had to be something. There had to be a foothold of reality somewhere in the dark.

Earlier in the evening, before the nothingness, the room had been empty and still, but its shape was still solid. The desk had been at its post, broad, strong, and important. The books were there, quiet and wise. The glow of amber whiskey flickered like flame in a bottle in the corner. As Bwrynn stepped through the timeline, she paused on the moment in which everything went dark. It wasn't all at once. At the opening of the room, near the warm mahogany door, she found a flickering moment just before the world was wiped away. The comforting radiance faded there first, retreating deeper into the den.

Without realizing, Bwrynn had turned her head in the direction of the fading world. The energy of the room hadn't just disappeared, it had been pulled out, sucked from the room into a single point. The muscles in her forehead twitched as she sifted through the nothingness. The darkness had an origin.

Her mind plunged deeper, searching smaller patches of the emptiness one by one. It wasn't long before she could feel the pull herself, a clenching weight on her temples, gripping and drawing her in. Bwrynn slurped a sharp breath, her mind sliding and tumbling faster towards the source. Her thoughts brushed away shadows, shouldering past them like gnarled brush in the black forest as she raced deep into the darkness.

With a final gasp she fell. It wasn't just her thoughts that toppled into the void, her body buckled in the physical world as well. A small and distant noise slipped from her lips before she crumpled to the floor in a mess of black cloak and black hair. She thought she'd heard Jaga shouting her name, but it sounded far away. It was comforting, she thought, that her name on his voice would be the last thing she would hear before slipping away forever.

With the central location of Kaddler's house and the cluster of first responders already on the scene, it was only a few minutes before Bwrynn was being carted out on an ER skiff. Paramedics were attaching medical injectors to her arm as they maneuvered her down the front walk. They were small squares with digital displays that flashed and surged as they read her vitals and introduced an ever-changing cocktail of stimulants and medication.

"She just collapsed," Jaga was repeating as he walked in hurried steps to keep up. "What happened to her? Can you tell me what's wrong?"

No one answered. There were a dozen things for them to do between the door and the ambulance, and a dozen more from ambulance to the hospital. None of them involved conjecture or consoling a panicked old man. As the injectors lit up and whined against her skin, the medics slid Bwrynn into the back of the ambulance and motioned Jaga back as they tried to close the door.

"I'm her mentor," Jaga responded quickly.

After a short and contemplative pause, the man offered a quick nod and gestured to the door. Jaga climbed inside and sat as near to Bwrynn as he could. He pressed up close and clasped her hand inside his own, leaning across the medic on the bench beside him. The injector on her bicep flared up bright and coughed out a repetitive alarm.

"Please," the medic said, pressing Jaga back with his arm. "This is sensitive equipment. If you jar her too much, they could misread her vitals and render an overdose."

Jaga's eyes went wide and sad as he drifted back on the bench. At first, he tried to keep just one hand on hers, then just his fingertips, then his hand simply hung in the air above hers before retreating into his lap. He wanted to be there when she woke up, as if she'd only fainted and would come to at any moment. He wanted his eyes in front of hers when she did. He wanted his familiar face to be the first thing she saw.

Jaga would explain to her what had happened. He would calmly ease her back to consciousness and help her get her bearings. He'd brush aside the dumbfounded paramedics and proudly inform them that Bwrynn had one of the most powerful and resilient minds in the city. They were fools to worry over something so slight as a dizzy spell. All these things played out in his mind while he stared at her still and shuttered eyes. The motion and the noise of the ambulance was muted while he clung to those thoughts, holding his breath, and waiting for a moment that would never come.

When they finally reached the hospital, the medics rushed her out the back and towards the rear entrance of the ER. Jaga remained in the ambulance, stunned, and lost. He tried to replay what had happened. He tried to find the event that caused her collapse, but his thoughts kept snapping back to the present. They were at the city hospital and Bwrynn hadn't woken up.

Without the same sense of urgency, he stepped out to the hospital driveway and slowly made his way to the entrance. Someone rushed past him, causing him to stumble aside, but he didn't see them. There were others all around him, rushing in and out, but they were only shadows on the edge of his tunnel vision.

'She's just a little girl,' he thought as he left the brisk morning wind and stepped inside the still and sterilized air of the emergency room. There was a small seating area to his right and a wide and endless hall ahead of him. She'd disappeared somewhere down its length, somewhere inside the scramble of noise and bodies, of intercom voices and fluorescent light.

'She's just a little girl,' he almost repeated the sentence to the receptionist at the desk. He cleared his blurring eyes and gave the woman as much attention as he could conjure. "Bwrynn Lucane?" he offered.

"Lucane?" she repeated back, strumming her pointed fingers across the holographic display in front of her.

"She just came in," he added.

The woman shook her head while pages of information danced off her big, round glasses. "It's possible she hasn't been entered yet," she said. "Are you family?"

Jaga stared quietly past the fluttering hologram and into the glass-saucer lenses on the woman's face. He didn't know how to answer. Was he family? Did he not know? Had he forgotten who he was? He finally shook his head and tried to moisten his lips with a dry tongue. "I'm her mentor."

"Her mentor? You're from the Legacy?"

He nodded, his face devoid of any of the pride or respect that the title would normally bring.

The receptionist was rising from her seat, plugging a few more keystrokes into the console as she did. "And what was your name?" she asked.

"Jaga Demain."

"Alright, Agent Demain, why don't you have a seat over there and I'll see what I can find out for you." Without looking up, she gestured to the strips of conjoined, vinyl seats in the waiting room, then stretched up a wide and practiced smile. It was a subconscious and fake expression, one that she'd trained her face to make after years behind that desk. It missed its mark and Jaga watched as she grinned at a coffee mug on her desk, her goggled eyes still scanning her display.

Jaga gave a half glance over his shoulder then responded with a nod before walking away. As he sunk into a lone and lonely string of chairs beside the window, he watched the receptionist swipe at one more command on her console. She mumbled something to her coworker and disappeared through a door at the back of the room.

The minutes bled together, forming a large, dull ache of time in Jaga's brain. Patients rose from their seats as they were called, and new ones filtered in to replace them. Many of them whispered to each other when they caught sight of the old man in the cloak with his knotty fingers woven together in his lap. He picked up on the obvious words; 'Agent', 'Legacy', and even 'Tsesh', but gave them no attention. His mind was on Bwrynn lying somewhere in the labyrinth of the hospital halls, no doubt plugged into a machine, breathing through a tube, her beautiful mind on full, holographic display for all to see.

"Agent Demain," a woman's voice came carefully through his reeling thoughts.

Jaga looked up, expecting to see the spectacled nurse with a sorrowful gaze, but instead he saw a cloak, a Legacy cloak. She was younger than him, though not by much, mostly in the eyes. They were kind, warm with concern around their outer edges. Her hair was a thick halo of auburn curls, and her face was round, soft, suspended up in an uncertain smile. Waking from his daze, it took longer for him to recognize the woman than it did her uniform. She was among the group that Bwrynn had scanned in the halls, the ones that she had insisted were hiding something, planning something.

"You," he responded simply.

"Me?"

He cleared his throat and straightened up in his seat, realizing that they'd never actually met. "I mean, I wasn't expecting another agent."

"Agent Rosewood," she said, "but you can call me Thisa." With another gentle smile, she gestured to one of the empty seats beside him. "May I sit?"

Jaga slid to the side to offer up more room. It was more than enough for Thisa's short and stocky frame.

She sat down and folded up the flaps of her cloak into her lap. "I was next on the scene at Kaddler's," she explained. "They told me what happened."

"She just collapsed," he explained as dry and colorless as a doctor might, "we don't know what caused it."

Thisa gave an understanding nod at the bustling hall. "Do you know what she was doing when it happened?"

"What she was doing?" Jaga's brow furled and he pushed a bit more space between the two of them. "She was doing her job. I'm sorry, but why are you here?"

Her thin eyebrows slid up and her lips squeezed together as if to say 'oh'. "My apologies," she said with a dainty hand against her chest, "I met Bwrynn yesterday in the cafeteria. I wouldn't say we're friends just yet, but when I heard it was her who'd been brought in, I simply wanted to check on her."

"You met?"

Thisa gave an affirmative hum and smile. "I'd heard of her before of course, but I'd never had the pleasure. She's a curious young thing, isn't she?"

Jaga laced his fingers back together and rested his weight onto his lap. "To say the least."

"So, do you know what she was doing? When this all happened, I mean."

Suspicion rose back up in Jaga's mind like boiling water. Bwrynn had had her own reservations about this woman and now, moments after her mysterious collapse, here she was asking questions. He wanted to turn her away. He wanted to scan her mind or mask his own. But he also wanted answers, and Jaga learned a long time ago that the people who are asking the questions are often the people who already have the answers.

"She was regressing the room," he said with a long and thoughtful breath, "trying to view what happened last night."

"Do you think she found something?"

The inquiry came too fast, and Jaga pulled away a little bit more. He shook his head and offered up a hand toward the deep hallway. "You're suggesting she picked up on something? Something that could have caused this?"

"It would seem to be the most obvious possibility."

"If it was, it's not like anything I've ever seen before. You?" He tacked on the question as innocently as he could, watching with a sideways glance for a physical response from her.

She seemed to see it coming and met his cautious eyes with her own. "Maybe." Thisa looked around the busy room, full of eyes pretending not to watch and ears pretending not to listen. "Let's get some air."

#

The morning chill had broken, giving way to the tepid compromise of midday. In the roiling cloudscape overhead, bursts of lightning snapped from one gray thicket to the next, splashing blue light across the white concrete of the hospital walls. The sound of humming cars seasoned the air. They created a barrier of noise as they crossed by the hospital entrance. It was a comforting din for Thisa, a buffer between her words and would-be eavesdroppers.

Nevertheless, she cast a casual and practiced eye around the area. There was a plain-looking man crossing the drive some twenty meters away. A few steps past him a nurse was tucked inside a corner beside the dumpsters. She was staring off across the lot while half-enjoying a stolen moment away from her work. Neither were in earshot. Across the way was the car lot, a deep and cavernous block of cement, full of shadows and dotted orange lights. Vacant vehicles filled nearly every space inside and amidst the shadows was a young woman struggling with a large bag while unlocking her car door.

Satisfied enough with their privacy, Thisa turned her attention back to Jaga. His eyes had been following her own, skipping from one stranger to the next, unconcerned with whatever they might be doing and whatever they may or may not hear. Caution and suspicion were traits of those with something to hide.

"You've heard the rumors I suppose," she said. Her tone was light and casual. They may as well have been strolling through a park discussing a film.

"Rumors?" Jaga asked. He assumed that she'd meant the conspiracies that filled the Legacy halls with whispered gossip but hoped to offer her the benefit of the doubt. Those were stories for children who reveled in mystery and fantasy, not a seasoned agent with any kind of self-respect or even a tangible grip on the world.

"Of course you have," she answered with a thin and sideways stare. "Rumors about Daemon, about his tower."

"Ah," Jaga said. He bunched up his lips, raised a brow, and nodded. "The whole black tower, secret laboratory thing. Is that what this is about?"

"You don't buy into it."

"I don't have to," he said. "It's just talk. People can think whatever it is they'd like. Imagination's not really my concern."

"What if it is?" she asked. Thisa jutted her chin at the emergency room door, prompting Jaga's attention.

"What? You mean Bwrynn?" His lighthearted pandering quickly hardened into serious attention. "You're suggesting that these supposed secret labs have something to do with what happened to her?"

"I'm not suggesting anything. I'm just saying that there's something going on here, and we're not being shown the whole picture."

"Something."

"Are you familiar with the executives?" she asked.

"Executives?" Jaga repeated back. "You mean Daemon's people? Valen? Faedra?"

"Kaelus and Caul, yes."

"Sure. They run most of the operations for the company. Why?"

"Have you heard of their abilities?"

Jaga stifled a snicker and shook his head, sifting through the gossip and banter that he'd picked up throughout the years. "I've heard they may have some psychic traits. So what?"

"Not psychic," she said. "Something else."

"Something else. What do you mean?"

"I don't know exactly." Thisa's voice quickly dropped from casual to cautious, whispering out the rest. "They can control people, warp their minds, even hide themselves from our psychic vision."

"What, you mean like the tsesh?"

She shook her head. "Not exactly. The tsesh can switch off their emotions, so—"

Jaga nodded and filled in the rest. "Right. No emotion, no psychic form."

"The executives though," she shook her head while searching for the words. "It's like they can manipulate the energy itself, make it do whatever it is they want."

Jaga would never admit that the idea fascinated him, even if it did. There was no way he wanted to start sampling from that buffet of conjecture. He'd seen where it leads, a downward spiral of vacuous questions. "What exactly are you getting at?" he finally asked, reeling in his imagination before she could lead it any further.

"Consider what you do know." Her tone had changed again. It was no longer a conspirator's whisper, nor was it the voice of pleasant mother. It was hard, almost forceful, stamping out each word. "Pramoore's father was abducting tsesh long before the Abolition wiped them out. Some say he was even experimenting on them."

"Those are just more rumors."

"But how many were ever heard from after their arrest?"

"That wasn't really my area. Why? You think he experimented on them to what? Give his executives powers?"

"I don't know," she answered quickly, "but if those labs do exist, I'm sure they'd hold the answers."

"The secret labs beneath Pramoore Tower." He nodded with bored condescension. The conversation had managed to come full circle after going nowhere.

"Psychics can't scan beneath the city," she said as if concluding a lecture.

"Yeah, because the tragedy of the apocalypse created a psychic cloud across the ruins. That's just a natural phenomenon, it doesn't mean—"

Thisa cut him off with impatient urgency. "If you were surrounded by psychics, but had a secret of your own, where would you hide it?"

"If," he repeated the word back hard. "And even if these secret labs exist, I still don't see how that has anything to do with Bwrynn."

Thisa jabbed a finger toward the door. "She's in a psychically-induced coma. No agent has the power to do that to her, and as far as we know, neither do the tsesh."

"So, what then? The executives? You're suggesting that they did this to her?"

She allowed a minute for the notion to settle in his thoughts. "They are the only ones who might have the power to do it."

"Assuming they even have the power that you're suggesting, why? Why go through all the trouble over an initiate?"

"What if Daemon Pramoore was involved in Kaddler's death?" She was whispering again, this time in a desperate and pleading tone. "What if Bwrynn saw something in those memories that she wasn't supposed to see?"

"Kaddler?" The name burst from Jaga's lips. "Kaddler was one of Daemon's most vocal supporters. Why would he have anything to do with his death?"

"I don't know. I don't know. But look around. The election is days away, the tsesh have returned, and now Bwrynn just happens to be put in a coma while investigating a sector lord's death?" She looked over each of her shoulders and her voice settled back down. "Something bigger is going on here. I know this is a lot of guess work, but we are missing a big piece of this puzzle and I need your help to find it."

Jaga's face cinched up with incredulity. Her theory was a flimsy string of speculation and fanciful ideas. There was nothing solid or substantial about it. Regardless, his mind plucked at each strand of its premise, and they all rang with a note of reason. As wild as it seemed, it did draw a straight line through the chaos and the questions. It was an ethereal tightrope stretched across a chasm of horrible possibility.

"I'm not asking you to believe me," Thisa added, placing a gentle palm against his chest, "but you're closer to Bwrynn than anyone. I'm just asking that you keep your eyes open." Her voice melted back to maternal care. "And be careful."

He hissed a breath out through his nose before nodding.

Contented with his simple response, Thisa wrapped herself up in her cloak and headed for the street. She turned to give him one last look before disappearing around the corner into the buzz of passing cars.

Jaga's eyes lingered on the street while his mind spun through the tangle of 'ifs' and 'maybes' she'd piled at his feet. He could see why so many agents had found this conspiracy appealing. It was rife with mystery and wild puzzles for them to solve. He shook his head. No. He only knew what he knew. Someone or something had killed Lord Kaddler. It was safe to assume that that same perpetrator was responsible for what had happened to Bwrynn. Anything beyond those facts was speculation and could too easily lead him further from the truth, if not further from reality.

His vision panned aside and angled up to the distant rise of Pramoore Tower, its black spires glowing faintly through gray haze. The dark clouds swirled above its peak, lashing out with violent whips of lightning as the skies waged their endless war against its arrogant stature. Jaga bit down behind closed lips, his muscles shifting beneath his beard. Finally, he let out another long and frustrated breath before turning around and heading back inside.

Across the driveway however, hiding behind deep shadows and blackened windows, Faedra Weiss had been watching him. She sat inside a glossy, corporate car, tucked between a tall van and a corner wall of the car lot. Her face was lit by dashboard light and her piercing emerald eyes that had remained locked on the conspiring couple outside the waiting room. Without so much as a twitch in her features, Faedra tapped at the comm on her wrist and added Jaga's name to her growing list.

CHAPTER 14

Daemon was staring down a list of names that spanned a full page on his desktop display. His eyes were black marbles, reflecting nothing back but the digital text. His mouth was sealed in a straight line, flinching every so often as if cursing without saying a word while he read the names. "This is all of them?" he finally asked.

Faedra was standing beside the broad, black desk, her hands clasped together in front of her. Her posture was stiff, like a soldier at attention, focused on an arbitrary point on the wall. "It's only a cursory search, but I confirmed these myself."

His brow shifted up. "I actually expected more."

"It's likely there are," she replied. "That's how these suspicions grow. Agents talk to agents, their imaginations ferment over time. I can have something more comprehensive in a few weeks."

"That's fine. These should be enough to quell the more troublesome elements." He swiped away the names and took a moment to smooth his eyebrows in the reflection of the black screen. A moment before he was satisfied, the office door chimed and drew his attention to the red light beside the door. With a quick tap at the console on his desk, it clicked and switched green.

The door slid open, revealing the broad figure of Kaelus filling its frame. "I have news," he said as he stepped inside.

"I have questions," Daemon answered back.

The cold look on Kaelus' stone face made it clear that he had no idea what Pramoore was referring to. "Sir?"

Daemon thumbed the black screen again and the door swept shut. The red light locked back into place. "Not a trace," he said, the words still bouncing against the executive's deadpan expression. "Your job was to erase any psychic energy from Kaddler's house."

Kaelus' eyes tried to shift together, but only drew shallow lines down his heavy brow. "That's what I did."

"Really? If that were true, if there was nothing there to find, then perhaps you can explain to me why one of our most promising agents is in the hospital right now in a psychically-induced coma." His tone grew louder but hadn't yet risen to shouting.

"I didn't put anyone in a coma."

"She was scanning your crime scene." He crossed the line to shouting and jabbed a conclusive finger at him.

Kaelus was stunned for a moment. His head dropped to the side and his eyes glossed over. "I had to draw in a lot of energy," he mumbled, presumably working out the reasoning to himself. "I had to create a strong void, but there's no way it could have affected her directly."

"Really?" Daemon spat back incredulously.

Kaelus' hardened glare rose back up and fired cold across the office. "It was a singularity. To identify the source of it would be like trying to find a single grain of sand in the desert."

Daemon threw his hands up then slapped them back down on his thighs. "Well, it would seem that she found your grain of sand."

He shook his head atop his thick neck that was cinched tight inside a crimson tie. "Even if she wakes up, she wouldn't have seen anything at the scene."

"*If* she wakes up?" Daemon asked, leaning forward on his desk. "You'd better hope she does. I had plans for her, Kaelus."

Kaelus was out of excuses and redirections. He couldn't fathom how an agent had fallen into the vacuum he'd left behind, but there was nothing to gain from defending it to Daemon. Instead, he huffed through his nose and rocked on his heavy stance before conceding to a shallow nod.

Daemon let him marinate in cold sentiment, filling the air with anger and anxiety. Finally, he broke the silence and held out a hand, palm up above his desk. "You said you have news."

Kaelus nodded again. "Reports from the attack at the diner." He tapped his meaty fingers on his comm then swiped the display upward toward Daemon's desk.

"Another failed assignment." Daemon's screens fluttered back to life, scrolling page after page of blue text against their mirrored surface.

"This is about the tsesh," Kaelus said, "and that woman he ran off with."

"The damsel in distress. Another one of them in disguise, most likely." Daemon scanned the text for news of the serpent.

"That was my first thought too," Kaelus said, nudging his nose at the documents, "but she wasn't. She was human."

He shook his head. "And how do we know that?"

"Because she used to work for us. Her name is Marianne Price. She used to manage a lab in Sector Four."

Daemon's black eyes tilted up slightly then returned to the display.

"We have detailed records on her," Kaelus continued. "She worked there for years; passed security scans every day. She was definitely human."

"Okay, so why would a tsesh break fifteen years of silence to save a human?" He muttered the thought to himself as he located the specific details of Marianne on the report. Then he muttered the answer. "He's in love with her."

"Mhm," Kaelus hummed in agreement. "She was a waitress at that diner too, real popular I guess. Some of the customers even mentioned that she'd recently started dating someone, some five or six months ago; some mystery man that no one knows anything about."

He'd captured Daemon's full attention. The report became foreground noise that he stared past to focus on Kaelus. "They're in a relationship."

"There's more," Kaelus added. His words had quickened, though almost imperceptibly. He sounded like a boulder might if it could get excited and talk. "We ran a background check on Ms. Price." He motioned for Daemon to dig further into the report, then continued to speak as he did. "Friends, finances..." he waited to finish until the look in Daemon's eyes assured him that he'd discovered what he was about to imply. "-medical records."

A long, steel silence crept into the room like icy water trickling into a cave. Beveled lines appeared around Kaelus' mouth, forming a satisfied smile on the brutish man.

Succumbing to the curiosity herself, even Faedra leaned in to read across Daemon's shoulder. On the display was an image of Marianne Price, a pretty, young blonde with smooth features and an unintrusive smile. Surrounding the image was every scrap of personal information she'd acquired in her life, an impressive amount really, for someone so young. Finally, she found the piece that Kaelus had referred to and that had captured Daemon's focus; medical records, including a recent visit to the hospital.

After absorbing the information, Daemon looked up, his eyes deep with insidious wonder. "Get me Dr. Cerrone." He pointed a finger to Faedra without looking at her. "And call a press conference."

# # #

Marianne spent the morning cleaning up the kitchen and double checking the gash across her temple. Staring in the mirror of her cramped bathroom, she'd dab the wound and wince as memory and pain stabbed at her brain. Most of the previous night was a fog of confusion and freeze-frame thoughts. She remembered her mouth being dry as she reached to tap Aldan Pharos on the shoulder. She couldn't recall the sound of the blast but remembered the bitter taste of plaster on her tongue and hazy silhouettes through dense dust. None of the sensations were in any kind of order and she finally gave up on stringing them together.

She returned to the kitchen and looked over the breakfast plates on the table. "I'm doing the dishes," she said casually to the room. The faucet chimed and turned on. At first it was a sputter of coughing water then, as the narrow temperature display above the sink climbed to 120, the stream filled out and pierced a cloud of steam as it filled up the steel sink with soapy water.

Gathering up the plates and flatware, Marianne looked up to the black panel on the patch of wall separating the living room from her bedroom. "Television," she said with a twinge of agitation as though the house should have already known.

The display panel flickered to colorful life. A red and blue background framed a well-groomed news anchor while golden text scrolled by, underlining his report. Marianne offered half a glance to the tv before stacking the dishes and turning them to the sink. They clanked and rattled before sinking beneath the dishwater. Marianne tapped at its surface, teasing and testing the water's heat then plunged into her wrists. She began clicking out a little rhythm with her tongue as she danced back and forth on the balls of her feet.

Behind her, the news feed droned on with the usual familiar monotone that fills a room; easily ignored, easily forgotten. Unable to piece together the chaos of the night, Marianne allowed thoughts of Akara to fade into the forefront of her mind. She lingered on an image of his face suspended over hers, his eyes piercing into hers, and a mischievous smile played across her lips. Then a single word snuck into her daydream and song, a familiar yet unexpected word, a word with a barbed hook that snags attention and doesn't let go; 'tsesh'.

Her wet hands slipped along the edge of a plate. It tipped sideways then cracked in half as it smashed against the edge of the sink. A sharp breath puffed from Marianne's tight throat. She jerked her hands from the water and held them up in disappointed surrender at the shattered dish. Grabbing a towel from the counter, she began wiping down her hands and turned to face the television.

"Turn up the volume," Marianne muttered absently. The television obeyed and the indistinct murmur of the broadcast hardened into words.

'We all remember the iconic video from fifteen years ago, when a tsesh attack laid waste to the 400 block of Sector Five, claiming the lives of more than two hundred civilians.'

The screen switched to a frantic, low-light view of green and black shadows. The image shook and jerked left to right as it chased a panicked man down a claustrophobic alley. Panting breath and pounding steps jumbled through the speakers, matching pace with the jarring of the camera. The fleeing man wore a long black coat and moved like a wounded animal as he stumbled over sidewalk trash and bounced his weight against the brick walls. When he finally reached the mesh fence at the back of the alley, the man seemed to spend a half-second examining the dead end before dropping his head in exhausted defeat.

A Legacy cloak stepped in front of the camera with a gloved hand rising from its folds and leveling a pistol on the cornered man. A jumble of voices fought for dominance among the cluster of off-screen agents as they ordered the man to surrender, but he didn't. They never did. His face stretched into a wide, open-mouth smile that carved out night-vision-green highlights and black grooves in his cheeks. Saliva hung from his joker's grin and a coughing laughter shook his body.

Slowly and mechanically, the man craned his head to stare down the camera, his eyes now serpentine and glowing. There was a thin slice of time pressed between the agents realizing what was happening and the moment that it happened. It was a split-second sound bite of stampeding screams and orders to fire. The tsesh's eyes flared with light that glared across the screen. Even his body seemed to glow in that final moment.

There were seven frames of fire and tumbling focus as the body of the tsesh erupted in white light, then there was a flash of static and silence. The image cut to a view from a distant street, this time in full color. Gray smoke and orange fire swelled into the sky, rising above the neon cityscape to meet the fierce lightning above. Buildings shattered and collapsed into the blast that swallowed them in pieces.

A torrent of billowing blackness rushed through the streets, enveloping storefronts, cars, and dozens of faceless and fleeing civilians.

The display went quiet and switched back to the somber image of the anchor. He sat in silence, his eyes fixed on the camera as though he were drinking in the imagery as well as the unseen response of his viewers.

'May we never forget those darker days,' he said as if finalizing a prayer. 'But even now those tragedies threaten to return.'

The camera slid left to make room for hazy pictures above the reporter's shoulder. Marianne mindlessly dropped her towel on the counter and lowered herself into a chair at the table, within arm's reach of the screen. The photos were mostly fog and dust, but she recognized the layout within them. They were still frames clipped from the security feed at Diedre's Diner. Each of the images seemed to focus on a shadowy figure inside the white haze. Beyond being recognizable as a human shape, the form had no distinguishable features. It was a faded silhouette inside pale-gray clouds. Some of the shots also included the large beast, its back webbed in electricity and its head cutting above the fog. As they continued to cycle through with a slow pulse, the reporter continued his script.

'These are just some of the images retrieved from the scene at Diedre's Diner yesterday. As you can see, the debris from the attack has obscured most of the details, but agents on the scene believe this figure here to be the tsesh that was involved.'

The final shot grew until it filled the frame of the television. The anchor continued to speak, but Marianne was no longer listening. She stared at the snapshot of her nightmare from the day before. It was chaos and ash, and a cloaked shadow wielding a sword, standing fearless in the center of it all. In the upper corner though, in a one-inch patch of pixels, Marianne saw herself, her closed eyes and bloodied hair lying helpless on the floor. She stared for a moment as if she'd died and was now looking down at her body. She turned back to the dark swordsman, then to herself, then back to him. The shape was blurred, but she thought she could make out the angle of his face. Was he looking at her? Her hand drifted upward to the television as if riding a wisp of smoke, and her fingertips slowly traced the pixelated demon who had saved her life.

# # #

Pramoore technology and Daemon's own influence allowed his presence to slip into every corner of Mallis Two. At a moment's notice and at his command, every monitor and hologram could display his angular face, his black eyes, and his glossy hair. Every speaker could carry his voice, whatever the message, into boardrooms and bedrooms alike. It mingled with low and rumbling music, prickling emotion, and seducing fear. Pramoore was synonymous with authority and what was innocently tagged as a press conference was, in fact, a voice from on high. It poured down upon the world like viscous oil, seeping into every home, slow, heavy, warm, just waiting for someone to strike a match.

Monitors would switch off sporting events and scheduled news, and the comms on every arm would blink out single note harbingers of his incoming message. His voice crept into every nook of the world, into private places, secret places, forgotten places.

Akara was pulled from his fragmented daze by the bold and simple tone on his wrist. The metal band of his comm was pulsing with a tiny amber light, with a long and lazy tone accompanying each flash. It was an emergency message, typically reserved for the announcement of dust storms and riots. Before he tapped at the band, Akara knew what it would say.

The hologram staggered to life above his arm. It was Daemon standing at a wooden podium, flanked by Faedra Weiss and Valen Kirsch. The stuttering chyron beneath them scrolled out the simple text, "Tsesh Among Us".

"Some of you have seen the news, most of you have heard the rumors." Daemon wasn't speaking to the reporters who were undoubtedly clustered before him. He spoke directly at the center camera, his umbral eyes piercing through the image and into everyone watching. "I came here today to confirm to you the truth. The tsesh have reemerged in our streets." He paused as the slow weight of his words descended on the masses, kicking up a clamor in the streets like dust beneath a fallen brick. "Yesterday afternoon, an unknown creature attacked councilman Aldan Pharos at a diner in Sector Six. Fortunately, the councilman survived unharmed, but it was a tsesh who stepped in to rescue him.

"It is unclear why these creatures would reveal themselves after all this time just to protect Mr. Pharos. We also don't know what his connection to them may be or how long they've been working together. I don't believe it's a coincidence however that, just a few hours after the attack, Sector Lord Kaddler, councilman Pharos' opponent in the upcoming election, was murdered in his home. The cause of death is still undetermined, but it does appear to be unnatural."

There was a swell of voices off-camera as reporters shouted over each other's questions, scrambling to be heard. Daemon let them battle for a moment before pushing them all back down to silence with a stiff, open hand.

"Over the past twenty years, the Dark Ocean Legacy has been unwavering in their duty to watch over us. Ever since my predecessor began their order, our city has known peace. We've felt secure. We've felt safe. It is precisely that dedication and efficiency which leads me to believe that we are in fact still safe. These snakes have not been living among us as they had in the past, but rather they've been hiding in our shadows, bartering backroom deals, only striking in our weakest moments, possibly even manipulating the political foundation of our city."

Another surge of questions clamored for his attention and this time Daemon gave a slow nod and finally chose one from the crowd. He pointed to someone without a word.

The other voices dropped away, and a young man's voice carved out from between them. "If the tsesh have been in hiding, what interest would they have in human politics now?"

"I would think that's obvious," Daemon replied. "Their crimes left them banished from our world. Now they're looking to reclaim it." The end of his answer signaled another flood of questions and he quickly pointed to another off-screen voice.

"If your agents have been as diligent as you claim," a woman said, "then how did they fail to find these tsesh in over fifteen years of service?"

Daemon had expected the question, but there was a short break before he answered. His eyes seemed to stab at the reporter with an unspoken threat before his thin smile wiped away their rage like blood from a dagger. "Legacy agents are unmatched in their psychic abilities," he said. "This latest generation is even more powerful than any before, but even they can't see everything.

"There are places in this world that remain hidden from us. The desert outside these walls, for example, is a mass of storms and psychic chaos, but even a tsesh couldn't survive for long out there. No, it's much more likely that these creatures have been living beneath our very streets, in the ruins of Old Mallis. The destruction from the apocalypse has left the old world masked in psychic energy and, while those ruins are also not very hospitable, they would make a perfect hiding place for snakes and assassins."

Daemon let the crowd bubble back to life. He didn't bother trying to silence them. Instead, he seemed to drink in their panic with a sly and satisfied smile. His attention turned back to the camera, leaving the roiling hysteria as a backdrop to his final message.

"We know from tragedies past that we cannot delay in our response. We cannot let these creatures take hold of our world. We must act, and we must act now. That is why I'm authorizing the immediate mobilization of our most powerful agents, sending them into the depths of Sector Six. They will root out these serpents as well as the identities of their human sympathizers. You have my promise that there will continue to be order and security in our streets."

Akara switched off the display with a tired and trembling finger. The small dorm plunged back into cold quiet and ambient light. "Sympathizers?" His father was right. The Legacy wouldn't just be coming for them, they'd be coming for Marianne as well. He felt the floor of his guts give out. He tried to swallow, but his mouth had dried up. Old Mallis was an easy sprawl of a hundred square miles, but Pramoore had already narrowed his search to Sector Six. He would find them. He would find her.

He snatched up his coat and stuffed his arms through the sleeves while crossing the room. Akara opened the door, and a storm of sound and agitated energy came barreling in. Tsesh were walking fast along the halls, plastic totes in their arms and duffel bags slung across their backs. He adjusted his collar and thumbed at the lapel, his gaze jumping from one person to the next.

Akara didn't bother asking them where they were going. It was likely they wouldn't know themselves. They were simply doing their small tasks in whatever grand plan the king had decided. Akara just offered simple greetings as he hurried past. "Basker," he said to one. "Treck," he nodded to another.

Halfway to the courtyard he found Malehk standing tall and still amidst a swarm of other tsesh. He was paying them no attention and tightening the holsters on his hips. Akara called out his name and hung a hand above the masses until Malehk turned to find him.

"There you are," Malehk greeted, tugging at the leather straps. He was crisscrossed in buckles and sheaths, more than Akara had ever known him to wear.

"Malehk," he replied, gesturing to the crowds, "what's all this?"

"Uh, precautions you could say," Malehk answered with a steady pan across the busy faces.

"Precautions. What do you mean precautions?"

"Well, after the... event," he served up the word with a cautious, open hand at the prince, "your dad has ordered everyone underground."

"Underground? We are underground."

"More underground. They're falling back to the old subway systems and pump tunnels."

"The sewers? His response is to run for the sewers? Why? You're okay with that?"

"They are falling back," Malehk emphasized while cutting him off and nodding his head to swarms of tsesh around them. "Me and a few others were chosen to stay behind; keep an eye out in case the Legacy comes lookin'."

"In case the— Malehk, of course they're coming. Staying here alone is suicide. When the Legacy comes down here, they'll just kill you. That's not a plan."

"Well then technically that's not suicide, it's murder," he replied with his cocky half-smile.

"I'm serious, Malehk. We either stay and fight together or we regroup together. As good as you are, if you stay up here alone, you'll just die."

Malehk clamped both hands on Akara's shoulders and leveled his eyes on him. "I'm touched by your concern, but it's gonna be fine. We're not lookin' for a fight. We're just hanging back until everyone else is clear."

"That's not what this is, and you know it. You don't leave a lookout when you're retreating." Akara paused to even out his voice then spoke as though he were laying out elementary tactics to a toddler. "The Legacy knows we're alive, all right? They will find this place. A single group staying behind provides nothing. It just gives them someone—" the sentence stopped as if chopped off by a cleaver on a butcher's cutting board. When he finished the thought, it was with a tone of revelation, "someone to kill." His eyes drifted away and suddenly he was only speaking to himself. "They only saw me."

Malehk's face bunched up at the notion and he replied with a shake of his head that seemed to be more of a befuddled twitch.

"Listen to me," Akara said, his attention snapping back and filling with urgency. "It's a decoy. My father didn't choose you to cover their retreat. He is leaving you here as bait."

"How is that bait?"

He continued as if he were out of breath and had only seconds to plead his case. "Pramoore has no idea how many of us are left, okay? They only saw me."

"So? So what?"

"So that's why my father is leaving you here. So that they have someone to find. They'll kill you and that will be the end of it. Pramoore gets his pound of flesh, and my father gets to go back to hiding." The prince's eyes locked wide and pierced into the ground as a frigid realization crashed across his mind. "This is my fault. That bastard is punishing you for helping me."

"Will you stop with all the dramatics," Malehk said. "This isn't about you. This is nothing. It's a simple spook job. I'll be meeting up with you in the Tunnel B pump station tomorrow morning, okay?"

Akara was frozen in place as his world of chaos suddenly began locking together, piece after piece behind his mind's eye. His father knew this was coming. He called it from the start. If Pramoore couldn't find the tsesh, he would find Marianne and he would use her to draw them out. As Akara's vision slowly began to regain focus, he formed a plan and tapped at Malehk's chest. "I have to take care of something," he said. "I'll be back in an hour. Don't do anything stupid."

"Hurtful," Malehk replied as Akara began heading across the yard.

"I mean it, Malehk. If you see agents, do not engage them." He shouted the final words across his shoulder as he broke into a sprint and pounded out to the broken streets of Old Mallis.

#

Akara had rushed to the surface, but his speed had slowed with his waning confidence as he crossed the sector to Marianne's apartment building. By the time he'd reached her stoop, his steps were small and shuffling. His hands were balled into fists with his thumbs rubbing hard across their knuckles. It was little more than instinct when he pressed the call button on the door-side panel. He hadn't even given himself the chance to work up the nerve for what he had to do. His pulse was still pounding in his chest, rattling his limbs with nervous tremors.

"Akara," her voice came through the speaker with a hint of surprise that quickly molded into excitement. "Back so soon. Hang on, I'll be right down."

When the speaker went silent, he tried to clear his throat, but a pained sound raked from his lips instead. He paced in tight circles at the top of the steps as though his feet couldn't decide where best to stand. In the flash of moments that he had left, he suddenly realized that he had no plan. He had no excuse and no idea what he would say to her. It was too late to think up a lie and it was impossible to tell her the truth.

The door opened. It was faster than he'd expected. She must have rushed down the hall. Her hair was still a mess, but her eyes glimmered their gorgeous sapphire smile. He was stunned by her. Whether he was caught off guard or remembering all over again how beautiful she was, he couldn't be sure, but his mouth and eyes locked open like a beast in headlights.

"Hi," she said simply, seemingly unaware of his panicked state and the terror that was tingling across his skin.

"Hi," he answered back in a hoarse whisper.

Marianne's smile filled out, becoming more deliberate as if she hoped to draw out more of a response from him. "What's up?"

He began to mouth her name, but it caught in his throat, and he retreated to a long sigh.

"Akara?" she coaxed. Her voice went soft and filled with concern. "What's up?"

"I have to tell you something," he began, his voice chopped into rippling waves, "and I hope— I mean— I have to say something."

Marianne cocked her head and fixed her stance as if preparing for a shockwave. "Okay?"

He huffed out another breath. His eyes dodged hers, searching for any random point on the cement at his feet to offer him a sense of stable focus. "This, um— this is— this isn't working out."

"This," she started to say back, answering before she'd processed what he'd said. Her tone faltered and her silken voice came back like fabric snapping on thin scaffolding. "This," she said again, "What's— what do you mean?"

"It's just-," he managed to clear his throat and suck in a breath. Akara was searching his heart for the conviction that had driven him here. This wasn't about him. He had to get her as far from his life as he could. He had to save her life. The world stopped and he slowly, deliberately looked her in the eye. Already he could see the shimmer of tears forming in their perfect corners. His mind begged for forgiveness as the words escaped across his lips. "It was never going to work out with us."

The first of her tears broke free. She pressed her lips together and shook her head. "What's that supposed to mean?" Her voice was broken now, fragments of song stitched together by creaking threads. "It is working out with us. It already is. Just this morning…" she gave up on the sentence before it could break apart into little more than tears and noise. She slid an open hand at him, gesturing like someone who had forgotten their lines in a play. "You're..." she tried the words once, then twice, then rushed them out together. "You were my hero."

"Marianne..."

"I made breakfast."

"I am so sorry." Akara's tone was graveled but sincere. The sound of his pulse was rushing in his ears, and he could feel his own eyes beginning to sting.

"No," she refused with terse lips while shaking her head. "It's something else, isn't it?" She thought back to the image on the news, to the gray beast and the creature that had saved her. Through the haze of her tears, she could see that shaded form again, staring at her defenseless form. Her words came quickly, strung together in a tightly knotted string. He had paused, so she tried the words again, "It's something else. I can see it in your eyes. You have to tell me."

Akara's own tears had betrayed him, painting glistening lines down his cheeks. "I'm sorry," he said again, "but this was always just a dream." He clenched his teeth hard to stabilize his voice. "And I have to wake up now."

"Akara, no." Marianne was wracked with shaking cries as if the words themselves were painful to utter. "Please."

"Goodbye, Marianne," He finally spoke the terminal word they'd promised never to say, then he turned his back on her and began descending the steps.

Everything around her spiraled away in a blur. He was leaving and if he reached the sidewalk neither of them would ever know the truth. She'd had a plan written out in her imagination, but she was out of time. She had to tell him. "I'm pregnant."

Akara paused at the last step, his head bowed. The words had reached his mind, but they couldn't touch his heart. His eyes had already slipped away to their golden, serpentine slits, and his emotions were wisping away like smoke in the wind. He considered what she'd said then slipped his sunglasses over his eyes and continued to the sidewalk, never looking back at the woman crying out his name.

CHAPTER 15

Jaga was sitting on a long bench in the locker room of Legacy Headquarters, working to lace up his last boot. Between the smell of sweat, the buzz of the lights, and the anxious heave in his belly, he was reminded vaguely of his youth, gearing up for the coming mission. Former classmates and fellow agents would be psyching themselves up, stomping their feet and slamming locker doors. He remembered the excitement they'd distill from their fear and the testosterone shouts they'd use to overpower their pounding hearts.

He used to look forward to those moments, reacting to a call and heading for the lockers. Sometimes they'd be summoned in pairs, oftentimes in groups, and the energy of camaraderie would become their shared pulse. Outside those concrete walls was the calm before the storm, and they were the storm. They felt invincible as only the foolish can.

All of that was gone. Jaga's thin skin and arthritic knuckles anchored him to reality. His gun belt bit into his hips and the pistols hung heavier at his sides than he remembered. There were no empowering barks of encouragement to puncture the heavy stillness of the room. Across the rows of steel lockers, even the youngest and hungriest agents were cocooned in quiet. The air was somber and repentant. This new generation, powerful as they may have been, weren't born into war as their veterans had been. This was thrust onto them, and they weren't ready.

His fists burned as he cinched the last knot in his laces. Jaga would have welcomed a shout of exuberance from the younger crowd who knew no better. He longed for the electricity that once crackled through his veins, but more so, he wanted the distraction. He wanted the noise to pull him out of his head and out of that hospital room where Bwrynn still lay unconscious. He wanted to feel like a warrior again because fathers can never be fearless.

"Two minutes!" Kaelus' voice blasted into the room, swallowing up even its own echo from off the ceramic walls.

Jaga snapped and smoothed his pant leg and rose to his feet while gathering up his cloak. Stepping around the corner, he saw the square and chiseled man, standing like an angry lighthouse at the locker room door. Kaelus was still wearing his narrow, crimson glasses, but in place of his pressed suit and silk tie, he was dressed for war. He had on black fatigues, adorned with the eight-armed star of Pramoore against a red field on his shoulder. His waist was clasped in a wide, leather belt with a flat-black buckle and holstered pistols hanging uniformly on either hip.

"Mr. Bathor," Jaga began as he crossed the room.

"Commander," Kaelus amended sternly with not so much as a glance.

Jaga hesitated at the impact of the correction then shook it off and continued forward. "Commander Bathor," he offered instead, "I wanted to ask you about the makeup of our squad."

The only sign that Jaga had caught his attention at all was a slit-eyed and sideways glance from beneath the glasses of an otherwise stock-still man.

"Sir?" he continued regardless. "Half of these agents are still in academics. They aren't even cleared for combat."

"They are today."

The brusque response punched another hole in Jaga's thoughts. His eyes flinched, but he shook it off. "Yes, sir, but what about file and formation?" He swept a hand to the room of mismatched men and women still buckling into their gear. "We've never worked together before. We can't just pile in with no plan. We'll need some sense of order down there."

Kaelus slid his eyes toward him again. "It's a simple sweep, agent. You'll be fine."

"It's not me that I'm worried about."

"Then we don't have a problem." The volume of Kaelus' voice filled up like a steel basin. "Because you are the only person you need to worry about. Composition is not your responsibility, and I did not ask for your advice."

"I understand that," Jaga started, "but if we go in—"

Kaelus turned his shaded eyes to fully face him now. He stiffened to a full and imposing height. "Agent Demain, you made a name for yourself back in the day. You killed a lot of snakes. That's commendable, but you still are and always have been a very small piece of a much bigger plan. You do your job. You get it done. Period."

Kaelus was a simple and hulking brick, both in stature and in dialogue. Pressing the issue would be brief and pointless, so Jaga simply bowed and said, "Yes, sir," before walking past him and into the hall. Heading down the sloped tunnel to the car park though, he couldn't shake the feeling that something was amiss. This assault was haphazard, and the assignments made no sense. He spared a moment to consider it, but his mind was soon back at Bwrynn's bedside. Kaelus was right, he just had to do his job. The sooner it was done, the sooner he'd be back.

#

Akara plodded, step-by-step through the streets toward the service elevator. His serpentine mind was clicking thoughts into place like a clock that was marching towards midnight. Marianne was pregnant. How was that possible? Humans can't bear tsesh children, they're biologically incompatible. He considered that she was lying, but she wasn't. He had heard that much in her voice. He considered that she was mistaken, that it wasn't really his, but she simply wasn't the type. She was always honest and unfaltering. With every angle filtered, the truth burned bare at the forefront of his brain. Akara Krosse, prince of the tsesh on the precipice of war, was going to have a child, a hybrid, human child.

There was another truth however, one that he knew as sure as his father would. The child would be a problem. It was an exposed wire that connected the royal line to the human world. It would ignite outrage throughout the surface, and it would give Daemon Pramoore a key to the front door of the last remaining tsesh. Something had to be done, but Akara couldn't see it. He found himself shaking off the slow creep of doubt and concern, the thin gray shadows of deeper and more dangerous emotions. The methodical thoughts of his cold mind seemed to misstep and slip, like gears skipping teeth in an engine. He couldn't fully grasp the situation. He couldn't reach past Marianne and the baby to the solution beyond. He opted instead to consult the king. Rhago would know what to do.

The elevator was just ahead, a squat silhouette past his glasses and a block further in the failing afternoon light. He locked his path and posture on the building, but it was soon broken apart by a storm of cars roaring past him on the street. Black, tinted Runcourtes, the signature fleet of the Dark Ocean Legacy. They barreled by, one after another, kicking up sound and smoke as they stormed the lot encircling the block beyond.

Akara stopped at the corner and watched as they surrounded the 6-4 maintenance building. Cloaked agents poured from the cars before the dust could even settle around their tires. A quick count tallied fifteen, heavily armed, and Kaelus Bathor was among them. The amber undertow of fate was rushing at them from every direction, pulsing as though it had a heartbeat of its own.

The last agent emerged from his car and paused as though he'd caught the scent of something on the wind. Even across the distance, Akara could see his eyes flicker with ghostly light as the agent swept a psychic mind across the street, snatching clips from every life it touched. Akara leapt aside, putting a stone wall between himself and the scan. With an unfeeling, serpentine mind, he would be nothing more than another brick, unreadable and insignificant.

He waited for the sweeping sensation to pass, watching as the wisps of fate spun in the wake of the psychic's inquisition, like stubborn smoke in a heavy wind. Coiling around his feet, the golden current urged him ahead, but the tsesh held his ground until he was certain that the way was clear. The agent's scan disintegrated, and the sound of an electronic door buzzed through the street. They were inside. They were on their way down.

Akara stepped casually from the corner and studied the black convoy parked around the silent building. The war was about to begin, and he was a half-step behind the coming wave.

A thought jumped uninvited from his lips. "Malehk."

#

The trip into Old Mallis was slow and sinking. Jaga was the lead agent of Bravo Squad, taking the second descent of the freight elevator behind Kaelus and the others. Across the sector, a half dozen other groups were following suit, penetrating the loosely mapped depths with the precision of high school stage directions. They'd been advised of a plan. It resembled a pincer maneuver with each team closing in on a vague destination in the southwest jumble of half-formed maps. The whole operation was an illusion of strategy with just enough substance to convince the inexperienced.

Methodical and battle-tested himself, Jaga still had no idea who he could count on. To his left was a rookie with his hands sending tremors through his rifle. To his right was a tired veteran who also didn't seem to know what the plan was, but visibly didn't care either. He wasn't at attention; he wasn't tense or poised. He was slumped against the side wall as if he were waiting in line for hot pretzel. Maybe he had the right idea. Maybe this whole expedition was nothing more than pageantry, a shallow show of force by Daemon Pramoore. They'd trudge through the shattered and haunted streets for a few hours then return to the surface with little more than hollow reassurance.

The mission was a patchwork of muddled concepts that were stitched together in a rush. Tension bubbled up like bile in Jaga's belly. It wasn't the nervous rush of adrenalin he used to feel, teetering over on the precipice of war. This was the heavy, quilted fear of uncertainty. They were willfully blind, and every clumsy move they made felt wrong. As his guts hollowed out, that sunken feeling was punctuated by the blasé stance of Alpha Squad lounging outside when the elevator doors finally slid open. They were kicked back on piles of broken brick, chewing strips of jerky, and laughing to each other over inside jokes. They weren't nervous. They weren't prepared. They were blissful idiots.

Standing inside earshot but outside of social chatter, Kaelus had his back to the overly casual squad. He was glaring across the buried horizon beyond. The red pulse of service lights tinted the steel canopy and sketched out across the tattered skyline ahead of them. He seemed angry at it all, his stern face carved into an expression of sour disdain. Even without being able to read the gritty man, Jaga could sense a fire beneath his surface, like a volcano desperate to erupt. Kaelus Bathor hated this place.

"Commander," Jaga shot out to him, hoping to lash a sense of formality around the group. He walked towards him, rifle stowed at his side, giving just enough attention to the uneven ground as he needed to cross the distance.

"Agent," Kaelus responded with a half-turned glance.

"The other teams are in position?"

Kaelus didn't answer. He looked west and nodded as if deciding off-the-cuff. "You'll take your team that way. Scout out five miles and report anything you find."

Jaga followed his gaze, examining the distant and tattered cityscape. There was nothing there, no landmarks, nothing of strategic value. Five miles would bring them flush with the edge of the crater, the stone brim of the underground city. "Yes, sir," he replied with over-emphasized subordination. "And Alpha Team?"

Kaelus turned abruptly on his heels to face him, like he'd been waiting for the question. His square head was cocked to the side. His voice was silent, but his posture growled, 'How dare you question me?' He took slow steps, back through the cluster of suddenly silent agents. He was a tiger amused by a mouse, stalking ever closer to the elder agent. Finally, his mouth clamped shut and worked to curve up into what may have passed as a smile on his chiseled face. "We'll be heading north," he answered as if it was none of Jaga's business. "We'll fan out and maintain the exit."

The roguish crew of Alpha Squad divided their attention between the two men, while Bravo shrunk behind Jaga. There was an anxiousness in the air, thicker than the dust and psychic fog that lingered in the ancient, static world. Whether their contest was across generations, rank, or social standing, Kaelus and Jaga stood evenly matched before their troops and those desolate streets.

Without implying any kind of surrender, Jaga offered up a simple nod, looking again to the bland stretch of their objective. He adjusted his cloak and nodded. "Yes, sir."

Kaelus was apparently pleased enough with the outcome and aped a matching smile. "We'll see you in an hour."

"One hour," he repeated back before turning to the men in his charge. "On me," he commanded. "Let's go." The last order had the bite of irritation, just enough for his troops to know that he hadn't submitted fully.

# # #

One mile out, Jaga's composure was showing signs of stress. His lips were locked shut and his breath was huffing through his nose while his pale eyes skipped from one dead building to the next. There was nothing there, and there was no reason to think that there would be. It was a broken and hollow place with no signs of life. He held up a practiced hand sign to halt his squad. They stopped dead center in a four-way intersection of the long-lost world.

"Sir?" a young agent replied softly at his side.

Jaga shook his head and panned another look across the landscape. "There's nothing here." He stretched a look across his shoulder at the rest of the squad. They were statuesque in their formation, trained soldiers, evenly spaced with their rifles at the ready. He appreciated the structure of the group amidst the chaos. Had they a plan, he may have even had confidence in their mission, but they didn't and so he didn't. They were blind and they were armed, and Jaga could think of nothing more volatile than that.

"Shouldn't we continue ahead then?" the young agent asked.

Jaga looked deeper to the west and saw nothing more than empty streets and crumbling walls. "This is a waste of time."

"We have our orders, sir."

"But we have no plan," Jaga snapped back. He thrust a hand toward the empty street ahead. "We have no direction; we have no information."

The agent considered his frustration, studying the scene as if to draw the same conclusion for himself. "What are you thinking, sir?"

He eased a slow breath from his nose and chewed at his lower lip. "I don't know. I don't know," he repeated in every direction. He began to plot out his thoughts, to lay them out aloud so that they could be sorted and organized, but a glimpse of his waiting soldiers hooked into his attention. Two of the other agents in their formation were looking to the north. They were fixated on a singular point and muttering amongst themselves. Jaga followed their attention and saw the hanging, black spire of the sub-basements beneath Pramoore Tower. It was a giant, obsidian drill aimed at the center of the forgotten world. The agent at his side seemed to notice and by the time Jaga turned back to him, he too was staring at the suspended monolith.

"What's your name, son?" Jaga asked, snatching back the young man's focus.

"Ellis Kyler." He seemed to ask more than he stated.

"Those agents," Jaga said, nodding toward the others. "Do you know them?"

Ellis allowed for a few beats of casual, innocent time to roll out before replying. "Yes, sir. We're in a few groups together."

Jaga opened his mind just enough to gauge a reaction without alerting the man to his intentions. "And Thisa Rosewood. You know her too?"

A lightning bolt had struck the young man's brain. It shattered his thoughts and forced him to chomp and swallow at his dry mouth while gathering them up like scattered marbles. "Uh, yes, sir. I've met her."

The steady, red pulse of the service lights ticked along above them, tapping in rhythm to the methodical thoughts and punching heartbeat of Jaga's growing suspicion. "And the others? How many of our squad are in these groups with you?"

"Sir?"

"Classes, study groups, training formations," he clarified. "How many?"

Ellis pretended to look across the row of faces behind them. Their stances formed a wedge that pointed ahead to their objective, though the individuals within the wedge were beginning to stir with impatience. Some of them remained oblivious while others locked expectant eyes with Ellis. "All of them I think."

Jaga's head spun toward them then back to him. There were hundreds of agents in the Legacy, and the seemingly random assortment of their squad was a surprisingly accurate cross-section of them all; new recruits, aging veterans, rising stars. They represented every facet of the organization, most of which had no business working together in any capacity. The chances of all of them ever coming together for any reason were slim if not impossible. This was the key he'd been looking for, the connection that made sense of their otherwise mindless assignment. They all knew each other. They all knew Thisa Rosewood.

"I'm about to make you very uncomfortable, Ellis," he said, creeping back toward the group, "but I need you to answer me honestly."

The young agent was struggling to lock down his unsettled mind. His head began to nod before he could eke out a verbal response. "Of course, sir."

After a long pause, Jaga pointed his chin at Pramoore's basement tower in the distance. "What do you think is beneath Pramoore Tower?"

A nervous snort blurted out of Ellis. He smudged his stumbling words together with filler sounds like 'uh' and 'um', and Jaga could feel his green mind scrambling like someone shredding evidence as the police were raiding their office space. "Beneath the— the um— beneath the tower?"

Jaga ignored his panic as all the jagged pieces of what he hadn't understood began to come together. "That's what I thought," he muttered. "This isn't a trap for the tsesh. This is a trap for us."

CHAPTER 16

Between the busy work and banter of Alpha Squad, no one had heard the elevator rise and descend once more. They were a mile away, unloading gear and cracking jokes, too distant and distracted to see the blink of the service lights or hear the sound of the electric door. The lift had brought a single passenger; a tsesh prince with golden eyes and a leather coat that snapped furiously as he rushed the distance towards them.

The radiant streaks of fate surged ahead of Akara like cobras made of light, ravenous for the rats that had invaded their world. They coiled around toppled walls and streaked ahead of the tsesh, cracking like whips. He obeyed their will, hurdling broken and ancient cars and stamping out a pounding pulse with his boots against the ruined street.

Akara's breath huffed in a trained rhythm behind the vented mask over his mouth. His muscles were saturated with oxygen, adrenaline, and the electric burn of anticipation. Just past the bent and powdered remains of an ancient bus stop, he could see his quarry. There were ten agents, each wrapped in their prideful cloaks lounging around a thick and looming support beam, one of hundreds that braced the canopy overhead. Akara spent a half-second analyzing their armaments, stances, and positions. In that snapshot he'd already planned his approach, but it was tinted by their lazy and thoughtless demeanors. They'd come to kill his people, to burn them from the world, and their relaxed postures signaled just how little the act would mean to them.

Light and sound blurred across Akara's senses. The hammering of his boots, the crack of his coat, and the rush of the wind all bled together into a building chorus, the sound-check of an orchestra moments before their performance. Only two sounds sliced through the crescendo: the whine of his pistol powering up and the smooth scrape of his blade against its sheath. When his determination was set, the streams of fate lunged ahead, blasting outward like daggers, each tendril locking on a separate target.

Akara leapt. The conductor raised his baton, and the orchestra went quiet. The agents of the Legacy had only a flash of time to see the masked assailant descending on them before it all began; before the first beat was struck.

There was a glint of chrome and blood. The first cloaked prey spiraled to the ground, his chest pumping a red stain across his white shirt. The tsesh fired two rounds through the crowd at another fumbling man. One in his heart, the second in his head. Akara had time for one more attack before the battle would begin. Another pair of gunshots blasted from his gun, dropping a third agent on the edge of the crowd. He flicked the blood from his blade with a quick snap. His eyes blazed bright. The battlefield filled up around him with the radiance of fate.

Rifles jumped to attention. Time, once so neatly divided into seconds, poured over them in a long, slow breath of smoke and sound. Akara moved forward in a rhythmic and steady dance as the gunfire erupted all around him. With every step, he'd swing his blade or pull his trigger. Each motion played out pre-planned, as though he'd fought this very battle a hundred times before. He would duck beneath glittering bullet trails as panicked shots fired past. The agents converged on him and any attack they'd dodge or parry would simply maneuver them towards the next attack.

As Akara wove through the blistering fray, his diverging paths, once so full of options, began to dwindle. His last remaining targets were holding firm at a distance, aware of his approach, with all their training now ramped up to its full potential. Kaelus Bathor was standing in between them. Akara's serpentine glare fixed on them, paying no attention as his blade sliced aside once more, cutting down the final close-quarter combatant. He unlocked his readied stance and stood to meet their weapons with audacious pride. His eyes glowed bright above his mask and dared them to shoot. They did.

Three bursts of fire blasted through the air, one each from the rifles of the remaining agents. Akara dodged two and slapped the third away with the flat of his blade. He dared them to fire again, and again they did. This time he ducked beneath them. They slapped into powdery bursts against the distant walls behind him, and Akara rose ever closer to his attackers. He spun his sword in his hand, readjusting his grip on its leather-wrapped hilt. The agents each took two steps back, their heads jerking back and forth amongst their slim, surviving ranks. Every time they fired the serpent only drew nearer. They grew reluctant to try again.

Then darkness crept in. It was a black worm in Akara's brain, slithering between crevasses and unlatching fastened thoughts. Marianne was the first to break free. Her silken face blanketed the forefront of his mind. Then came his unborn child, still a shadowy question spanning across the future. Then came Malehk and then the king. Akara's forward motion stopped, and the searing righteousness of fate faded away around him. His eyes went dark and round, then turned toward their invader. Kaelus was taking slow, golem-like steps into the battle, his eyes bubbling with a blue light. Somehow, he had stricken Akara's tsesh mind, stripping it away and reducing him to nothing more than a mortal man, filled with questions, doubt, and trembling weapons in his hands.

Another gunshot burst through the air. Akara's shoulders jumped at the sound and his sword and pistol both tumbled from his grip. His breath had been punched from his lungs and he scuffled back a step. The left side of his stomach filled with a creeping, icy puddle and the taste of blood belched up into his throat.

"Was it you?" Kaelus asked in a calm and sonorous tone. His eyes still twitched with light as he hissed a breath through his nose like a disappointed father after curfew. "Are you the one who's been coming up to my world and causing all this trouble?"

Akara wasn't sure if he'd meant to respond but drawing in a breath only kicked up bubbles in his airway, now full of coppery bile. He coughed a wet cough through the vents of his mask and allowed himself a downward glance at his ribs where his shirt was wet with blood and sticking to his skin. His hand had clamped around the bullet hole in the fabric but did little to stem the torrent of the seeping wound.

"You're extinct," Kaelus continued, drawing closer as Akara dropped to his knees amidst the blood and rubble. "You have no place in this world. Why haven't you accepted that like the rest of your kind?" He grunted the final word while hammering a solid, boulder-like fist into Akara's face.

The force of the blow split the skin around his eye and wrenched Akara's spine sideways. His ears rang out deaf and his body twisted and fell into the dirt. His wide eyes searched the ground and his free hand swept for his fallen sword. When the ringing faded, a throbbing sound filled his ears and his vision wilted out of focus. The scene broke into a kaleidoscope of shapes, with just enough detail for him to see Kaelus raise a pistol to his head.

"Kaelus!" a voice called out from some unseen and distant point. Akara didn't bother to look.

Jaga and his disparate battalion were approaching from the long westward street, still holding to a loose semblance of their trained formation. As they emerged from the dusty horizon, they were visibly surveying the ground, noting the dead bodies and scattered gear. Jaga however, remained focused on the kneeling man and the pistol held to his head.

"That's commander," Kaelus corrected him again.

Jaga stopped his troops at the edge of the conflict. His heart thumped heavy at the sight of the tsesh. It was an image he'd seen before, a defeated tsesh, cornered and captive. He knew what they could do. He knew what the outcome would be: death. Jaga took a half-step back, the muscles in his body preparing to flee, to sprint from the scene before the inevitable explosion. His breath caught in his throat, but slowly began to relax as he realized that nothing was happening. It had been nearly half a minute, more than enough time for a tsesh to erupt and destroy them all. He drifted another gaze toward the defeated prince and studied him. "He has no power," he noted aloud yet to himself.

"Of course, he doesn't," Kaelus said with a cocky smirk. "If he did, we'd all be dead by now. Isn't that right, snake?"

"But how?" Jaga asked. "How are you doing that?"

Kaelus flicked his blue-static eyes at him, but only for a second. It wasn't enough to free Akara from his oppressive, mental hold.

"You can negate their abilities." Jaga was still narrating to himself, but his thoughts raced back to Bwrynn, lying on that hospital bed, lost inside her mind. He thought for a moment of what Thisa had suggested, that the executives could control psychic energy.

"I said one hour," Kaelus called out to his side while smugly thumbing his pistol grip. "You're early."

"I'm efficient." Jaga didn't appear interested in the coming execution, but he did look past it to the stacked crates around the underworld's support beam. He squinted behind his glasses until he could make out the thin wires snaking out from them, each leading to a single box mounted on the steel surface of the pillar. The small box had a touchscreen display and four rectangular panels that were blinking the digital eights of an unprogrammed timer. He waved the barrel of his rifle at the device. "Commander, what is that?"

Kaelus held his pistol inches from Akara's wobbling head, turning his attention to the device. "That," he said slowly and definitively, "is the mission."

"It's a bomb." Jaga rushed the words in rapid contrast to Kaelus' slow manner.

"Yes. It's a bomb."

"You were never actually looking for tsesh, were you?"

Kaelus huffed a shallow smile at Akara's gasping face while Jaga pieced together the puzzle of their mission. "And yet we found them," he said, gesturing toward the kneeling prince.

"It was meant for us, wasn't it? Daemon thinks we've gone rogue, and he sent you to kill us." Jaga tightened his grip on the rifle but didn't raise it from its readied position. Not yet. He only waited half a beat for the answer that he knew wasn't coming. "So, what then? You were going to lead us here and blow us up? You were going to destroy half the city?"

A buzz of stupefied questions churned up within Bravo Squad. They glanced around at each other, each one asking if the others knew. None of them did, but Jaga had managed to figure it out.

"Going to?" Kaelus finally turned to face them, his gun arm still straightened at the tsesh and his eyes still fluttering with abyssal light. "I have led you here, and I am going to kill you." He cocked his head toward Akara. "And the world will believe that it was this thing that did it."

Jaga's rifle jumped up and locked firm in his hands. His cool eyes cut down the length of the barrel, now leveled on the mountainous form of Kaelus Bathor. Behind him, he heard the rest of his crew follow suit. Robes shuffled and weapons clattered and hummed to life as they all took aim. Jaga slipped a quick look to the three surviving agents of Alpha Squad. "Did you boys know about this?"

They didn't respond except to fix their stances and turn their rifles on Jaga and his soldiers. Jaga didn't try to hide his disappointment.

"Of course they knew," Kaelus answered for them. "Everybody knows. You traitors aren't as covert as you think."

"Traitors?"

Kaelus pressed his gun hard against Akara's head. "We're already done here." The prince rolled his face from the pistol and turned a glazed look at the hazy mass of Jaga and his troupe, his mask still dripping with bloodied spit.

In a half second, Jaga locked eyes with the tsesh and tumbled into his soul. Akara was a desperate man like any other. In his short and secret life, he had felt fear and love. He had experienced joy, he'd fought through anguish, and he didn't want to die here on his knees.

"Commander," Jaga offered quickly, raising an unarmed and contrary hand, hoping to thin the heady tension. But he wasn't fast enough. The gunshot split into echoes on the air, clapping at everyone's ears and forcing them all to wince.

But Akara hadn't been killed. He was still kneeling in the dirt, his cinched face as confused as all the others at his own survival.

Kaelus' hand however sprung up to his neck and clamped down hard. His teeth ground together in a furious sneer as blood pumped out from between his fingers. His head snapped to the side, tugging at the fresh wound until his blurring vision found his attacker.

"Oh no," Malehk chuckled as he drew closer to the crowd. His eyes were dark and wide with surprise. The rest of his face was covered in the signature, slotted mask of the tsesh. His sizzling pistol was still breathing smoke while trained on Kaelus. Malehk shook his head in disbelief and raised his free hand. "I swear, I'm usually a much better shot. I did not mean to do that." He slowly drew his sword. His playfulness melted away and his eyes sharpened into slits, blazing with violet light. "I'll get you with the next one."

With all attention turned to Malehk, Akara found the sword at his side, gripped it tight and swept upward. The blade cut deep through the sleeve of Kaelus' expensive suit and severed tendons across the back of his hand.

The hulking executive flailed backwards into the dust and rubble, a pained growl tearing through his teeth and blood spitting across his lips. Akara's mind instantly began to calm. His fragmented thoughts started locking back into place and his eyes returned to their steady, serpentine glow. The pain in his side eased back and the rippling gold of fate burned back to life around him. He snatched up his gun and sprung to his feet, leveling the sword at Kaelus and the pistol at Jaga.

Jaga responded first by hoisting his rifle in defense, but immediately thought better of it. He released the weapon to dangle at his side and raised his hands in surrender. "Wait," he blurted out. "Just wait. He was going to kill us too."

Akara tapped the controls on his gun and the blue lights along its side flashed to life. His mind went to work on the variables of their circumstances, but he could feel his strength waning. Blood loss was giving extra weight to his weapons and his arms were beginning to tremble. He estimated that he'd have only fifteen seconds to resolve the situation before he'd be too weak to stand. Could he kill them all in fifteen seconds?

He'd used one second to weigh the situation when Kaelus groaned and ambled to his feet. Akara realigned his sword, angling the tip of the blade up at the brute's wide and red-stained chest. Kaelus simply sneered and tapped a bloody finger to his comm. The subtle, electronic beep whipped everyone's attention to the pillar. The blinking timer went dark, then returned with a ten-second countdown; 9, 8...

"Fall back!" Jaga shouted to his squad. Their weapons dropped to their hips and the agents spun and sprinted back the way they came.

Kaelus grimaced at Akara then turned to flee himself, his remaining soldiers trailing after him. The tsesh followed suit, racing in the direction of a sealed passage that they knew would lead them into the sewers.

The hole in Akara's belly tore open wider as he ran, spilling cold blood down his side. His limbs were going numb. His feet were landing heavy on the pavement, sending shockwaves up his hip to bite at the wound. He choked back a wad of metallic blood and growled through another breath. He counted down in his head, measuring five jolts of pain for every second that passed.

3... 2... 1...

The bomb sucked in all sound for a slow and sluggish moment. It was one more breath through slotted masks. It was one more frantic step along the broken street. The world stopped. Then the explosion spewed out all its gathered noise at once, tearing outward like a scream in every direction and shaking the dusty air of the subterranean world. The pillar vanished in a plume of black smoke and white fire that quickly billowed out to swallow nearby buildings. The howling groan of bending steel poured down from the canopy. Girders broke loose and stone rained into the rising flames.

As the beam broke loose, it yanked a chunk of the surface world down with it, like a weed being pulled out by its roots, only this time it was the root doing the pulling. Buildings of concrete and glass were pulverized and dumped into the chasm. A roar of chaos punched into every corner of the old world, filling it up with smoke and powder. The hole in the canopy crumbled ever wider until it had chewed and swallowed nearly a hundred meters of Mallis Two. A dense halo of soot washed outward, blackening the ruined world, and burying it in darkness.

Malehk pulled open the barred entrance to the sewers, allowing Akara to tumble in ahead of him. The prince collapsed and cracked his shoulder on the damp floor. He risked the pain in his side to reach up and pry the mask from his face, revealing a blood-filled mouth of gritting teeth. Malehk followed him in, closed the door and turned his back to the bars. His eyes blazed with their purple light as he flared his long coat outward. Harnessing the energy around them, he created a wall of kinetic force, pressing back as the blast of debris began pelting the door.

When the chaos finally rumbled back to muted echoes and the distant clatter of stone cracking on stone, Malehk relaxed his power and lowered his arms. Akara was looking up at him with human eyes, struggling to keep his pain from screaming out his mouth and shattering his teeth. He hissed his breaths and managed an approving nod.

Looking beyond his friend however, movement caught the prince's eye. Through the settling smoke outside, he saw the familiar lights of the maintenance elevator as it made its return journey to the surface. Kaelus had survived.

Chapter 17

The explosion deep beneath the surface of the world had shaken Marianne's small apartment. Picture frames rumbled loose from their hooks. Dishes had rattled from the drying rack and smashed against the floor. A shuddering and yawning crack had crept up the wall and crawled across the ceiling, ripping free one of the mounts on the light fixture. The bar of sputtering and flickering glass swung down and sliced the air above her kitchen table.

When the howling and roar of the devastation finally stopped outside, Marianne was huddled beside her bed, cradling her belly with one hand and pulling her knees in like tightened armor with the other. Her head was tucked down, and her eyes were clamped shut. As silence bled back into the room, she became frightfully aware of her own panting breath and pounding heart.

She sucked in a lungful of shaky air and blew it out in a steady wind across her lips. Still speaking into her knees, she reassured herself several times, "It's okay. It's over." Unconvinced however, she waited another full and trembling minute before she left the floor. Her limbs were weak as she stood up. Her legs could barely hold her, and her arms were uselessly slapping at the bedside table in search of balance and support.

Marianne huffed a few more breaths while smoothing her clothes. She told herself that she was overreacting. Whatever had happened was a one-off accident and now it was over. For all her assurances though, something else had shaken loose inside of her. A pit had opened in her guts and was whispering to her over and over that something terrible had happened.

Working to swallow the dry dread in her throat, Marianne focused on breathing through her nose and putting one foot in front of the other. Crossing the room, she stopped at the terrarium on her way to the door. It was still intact, not a speck of soil out of place. Inside, the sanguine rose was nearly in full bloom. She allowed a single breath across her lips as they curved up into a smile, but it was a fleeting joy. Reminders of the day curled up into her thoughts and that chasmic hollow in her stomach forced her smile to press tightly shut. Tears welled up in her eyes again, and all she could think to do was brush her fingers down the smooth glass once more.

Shaking her head, her blonde curls tapped across her cheeks. Marianne cleared her throat and her mind and turned to leave the room. In the kitchen, the dangling light was still flickering, clinging to its last few volts of life. The gash across the ceiling was two inches wide and had dumped a trail of plaster and powder across the table and floor. Mindlessly steadying the swinging light and brushing the remains of a plate to the side with her foot, Marianne crept toward the window.

Already she could see the column of smoke spiraling up between the buildings. Its monstrous image somehow gave her comfort. Whatever happened had happened somewhere else. It was in the distance, and she could see it, and that meant that it wasn't her fault. It wasn't a dark vengeance let loose on her life. It was a tragedy that had come and passed. It meant that she could help.

When she finally reached the window, she saw just how widespread the disaster had been. Meridian Boulevard was in flames, and the static stamp of the skyline she'd looked out to a hundred times before was somehow different. Beyond the horror of rising flames and smoke, the line of the horizon had changed. Buildings that were there before were gone. They hadn't gone dark in a blackout as she'd seen before. They hadn't been damaged in the quake or caught fire. They simply weren't there. She wasn't sure just how many had gone missing, but it was enough to make the world outside look foreign and strange. It was no longer the city she'd known the night before.

The twist of raging smoke was hypnotic. It reflected in her glassy and trepid eyes, flecked with the distant flames of the burning world. That feeling returned in her core. Her stomach felt heavy like a balloon filled with icy water, and hopelessness taunted her recessed thoughts. Marianne wasn't sure how long she stared at the catastrophe outside, but it was at least long enough for emergency services to arrive. She saw their flashing lights between the alleys, and silently thanked them for their expedience and courage.

She had to help. Whatever horrors awaited her at the scene, Marianne knew that there would be chaos. People would be hurt. People would be frightened. She could stay clear of the responders while still lending a hand in whatever capacity she could find. If for nothing else, she hoped it would quell the sinking in her stomach.

As she began to step away from the window however, a glint of light blinked in the street below. It was almost nothing, but it was just enough to catch her eye. Looking down, she saw a sleek and polished Runcourte parked at the base of her building. Through its tinted glass she thought she saw someone moving inside, but then they were gone. It was a still and silent car, doing nothing and offering nothing of significance, but she'd never seen it there before. Its presence dumped a heavy weight on the alien ambiance of the world outside, and Marianne's guts ground together inside of her again.

# # #

"Did you see them die?" Daemon's voice was far less rigid than usual. It was bubbling with a restrained rage as he punctuated each segment of the question with a knife-hand in the air. He was pacing the floor of the infirmary, his presence flooding the room though his eyes were distant, piercing and plotting.

Kaelus was bleeding on the starched sheets of a narrow bed against the side wall while masked doctors worked to clean and stitch the wound in his neck. His expression remained stone and serious, even as surgical staples were clamped into place across the hole in his neck. "There wasn't time," he replied. His voice was a muted growl, like a bolt of fabric being torn in half.

Daemon was smudging his thumb and forefinger together in front of his lips, taking in the answer as if deciding where to file it. "There was time enough for you and three of your agents to flee."

"We were ambushed by two tsesh. I nearly had them, but Agent Demain suspected something. He came back early."

"And now?" Daemon asked, turning to face him. "What do you think he... suspects now?"

Kaelus didn't respond. His eyes just shifted sideways as another staple was fastened into place.

Daemon turned toward a dark corner near the door where Faedra had been observing the two with a sly smirk of amusement. He pointed at her then swept his finger to the door. "Find him," he said. "Whatever it takes."

"I can find him," Kaelus cut in with a achy groan as he sat up. He dabbed a hand against his neck then checked his fingers for blood. He scowled at the doctor then swung his legs over the edge of the bed. "He's an old man with no resources."

"He's a trained soldier hiding inside an invisible city," Daemon corrected with a pointed finger. "Brute force was clearly a miscalculation, and Faedra," he paused mid-sentence and accentuated the name to let it burn in Kaelus' ears. "She will take over with a bit more finesse." He reiterated his command to her with a nod. Faedra slipped on a serious expression, still highlighted with upturned corners of content and amusement. She responded with a shallow bow before disappearing out the door and into the corridors of the tower.

While Daemon was presumably planning out his next course of action with his head lowered and his back to the room, Kaelus rose to his feet. His large hand was still patting at his wound, and the tangy taste of blood was clinging to the back of his tongue. "So, what do you want me to do?" he asked with less bravado than usual.

Daemon turned to face him. He cocked his head, briefly inspecting the doctor's work. The wound was sealed, and the staples were straight. With Kaelus' genetic advantages, he'd be fully healed in a week. "You," he began, straightening his posture and looking up at the brute. "You'll do nothing."

"Nothing? This fight has just begun—"

"Exactly," Daemon said, biting off the end of the sentence. "Which means that your opportunity to prove yourself may yet still come, but until then, you will do nothing. You are useless until I say otherwise."

Kaelus bared his full mouth of pearled teeth, grinding them together inside a sneering mouth. His fists clenched at his sides and his ears filled with rage and the rush of his pulse.

Daemon didn't move. He barely seemed to notice. "Go get changed," he said with the wave of a hand, "then get started on your report."

Akara sprung up from cold concrete, unaware of how long he'd been unconscious. His mask was gone, and the cool taste of mildew was thick in the heavy air. Several tsesh were nearby. Two were crouching beside him and the others were standing in the dimly lit room around them. Malehk was there, unmasked as well and speaking with the others. His eyes, now dark and human, turned toward the abruptly awakened prince.

Akara's shirt had been pulled open and the tsesh at his side was fastening a large patch of gauze over his wound. The bullet hole had bled through the bandage, though it appeared as though the bleeding had stopped. As his senses focused one-by-one, he was reminded of the blast from Kaelus' gun, and the pain rumbled back up beneath the gauze.

"What happened?" Akara asked anyone who might respond.

"You passed out," Malehk answered, "and I heroically carried you down here."

As his vision cleared and the edges of his surroundings sharpened, Akara glanced around. He didn't recognize the place. It was a cubic, windowless room made of smooth, wet bricks. There was a single steel door to his right. It was the kind of heavy steel that you know from looking at it will creak and groan under its own weight when you open it. To his left was a large machine woven into the wall with wide pipes. It was a mass of broad tanks, steel plates, and oversized bolts, all lacquered in red, chipping paint.

"Where are we?"

Malehk popped his attention around the room as if he'd only just noticed where they were. "I'm not sure. Used to be a pump station or somethin', but for now it'll have to pass for a hospital." He shrugged. "At least until we get settled in."

Akara closed his eyes and dropped back on his elbows, his chest deflating with a long breath. "So, we've managed to sink even lower."

"Oh, I don't know. It's got some charm." Malehk tossed a thumb in the direction of the door. "I managed to section off a couple subway cars for our rooms. They're pretty cozy."

The prince just stared at him through slitted eyes.

"Hey, you were just shot in the belly and survived," Malehk said, wagging his finger at the wound. "Things could be worse."

"Where is he?" Rhago's voice was muted, hammering against the steel door outside.

Malehk's head slumped. "Timing," he stammered as if the word was meant to be part of a longer sentence.

The door squealed on its hinges as the king pushed through and stormed inside. Kade lumbered in beside him, his expression calm and somber, as if apologizing in advance to everyone they passed. Rhago shot a look around the room, stabbing at everyone he saw until he found Akara on the floor.

"You," he scolded.

Akara's eyes drifted to the side, awaiting the inevitable.

Rhago closed the distance between them. "How many times do we have to do this?" He kicked his son's foot aside, scraping it along the floor and tugging painfully at the fresh wound in his side.

Akara let out a grunt and pressed his eyes shut until the jolt of pain passed, then returned a defiant glare at his father.

"What exactly is wrong with you?" the king demanded. "Will you not be satisfied until you've gotten all of us killed?"

"I was doing what you asked," Akara said, blowing a steady wind from his lips to even out the rising ache in his stomach.

"No," Rhago fired back, "you were doing the same thing you always do; whatever it is you want. I don't recall ever asking you to engage the Dark Ocean Legacy or risk giving away our position."

"They were already down there," he tried to explain, but Rhago silenced him with a raised finger.

"You were to take care of that human woman then come back! But instead, you rushed in and started shooting whoever you could find, picking an untempered and hopeless fight! And then you run away and come back here. How do you know you weren't followed?"

"We weren't," Akara offered meekly.

"I sent Malehk to watch for agents," he said, jabbing towards Malehk who was fidgeting on his heels.

"You sent him to die," he shouted back. "You wanted Pramoore to find him. That way he would have his war, kill a tsesh and assume that Malehk was the last."

"If Malehk had died protecting our people, he would have been twice the tsesh you'll ever be."

A snarl ground through Akara's teeth, partially spawned by pain and partially from frustration. "Running and hiding," he snapped. "That's all you ever have us do. Crawling like rats. But we're not all cowards!"

Rhago moved in a flash, faster than his age should have allowed. In a heartbeat, he was hovering over the prince and slapping a heavy hand across his face. Akara twisted to the ground, his limbs banging against the bricks to catch himself. The tsesh who had applied the bandages made the mistake of shouting, "Sir", but she was silenced by a furious glare from the king.

A flash of white pain blotted out Akara's vision. He felt his wound twist and tear beneath the gauze and his bare skin slapping at the concrete. Blood trickled across his tongue, oozing from the gash that had been cut open against his teeth.

"You were a baby when they were hunting our people," Rhago said, standing up above his son. "You have no idea what they did to us, what our people had to endure. Your mother was—" Rhago stopped himself before the sentence could flee from his lips. It was as if he was about to say something that even he might regret, or something he simply didn't want to recall, a memory too dark to conjure by speaking it aloud. His face simmered down to a steady and stoic expression as he actively calmed his demeanor. "Perhaps it was a mistake for me to shield you from those horrors. You can't possibly appreciate what is required of us to keep our people alive."

Akara spit the pooling blood from his mouth onto the floor and strained his muscles to press himself back up and against the wall. He rolled his head along the brick, shaking it in tired disappointment and surrender. "We're not alive," he mumbled. He gestured with a weak hand to the ceiling. "We're already buried."

The king's deliberate composure held him in place, seemingly impervious to the prince's insolence. "And that is where you'll remain. My own guards will see to that from now on. Your time on the surface is over."

After a sharp, judgmental scowl at the other tsesh, Rhago turned to walk away.

A sharp chortle coughed up from Akara's lungs and his lips curved up in a bloodied smile. "She's pregnant." He wasn't sure why he'd said it. Maybe it was defiance, or perhaps it was a way to let his father know that there was a piece of him that the king could never touch. Mostly though, he just wanted to hurt him. He wanted to see the look on his old and angry face.

Rhago didn't give him the satisfaction. He simply looked to Kade who in turn looked to the prince. Then they both just left. Not a muscle flinched, not a word spoken between them. Akara was left on the floor with all his secrets laid bare and fresh blood spreading out across his bandages.

# # #

Bwrynn's hospital room was quiet, save for the steady and lonely beep of the machines around her. The walls were starch white. The curtains were an anemic shade of blue. To the side of her steel-framed bed was an empty chair of stiff, pale-gray vinyl and an end table made of white plastic woodgrain. The room was static and sterile. Everything from its novocaine-flavored air to its sickly, pallid lighting. It was less like a place where people went to heal and more like a place where they went to disappear, a room between worlds, devoid of life and connected to nothing.

Bwrynn was lying in the bed beneath a thin sheet. A needle was planted in the back of her hand, leading a tube of measured medicine into her veins. Around her forehead was a halo of flickering metal squares that mapped her mind and cast a rotating image of her body and brain to the monitors around the room. They chimed out a single tone with each new scan, the robotic heartbeat of her digital anatomy.

The hallway door hissed open, letting in a conversation already underway between the nurse and Faedra Weiss.

"What kind of treatments have you been using?" Faedra asked, her head cocked toward the holographic data floating above the nurse's wrist.

"It's all preliminary right now," she replied, motioning across a strip of text. "Scans, bloodwork, that sort of thing. We did, however, start her on a small dose of quetilone."

"The antipsychotic?"

"It also suppresses the psychic part of her brain." The nurse pointed to three different monitors throughout the room. "Whatever happened to her, it created a void in her synapses. It's a mental wound that her psychic mind is constantly trying to fill in. It's not unlike internal bleeding, except in this case, it's her thoughts that are bleeding out."

"So you're trying to stop the flow," Faedra concluded with a nod from the nurse. "Do you mind if I sit with her for a bit?"

"Not at all," she said, gesturing to the uncomfortable-looking chair.

Faedra walked with the hollow clack of stiletto heels to the foot of the bed and waited for the nurse to leave. After the airy swish of the door sealed them in, she turned a far more serious look to Bwrynn's unconscious form. The young initiate was slack and pale, her hair twisted heavy and limp around her face. Faedra however was a blaze of color beside the placid girl within the blanched room. Her thick hair gleamed beneath the overhead light, burning with fiery color while hiding deep sienna within the folds of its curls. Her wet, red lips cocked up in a smile and her emerald eyes sparkled and danced with verdant light.

"Bwrynn Lucane." She touched a gingerly hand to Bwrynn's foot and traced up to her knee as she rounded the bed. "The rising star of the Dark Ocean Legacy. People have been so impressed by you, haven't they?" She leaned into hover above Bwrynn's face as though she were studying an unearthed artifact. The light from her glowing eyes painted green, rippling patterns down the young girl's cheeks. "Now look at you, betrayed by your own power."

Faedra turned to examine the medical machines around them, studying the IV bags and the pulsing readouts. She ran her fingertips along the plastic and metal. She had no academic interest in the science behind it all. She was simply intrigued by the ballet of images now keeping the girl alive.

"Still, it's not all bad," she said, her eyes playing across a model of Bwrynn's frontal lobe. "You may have gotten yourself burned out there in the real world, but that impressive little mind is still in there, isn't it? A deep pool of energy. Untouched. Untapped." She illustrated the words with a rap of her sharp finger between Bwrynn's sleeping eyes.

"Let's see just how powerful you are." Faedra's gaze burned brighter, tinting all of Bwrynn's face with a fluttering green glow. Her fiery mind lashed and crackled at the thoughts that were locked inside the coma. "Let's find your master." She spoke in the whisper of a parent reading a bedtime fable, though her voice still echoed in the air, as if it were booming from some far away mountain. "Somewhere far beneath the city, hiding in the fog of ancient ghosts. Jaga Demain. Where is he?"

Chapter 18

Adrift in the void, between the coiling smoke pillars of her thoughts, Bwrynn had lost track of the outside world. How long had she been there? There was no way of knowing for sure. Her head was filled with fleeting shapes and half-formed questions. There was nothing solid or substantial, nothing for her eyes to hold onto or her hands to grasp. There was no sense of movement or direction, no beginning or end. This was the world, all that she could dream or remember, endless in every direction. Nothing was good. Nothing was bad. It was a numb desert of gray unknowing.

In the haze of her yielding melancholy, she didn't hear Faedra's thoughts when they crept inside. She felt them though, tugging at the overlooked pieces of her listless will. They were a prickling in the back of her brain, coming as an urge to pluck at the strings of her mind. They were a button she wasn't meant to press, a sneeze behind her eyes that tantalized freedom through expulsion.

Hardly a thought had passed before Bwrynn reached out to the creeping whispers. She felt the silk of their presence in her fingers. She marveled at the elegance of their form and the confidence of their direction. They were substance and power in a world of thin veils and doubt. Moments later she was diving into them.

The emerald wisps plucked at her thoughts as if they were grooming them, or perhaps they were looking for something. Her eyes twitched behind closed lids. There was an insistence growing inside of her, a desperation swelling into rage. Bwrynn tried to pull back, but the intruders had her now. Faedra's grip tightened on Bwrynn's mind, shoving down inside her and rummaging around for secrets.

Bwrynn tried to bite down, but she couldn't move. She tried to cough, to expel the tendrils from her body, but she only managed to twitch a few muscles in her face. The whispers grew, overlapping and repeating in her head. They unraveled her consciousness bit by bit, like threads being pulled from a sweater. 'Jaga.' It was the only formed thought that Bwrynn could find. She couldn't tell if it was Faedra's desire or her own, but she knew she had to find him.

She plunged into the depths of the world, wrapped like a body in a tarp by Faedra's persistent command. Bwrynn's eyes began to ache, and she was sure that somewhere she had them squeezed shut. In the catacombs of the world however, her awareness was a broad mass of flashing images. There were phantom figures all around her, laughing, screaming, crying. They had no solid form, but in her wounded and ethereal state, the specters were just as real as Bwrynn. They swarmed around her. They filled her presence and blurred the lines between them and her. In the psychic swarm, Bwrynn was losing sight of herself. She was becoming a stranger in the crowd, her image chopped up between the passing wraiths as they tangled back and forth in oblivious lives.

'Jaga.' The name slipped across her ears. She wasn't sure if she'd heard it in the crowd or if she'd spoken it to herself, but it caused Bwrynn to lunge ahead. Her thoughts reached out ahead of her but were quickly snatched back. She lurched left then right, but each time, her extended mind sprung back and closed in on her. It felt as though she were wrapped in tar, reaching out to the passing crowd for help. But she was invisible. They swept by her one by one, each of them chipping off a piece of her as they went.

The ache in her eyes swelled up into pain, heavy and gripping, that crackled outward like a spiderweb in her brain. The corrosive mist of the underworld was whittling her away, forcing her to cling to the pearl of her identity as she disappeared piece by piece.

"Jaga?" she whimpered inside her mind as Faedra peeled off strips of her consciousness and fed them to the wraiths.

"Where is he?" Faedra's voice demanded, raking emerald claws down her back.

"Jaga?" Bwrynn cried again. She huddled around the glimmering orb of herself, clutching it close inside her chest. "Jaga, help."

"Show me where he is." Faedra had cast aside all sense of deceitful niceties. Her voice was forceful and furious as she tore through the thin layers of the young girl's soul.

Bwrynn clenched her psychic eyes. She squeezed the shimmering ball of her identity as her hands began to dissolve. "No," she whispered painfully. "Jaga?" The jeweled razor of Faedra's mind scratched the smooth surface of the orb. Bwrynn bit down hard as light poured out from the ball and all the memories of her short life shattered outward.

Somewhere in a hospital bed on the surface, a tear slipped down the cheek of the sleeping girl. Machines blared out their sirens all around her as Faedra looked on with fiery intent and glowing eyes. The girl was silent, but in her mind, she screamed a chilling scream. Then the alarms around her body stopped, leaving only the flatline tone of her still and broken heart.

Inside her mind, Bwrynn had lost the final pieces of herself, but she slipped free of the mist and hungry specters. Faedra was gone and she was drifting upward on a silken breeze. She rose above the ruins and the concrete streets, then slipped up and beyond the glass panes and neon edges of Mallis Two. In the brief flicker of a single thought, she ascended into the churning storm that covered the world. The clouds fluttered across her psychic eyes and lightning flashed in violent spikes all around her weightless form.

She wasn't afraid. More than that, Bwrynn had shed the wiry mesh of fear that had always surrounded her when she was alive. It was an iron net that had been such an integral part of her body, she'd never even known it was there. Perhaps she had suspected from time to time, but now that it was gone, she realized just how much of her it had taken up. As it broke away though, she found herself unfettered and free, a warm and powerful breath joining with the wind.

She watched the bursts of lightning around her incorporeal form with a new kind of wonder, wide-eyed and quiet. Her mortal shell had been broken open and all the curiosity that had eked through in her life was now exposed and drinking in all the marvels of the world. Her mind was newborn and ravenous.

Another moment passed and she was beyond the storm. It swirled beneath her feet, pulsing with its silent boil. Above her, the gray had dissolved and given way to black. Bwrynn looked up from the clouds of her world and saw the boundless dark of a true night sky, bejeweled with the glimmering light of countless stars. Lumbering below with a lazy rotation, the old world curved out wide in a writhing sphere of ash and muted light. It was broad and angry, but amidst the endless stretch of the night, it was almost nothing at all.

Her psychic glow reached out to the fathomless void, plunging headlong into eternity. With every inch, every mile, every light year she stretched, her mind filled up with insight and awareness. With the last diamond of her physical self twinkling down to a grain of sand, she stared out at the profound darkness of space and whispered her final thought. "The Dark Ocean."

Then there was pain. An electric jolt seized her thoughts and shoved them back into her mind. Bwrynn's senses spun in every direction, twisting the stars into streaks of light. Another jolt, this one cracked against her chest and cut out the shapes of her arms and legs. She looked down again. She was back above the planet. The gray storm was twirling beneath her feet like hungry blades. Lightning leapt up and whipped at her raw, bare skin.

Bwrynn could feel her teeth again. They were biting down and grinding out a pain inside her head. She could feel the exposed wires of her nerves, burning beneath her flesh. Then she felt her heart. It was punching at the mausoleum walls of her chest like a man who had been buried alive. Another blade of lightning jumped up and burned into her feet. It wrapped up her leg and jerked her back into the storm below. The clouds overtook her, and she fell, smothered in smoke and blinding madness.

Reality closed in around her. The vastness of the Dark Ocean was gone. Her limitless wonder was cut off and cauterized at the edges of her brain. There was a final flash of speed and light, and then the world went still. She could hear voices somewhere in the distance. They were unfamiliar and mumbling as if behind thin walls. A firm and steady noise rose to greet her, to welcome her back inside her tiny body. It was the arrogant pulse of hospital machines, beeping out the monotonous heartbeat of a girl come back to life.

# # #

Five agents had survived the explosion. Jaga quietly counted their dirty and exhausted forms. Their postures were wilted against the brick walls of some forgotten city block, with only their aching and rubbery limbs to prop them up. The worst of the battle had passed, but the worst had been bad enough. The explosion that Kaelus set off had brought down a half mile of concrete and glass to bury them. One of Jaga's men had been incinerated in the blast. Three more were crushed by debris as they fled. The unfortunate survivors were now buried and betrayed, abandoned to the depths of the world where Daemon Pramoore cast all his enemies.

Ellis was among the survivors, the only one, it seemed, with strength left to stand. He turned in short paces, nodding his head and raising his hands before slapping them down to his sides. "Well, that's it then, isn't it?" he mewled. "We were right. We were right about Daemon. We were right about Kaelus. We were right about all of them."

"It would seem you were right about something," Jaga groaned. He was leaning his weight on a windowsill, stretching a dull pain out across his lower back. His long legs felt useless beneath him, aching around their joints, and burning in every muscle. "Though we can't really be sure of what."

"Everything," Ellis answered with a sweeping hand toward the hanging cloud of smoke behind them. "We figured it out and they tried to have us killed."

"What?" Jaga snapped with frustration. "What exactly did you figure out?" When Ellis didn't answer right away, he prodded further. "Do you even know?"

"Yes," he fired back then paused to collect his thoughts. "The secret rooms beneath the tower. Daemon's lab grown freaks."

Jaga's eyes fell shut and he unlatched a pained breath from inside his lungs. He held up a hand and patted at the air to slow the conversation and soothe both of their nerves. "We don't actually know any of that."

"Are you kidding?" This time Ellis flung both hands toward the destruction in their wake.

Jaga shook his head. "All we know is that you all shared a common suspicion of Mr. Pramoore; a trait, it would seem, that he did not appreciate. It doesn't mean that you were right. It just means that you were disloyal."

"Disloyal? The man just tried to kill us."

Jaga's thick brows flicked up. "I'm not saying I don't agree with you. I'm just saying that we don't have all the facts just yet."

"Well then, I say we go get em." Ellis jabbed a finger at the black, basement tower. "Break into the tower from below and see what he's been hiding."

Another agent piped up from within the tattered group. "Are you crazy, man? Ellis, the guy just dropped a city on us. You don't think he'd be prepared for that? Do you honestly think we'd stand a chance just smashing our way in there?"

"So we break into teams—" Ellis started, but Jaga was shaking his head and wiping the idea from the air with his hands.

"Your friends are right," he said. "If Pramoore has been onto you for this long, he's most certainly prepared himself for any kind of direct assault."

"Well then what do you suggest we do?"

Jaga pressed himself onto his feet, ignoring the taut wires that throbbed in his muscles. He took slow steps while staring up at the distant hole in the canopy. "Nothing," he muttered to himself.

"Nothing?"

"I understand that you're angry," Jaga said before the young man's impatience could boil over. "I'm angry too, but we both know from our training that it is action, not reaction, that can lead us to the truth. We need more information."

"Like what?" Ellis spat the words.

"Like why now?" He finally turned away from his thoughts and the destruction overhead to look back on the disheveled troops. "If he's known about you for all this time, why wait until now to do anything about it?"

Ellis shrugged. "Opportunity. He needed a scapegoat. There's no doubt that he'll blame that explosion on the tsesh."

"That's very astute," Jaga agreed, "and you're probably right." He turned to look back at the hole. "But our last conflict with the tsesh lasted for years. He could have waited. This was rushed. Sloppy." His cool eyes sharpened into focus as revelation struck him like a bolt from the storm. "The election."

"The sector lords?"

"The election is tomorrow." Jaga's gaze darted back and forth as he pieced the puzzle together in his mind. "Bwrynn and I were investigating Lord Kaddler's murder when she collapsed into a coma. Thisa had suggested that it was the work of Daemon or one of his executives."

"Kaelus," Ellis added, sharing in the epiphany.

"I thought she was being paranoid."

"Okay, but why Kaddler? That guy's been one of Pramoore's bootlickers for years. Why would Daemon want him dead?"

"Because this isn't about support from the lords," Jaga said as the answer stumbled into his mind. "He's framing the tsesh for the attacks and making it look as if they are working with Aldan Pharos. He doesn't care who wins. He just wants to rattle the city's faith in their leaders."

"Okay, but why?"

"So that he can take over for himself."

"Whoa," Ellis smirked and shook his head. "Take over? That's a pretty big leap, even for me. It would take a lot more than some shaky confidence to overthrow the sector lords."

"Yes, it would," Jaga said, his eyes returning to the broken dome. "Which is why I think that this is just the beginning."

Ellis' mouth went dry, and his eyes followed Jaga's to the settling billow of smoke. He began several sentences but couldn't seem to fit words into any of them. Eventually he was able to ask, "Then what about us? We didn't know any of this. Why was he in such a hurry to eliminate us?"

"Because you were right." Jaga turned his attention to the hanging spire. "The key to all of this is in that tower."

Excitement buzzed through Ellis' body. The validation of a skeptic like Jaga Demain had smoothed the jagged edges of his paranoia and filled his chest with bitter relief. He quickly found however, that he couldn't enjoy it. His intangible world of conspirators and secret assassins was suddenly all too real, and he had awoken inside its black core. "So, what do we do?"

"We need to regroup," Jaga answered with an abrupt and hardened sense of determination. "Kaelus was able to mask his intentions from us, but the others may have been tipped off sooner. We need to find out how many of us there are, how many survived."

Jaga moved with rekindled urgency back toward the group but stumbled after two steps and dropped to his knees. After breaking his fall, his knotted hands jumped to his temple. There was a voice inside his head, like the echo of an expired scream. It was Bwrynn, calling out his name. The psychic cry offered no sense of distance or direction, and as quickly as it began it was cut short and silenced.

"Bwrynn," he whispered to the ground.

"Master Demain?" Ellis inquired softly.

"They have her," he said, forcing himself to his feet.

"Who has her? Pramoore?"

"They're going to take her from the hospital. I have to stop them."

"Whoa, whoa, whoa," Ellis maneuvered in front of him as Jaga tried to weave around the younger and nimbler agent. "Hey, we all know what that girl means to you, but it's like you said, we need to think this through. We can't just react, right?"

"This is different. They're killing her. If I don't stop them before Pramoore takes her into custody, she'll be lost forever."

"That's exactly what they want you to do." Ellis planted his open hands on Jaga's chest as gently as he could while still holding him in place. "This is a trap. Pramoore knows that we survived and they're trying to use her to draw us out."

Jaga pulled the young man's hands from his chest but made no further attempt to push past him. He sealed up his lips and darted his eyes back and forth as his mind tested scenarios. He knew that Ellis was right. He'd be walking into a trap and allowing Daemon to finish off the sparse remains of the rogue agents.

"I'll go alone," he offered with haste. "They don't know how many of us made it, just me. I'll go and you five can stay below. Search for any other survivors. In two hours, everyone meets back in this spot." He pointed decisively at the ground. "If I'm not here, then take everyone to some place secure, something defensible, with strong psychic energy."

"But Master Jaga—" Ellis tried.

Jaga handed over his rifle then landed a consoling hand on the agent's shoulder, lowering his gaze to look him in the eye. "If I can find you I will. We can survive this."

#

Akara was sitting atop a pile of coarse blankets on a bench seat in the back end of a subway car, one foot on the floor and the other planted on the tattered padding beside him. The seat was long enough for him to lie down had he wanted to and would likely be serving as his bed for the foreseeable future. The fabric looked as if it'd once been blue but had aged into a kind of gray pastel. Although it was torn in several places, it was comfortable enough. The rest of the car was surprisingly intact as well, with only small patches of rust beginning to show around the bolts and seams of the white metal.

Somewhere in the deep tunnels around the dormant tracks, a handful of tsesh were working to restore power to their newfound patch of the underground. For the time being, Akara was left in the puddle of blue light from a lantern on the adjacent bench. His amber eyes panned across the monitors and lights that lined the room. They were all dead and gray, silent plaques from a world once filled with light. Beyond a few with cracked screens or broken filaments though, he suspected they may still have a bit of life left in them.

He craned his shoulder up, stretching out the stitched skin at his side and thinning out its throbbing ache, stopping just short of tearing the wound. His snake eyes helped with the pain. Without the instinctual panic of emotion, Akara was able to reconcile the burning patch in his ribs and keep it contained to a pin prick sensation. His subconscious mind had also been busy energizing the affected cells, accelerating their healing process. Within a week the bullet hole would be gone, leaving behind only the red patch of a new scar.

The slow pulse of fate wound through the long darkness of the subway. The golden wisps were acting stranger than usual. It was bizarre that fate would 'act' in any way at all. It was a natural force, like magnetism, wind, or electricity. The notion that it would behave in any kind of sapient capacity was uncharacteristic, yet Akara was certain that it was. Its subtle strips of current were twitching against corners and vibrating with subtle tremors as if a bass drum had just pounded through the air. Akara picked a strand at random and studied it as it inched along the lower rim of the window. The yellow glow flickered up at the glass, almost like it was tapping it or testing its integrity. He was fascinated by the scene, hypnotized by it. Fate had always moved with sense of intention, even with determination, but this was different. It seemed willful and alive.

The hollow echo of boots against the metal landing rang down the shaft of the car. Akara turned his head from the dance of fate and saw his father entering at the front of the room. The king had cleaned himself up, now dressed in his favored, white suit. His golden ring of royalty swung on its chain with each step, bouncing against a cornflower tie and kicking back tiny glints of light from the lantern. Rhago's hair had been tied back, a waterfall of white, bound by a leather band and a golden knot at the back of his head.

Kade wasn't with him. He was alone. It wasn't unheard of, but rare enough to draw attention even on the most peculiar of days. Whatever reason the king had for leaving his right hand behind, it signaled the significance of his visit. Good news or bad, he was there for something important; the unborn, half-tsesh child.

Akara adjusted his posture, dropping his foot to the floor and sitting up as straight as his wound would allow. "Father," he addressed, offering a nod before returning to a more stoic, face-front pose.

"Akara," the king responded with soft professionalism diluting his voice. He walked with mindful steps as if the floor of the car was littered with debris even though it wasn't. His old hands brushed down the pole grips as he passed them and his head oscillated across his path, analyzing the layout. "So, this is to be your room?"

"It's as good as any."

Rhago nodded in dull agreement then maneuvered to the seat across from his son. He grumbled a breath and swatted dust from the cushion before tugging up his pant legs and sitting beside the lantern. The light rose up to meet him, casting crags and shadows across the lines in his face. His lips were bunched up with a kind of sour disappointment and a strained breath hissed from his nose. He flicked his chin at Akara. "How's your wound?"

"It's healing. I should recover in a few days."

The king bobbed his head while looking idly around the room. He seemed to be searching for another bit of small talk, but the subway car had little to offer in the way of conversation. His focus finally settled on the floor, and he spoke to the space between his feet. "You've put me in a difficult position."

"I know I have," Akara said without feeling. "That wasn't my intention."

"This child," he began then shook his head and clamped his mouth back shut. "It's a threat to all of us."

"In what way?" Akara's serpentine eyes twinged with a hint of genuine curiosity.

"In the same way that its mother is, the same way that any attachment to their world is."

"That's not an answer."

The tense and cautious concern melted from Rhago's face. His expression stiffened back to his more characteristic austerity. "Daemon Pramoore." He fired the name like a bullet from his tongue. "We tried to defend ourselves against his father and it nearly destroyed us, and with each new generation, their power, their influence, and their hatred for us only grows stronger. There is nothing he won't do, nothing he can't do to exterminate every last one of us."

Akara stared with unblinking and amber eyes. Rhago realized that his son's unfeeling mind was impervious to any painted picture of violence or impending threats, so he chose a more specific path.

"He will abduct your woman. He will abduct your child. He will torture them both until you reveal yourself. He will do it in plain view of the public and they will cheer him on and applaud your execution."

"That isn't the world I've seen—" Akara started, but Rhago's composure snapped like a rubber band.

"I have seen it!" he bellowed. His voice and rage filled up the cramped room and scattered the glow of fate like roaches from the light. "And I don't care about your feelings. My concern is for our people, even if yours is not. While I am king your experience means nothing."

There was a long pause while the violent burst of echoes faded from the chamber. Akara remained cold with a silent stare that followed his father as the king rose to his feet.

Rhago smoothed the wrinkles from his suit and brushed the tension from his shoulders. "You will leave tonight," he said. The civility had returned to his voice, but without the soft edges of compassion. "You will enter the woman's home and terminate the pregnancy."

"Terminate?" There was the smallest crack in Akara's voice, a flicker of emotion in the callous dark.

"The mother will be allowed to live, but only because her death would arouse suspicion, and that is a risk we cannot afford right now." He raised a finger and leaned in towards the prince. "Her life however is paid for with your fealty. You will never speak to her again. You will never think of her again. The moment you endanger us again, I will kill her myself."

Akara's tongue worked at the dry corners of his mouth, but his expression was blank and static. The king's words poured through his mind like lava carving through cold stone. He blinked once then stood to face his father. "I understand," he answered simply before turning for the front of the car.

As the young prince left the lantern's light and faded to a silhouette in the shadows, Rhago's eyes twitched. His lips parted and his hand raised up halfway. "Son." The word slipped from his mouth almost as if by accident, but Akara was already gone. He'd disappeared into the tunnels beneath the world to prepare for his next mission.

CHAPTER 19

The elevator to the surface world was slower than Jaga would have liked. It was louder too. The groan of cables and pulleys poured into the lift as the subterranean world slipped further away below him. More out of absent-minded habit than nerves, he pressed the controls on his pistol and read the small display, '100%'. He'd installed fresh rounds before their mission and had yet to fire a single shot. Unspoken on a shaky breath, he hoped to keep it that way.

When the doors finally rolled open inside the small building on the surface, Jaga tugged at the shoulders of his cloak, covering the weapon on his hip. He stepped into the dark and dusty air of the maintenance room and headed for the door. He was about to press at the controls but stopped midway. He ran his hands down the surface of the door while his cool eyes studied the frame as if searching for a hidden message.

Letting go of his tension, Jaga's eye glimmered with faint light and his mind reached out to the city beyond those concrete walls. Even the psychic mindscape of the surface felt cleaner than the world below, unpolluted by tragedy and ghosts. He let his thoughts spiral around the street and sidewalk outside until he found exactly what he'd expected and exactly what he'd feared; the lambent mind of a Legacy agent stationed outside. They were waiting for him.

Jaga's thoughts skirted the perimeter of the sentry's attention. They weren't alarmed, expectant, or even actively aware of their post. It was an agent who'd been stationed to watch an abandoned building in the middle of the night. They were bored and inattentive. Dipping into the rim of the guard's focus, Jaga picked up the images of the street corner, the cold stillness of the midnight air, and the randomized parade of headlamps and taillights.

He wrapped himself in the imagery, painting over his own appearance with the bland ebb and flow of the night. Dabbing his presence at the back of the agent's mind, Jaga slowly desensitized the psychic to his presence. When he finally opened the maintenance building door and stepped out to the street, he was nothing more than a passing car or a tumble of trash on the wind. The agent didn't even bother to look.

Tightening his cloak against the chill of the night, Jaga walked past the Runcourte, giving a half-glance to the agent inside. She was a middle-aged woman who was rummaging through a bag of fried chips, searching for one in particular. She never even turned her head to the master agent as he crossed the street beside her and headed inward to the city.

Jaga took a mental note of the orange glow of fire against the stormy sky. Only a few winding streets in, emergency workers were still battling the flames of the decimated city block. He could hear faint sirens running through the crevices of the ambient noise of the city. The chaos would offer him some protection, but only if he moved quickly. He raised a hand to a passing cab and offered the driver inside a generous tip if he could find the quickest route to the hospital.

# # #

Akara was crossing the rocky and silent landscape of Old Mallis alongside five other tsesh. They were all wearing their long, leather coats, each with pistols strapped beneath the folds. Three had already shed their emotions, treading the path without feeling and glancing aside from time to time as an isolated streak of golden fate would slip by.

The prince was among the snake-eyed majority of the group. His unburdened mind allowed him a clarity that his emotions never would. Ahead of him, Basker was carrying a bulky briefcase with an electronic lock. Inside were the drugs and devices that would be used to carry out their objective; eliminate the half-breed child and level the playing field against Pramoore and his agents. Nothing within their reach could undo what had been set into motion, but at the very least they could remove one of Daemon's advantages over them.

The ache in Akara's side began to stretch around his ribs again and he forced himself to look away from the case. He directed his thoughts to the task at hand and focused his energy on repairing his wounds. From a tactical standpoint he should have stayed below. His injury made him a liability to the group if they were to encounter any trouble. But his father had been right, this was his fault, and it was his responsibility.

"Akara," Malehk's voice pulled his attention back and behind them. The prince turned to see him running across the broken streets, his coat spiraling at his back and cracking in the air as he jumped the hurdles of the ruins.

"Malehk," Akara simply noted as his friend raced up to join them. "What are you doing here?"

"Me? What are you doing here?"

"We have an assignment." Akara motioned toward the others and the heavy case.

"Yeah, I heard. You can't possibly be okay with this."

"What I'm okay with is irrelevant," Akara replied, turning back to their steady march forward. "This is what needs to be done."

"Akara, this is Marianne we're talkin' about."

"I'm well aware of who it is."

"And you're just gonna go in there and kill her baby? Your baby?"

"You're being dramatic," Akara said over his shoulder. "We're terminating her pregnancy. The alternative would be far worse."

"Says who? Marianne? Are you gonna ask her what she wants?"

"Of course not. Marianne will be rendered unconscious. In the morning she'll believe that she lost the child naturally. Her grief will pass, and she will live on." He turned and gave his friend a puzzled look. "This is the right thing to do."

"Is it? Have you seen fate tonight? Have you seen how it's moving?"

Akara panned another brief look around their environment, noting the unusual movements of the amber light. "I have."

"So, shouldn't that tell you something? Doesn't that suggest that maybe we're doing something wrong?"

"That's precisely why you can't see it when your mind is distracted by emotion," Akara explained academically. "Fate doesn't suggest anything. It simply moves forward from one source to the next. Our duty is to follow that path and remove any obstructions. That's all."

"So that's what she is to you? An obstruction?"

"Malehk, don't mistake my obligation for callousness. I understand what it is that we're doing and how it will affect others, but our emotions do not change the facts. This is our safest path forward."

"What if it's the Sasha Kel?" Malehk blurted out.

Invoking the prophecy caused all the tsesh to stop, the last of which was Akara. He turned to face his friend whose arms were shrugged up and his head cocked sideways. A stiff silence rippled through them as Malehk waited with pleading eyes for acknowledgment. They offered none. They only stared.

"Well, we don't actually know, do we?" he eventually continued. "Marianne shouldn't even be pregnant, right? Humans and tsesh are incompatible. And now fate suddenly starts acting up and fumbling around? What if this is how the Dragon Child is born?"

"Now you're being childish," Akara said dismissively.

"It's one of our oldest teachings," Malehk replied, leaning forward and into the words. "Even objectively you have to respect that."

The others had begun to look around at each other as if testing the weight and validity of his theory. The prince thought only of his father and their clear path forward.

"There is no way of knowing that," Akara finally answered for the group. "And even if we did, you yourself have said that there is no way of controlling it. We don't command fate, we obey it. If this child is the Sasha Kel then there's nothing we could do to stop it. Those are your words. And if it is never born then it was never meant to be and was therefore not the Sasha Kel."

Malehk's mouth slowly pulled up shut like a drawbridge. His eyes drifted far away for a moment then, as if placing a bet on his theory, he nodded to the prince. "I'm coming with you. It's my duty to protect you anyway, right?"

"Only with a clear mind," Akara said with a pointed finger. "If you come along, you will shed your emotions and not interfere."

He nodded again, this time with a hint of submission to Akara's royal standing. When the tension faded and Akara gave Basker a signal of approval, they continued on.

Basker switched the briefcase to his off hand then motioned with the other to the distant elevator shafts and the canopy overhead. "The scouts say Pramoore's got agents at every major exit, so we gotta take the long way up. We'll take the service elevator to the mechanical level then into the labyrinth. We'll be coming up in a warehouse on 85th. We've got some vehicles waiting for us, so from there it should be a short drive to our destination." He craned a look specifically to Malehk. "The election ceremony starts pretty early, and the streets will fill up fast, but if we stick to the plan..." Basker's eyes drilled into Malehk, waiting for the words to strike his mind before continuing, "we should be back home long before that happens."

"What?" Malehk asked defensively.

"Let's go," Akara added. Then they were on their way.

Jaga had the cabbie drop him off around the corner from the hospital. He tapped his comm and left a generous tip before stepping out to the midnight streets. The traffic was thicker there, in the heart of downtown, and Jaga welcomed the many moving parts of the nightlife. On the outskirts of the sector, near the 6-4 maintenance lift, he'd felt exposed, the only living thing that dared be out so late.

Watchful eyes are always drawn to movement and tonight Jaga had more than his share of predators in the streets. There, in the center of Six though, he was an insect in a swarm, masked in a flurry of life.

He steadied himself with a breath, his eyes set on the glowing corner near the emergency room entrance. In a few short steps he'd leave the safety of the swarm and step into the eye of a storm. He'd be exposed again, and he knew that they'd be waiting. His foresight and his nerves on the edges of a razor were his only advantages now.

Lightning crackled across the section of sky between the buildings overhead and tinted the edges of the city blue. The master agent wrapped his hand around the pistol-shaped folds of his cloak, promising himself that he wouldn't need it, but reassuring himself that it was there. A few short steps and a dozen hard hammers of his pulse later and he was at the sliding doors. The parking lot was dark, but the hospital entrance and the corridors inside were glaring with brassy light.

Jaga let his mind flitter outward, creeping into unseen corners, and listening for hushed secrets in the sparse minds inside. There was a physician sizzling with frustration, a nurse with single-minded concentration, and a mother projecting imagined outcomes of her child's surgery. There was nothing of Bwrynn. There were no whispers of secret plans to spring on Jaga when he entered. It was an ordinary hospital on an ordinary night.

Although he didn't trust the stable footing of the casual room, Jaga stepped inside and let the doors hiss shut behind him. The receptionist barely acknowledged him. She tilted a brief glance up, between a countertop cactus and directory monitor, then dropped her eyes right back down to her work. He saw the mother as well. She was seated in the waiting room, flipping absently through text articles on her comm and doing an impressive job of hiding the worry for her child.

Still there was nothing, no rise in tension, no forced indifference. Whatever trap Pramoore's people had laid, they'd kept it to themselves. Regardless, Jaga wanted to raise as little attention as he could. He walked straight past the receptionist, offering a cordial nod before moving into the long hollow of the stark white halls.

The third floor was where they treated mental trauma and psychic patients. As he stepped from the elevator, Jaga kept his psychic mind subtle and slow, knowing that any agents or executives would be able to sense his prodding were he to delve too deep. A quick thought would slip inside a room then recoil back and brush a passing mind. It was slow and the information incomplete, but Jaga searched for any flickering sign of Bwrynn or hidden agents. There wasn't a whisper out of place. The hospital was clockwork and the people inside were cogs.

Jaga paused before the next corner. Something wasn't right. Beyond knowing that this was a trap and yet there were no traces of its workings, there was something else. The deeper he ventured down the halls, the more static things began to feel. They felt shallow and superficial, almost simulated. Risking a bold approach, he released his constraints and plunged his mind into a nearby doctor at his desk.

The physician's thoughts read in simple notions, one at a time, like an old printer scratching out a document. He was focused on a medical scan. His mind then moved on to possible medications, then to his next appointment. The information slipped out clean and concise. There were no thoughts of his home, no distracting memories, or concerns of family. There was nothing confused or tangled or messy or anything else that made someone human. His mind was being controlled. His thoughts had been sterilized and filtered then poured back into him.

No one had that power. A hundred agents couldn't pull it off. Jaga was among the most powerful psychics in the Legacy and even those who were above him could never control a mind so completely. To control an entire building, filled to its walls with science and psychosis? The idea at its very premise was absurd.

He continued down the hall, his eyes unblinking and his psychic energy frisking every mind he crossed. They were all still different, but they were all the same, trickling, and unwavering. They were puppets unaware of their own psychic strings. This was a trap. Someone was waiting for him, and he had greatly underestimated who they were.

Around another bend, he picked up the familiar and humming warmth of his pupil's mind. Room 326. The second door from the end. Her subdued and sleeping thoughts were drifting like a heavy fog from behind the door. Bwrynn was unconscious but alive, cocooned in the blanket of a dreamless sleep. Jaga stopped at the intersection, reeling back his probing mind. He turned away from the door and faced the wall. He whittled his psychic energy down to its most simple and silent form. He pretended to study a touchscreen map on the wall while the thread of his mind crept into room 326. Gingerly at first, Jaga studied the room, prodding every corner with the needle of inquisitive thought. He searched for anything out of place; an unusual pattern in Bwrynn's emotions, a fading sense of aggression, anything. There was nothing. Aside from the comatose girl the room was empty.

Regardless of what his psychic vision told him, he knew in his gut that they were there. They were waiting. It was a hard-learned lesson he'd picked up in his youth while battling the tsesh. Despite what you're told, despite what you want, the truth is sometimes hiding in plain sight. It's in the most volatile of times that you're better served by trusting your instincts.

Jaga turned to face the room just ten yards down the hall. The white steel door was sealed shut with the room number glowing on its face. Just above the text was a wide bar of a window that offered a scalped view of the dim-lit walls inside. It wasn't much to work with, but more than enough for Jaga's needs.

He shut his eyes and conjured up all the warmth and shape of his psychic form. The energy writhed around his body, mimicking his shape as best as a tangle of yarn might do. The manifestation was lacking in detail. It had no features, and its arms were vague impressions of limbs. It was invisible to the normal spectrum, but it still might pass as Jaga to the eyes of a psychic mind. He ushered the phantom ahead, directing every twinge he felt of nervousness and caution into its presence.

The door remained closed, and he couldn't force it open, but Jaga hoped that whoever might be watching was only watching with their mind and not their eyes. The wraith passed through the wall and drifted into the room. No trap was sprung, but its components gave themselves away. As soon as Jaga's psychic decoy neared Bwrynn's bed, he felt the flare of Legacy minds blaze to life. They lasted only a moment as they realized their mistake, but it was enough for a master to count them. Four agents, all hiding behind the doors of the adjoining rooms.

Jaga released the decoy, allowing it fizzle out to the ether. Then, with half the thought and focus, he created another, a vague shadow that he cast aside to wash down the hall. Then he made another, and then another. As he himself moved for the door, Jaga flicked away a new psychic specter with every determined stride. After only a few measured steps, the corridor was filled with half-formed thoughts and dim memories of his life.

The door slid open, and he could feel the trembling of the agents that flanked him through the walls. Ahead of him, in the center of the dark room, Bwrynn lay asleep on the bed. Holograms of her vital signs played out like advertisements in the Central Plaza. Keeping his own intentions small and subdued, he moved quickly to the helpless girl and began unplugging the tubes and wires from her skin.

The two side doors whipped open and four cloaked agents poured into the room, pistols drawn. Faedra followed them in on slow and clacking heels. The room was empty, as was the hospital bed where Bwrynn had laid unconscious only seconds before. The agents snapped the aim of their guns to every shadowed corner, every door, and even the sealed window beside the bed. There was no one there, not their bait nor their prey.

Faedra slid her fierce and glowing gaze across the bed and to the door. "Where are they?" she asked with a slow and harmless voice, the way a spider might invite a fly into its web.

One of the agents piped up. He lowered his gun and stepped to attention in front of Faedra. "There are still ghost images in the hall, but I'm sure he was here."

"Obviously he was here," she said, sweeping a hand to the empty bed. "Go find him before Daemon learns that you lost both his prisoners in a single operation."

"Yes, ma'am," he answered with a bow and a long step toward the door.

"Wait," another agent said. It was Bryce Bishop, the spiky blond with a tattoo across his eye; the same youthful student who had first seen Akara in the diner.

The others all stopped mid-stride and Faedra turned to face him. "Agent Bishop?" she acknowledged.

Bryce shook his head and moved slowly toward the foot of the bed. "Master Demain is old. He isn't strong. He isn't fast." His cold eyes studied the empty bedsheets in front of him. "But he is smart." The young psychic's mouth twisted up into a smile and he aimed his pistol at the center of the vacant pillow.

"Agent, if you have something to say..." Faedra started.

Bryce didn't answer. His smile grew wide and toothy as he flicked the switch, charging the gun to life. Before he could pull the trigger, the imperceptible haze in the forefront of his mind began to clear. As it did, two figures appeared in front of him, vibrating into view like heat wavering atop a hot road. It was Bwrynn, still asleep on her bed and Jaga Demain, hunched over her with one arm raised in surrender.

Faedra cocked a look at them and smiled. "Impressive insight," she congratulated Bryce as she passed by him.

"Thank you, ma'am," he said with his smirk still smudged across his face.

"Master Demain." Faedra locked eyes with the defeated old man. "You don't disappoint. You're just as clever as they say. But this outcome had already been decided before you arrived." Without turning away she called an order to the others. "Take them both."

Chapter 20

The tsesh made their way through the iron labyrinth just beneath the city. The mechanical level was a maze of ductwork, pipes, and hissing machines all bolted to the belly of Mallis Two. It housed the access points and control panels for the city's life support systems; air filtration, water recycling, septic pumps and the like. The path from the ruins to the surface was cramped and winding, but it was safer than the elevators. The unlit and twisting route allowed the tsesh to emerge at any point in the city and Basker led them through it as if he'd walked the path a hundred times himself.

He was right. They emerged from a manhole in the cement floor of a wide and hollow warehouse near the edge of the sector. The only windows were small and forty feet up near the ceiling. They were coated in a decade of dust and neglect and flashed with the dampened brilliance of lightning outside. The thunder drummed against the thin walls of the building, rippling the heavy sound through the dry air inside.

There were a few large and forgotten items covered in dirty, plastic tarps against the wall, otherwise the warehouse was nearly empty. Its only occupants were the five leather-clad tsesh crawling from the floor and two polished sedans that were parked behind a wide, roll-up door. Basker nodded to the cars, and they all crossed the long distance to climb inside.

It had begun to rain outside. It fell in fat drops that spattered on the windshield like an onslaught of tiny water balloons. The muted roar of the storm surrounded them as they crossed the city streets, trapping them inside the dark car with only the sound of the wipers whining as they battled the downpour.

Akara had joined Basker in the lead car. Malehk had followed him and climbed into the backseat. They were halfway to Marianne's when Akara turned around. Malehk was staring deadpan back at him.

"Malehk," he said, his voice cold and simple.

Malehk shifted his jaw and studied his friend, but there was nothing there to see. Akara was locked behind his serpentine eyes and only the golden gaze of the prince remained. Malehk chewed at his tongue and flicked his eyes to the side.

"It's an order," Akara added before activating his steel mask. Its panels slid out and around his face, clacking into place until only his glowing eyes remained.

Malehk huffed a breath. His eye twitched before he finally released his emotions. They faded away from him like steam and his eyes glimmered into violet slits underlined by his silver scales. As his acknowledgment of duty replaced his feelings, Malehk retrieved his own mask from his pocket and snapped it into place. The rest of their journey was done in silence, with nothing but their hissing breath behind their masks and the wipers battling the ceaseless barrage of the storm outside.

The drive was short, but it was after midnight when they finally arrived at Marianne's apartment. The two sedans parked in a line outside and the car doors opened and shut in quick succession as the five tsesh billowed out to the sidewalk. They were masked apparitions with their burning eyes and long black coats now glistening in the rain.

Basker pulled the briefcase from the trunk, the orange fire of his gaze casting a stone look of indifference at the prince. Akara gave a quick glance to the case then turned his attention on the door. The others had already climbed the steps and were hacking into the electronic lock. The door flashed green and opened. They filed inside one by one, shaking off the rain as the door locked shut behind them.

Eight floors up in the packed silence of the elevator reminded Akara of his decent into Old Mallis after a date with Marianne. His stomach sank beneath the motion of the lift and the pain in his ribs began to tingle beneath his shirt. He winced his amber eyes and sucked in a breath of filtered air through his mask. The tiny motions would be insignificant in anyone else, but from an unfeeling tsesh they were wildly out of place. Standing at the back of the group though, Malehk was the only one to notice. His head turned a half degree to the prince and his purple eyes locked on him. It had passed. Akara had turned back into stone and was staring ahead with glowing intent.

The doors slid open, and they made their way down the hall. Akara nodded to the apartment door, and they all piled up around it. After a few swipes of a comm, the door unlocked, and they were inside. Her apartment looked different than he'd remembered. It was dark and silent, and the endearing knick-knacks and clutter were devoid of their usual nostalgia. The cramped cluster of rooms felt as though they belonged to a stranger, or as if they'd been abandoned altogether.

The glow of fate was pouring toward the bedroom door like water circling a drain. It twisted up and traced the door frame, wrapping around the faint orange glow from the terrarium light inside. Malehk looked to the prince who gestured toward the door. The others obeyed, walking in silent steps through the ring of fate and filling up the tiny bedroom beyond. The rain was pattering at the window, watering down the lightning and neon of the city outside, drumming a stampede of sound into the air.

Marianne was sleeping on the bed, bundled inside her thick comforter. Basker and the others hardly noticed. They simply placed the briefcase on her dresser and began retrieving its components. Akara ignored them, his glowing eyes settling down on the quiet curves of Marianne beneath her blanket. He walked past Malehk and approached the bed. Fate was drawing lines across the floor. It wound up her bedposts and traced the edges of her body before spiraling around her belly in a halo of light. He watched the golden ring for a moment then turned his attention to Marianne. There were streaks of speckled makeup along her cheeks and dark stains on her pillow where she'd cried herself to sleep.

Akara's hand seemed to reach up on its own, hovering toward her slowly as if she were made of delicate magic that might burst at the slightest touch. His fingertips were nearly to her cheek, but the movement summoned back the pain in his side. He slurped in another pained breath and recoiled his hand. The bite in his ribs had jerked him back from his mesmerized state and resharpened the edges of the unfamiliar room.

Basker stepped between them with a syringe in his hand. It shook Akara back to reality and he stood up and backed away as the needle stabbed into Marianne's shoulder. The anesthesia worked quickly, drawing little more than a flinch and a flutter in her eyes before she drifted deeper into unconsciousness.

Marianne's lips parted a bit and her head rolled along the downy plush of her pillow. She seemed as though some part of her was trapped beneath the drugs, unable to break through the surface of sleep. Basker turned her onto her back and stripped the blanket from her body, holding out his hand to one of the other tsesh.

Akara had been taking slow and mindless steps backward until his heels tapped against the wall near the door. Malehk was there, his eyes watching the movements of the prince the way you'd study a grizzly stranger who'd just crept into your favorite pub; cautious, suspicious. Akara gave a brief and sideways glance to him then turned back to watch the others work.

Basker pressed the barbed surface of a medical injector into Marianne's arm. It immediately sprung to life, first with a blast of lights then settling down to display a stream of vital information. Her temperature, pulse, and respiration played out across the small screen as Basker synced the device to his comm and began programming it for the procedure.

Tension coagulated inside Akara's throat while he watched them prepare. He cleared the phlegm with a subtle growl behind his mask and turned another look at Malehk to see if he had noticed. He had. His serious and violet eyes turned cautiously again to the prince who seemed to be showing signs of stress. He was acting like a man who was rushing to patch the cracks in a dam as it slowly came apart. It wasn't just uncharacteristic, it was impossible for a tsesh without feeling.

Akara ignored his curious friend in the corner of his eye and concentrated instead on the operation. Basker was still sliding holographic bars on his comm, and Marianne was still stirring in her synthetic sleep. Her mouth moved again and Akara was sure she was trying to form a word. He narrowed his eyes and focused on her lips but couldn't translate their movements.

At the edge of his vision, he saw the injectors flashing an affirmative green as Basker finished his calibration. His gaze flicked aside then returned to Marianne's lips, staring so hard that his eyes began to burn. He reached up to rub the dust from his vision and the movement pulled at the stitches in his wound. He winced and grunted and recoiled back, this time drawing the full attention of everyone in the room.

Malehk swung his head to the prince. Basker and the others shot burning glares over their shoulders. Even Marianne rolled her head to the side, her groggy blue eyes fluttering open.

Malehk's serpentine stare went wide with an unusual expression. "Akara, no."

That was when Akara noticed. The winding ribbons of fate were gone, replaced by the delicate orange light of the room and the burning pain in his ribs. His emotions began pouring back into his mind, filling it up with horror and icy water.

"Akara?" Marianne's voice whispered across the room. "You're back."

His head snapped forward to see her staring into his dark and human eyes. His own voice eked through his mask. "Marianne?"

Her vision blurred and drifted around the room, catching the shadowed figures beside her bed and the injector planted in her arm. "Akara?" she said again, this time with a rising tone of fear and confusion. She whimpered and struggled to lift the dead weight of her arms.

"Marianne," Akara repeated aloud with a single step forward. The bullet hole bit at his side again, twisting him over.

She was waking up, breaking free of the anesthesia, and struggling to understand the shapes in her room. "Akara," she cried with urgency. "Akara, help."

"Marianne!" he ignored the pain and rushed toward the bed.

Basker leapt up and shoved an open hand forward, trying to stop the prince's advance. As he did, Marianne lurched back and away from him. The injector in her arm screamed and flashed a blur of scarlet text. She was shouting for help and laboring to escape the heavy weight of her body.

"No, stop!" Akara yelled past them to her flailing form.

Basker drew his pistol and aimed it at the storming prince. Akara slapped the weapon aside, forcing out a clap of gunfire that filled the room and punched a hole in the back wall. Marianne screamed and recoiled from the sound. The tsesh twisted around each other, the gun blasting out two more rounds while the injectors blared their alarms between the echoes. Amidst it all, Akara heard Marianne gag and gasp for breath. Panic snared his attention long enough for Basker to twist the barrel of the pistol into his temple. In a flash, Akara knocked it away and hammered a steel fist into Basker's jaw. The large tsesh crashed to the floor, his gun coughing out a final round into the wall as it slid across the room.

Plaster dust and gun smoke was glittering in the air, hanging, and twisting like thick smoke in the wind. The other tsesh drew their weapons and turned to intercept the prince, but Malehk intervened. He snatched his gun from his hip and skated between them, his purple eyes glaring down the sights at the tsesh who would dare to move against their prince.

Ignoring the others, Akara dropped to his knees beside the bed and tore the mask from his face. The screen of the injector was pulsing bright red and screaming. He pulled it from her arm, leaving six trails of blood from its needles, then looked to her with bloodshot eyes. "Marianne?"

A deep breath ebbed from her chest and her eyes trembled then opened. "Akara," she sighed out long and soft. "You came back."

"Yeah. Yeah, I'm here," he said with a frantic whisper. Tears were pooled in his eyes and tumbled down his cheeks when he blinked.

"Oh, Akara, don't cry." She raised a sleepy hand to his cheek and tried to smile. The glittering blue of her eyes had gone dark. The chaotic amalgam of drugs was working its way through her blood, overwhelming her body, and burning the memories from her mind.

Akara could see her light fading. "Marianne," he repeated over and over. "Just hang on."

"It's okay," she hushed as a mother might say to a child, "it was just a dream."

"No. No, Marianne. It's not."

"Shh." Her strength slipped away, and her hand fell from his face, slumping to the quilt at her side. With her last breath and her last thought, she whispered, "Goodnight, Akara."

"Marianne?" he said again, waiting for her voice to return. His breath shook and he began rocking on his knees. "Marianne?" Akara's expression was strained with agony, his tears pouring down fresh lines in his seized and trembling face. He tried to say her name again. He tried to say anything, but only a crushed and airy breath could escape from his throat. She was gone. Her face had gone slack and her eyes relaxed open without even a hint of their loving, sapphire shine.

Malehk allowed his attention to move away from his attackers and settle on his friend. The prince slowly rose to his feet and stepped back from the bed, his body convulsing atop his sobbing breaths. Drool hung from his lips and blood had begun to spread out beneath his shirt. He turned to stare into Malehk's serpentine eyes. Without a word, Akara begged him for help. He begged for miracles and answers. He begged for the night to be undone.

His friend could offer nothing, and when Akara realized that, he also realized that Malehk wasn't looking at him. He was looking past him to the faint orange glow at the side of the room. He followed the frozen stare and turned to see the terrarium where Marianne had grown her rose. It was dead. Its stem was wilted over, and its petals were shriveled and gray. An emotion that Akara couldn't understand gripped his throat and threatened to strangle him. He couldn't breathe. His stomach tensed up into stone and he couldn't release it. When he finally managed to close his mouth, his teeth ground together, clenching to the edge of shattering, and pressing spikes of pain up and into his skull.

Akara coughed out a feeble whimper. It wasn't the lamenting of sadness or the sobbing of pain. It was the stifled cry of grief laid bare, of a world undone and a man unmade. It was the extinguishing of a light that's often overlooked, an imperceptible glint that can only be seen in our darkest days. It was the sound of hope leaving someone's heart.

Then he stopped. His face still frozen and contorted, Akara turned back to look at his friend. Through Malehk's eyes, the prince was ablaze with the fiery light of a fate betrayed, but Akara felt nothing. He saw nothing, only a cold, dark room in the corner of a lifeless world. Without a word, he picked up Basker's gun, looked one last time to Marianne, then left the apartment and stepped into the storm.

# # #

"Father!" Akara's voice flooded the brick tunnels beneath Old Mallis. His footsteps marched like war drums echoing down the corridors. His coat flayed out around his silhouette, catching the wind of his determined pace like a flag on the battlefield. Basker's pistol was clenched in his hand, gripped so tightly that he'd forgotten it was there. It was nothing now but an extension of his body and his rage. "Father!"

The drive back from Marianne's was a blur in his memory, nothing more than streetlights and streaks of rain. He couldn't remember getting into or out of the car. He couldn't remember what had happened to the agent outside the maintenance lift and he forgot to count the eighteen second decent into the ruins. He was trapped inside his mind, drifting in darkness while everything around him faded to gray like Marianne's jeweled eyes. His past, his future, all the pillars that had propped up his life were gone. A piece of him knew where he was going. While he wailed in the silence of his grief, some driving force that stamped out the beat of his boots knew what he was about to do. The rest of him no longer cared.

Akara kicked open the steel door of his father's makeshift office. It was a square chamber of rusted pipes and red brick with a square pool of water in the corner that drained out through a barred alcove near the floor. Rhago was there, sitting at his desk like he would on any other night, still dressed in his white suit that carved him out like a beacon against the murky bronze of the room.

Kade was there as well, his burly stature leaning over the desk, staring at the tedious feed of the holographic display. He jumped up straight when Akara stormed in, and the heavy door screamed on its hinges and slammed against the wall.

"Akara," Rhago barked. "What are you doing?"

"She's dead!" he shouted back. "Marianne's dead!"

Rhago's eyes flickered wide for a fraction of a second and he shot a glance to Kade whose expression had gone slack.

Akara was pacing in short circles, his face twisted in pain and dripping with tears and trembling spit. "This was what you wanted all along, wasn't it? Marianne gone, and me locked away in darkness. You killed her!"

Kade eased an open hand up at him and patted at the air. "Akara, just calm down. Explain what happened."

A pained squeal peeled from his lips. His stomach was a knot of muscle and stone. He pressed both fists against his temples, one still white-knuckled around the pistol.

Kade stepped back at the sight of the weapon and Rhago's chair scraped along the floor. The king began to interject with his authoritarian tone, "Son, you don't—"

"Shut up!" Akara jabbed the gun at him. The ribs of the barrel filled with blue light and weapon hummed to life, forcing Rhago's hands to leap up from the desk. Akara stared deep into his father's widened eyes. The fear piled a sense of power and confusion into his already crowded mind. The pistol bobbed in the air, and he pulled it back as though he'd just remembered it was there. He rapped the barrel against his head and returned to his pacing, gasping through the strained muscles in his neck and the throbbing lump in his throat. "Why?" he groaned out long and slow.

"You know why," the king replied. "She was a danger to you. She was a danger to us all." He made a sweeping motion to the imagined tsesh that were scattered in clumps throughout the sewer.

"No, she wasn't!" Through his strained and teary eyes Akara could hardly see his father anymore. He was only a vague, white shape behind the desk, no features or expression, just the blur of the thing that had hammered his life into its twisted and tortured form. He shook his head at the thing and repeated, "No she wasn't."

"Fate always finds its way down here. It always has." Rhago spoke as if he were prefacing a lecture. "Any interaction with the surface will always lead back to us. That's just the way it is, the way that it's always been."

"I loved her."

"Oh, please. Love." Rhago spat the word. "You were bewitched by something you didn't understand."

"You don't know what we had," Akara screamed as if his words might cauterize his father's insult. "You don't know anything. You've never loved anyone other than yourself."

"Don't you dare presume to lecture me on life." The king's voice grew bold and angry. He was no longer explaining himself, only defending and attacking. "I lost your mother to these same childish whims. She died because we trusted the surface world."

"She died because you were afraid to fight for us!"

Rhago's expression flared with a rage so bright that he himself was caught off guard. He heaved a breath through his broad chest to calm himself before something terrible was allowed boil over. He smoothed out his white suit and tried to steady his voice. "You broke the laws of the tsesh. Perhaps now you understand why they exist. Her death is not on me." Rhago punched the last word with conviction to remind the prince of his role in their plight.

Akara's eyes flashed furious and lucid, bearing down on the king. "Why?" This time the word poured out like lava. "Because I didn't want to live your life? Because I didn't want to crawl on my belly in the sewers like an insect?"

"I was keeping you safe," he snapped back. "This affair of yours—"

Rhago's trite reduction of their relationship brought Akara's gun arm back in line with his father's head.

The king rose from his chair and stared down the barrel. "You were acting like a spoiled child with no regard for the consequences of your actions. You still are."

"You would have us all buried alive, and you would call it safety. An unseen life? You're not a king, you're a coward. You've condemned us!"

"You have condemned yourself!" Rhago screamed back.

Akara's face went cold. A fresh well of tears filled his eyes and his mind fell backward into memories, into that bedroom, to the soft red light of the rose, the warm and heavy blanket, and the sapphire smile of the woman who had loved him. "Yes, I have," he whimpered. Then he squeezed the trigger.

BOOM.

"No!" Kade's voice barreled through the echoes of the gunshot. He lunged ahead to catch the king, his blood already spattered across the dark skin of Kade's face. He kicked the chair away from the desk and eased Rhago's limp form to the concrete floor. Warm blood was pouring out the back of Rhago's head, filtering through his white hair before spilling between Kade's fingers. "What did you do?" He repeated the question several times, his trembling hand lingering above the bullet hole in the center of Rhago's blank stare.

Two more tsesh rushed into the room with their swords and pistols drawn. Their faces were masked, and their eyes were already glowing with cold intent. They surveyed the office and pieced together what had happened but made no move against the prince. They stood poised in the unprecedented scene as if waiting for someone to tell them what to do. The order came as a passive wave of Kade's hand while he cradled Rhago's body in the other. The guards' weapons relaxed to their sides, and they stood at attention to block the door.

Akara's arm wilted, the smoke from the gun coiling up and around his nose. He stared with wide, wet eyes at Kade rocking his father's corpse. A flood of emotion poured like ice water into his heart, rushing in too quickly for him to identify any single one. He dropped to his knees and looked on as if he'd only just arrived to find his father dead. "Kade?"

"He's gone," Kade whimpered over the limp king.

"Kade, why?" Akara's voice was clenching up in his throat. "Why did he hate them so much?"

"You never understood."

"Then tell me!"

"Your father didn't hate the humans, he loved them," he suddenly bellowed with a stern glare at the prince. "Your mother was human!"

The words punched Akara in the gut, forcing breath and tears from a frozen face. His words came out slow, only mouthed at first until the strength in his belly returned. "No. No, my mother was queen of the tsesh. Nadina Krosse."

Kade sniffled and hugged Rhago's head to his chest. "You stupid kid. Your mother was Nadina Frey, and she was human."

Akara's mouth made the word 'no', though he wasn't sure if he'd said it. His head shook and his eyes flickered off to some distant horizon. "No," he finally heard himself say. His gaze returned to the room and to the fallen king. He didn't just see his father bleeding out in someone's arms. He saw himself. Blind fury rushed up inside of him, birthed from some unknown place in his heart. The sound he made as it erupted from his twisted lips wasn't human, nor was it tsesh. It was primal, ancestral, an agonized howl that exploded through the dark tunnels of a forgotten kingdom.

Chapter 21

Throughout the night the rain had covered the city and dulled its lively buzz to a muted roar. It wasn't until early morning that it let up, petering off like a tap slowly wrenching shut. By the time the sky had ebbed back to pale gray clouds and fluttering sheets of lightning the rain had stopped completely. The glass towers of Mallis Two were shimmering. Cars were glistening and vibrant as the populace eased into its morning rush. The packed, commercial heart of Sector Six was alive with neon ads that danced in the splashing reflections of sidewalk puddles.

It was more than a new day. It was more than a fresh, petrichor breath. It was Election Day, a day when rules were rearranged and fresh faces replaced those that were old and tired, out of breath and out of touch. It was a day that hummed with electric animation, when every conversation was spoken with the sharpened edge of tension. The bleak worries of the past were scraped together, divided, and boxed up into black tie bundles that the citizens could cheer for.

As the city swelled to life, its population began to pool into the neighborhoods surrounding the courtyard of Pramoore Tower. Lines of traffic slowed and stiffened throughout the streets, blocking every thruway and decorating the air with a symphony of blaring horns. Large transit ferries warbled between the buildings twenty feet above the cars, hauling load after load of passengers toward the plaza. They'd drop them off fifty at a time, then ascend and growl back to the outskirts for another batch.

The festivities consisted of eight grandstands, each no more than a mile from the next that wound a tight circle around the central courtyard at the base of Pramoore Tower. Every patch of pavement was filled with kiosks and tents, and every space between those was packed with emergency vehicles and bustling families.

Daemon had made his rounds early on, stepping from his limo at the edge of each plaza with Faedra at his side. He'd smile a synthetic smile and shake a few hands before shuttling off to the next sector. This year they'd ended their route in Sector Six. With the assassinations and the emergence of the tsesh, the oft forgotten Six had become the brand-new focus of the city. The people's excitement with their own election had become a rerun of every election passed, but their preoccupation with the outcome of Six was new. It was exciting and dangerous and could reshape the future of them all.

The executive seats were in a sleek, raised platform twenty feet from the ground. It had a sloping base of black glass and metal that curved up to a beveled cube that was surrounded in blue lights and bulletproof glass. The elevated position offered Daemon and his troupe an unobstructed view of the stage as well as the amassing crowd. From the ground, passersby could see them taking their royal seats. At the back, Kaelus was a white marble statue in a navy suit standing guard at the door. The bandage across the side of his neck was a harsh contrast to his dark and formal attire. Seated in front of him was Daemon, staring intently at the crowd with his obsidian eyes. Faedra was poised and proper in her seat to his left, her fiery hair pinned up and dropping only precise orange curls down her slender shoulders. To Daemon's right was Valen, wearing a brown suit, his face masked in his permanent expression of hawk-eyed indifference.

Daemon slid a hand down the purple silk of his tie and settled back in his seat. "At last, we're at the end of all of this. Is everything ready?"

Faedra nodded without looking. "Caul is in his office waiting for your order."

"And the seditionists?"

"Security is tighter than it's been in years," she said. "If there are any rogue agents left alive, it'd be too soon and too dangerous for them to make a move on the ceremony."

A low smirk crept up on Daemon's face. "Perfect."

#

Jaga was sitting on a vinyl mattress that had been planted atop a steel cot in a tiny room. It wasn't a prison in the conventional sense. It was more like a containment cell; two walls of concrete and two of tempered glass, boxed together in the back corner of a lab on the upper floors of Pramoore Tower. It was a tiny chamber, just wide enough for him to lie down on the cot or to pace in tight circles in front of it. He'd spent the night alternating between the two while Bwrynn slipped between sleep and foggy consciousness on the other side of the room beyond his cell.

It had been a long and contemplative drive back to the tower. Jaga had stared out the tinted windows of the car while working out what fate the agents may have had planned. Daemon wanted him dead, that much he knew. But Jaga was well-known in the sector, and their arrest at the hospital had kicked up quite a bit of public dust, making a private execution all but impossible anymore. No, he suspected that he'd simply disappear behind some laboratory curtain until his name faded from common lips. He would vanish and be forgotten just like the countless tsesh he'd condemned to the very same end. 'Befitting,' he thought, 'if not a little poetic.'

But the night had passed without a word, without a weapon drawn, without so much as the prick of a syringe. Morning was well underway, and Jaga was still alive, still locked in a tiny glass box, and still wondering what might come next.

Two guards had been assigned to them. They weren't police, nor were they agents of the Legacy. They were private security; polished thugs recruited a dozen at a time by some underpaid headhunter on the ground floor. The guards paid little attention to Jaga throughout the night and even less to Bwrynn. They were there for the paycheck, nothing more.

Jaga had been staring at Bwrynn while he thought, but finally turned his focus on the guards. His eyes danced between them with sinister intent as ideas took shape in his mind. He glanced up and noticed the strip of bored holes in the glass near the ceiling of his cell. They were meant for air circulation, but it also meant that the guards could hear him.

His face slumped into a practiced expression of lazy indifference like an actor about to perform a somber scene. Jaga rose from the cot, his slow demeanor masking the flurry of psychic power that was winding up in his mind. "Excuse me," he bobbed his chin toward the nearest guard. "Do you have the time?"

"Quiet," the other man demanded then looked to his partner. "Don't talk to him."

'Don't talk to him?' Jaga thought. The guards no doubt knew of his position in the Legacy, possibly even of his reputation as a hunter, but to avoid contact altogether? They hadn't been ignoring them because they were lazy. They were under orders to avoid interaction. There are many superficial reasons to avoid a situation; fear, anger, disinterest, or distrust, but beneath them all is a single truth. They weren't prepared for it.

Jaga's mind went to work as he spoke again, this time lashing his words together with psychic intent. "Aren't we going to be late?"

"He said be quiet," the man replied, cracking open the door to his mind.

"I'm hungry," Jaga continued. "It's already ten after nine."

The guard turned sharply toward him and scowled but didn't advance.

"And we still haven't eight."

The scowl began to twist, curving up in confusion.

"I said quiet," the other man snapped, but his voice seemed far away.

"I haven't eaten since seven last night," Jaga went on, "at that diner on six."

The entranced officer formed the word 'five' with his mouth as if he were thirsty.

"It may have been five," Jaga confirmed with a comforting nod. "Isn't that what you're here four?"

"Four?" he asked dumbly, taking one step forward.

"The three of us are going downstairs," Jaga said, slipping the psychic marbles along the string of words, tripping up the simple guard to slow his comprehension. "Your friend can come two."

The man was ambling forward on slow and heavy feet, his mind sifting through a haze of numbers and psychic gibberish. He was two steps from arms-reach of the door, but his partner had taken notice and shouted, "Hey."

One more step.

"I'm hungry," Jaga repeated softly, "I can't be the only... one."

The wits of the guard were lost in fog, his eyes distant and glazed as he took the final step. His partner jumped up behind him, shouting out sounds that fell flat before they could reach the young man's mind.

"Open the door," Jaga ordered.

He pressed his thumb against the controls, unleashing a loud buzz into the room.

The guard at the back was rushing toward them and wresting his gun from its holster. "Aiken, wait! What are you doing?"

The moment Jaga heard the click of the lock he smashed his foot against the door, kicking it open and into the face of the dumbfounded man. His nose popped a splash of blood against the glass as he was rattled from his daze and toppled backward to the floor.

Jaga jumped from the cell and pivoted around the door, ducking behind it as gunshots flooded the air and a storm of bullets hammered at the glass in front of his face. A web of white cracks splintered out around his vision, becoming wider and thicker with every shot.

He dropped to one knee and yanked the pistol from the unconscious man's belt. Another three shots blasted at the glass. Jaga sucked in a steady breath and huffed it out. His eyes twinkled with power, and he fired a wave of psychic energy at the gunman before kicking the door aside, raising the gun and shouting, "Stop!"

It was a brief hesitation, barely long enough for the echoes of the gunfire to fade away, but it was more than Jaga needed. He lunged forward, twisted the man's gun arm away and punched the hilt of his own weapon into his throat just beneath the jaw. The guard's eyes rolled up and he dropped like dead weight to the floor, his gun scraping and clacking across the tiles.

Jaga double-checked the two men with a quick glance to each then rushed to Bwrynn's bedside. He didn't know the building's layout beyond the door, but someone would have heard those shots and they'd have only seconds to escape.

# # #

Akara was sitting on the metal lip of a subway platform, his feet dangling over the edge and hanging above the dead tracks. His hands were clamped together in thick, metal cuffs and two armed tsesh were standing over him on either side. His head was hanging to his chest, his human eyes examining the handcuffs through the rogue strands of long hair that had escaped his ponytail.

The tsesh had managed to restore small pockets of power throughout the underground system, and weak yellow bands of light now fluttered back and forth from life around the crowns of the station's pillars. The air was humid and dirty, glittering in dusty sheets along the dim yellow rays. The world felt like it was made of cardboard, thin, dry, without texture or temperature. Akara, the would-be prince of the tsesh was little more than a paper doll, dressed up and moved around like a two-dimensional plaything for people who never cared.

He opened and closed his fist. The skin of his palm still tingled, and he swore he could still feel the grip of the pistol in his hand. He couldn't remember squeezing the trigger or the recoil of the gun when he shot. His memories were a mess of still frame photos scattered across a floor. Individually, he recognized each moment, but they were all out of order and, try as he did, he couldn't get them to make sense.

His father was dead. Marianne was dead. His unborn child was dead. All his tethers to the world had been cut. He was lurching in the wind with no sense of direction and no safe place to land. As near as he could tell, he was dead too. He just had to keep on living afterward. But the day was still young.

The shriek of rusted hinges pierced through the station. Across the tracks, in the failing light, Akara saw Kade emerging from one of the black doors down the tunnel. The large, bearded shadow of a man walked slowly toward them with a solemn look wilting the bold features of his face.

Kade's feet fell in heavy clops on the concrete. He glanced up then waved away the two sentries with a flick of his fingers. They granted a courteous bow before disappearing down the tracks, leaving the young prince alone with the somber giant.

"Why didn't you tell me, Kade? Why didn't anyone tell me that my mother was human?"

He sighed a long and ancient breath as he stepped beside Akara then tugged up his pant legs and lowered himself with a groan to sit beside him. Kade's voice was a deep river of warm chocolate; slow and smooth. "Most of the people who knew were killed in the Abolition. The few of us who remained were sworn to secrecy by your father."

Akara shook his head. "But why?"

He shrugged his mountainous shoulders. "It was a different time. There was a lot of tension between the humans and the tsesh, and no one wanted to be the guy who tipped the balance."

"But the whole reason they hunted us was because we were genetically incompatible, a flaw in a closed society."

Kade snickered. "Yeah, that's what the last Pramoore led with. Built his whole image on it in fact."

"So why didn't my father just tell them?"

"He did. Of course, he did. Your father thought he could stop the whole thing before it began. He believed his love for Nadina could save the world."

"So, what happened?"

Kade's thick brow slid up and he puckered his lips. "Nothin. The Legacy came after us harder than ever. Pramoore took a particular interest in you though." He wagged a finger at the despondent prince. "We don't know what he had planned, but he was desperate to get his hands on a half-breed." Kade's tone went soft as the memories seem to play out behind his eyes. "He took your mother, tried to use her to lure us out."

"Just like my father said."

"Almost worked too. We knew it was a trap, but we all loved that girl. Ain't nothin' we wouldn't have done to save her." His voice withered to a faraway whimper. "And she knew it. In the end, she sacrificed herself to save you, to save all of us." He heaved a breath and turned his head to the ceiling to keep the tears inside his eyes. "For all the good it did."

Tears trickled to the tip of Akara's nose before falling to splash on the cuffs that bound him. "I'm sorry, Kade." Grief finally overtook him and contorted his face. He wept deep and heavy. "I'm so sorry. I'm sorry for everything."

"Hey," Kade consoled him, wrapping a large arm around the prince, and pulling him into his chest. His own tears slipped from his eyes and glistened in his wiry beard. "We're gonna figure this out. We'll get through it like we always do."

"But my father..."

Kade bobbed his head in sharp nods, pressing his damp lips together. "I know. I know. It's okay. The truth is, the Rhago I knew died a long time ago."

"There's nothing left," Akara cried into Kade's giant body. "I've lost everything."

"That's just how life works, ain't it? For all of us. Eventually it will always cost us everything."

They cried together for a long time, their sniffles and sobs fading down the tunnel into whispers in the dark.

When Akara felt that he had wept enough, when there was no more purpose to it all, he rolled his face from Kade's chest and stared blankly into the shadows across the way. "Are you going to kill me?"

Kade coughed a sound that was somewhere between sorrow and laughter. He squeezed the young prince tighter, almost as if he meant to purge the notion from his very bones. "No," he answered. "No, of course not. Quite the opposite in fact."

Akara leaned back, wiping his tears with the backs of his hands. He didn't ask, but the question was clear on his face.

"C'mon," Kade finally answered, retrieving a small key from his pocket. He pressed it into the handcuffs and released the prince. "We gotta get you cleaned up."

"For what?" he asked, rubbing at the red marks the cuffs had left behind.

"For your coronation."

"For my coro— what?" The response leapt out loud from Akara's lips. "My coronation?"

"You're Rhago's only heir."

"But Kade, I..." Akara stopped himself. He couldn't bring himself to speak the words. He couldn't admit out loud that he'd murdered his father just a few hours before, as though if he kept it to himself, kept it from the open air of the world, then it wouldn't be real.

"Yeah, I know," Kade offered sympathetically. "But in the end, none of that matters. All that matters are those scales." He pointed to the prince's eyes then began maneuvering himself to his feet, pressing his hands into his knees and groaning like a lumbering machine. "Like you said, we don't got much left anymore, but at least we got that. The black scales of the royal line. That's the way it's always been and, especially now, we need that to mean somethin'." He plunged a meaty hand to Akara and smiled, his beard still twinkling with his tears.

Akara nodded absently and took his hand without looking up. "Okay."

CHAPTER 22

Jaga's momentum crushed against a large window at the end of a hallway high above the city. His chest was heaving over panting breaths. His heart was pounding in a rushed but steady rhythm, responding to his sprint down the hall, the uncertainty of their escape, and his concern for the groggy young girl under his arm.

Bwrynn was awake, though she hardly seemed aware of it. Her head was heavy and rolling around on her neck. The world was a blur of washed-out shapes and streaks of light, rushing forward and back, tugging her through doorways and stairwells. There was a bulging pain at the base of her skull, bulky and throbbing like someone had pumped a blood vessel full of clay. It kept her senses from reaching her brain, and her brain from reaching her body. She struggled to move beyond it, to clear her head of vertigo and focus on a single point. She'd try to close one eye, but the other always followed. She felt her head wobbling recklessly on her shoulders but had only the strength for one limb at a time, and from what she could gather of the situation, her legs needed priority.

Jaga cupped a hand around his eyes and peered through the window. They were halfway down the tower and standing along the western wall. The shining gray awning of the main entrance was several hundred feet straight down. Beyond the front steps, he saw the swarming crowd in the plaza. It was a kaleidoscope of colored dots and pop-up tents that danced with glowing ads and brazen logos. Distant holograms twirled images in the air; smiling sandwiches, dancing bratwurst, and balloons wiggling in digital wind.

"The Dark Ocean," Bwrynn mumbled into her chest.

It was the first thing she'd uttered in days, a welcome sound that pulled Jaga's attention back inside. "What?"

"It's everywhere. It's all around us."

"Yes, Bwrynn. Yes, we know that, but right now we have to keep moving."

"Jaga?" his name crept from her lips in a whimper as though she was seeing him for the first time. The pain in her skull cinched her eyes into slits and pressed her tongue to the roof of her mouth.

"Yes child, it's me." He pulled her close and brushed his hand down her cheek, "I'm here."

"We're not alone." She nearly sobbed the words, her frightened and desperate tone rattling deep into Jaga's nerves and prickling at his skin.

"I know. I know," he repeated in as comforting of a voice as he could muster while his cool eyes snapped around the hallway. Twenty feet ahead he found an intersection with the words 'stairs' glowing above it. "Come," he said, ushering her along beneath his arm.

"They're out there," she mewled. "They're everywhere."

Jaga rushed them past the intersection to a steel door and peered through its slit of a window. The stairwell was empty, a hollow chasm ringed in metal steps that plunged downward at least twenty floors.

Voices came tumbling down the hallway, frantic guards barking orders, their boots strumming out thunder against the ceramic floor. With half of his mind, Jaga heard their commander order them to lock down the building. They were splitting up and spreading out. It would only be a matter of minutes before every door in the tower became a steel barrier, magnetically sealed. He glanced back into the stairwell and wondered how many floors they could make it before the lockdown was initiated. There were no shadows and no cover. He'd have to be quick. A naked tunnel was the last place they'd want to be trapped, but he had no other choice.

"Let's go," he instructed, hugging Bwrynn close as he pressed the controls and the door slid open.

"The world," she muttered, shuffling sideways beneath his panicked pace. "The world is so big. I can't..."

Anger was piling atop the fear in his belly. To hear Bwrynn terrified and maundering against him, to see what they had done to her pure and beautiful mind was testing his poised facade. He slung her arm across his shoulder and hoisted as much of her weight as he could manage. They began their descent. His heart was racing faster than his hurried feet that tromped out echoes in the silent stairwell as they raced toward the ground.

# # #

Daemon scanned the crowd beneath his elevated balcony with black and narrowed eyes. The hovering ferries still worked to shuttle people in, but the plaza was full. Beyond the tight paths that allowed people to pass from one crowd to the next, the citizens were packed together in dense clusters of mishmash lifestyles. Doctors squeezed past housekeepers. Grocery clerks shouldered through bundles of first year students. They swarmed around the vendor booths and piled up in front of the stage where a band had begun to play, though the music was lost in the babel of the crowd. It was a sugar coating to dress up a rolling mix of sound.

At the edge of the plaza sector security officers were holding a line between the spectators and a thin, metal barricade. Just past them was a private lot, now dotted with sleek, navy patrol cars and polished limousines. The election candidates and their staff were rehearsing speeches in quiet rooms, locked away from the crowds as tensions rose to critical mass.

"It's time," Daemon uttered plainly.

Faedra glanced to Kaelus near the door at the back of their balcony then tapped at the comm on her wrist. "Doctor Cerrone," she said into the device. His voice hissed back a response as she rose to her feet and took a single step toward the window. The sky rumbled and lightning stabbed at the peak of the southwest tower. Shadows crept in around Faedra's face, then her eyes began to glow with green light and drifting steam. When her mind latched on to every slumbering beast inside the spire, she raised the comm to her lips. "Wake them."

# # #

The shadow beneath the city was thick, pressing back against any source of light until all that remained of them were tiny orbs of orange glow around every lamp and flame. Candles were reduced to pin pricks, casting desperate flutters into the dark that brushed across steel masks and serpentine eyes, the apathetic gaze of a half-hundred tsesh.

They'd gathered inside an abandoned subway station. The vacant room was tall and broad in every direction, though the heavy darkness had filled it up with claustrophobic shadow. Some of the tsesh were there to guard the doors, others were there for ceremonial duty, but they'd all arrived to mourn the passing of King Rhago and to celebrate the coronation of his son, Prince Akara.

At the center of the station, Rhago's body had been placed on an altar. He was dressed in his white suit and blue tie, and his hair had been taken down. It now framed the quiet serenity of his face like a mane of silk and snow. The dead king's hands were clasped together on his chest and his closed eyes were underlined by the black scales of his family line.

Candles had been placed on the floor around the altar and stretched outward in every direction drawing eight lines of flickering light on the floor. The tsesh who were granted permission, either through rank or favor, stood between the lines. They each were dressed in the long coats and vented masks of their people, and they looked down on the king with scaled and glowing eyes of every color. They watched as the warm light of fate coiled out from the body and snaked around the room.

The funeral of kings was getting old and thin, now little more than a ghost itself. No one could be sure of where the ceremony had begun.

None of them knew the symbolism involved or even the proper words to speak. The gathering was an echo of a forgotten time, the shadow of a kingdom that none had ever seen. It was something they'd learned from their parents and their grandparents, a ritual passed down through the ages. Each generation would repeat what they remembered, glossing over the trivial parts or forgetting a step or verse.

The tsesh carried on regardless. The liturgy didn't matter. They simply needed a chance to grieve, to mark the passage of time like a tally carved on a prison wall. Kings would die. Princes would be born. It was the turning wheel of a derelict life, and they would continue its rotation until they were whittled away to nothing.

Akara stood at the edge of the platform, his back to the subway tracks and his golden eyes fixed on his father's body inside the crowd. Kade was close to his left, a symbol of the previous king and the last remaining piece of Rhago's reign. The two of them watched in solemn silence as the other tsesh stepped forward to lay hands on the body and bow their heads.

To Akara's right was Malehk, the assigned protector of the prince who would soon take on the role as his advisor. He watched the gathering as well, but his mind was set instead on the movements of fate around them. It was his duty to witness its response to each of the chosen tsesh, to determine their importance and their significance in the coming days.

More than half the tsesh had already paid their respects, but so far Malehk had seen nothing of merit. The slow wash of fate seemed listless at their feet, disinterested in the fallen king and those who had survived him. The tsesh were fading away and fate itself seemed to know it. Regardless, Malehk carried on, his focus unwavering. Akara would be king, and together they would rebuild all that they had lost.

When the final tsesh had raised his head and moved away from the altar, Akara and his companions stepped forward. They moved in unison down the path of candles until they stood at Rhago's feet. As expected, a steady swell of fate climbed up to greet them. It trailed around Malehk's hands and crawled up to Akara's mask. Another ribbon of light followed Kade as he moved to the altar's head and removed the amulet from around Rhago's neck. The gold pendant twirled beneath its chain and splintered the candlelight into fragments of blinking stars.

Kade returned to the young prince who closed his eyes and lowered his head. As the royal signet was clasped around his neck, the amber glow of fate poured into it. It became a whirlpool of radiance, growing deeper and wider until the amulet itself couldn't be seen. When Akara raised his head again he was a king, shining with the beacon of destiny.

Then something happened that had never happened before. The amulet flared with blinding radiance just as a wave of luminous fate surged up every wall around them. The station was flooded with golden light. The tsesh reared back, squinting, and shading their eyes from the overwhelming vision. Many turned to Akara, but his features had been washed away, lost in the glare of the amulet.

The new king himself scanned the area. He looked to Malehk and then to Kade, but each of them was little more than a silhouette, haphazard smudges on a canvas of raging white. Indistinct shapes bobbed and swayed across the room like marionettes on slack strings. The tsesh were scrambling between each other, lurching back and forth as if to dodge the light.

Then there was darkness. Fate plunged out every door, rushing upward and away to the ruins before dissipating into the air. The remaining strips of its presence seemed oddly dim against the memory of the blaze, and a stir of whispers was rising up among the tsesh. They were soon quelled by a distant sound, a mechanical sound.

The groaning of a great machine bellowed out above them and rumbled down through the catacombs. Malehk was the first to draw his gun, sprinting for the door and heading to the surface. Akara and Kade were close behind and a crowd of tsesh followed suit.

They launched through the steel gate and rushed into the familiar stale air and red light of Old Mallis. As they each emerged in turn with weapons at the ready, their black coats formed a leather wall of unity that guarded their new makeshift home. Luminescent, slitted eyes searched the distance crags and spires of the ruined world, searching for the source of the sound.

"There," Malehk said with a finger aimed to the distant border of the world.

It was just below the border wall of Mallis Two, the mechanical root of the southwest tower. Rock and dust kicked loose as the steel cylinder face of the foundation came to life and rotated against the surrounding stone. Lights began to sputter and shine inside the haze of raining dirt. Sheets of metal, once thought to be structural or decorative were grinding awake with groggy purpose.

Malehk's thoughts returned to the conversation he'd overheard inside the tower. He remembered Dr. Cerrone's talk of bio-wraiths, stolen souls that were reforged into monsters and brought to life by the storm. As he watched the precision of the churning machine, and saw the way that fate crackled like lightning along its face, he suddenly realized what was coming. "Bio-wraiths."

Akara turned reluctantly to face him. "What?"

"The creatures I told you about. The things that Daemon's been growing in his lab." He nodded to the machine. "They're waking up."

"The election." Akara tilted his attention to the city overhead. "How many are there?"

Malehk cocked his head and shrugged. "I don't know." His eyes were fixed on the shifting wall and his muscles were prickling to life. "Maybe one. Maybe ten." He thumbed the switch of his gun and flipped the hilt of his sword back and forth in his palm until he found a comfortable weight. He turned to cast a flowing gaze across the tsesh at their backs. "But you defeated that creature in the diner. I believe these are the same. We can handle them."

The diner. Akara's memory toppled backward to that night. He could taste the bitterness of plaster in the air. He could hear the roaring and the screams, and he could feel the recoil of his gun as it spat round after round into the beast. He remembered Marianne. He remembered the blood trickling down her pacific porcelain face. His emotions hammered at the back of his serpentine eyes and howled for release, but he ignored them. His heart was a callous warden, unmoved by the wailing of the damned.

He pulled his mask from his face and looked over his shoulder at the expectant tsesh, glimmers of fate swaying all around them. Their eyes were as cold and focused as his own, ready to move on any order he gave. And suddenly, the weight of his commitment dropped down upon his shoulders. It nearly stole his breath and shook the golden light from his eyes. They could die. They could all die but for a single word from his lips.

"Move everyone down below," he said.

The order hit Malehk like a club to the back of his head. In a single motion he plucked the mask from his face and turned to face the king. His eyes dimmed and faded back to their human shade. Emotion, mostly confusion, crumpled over his brow and he formed a long, single word that filled his mouth for the full duration of the movement. "What?"

"Seal the doors," Akara continued, "and cut whatever power we have. Operate as quickly and as quietly as you can."

"You're hiding?" Malehk forced the words into his friend like the insult they were meant to be.

"These creatures aren't coming for us," Akara explained. "Daemon is attempting to disrupt the election. This is a human matter. I'm allowing it to pass."

"By hiding."

"This is my first act as king, Malehk. Don't let your first act as advisor be that of insubordination."

"Insub—" Malehk choked on the gall of the words, his head teetering on his neck. "Are you kidding me?" He leaned in and swept a hand to the rumbling machine. "We can do this, Akara. We can stop this. We can actually make a difference for once."

"That's not my concern. Nor is it yours. My duty now, our duty is to keep our people safe. That's all."

"That's all? What are you talking about? That's not you, that's your father talking."

"My father was right." The response leapt from Akara's mouth more forcefully than he'd intended. He took a moment and a slow breath to shutter his emotions. He evened out his tone while never breaking eye contact with his friend. "He was right, Malehk. He was right about everything. The best I can hope to do is to protect our people as well as he once did."

Malehk felt his insides wilt and his posture slump. He shrugged his weapons in the air and looked into his friend's fierce, unfeeling eyes. "Akara," he tried to plead.

The fledgling king stared back at him and, for a moment, Malehk thought he saw the panic of a drowning man. Akara was losing himself, and there was nothing he could do.

"Malehk," Akara spoke in a soft and remorseful tone, then paused and took a breath. "How does a tsesh dodge bullets?"

"Akara, don't," he whispered back. "This can't—"

"How does a tsesh dodge bullets?" he asked louder, speaking now to the others at his back.

"By being where the bullets are not," they answered in practiced unison.

Malehk closed his eyes and bowed his head.

"How does a tsesh see the light of fate?" the king continued, acknowledging the congregation of his kingdom.

"By standing silent in the shadows."

Akara looked back to his friend. His voice came forceful as if he were drilling the words into Malehk's eyes. "How does a tsesh cheat death?"

All but Malehk answered. "By living an unseen life."

When he was satisfied with the response and its impact on every tsesh, Akara lowered his volume and spoke succinctly to his friend. "Get below. That's an order."

CHAPTER 23

An alarm buzzer wailed through the halls of Pramoore Tower and filled the air of the stairwell, drowning out the stampede of Jaga's steps. Inside the noise, he heard the loud thunk of breakers switching off. Above them, the yellow lights that lined the walls were blacking out, only to be replaced by a blood red glow a moment later. With every punch of the breakers, the fog of black and red shadow dropped another ten feet. The lockdown was beginning, and Jaga was on a landing between floors.

"Hurry, Bwrynn," he pleaded under his arm.

They rushed down the concrete steps with Jaga, for the most part, hopping on one foot as he held up the bulk of Bwrynn's weight on his other hip. His free hand gripped the black steel of the banister, chomping forward with every step. They rounded one corner then another. One more turn and ten more steps and they'd reach the nearest door. It wasn't the ground floor, but it was close enough. If they could reach the hallway beyond, they might find a fire escape or at least a place to hide. Jaga's muscles were burning with adrenaline and fire, and he wasn't sure how much longer he could carry Bwrynn's half-dead weight.

He lost track of the descending darkness above them. His eyes were locked on the green light of the door ahead. Jaga's weight slammed one foot at a time down the final rise of stairs. He rushed to the door's controls and slapped his fingers at the green panel. It spat back a growling tone and flickered red. He pressed it again, less hurried this time. It growled again and the red light flashed as if to remind him it was there.

He stuttered the half-formed sound of 'no' over and over as he jackhammered his thumb against the button, each time with the same result. It wasn't until the booming sound of the breaker filled the level and red light poured in around him that Jaga gave up trying. He puffed a fearful breath and cranked his head in every direction.

Over the railing he saw the bottom floor. He saw the darkness and the crimson glow as it swallowed up the lights and sunk below them. Looking up the stairwell shaft, he could see shadows in the fresh red light. An army of boots was pounding down the ring of stairs. It was only a matter of time.

"Come on," he muttered absently to the girl beneath his arms.

Bwrynn worked to get her feet under her, each bare foot tripping behind Jaga's rushed pace. His urgency buzzed like electricity in her brain. She slid another foot forward and felt the cold concrete flat against her foot. It was tugged away again, and her toes were soon slapping the edges of steps as Jaga rushed them down the stairs.

All around them, in the staircase above and the rooms outside the door, urgent minds were peering around corners and creeping through darkened halls. She felt them looking for her. She saw poorly imagined pictures of herself in their thoughts. She saw their intent to shoot her, to tase her, to tranquilize her. All of them, every hungry mind was proud and angry, desperate, and afraid. Swallowing Bwrynn up in the shadows of their world was all that they could think. There was nothing more beyond that thought, nothing past that future.

Bwrynn's eyes slit open and tried to make sense of the hazy shapes that pursued them from above. They were human. She was sure of it. "Jaga?" she mumbled. He didn't look. She worked to get another foot beneath her, to relieve some of her weight from his arm and to make him proud of her again. She couldn't be sure, but she thought she felt herself take a step. "Jaga, where are we?"

"Pramoore Tower," he replied, short of breath. "We have to escape."

"Escape," she repeated back. Her head slumped back, and her eyes scowled up the stairwell shaft. Bwrynn waved and flopped a finger at the pursuers. "Who's... people."

Both her shoulders pounded hard against the wall, an impressive attempt by Jaga who was trying to prop her up. They were on the bottom floor. Bwrynn could feel the stability of the ground beneath them and the firm grip of gravity on her body. She could feel the world stretching out sideways all around them. "That feels nice," she muttered. She managed to raise and tap the ball of her foot on cool cement floor. "I like the ground."

The door buzzed indifferently as Jaga rapped his fingers against the controls. His breath was more sound than whispered air. He fired a look across his shoulder while he continued to thumb the button.

Grabbing Bwrynn by the shoulders, he shoved her into the corner and caged her in with his body and arms. His focus was jumping between the guards, now just one floor above them. His mind was dabbing at their thoughts, tasting them for weakness.

Bwrynn was buried in darkness and the smell of her master's clothes. His energy was a mesh of fire in front of her, spotted with gaps and holes as he tried to spread it thin to protect her. He was growing weak, and she could feel it. The warmth of his mind was fading like an early morning firepit, still smoldering with ash and embers from the night before.

The rampaging minds above them were close. She felt the thick molasses of their hate clotting in the air and seeping down to find her. Jaga wouldn't be able to separate them. He wouldn't be able to pierce the single-mindedness of their pursuit. He would fail. He would die.

"Jaga," she whimpered from the corner as their inevitable fate ground itself into her mind. She tried to open her eyes but saw only patches of crimson light around the shadow of her master's body. "Don't," she begged. She felt the soldiers' eyes. She felt the aim of their weapons. "No," she tried again, clawing her fingers against the tight walls of the corner. But the future was already playing out. They were going to kill him.

"NO!" Bwrynn screamed the word so loud that she wondered if she'd ever really spoken before or if she were only now giving birth to her voice. The world rippled outward with her shout, and she felt the lump in her skull swell and break loose. Fire filled her brain. The wall behind her cracked and buckled. The soldiers made futile attempts to scream, but every note had been cut short. The door lock buzzed and sputtered, its red light flickering behind shattered plastic, and the door itself howled and broke open as though it'd been hit by a car.

It was quiet again. There was only Jaga's breathing. He was terrified and tense, but he was breathing. Concrete dust tickled Bwrynn's arms and clacked pleasantly to the floor at her feet.

Jaga spun wide-eyed back to Bwrynn. "What... what was..."

"Escape," she mumbled before tumbling back to half-consciousness.

Jaga gawked at the bowed door and pulverized concrete around it. He swallowed a gaping mouth of saliva and dust then scooped her up in both arms. Stepping sideways into the carpeted halls, Jaga rushed her toward the lobby.

#

The coolness of morning and the previous night's rain had finally begun to shift toward tepid. The Election Day festivities and the heat of a thousand bodies had started to warm the plaza, adding more spring in elderly steps and more dance into youthful legs. People were smiling, waving to friends across a sea of strangers, and any attempt to pull the thread of a single voice from the tapestry of noise would undoubtedly reveal laughter and cheering.

Election Day was more than a political affair. It was more than a paid holiday or long weekend. It was a day outside of time, outside of the tension of a sluggish grind. It was a day when the citizens could step out of their ruts and into their lives. How much of that concept was by design and how much was by choice wasn't always clear. The weight of an unlit life grows heavier with time and after a long string of years, those who carry it will seek out even the faintest slice of respite.

When the sector lords had declared it a holiday it was no doubt an attempt at self-promotion, to wrangle smiling voters and wring a few last drops of taxpayer money into their coffers before their term was up, but it didn't matter. The people saw an excuse to escape their solitude, to gather with friends to brag about accomplishments, to spend money and eat expensive food. It could have been any day, but if the lords wanted to pretend it was about them, no one was going to correct them.

An MC's voice chased off the last few notes of a song. The lead singer howled. The crowd cheered. The MC patronized them with a poor attempt to duplicate the howl, and the people roiled down to a cafeteria roar. As the band began clearing their most portable gear from the stage the MC offered them a nod and a polished and pearly smile.

He was a narrow man, middle-aged but balding. What remained of his hair was thinning but still dark and matched the thick mustache that stretched wide over his practiced grin. As he began to speak, his voice was little more than an electric mumble through the oversized speakers. He addressed the crowd and thanked the band. Then, without segway, he fumbled into his opening speech. He'd no doubt toiled over his comm while writing it, scrutinizing every word for months. In the end, of course, he'd managed to write the same speech that every MC had written for the last fifty years. His job was important, it was an honor to be chosen. There was no sense in mucking it up with flavor or significance.

Above the rumbling din of the crowd, the MC did manage to pique an ear or two with his mention of Kaddler's assassination, the attack on Diedre's Diner, and of course the tsesh. It had been an eventful election year, and he managed to rope it all together into a heartfelt toast to patriotism. The crowd had their own opinions, though most of them were shattered into segments; some were cheering, some were booing, some were even shouting conspiracies. It all bubbled together into a gray ideology of 'the tsesh are bad' and 'don't trust the government'.

When the MC finally reached the bottom of his holographic notes and cinched off the opening speech, his tone switched to that of a game show host. He leaned in close to the microphone and swept a dramatic hand to the back of the stage and announced, "Aldan Pharos!"

The introduction and appearance of the youthful politician broke the dam on the rising tide of cheers. The people shouted for the rising star as he entered the stage, and he drank it in with a wide smile. Aldan waved to the crowd, occasionally singling someone out with a grin and pointed finger as he made his way to the podium. He let the applause cascade over him and fill him up with energy and adoration for a long moment of broad waving before finally patting the audience back down to ambient chatter.

"Wow," he chuckled into the mic. His smiling face was captured and projected throughout the plaza, and his voice echoed against itself when he spoke. "We're finally here," he said with uplifted arms, "and what a road it's been."

Daemon was a statue in his seat, staring down Pharos with cold indifference and barely a twitch in his upper lip. "Where are they?" he asked with impatience boiling in his gut. Faedra didn't respond, her searing eyes and focused mind locked instead on the horizon.

A subtle buzz and flash of red light on Daemon's comm pulled his attention away from her. He tapped and scowled at his wrist. "Yes?"

The response was broken and filled with static, but Daemon heard enough. "Prisoners," and "escaped". His black eyes shifted to the side window of the balcony and stabbed through the mass of people toward Pramoore Tower. He saw them. Jaga Demain was limping across the street with the limp form of Bwrynn Lucane in his arms.

"Kaelus," he ordered with muted panic. "It's Demain. Take care of it."

Kaelus followed his eyes to the escaped prisoners then turned a nod over his shoulder. He drew his pistol with one hand and pressed the door controls with the other before slipping out to the stairway to the ground.

Daemon ground his teeth at Jaga then turned impatiently back to Faedra. "Where are they?" he asked with a bit more agitation. Faedra still didn't respond.

On the stage below, Aldan's speech was reaching its energetic middle. "-a fair society," he said proudly to the crowd, "a balanced society for everyone. When I take that seat in the-"

The speakers crackled and shrieked out feedback. Holograms flickered and swayed throughout the plaza as the ground shook and a sound of thunder crashed in sideways from the street. Heads turned and as the tremor faded, silenced rippled through the festival. It was a long razor blade of unease and bated breath. Automated music trickled from the meek speakers of the food tents, mocking the quietude of the festival. Fearful whispers snaked through the fairgrounds, but all eyes remained on the source of the rumble to the south.

Silence can only last so long. It swells beneath knotted nerves and impatient ears, growing thick and audible. Eventually it would burst and be swept away by a storm of sound, erased as though it had never been. That was the stillness of the plaza, growing fat and heavy atop the crowd. Reinforced by haunted memories and present fear, it expanded beyond what any normal quiet could be. It had to break, and it finally it did, but not in the way that silence should.

A monstrous roar barreled through the air, deafening the muted masses. It was a sound of rage, of blind fury. It was a harbinger of chaos and reckless death.

A brick wall, barely south of the road, exploded in a burst of powder and jagged stone. Inside the core of the eruption, a black beast leapt out to the street. Even on four legs, its head stretched upwards of ten feet. Its body was a tight weave of dark scales that bristled out behind its head in a glistening, bladed mane. A long tail cracked like a whip behind its haunches as it stretched a long, muscled body into the open air. The beast turned its head to face the crowd with four green and piercing eyes. It spread its fanged jaws wide and roared again.

Two more hulking creatures crept from the hole in the wall, snarling and snuffing at the lingering dust. One was covered in coarse, brown hair and wore its skull on the outside of its head. The jawbone flared out like gills at its neck, and the empty sockets cast a reaper's stare around the street. It shrieked and barked, clacking its skeletal mouth open and shut, revealing row after row of needle-like teeth.

The third creature was bipedal, crouching to fit through the hole before finally rising up to a looming fifteen feet. It looked as though it were made of knotted wood and twisting vines. The contours of its body slithered like worms around areas that might have been muscles. It had two long arms, tipped with wriggling fingers that grazed the ground around its cloven feet. It had no head where a head should be. Instead, it bore a black sphere in its chest, trapped inside a ribcage of wooden roots.

Before long, more monsters emerged onto the street behind the others. They were draped in smoke and shadows, assuming countless hideous forms. Each of them was facing the mass of paralyzed onlookers, crouching, twitching, and chittering with hungry anticipation.

The corner of Daemon Pramoore's mouth snuck upward into a sly and insidious smile. He rose from his cushioned seat high above the festival and approached the window to stand beside Faedra. Her expression was rigid porcelain and burning with emerald eyes, her focus locked on the alley of beasts.

Daemon puffed a proud and victorious breath of relief. "Do it."

Chapter 24

Jaga was running for the gap between the aluminum barricades, hoping to slip inside the festival and disappear in the bustle. He was carrying Bwrynn in his arms, her small, limp body still loosely draped in the pale blue hospital gown. Of course, people would notice an old man carrying an incapacitated and barely-clad girl. It was a compromising image and both he and Bwrynn had been on full display in the news for the past day. Regardless, the festival was a forest of bumbling eyes and noisy lips. He was confident that he could outmaneuver any attention he picked up along the way. The people were cover. They were protection, and their minds could be assets should he need them.

The security stationed at the entrance had their backs turned. Jaga noted the brush of luck and sidestepped between the railings to the edge of the crowd inside. Bwrynn stirred in his arms, and he cupped her head in his hand and pulled her close to his chest. He risked a quick glance down and saw her eyes fluttering awake.

"Bwrynn," he whispered with short breaths. "Bwrynn, can you move?"

She mumbled half his name and struggled to turn her head.

Jaga quickly searched the area for a place to sit, something hidden away, something opposite the distant stage where eyes wouldn't bother to look. He settled for a vacant, metal bench. Dragging himself across the distance, he placed Bwrynn on the seat as gently as his burning arms would allow. He slid onto the bench beside her and wrapped a protective arm across her shoulder.

"Bwrynn, please," he spoke with quiet urgency into the small space between them. "You must wake up. You have to clear your mind. I cannot help you."

"Jaga," she managed to utter as her vision began to return. "Where are we?"

"We're in the—" Jaga's head spun to address their location, but his words stopped short, his breath deflating between his teeth. Something was wrong. No one was moving. Everyone was frozen in place with their backs turned to them. Their minds were pulled away by something else.

A violent and pained shriek pierced the air, slicing upward from somewhere to the south. It sounded bestial and ravenous. The high pitch of the howl poured ice into Jaga's veins. Then it was joined by other sounds, distant animalistic roars and a stampeding and rolling thunder. The storm of sound became laced with panicked, human screams and the crowd flashed back into motion. They twisted in every direction, tripping and pushing each other over as the packed mass of people ballooned outward toward the exits.

"Bwrynn," Jaga repeated sharply, jostling her narrow shoulder. "Bwrynn, you have to wake up. We have to go."

Some of the more distant screaming changed. They were no longer the sounds of fear, but of pain. Noises were being punched and torn from people's lungs, their twisted howls spattering onto surrounding witnesses.

"Bwrynn, now!" He tried to lift her weight again, but his strength was gone, and his adrenaline used up.

"Master Demain." Jaga knew the voice; deep, proper, and far too calm. It was Kaelus Bathor. He was walking towards them with his gun swaying casually in his hand.

"You're a fugitive," Kaelus said, using his pistol to point at them. "How'd you get out of your cage?"

Jaga's hand swept up, aiming his stolen gun at Kaelus. His muscles were still burning from their escape and the extended weapon was trembling at the end of his tired arm. His eyes weren't angry or narrowed, they were wide with surprise and concern. It was hardly the image of a threatening man. Kaelus and Jaga both knew it.

"Kaelus," he said, slipping out intention through his silvery-blue eyes. His mind searched for a barb or an outcropping in Kaelus' mind, something to latch onto or to tug at. There was nothing. His thoughts were smooth, cold, like a large sphere of polished stone. He was featureless and impregnable.

"Really?" Kaelus responded with a smile, not bothering to lift his own gun. "Your mind games aren't going to save you. I'm immune. I could pluck that power from your head if I thought it might be fun."

Jaga's thick eyebrows pinched together. "How?"

"That is my gift," Kaelus said. "To wipe away your bluster and see you for what you are, a weak old man." His mouth shifted into a toothy smile, sated by the bewildered look on Jaga's face. "I'll tell you what," he said, "leave the girl and I'll give you a head start."

The horrifying screams continued to bulldoze through the plaza, dividing Jaga's attention between Kaelus and some unseen threat that was coming their way. Gunshots from sector security were popping in sporadic bursts inside the panic.

"What is..." Jaga winced and shook his head. "What's happening?"

"What, that?" Kaelus turned toward the scrambling crowds at his back. "That is the end of—"

BOOM! The bullet punched through his shin and split the bone. Kaelus yelped and dropped to one knee and one fist in the dirt. Jaga rose to his feet with the smoking gun in one hand and Bwrynn in the other.

"I don't care," Jaga said, taking slow steps away from the fallen and bleeding man. "You will not touch her again. Do you understand?"

A food tent exploded beside them. Shredded fabric and twisted metal blasted outward. Jaga, Bwrynn, and Kaelus were all splashed with fryer oil, splattered meat, and red pieces of the attendant who once stood inside. An enormous beast rose up from the wreckage and pounded its fists into what remained. It was a giant wrapped in tight, gray skin. Its face had no eyes, but a wide and grinning mouth. Behind its muscled arms, four more, thin and spider-like, sprouted off its back and snapped in the air with sharp and pointed talons.

Jaga turned his gun arm and immediately began firing at the beast. The bullets ripped into its torso, but the creature didn't seem to notice. It shrieked at them, and its fanged maw shuddered as if it might have been laughing. The head swept downward and smiled a dripping grin at Jaga.

Pulling Bwrynn away, Jaga pointed the gun upward beneath the monster's jaw. The shot exploded from the barrel and spilled black blood into Jaga's hand. The creature lurched back and screamed, shaking its head, and clawing at the wound. Jaga ducked beneath its gangly, extra arms and ran into the crowd, grateful to find Bwrynn supporting most of her own weight. Her steps were slow and uneven, but she was awake.

The howling creature pitched its head, pouring its oily blood across the ground as it searched for its quarry. It found only Kaelus, bleeding in the dirt. Its grin opened wide, revealing a striped tongue that was lapping at the teeth inside.

Kaelus fell backward and kicked at the ground, shuffling away from the beast. "Faedra!" he shouted. A moment later, the monster spun its head again, looking back into the swarming masses. It gave one last look to Kaelus then turned and rushed back into the fray.

Jaga was shouldering his way through the crowd, tripping over bodies and debris, and turning quick glances across his shoulder. The creatures were everywhere, each bigger and more hideous than the last. People were twisting and weaving between one another trying to escape, each time finding that their path was blocked by another horror. Keeping his head low and Bwrynn close, Jaga raced through the plaza, occasionally lifting his gun, but never pulling the trigger.

"Jaga," Bwrynn whimpered beside him. She was jogging in short, quick steps to match pace. "What's happening? Where are we?"

"Come, child, keep up," he answered with another tug of his arm.

Another beast sailed through the air and slammed into the ground in front of them. This one looked almost human, like a massive, bare-chested man with thick bones beneath wet skin. Its arms were too long though, and its legs too thick. The heavy brow and wide cheeks masked its eyes in shadow, but long, narrow teeth protruded outward from its mouth and wiggled in the light. Small holes opened in the flesh around its neck and a bouquet of slithering tentacles poured out, licking at its chest, and snapping at the air.

Jaga quickly fired at the hulking brute. It flinched and howled then swatted at the gun with unnatural force. Jaga screamed, feeling the bones in his hand snap like twigs and the flesh burn until it went limp and numb. The gun rattled to the ground. He retracted his wounded hand and pressed Bwrynn back with the other, placing himself between her and the monster.

It reared back, its tendrils thrashing around its face. Jaga tensed his muscles and bared his teeth. Then gunfire rippled through the air. Already leaning back, the monster stumbled and flailed, bursts of oil exploding from the bullet holes appearing in its chest.

"Jaga!" Bwrynn shouted behind them.

He spun to see where the shots had come from. There was a pickup truck racing into the plaza, kicking up dust in its wake. Thisa Rosewood was behind the wheel and the young Agent Ellis was leaning over the rim of the bed with a blazing rifle in his hands. He squeezed the trigger again and unleashed another barrage of fire into the screaming monster.

"Come on!" Ellis shouted between bursts as the truck slid to a stop.

Glittering streaks of bullet trails zipped between Bwrynn and Jaga, perforating the door of the truck with the hollow sound of a metallic drum. Jaga swiveled his head and saw Kaelus limping across the field. His broken leg was dragging behind him and his stern face was set firmly on the agents.

"Go!" Jaga ordered, shoving Bwrynn toward the truck. She hobbled to its side and took Ellis' hand as he pulled her aboard.

Holding up his shattered hand like a broken wing, Jaga dove down and grabbed his gun from the dirt.

"Jaga, come on!" Bwrynn yelled from the back of the truck, but he'd already aimed his pistol. His head tilted to the side, looking past the gun at Kaelus as he activated the weapon.

The man-like monster had regained its footing and lunged forward. Five of its serpentine tentacles stabbed through Jaga's back and burst from his chest. The pistol fell from Jaga's hand, though he couldn't understand why. He saw a flash of lightning overhead, but he couldn't hear the thunder. He couldn't hear anything in fact. There were no screams, no shots, no shouting, only the sound of his own blood rushing through his ears. Copper and bile filled his mouth, burning his tongue and uncontrollably spilling from his mouth. His legs buckled and he slumped forward, suspended in the air by the tendrils of the beast.

"JAGA!" Bwrynn's voice clawed up her throat and expelled from her lips in a hoarse screech. Beside her, Ellis unleashed another wave of gunfire. They sounded more sluggish than before, slower. The world went dim and ebbed to a crawl around her. She couldn't feel her body in the space around her. She couldn't feel the starched gown on her skin or the rust-pocked metal of the truck beneath her feet. She felt weightless, formless. Bwrynn recognized the sensation. She'd felt it once before, in the moments before she'd died.

A blade of lightning sliced the sky in two, cutting over the plaza and crackling at the tip of the southwest tower. The tower surged with blue light and the hum of electricity could be heard above even the chaos of the festival miles away. A cold wind swept through the dust and bodies of the fairground. It shoved Ellis back against the cab of the pickup and gathered up the dark curls of Bwrynn's hair.

A shallow whirlwind of blood and dirt spun up around the truck. Bwrynn drifted to her feet as if being lifted by the wind itself. Anyone near enough had their breath stuffed back into their lungs, leaving them gasping and squinting against the maelstrom.

Bwrynn glared with unrestrained ferocity at the creature in front of her, the monster that still held her master's body in the air. Against the gale force winds around them, even the tendrilled beast was guarding its face and stumbling back. It tried to growl and snap at the girl, but the winds stripped the sounds down to little more than a suffocating whimper.

The tentacles were pulled from Jaga's body, dropping it with a wet thud into a puddle of blood. The monster struggled to lash back at its latest victim, but it had lost control. Its feet kicked and scraped at the dirt as it was slowly lifted from the ground. The creature floundered and flapped its limbs in the air, snapping its teeth toward Bwrynn. It craned its head left and right, watching as its arms were stretched out wide. Its flailing movements were stretched out thin to violent shaking, and then a panicked shudder. The monster screamed one last time before its body was torn in half, split jaggedly down the middle in a spray of black mist and spilled organs.

Hovering in the place where the monster once hung was a glowing crystal, still dripping with its oily blood. Through the whipping locks of her wild hair, Bwrynn's eyes burned into the floating jewel. Her teeth ground together, and her lips stretched back, trembling with rage. She screamed and the crystal cracked and shattered into a thousand glittering pieces that streaked away and clattered to the distant ground.

In his raised bunker above the crowd, Daemon's eyes were growing steadily wider. He gawked at the fury of the whirlwind below. The winds were pounding at the walls and shaking the balcony. The bulletproof glass of the window was vibrating in front of him.

"Faedra," he stammered in as calm of a voice as he could muster. "Faedra, it's Bwrynn. Stop her."

Still, she remained silent. Her eyes were burning their deep green light and a single drop of blood trickled from her nose and down to match her ruby lips. Her mind was focused on the chessboard battle below.

The creature nearest to Bwrynn was the wooden giant with a black sphere in its writhing ribs. It abruptly spun and began stampeding toward the young girl inside her psychic tornado. Bwrynn's eyes flicked to the side and saw it coming. She plunged a fist in the direction of the giant then flared her fingers out wide. The black sphere in the monster's chest exploded, sending obsidian shrapnel tearing through its body in every direction.

At the whim of their controller, the remaining creatures in the plaza stopped what they were doing. Bodies hung, half-eaten in their mouths, children cowered in the shadows of their descending hooves. Then, all at once, the beasts turned and ran for the truck in the center of the battle. The dirt cyclone grew until all that could be seen inside was the shadow of Bwrynn and the flashing muzzle flare of Ellis' rifle.

Tents and pop-up sheds exploded in a row like a bursting string of lights. The debris from their walls shredded three more of the monsters, who dropped and slid through the gravel, breaking into several meaty pieces before they stopped. Others were simply thrown back by an invisible force. One crashed through the stage, tearing a splintered gash through its floor, and another punched into the side of a news van that buckled backwards from the blow.

The howling winds peaked at a deafening roar before dissipating to a haze in the air until all that remained was Bwrynn screaming in agony and rage. The whirlwind collapsed, leaving a spiral pattern in the ground around the truck and Bwrynn dropped heavily into the metal bed.

Ellis tried to catch her, bracing her fall with the crook of his arm. He looked once to her unconscious face, then turned back to the wave of monsters still closing in on them. He unleashed another burst from his rifle. With only one free hand to hold the weapon, its recoil rattled through his body and shook the gunfire into a wide arc. He spun his head to the front and shouted, "Thisa, go!"

The truck's tires spun dark trenches into the spiral pattern around them. It fishtailed in the loose gravel before finally catching traction and plowing ahead through the plaza. Thisa cranked at the steering wheel, dodging the wounded civilians, and clipping a beast in its long and outstretched knee. They cut through the length of the grounds and crashed through the mesh fence at the other side. The tires squawked as they dropped from the curb and snagged the pavement, and the truck sped away in a stream of lingering dust.

The beasts howled in a circle at the center of the festival beneath Daemon's watchful and twitching eye. Security officers resumed their gunfight against the creatures, who quickly went back to stalking the remaining people. Daemon turned his back on the scene and raised his comm to his frown. "Send in the Legacy. Let's wrap this up."

Chapter 25

In the shadows of Old Mallis, beneath the northern edge of Sector Six, a pair of tall, steepled doors groaned open, swinging as quickly as two half-tons of ivory can. The red haze of the underground world bled inside on beams of lingering dust. It mixed with the amber light inside, the glow of twenty lanterns strategically placed throughout a wide and cavernous room.

The far end of the room, opposite the doors, was raised up three steps to form a low stage. The space between was filled with long, polished wooden bench seats and broad aisles of pearled tiles. The windows that lined the side walls were boarded up haphazardly, leaving only a vague impression of their tall and narrow shapes. Above the center of the stage was a centerpiece window, enormous and round. It may have contained a patchwork image once, but all the glass had long since been destroyed. Now it was nothing more than a wide eye at the head of the building. Its only view was a dirt wall, the inside edge of a crater that had swallowed up the ancient city.

A sparse population peppered the room. They sat in small groups on the benches and the steps to the stage. They crossed the room from one side door to the next, venturing off to deeper halls in the old building. Most were dressed in street clothes; blue jeans, sweaters, and sneakers, but some were cloaked in Legacy robes. They wore them without thought or pride, without any real purpose other than to stave off the subterranean chill.

Thisa hurried through the open doors with Bwrynn hobbling in short steps beneath her arm. Ellis came in behind them and ushered shut the giant doors. Their entrance stirred up a mild commotion. The wayward citizens of the underground rose to their feet, some rushing down the aisle to meet them.

"Bring Doc," Thisa ordered to no one in particular. A youthful man at the back bobbed a rapid nod and slipped off to one of the darkened halls.

"That's Bwrynn Lucane," another man said as Thisa eased her onto the nearest bench. "What's wrong with her?"

Ellis approached with a snort. "A lot, I'd say."

The other man scowled at his snide response, sapping the color from Ellis' cheeks.

"But uh, I'm not really a doctor, so..." Ellis let his presence and his words fade off into the background.

Bwrynn turned a wilted look at the stranger who was eyeing her. "What is this? Where are we?"

"You're safe," Thisa answered in her soothing, maternal voice.

Her eyes explored the high ceiling and foreign walls. "I don't recognize... we're underground?"

"In Old Mallis, yes." Thisa gave a side-glance to the room. "Think of this as a safe house. Some of us have been coming here for years, stocking it with supplies. We've got a very good medical facility, and Doc is one of the best. You're going to be okay."

"Jaga," Bwrynn suddenly realized aloud. "Where is he?"

Thisa turned one look to Ellis, then to the small group that had accumulated around them. She'd expected the question and she'd answered others just like it more times than she cared to count. This one felt different, delicate, like a sculpture made of ash. "Just focus on regaining your strength."

The evasive response sent jolts into the others. They stifled their gasps and strained their composures to mask their shock. They may as well have screamed it; Jaga Demain was dead.

The thoughts and reactions plunged into Bwrynn's mind and cut out pieces of her heart. 'Dead.' 'Master Demain.' 'Jaga's gone.' 'They killed him.' Her brow tensed and creased, and tears began to pool in the darkness of her eyes. Her lips began to tremble as she shook her head and stared up at Thisa. "They killed him?"

Thisa's eyes softened, her lips seemed to kiss the air, and her own tears began to well up. "I'm so sorry, Bwrynn."

Bwrynn's soft face was twisted with growing despair. She looked all around her, searching for a familiar face but found no one. She was alone in a room full of strangers, dull eyes that didn't know her. Her breathing became audible and coughed upward inside her heaving chest. She wanted to say his name, to call out for him, but she was afraid of what the sound might do to her, or worse, it might make it real. With nothing to say and no one to say it to, Bwrynn fell forward into Thisa's lap. She clutched her fists inside the tangled curls of her own hair and tried to hide away her mind as the sobs crashed through her body.

# # #

Malehk had done everything that Akara had asked. He'd returned to their underground sanctuary. He'd reinforced the secondary doors and trimmed their power consumption down to its bare minimum. He'd hidden away all trace of their existence and tucked in the tsesh to sleep forever once more in the shadows. He worked for hours alongside the others, transforming a tangle of subway lines and sewer tunnels into an obfuscated fortress that none would ever find. Then he did what he'd always done. He snuck out. He topped off his flask of whiskey and slipped away while the king was distracted by subjects and duty.

The city was growing dark and cold again by the time he'd reached the surface. The battle was long since over. There was no sign of the creatures they'd seen below, only defeated people. Heads hung lower. Voices were quieter. The cars drove by slow and aimless. The neon lights and holograms that packed the sidewalks formed an oil painting of muddled colors on the still-damp streets, and every projected news feed repeated the same message in a hundred different ways.

The attack on the Election Festival was tragic. It had claimed the lives of thirty-seven people. Among them were mothers and children, elderly and first-time voters, councilmen and security. Similar attacks had happened in every other sector at the very same time. That meant it was coordinated, deliberate. From there it was a short walk to laying the blame on the tsesh.

The government was in ruins, hardly enough members remained to even hold a vote. Those who had survived were holed up in a secure room inside Pramoore Tower. Apparently, they were holding an emergency session, a Sector Convention to decide what to do with all their broken pieces. Malehk already knew what was about to happen. It'd been hinted at in every broadcast and muttered a bit more plainly by every passerby. The eight councils would grant the Legacy broader jurisdiction and, by association, Daemon Pramoore would have emergency power over the city. After all, when sector security had failed, it was the Legacy who swooped in to save the day.

The people on the street were keeping to themselves. It was a deliberate and active isolation. They'd gather in their familiar cliques and lob hinted accusations at anyone who wasn't them. Malehk could hear the trepidation in their voices, clumsy bricks of paranoia ripping through the thin parchment of their intellect. Once they had enough of them, enough building blocks from like-minded fools, they'd build a wall around themselves, dense enough to feel safe, tall enough to blot out reason. It was a rigid patriotism that had already begun stitching itself across a mourning city like scar tissue over a wound.

With every sideways and suspicious glance, Malehk's pace picked up. Around every corner was a Legacy patrol and the raised brow of suspicious men. Even the less-traveled streets were beginning to feel crowded and claustrophobic. After dodging another Runcourte, Malehk turned down a vacant back alley and sighed heavily against the welcome sound of his lonely footsteps. The tinted car crept past the alley's mouth. Malehk didn't look. He twisted off the cap of his flask and tipped back a mouthful of burning musk.

As he replaced the silver stopper and hissed a breath of whiskey fumes, his eyes remained upward. The buildings on either side of the alley stretched upwards fifty feet. Beyond them was nothing but fading gray and storm clouds. The rooftops would be as good a place as any for a lungful of air and a belly full of liquor. He shrugged to himself and made his way to the fire escape.

The thunder sounded louder from the roof, a naked and angry noise unfiltered by concrete tunnels and prattling people. Malehk liked it. It felt as though he could shout back if he'd wanted, have a proper argument with the storm. He could scream curses at the lightning and blow back against the wind. He could blame it for everything that had happened, the attack on the festival and the slaughter of all those people, the cowardly introversion of his friend and the death of his child. That's all anyone really wanted, someone else to blame, for their fear, for their suffering, for all the shambles of their lives. Malehk could have howled until his voice collapsed, but he didn't.

He dropped the heavy weight of his body and his grief on the humming edge of an electrical box and scraped the heels of his boots through the dust on the rooftop tiles. A cold wind carried the metallic taste of desert sand to his lips and the thunder rolled back to regroup on the horizon. He took another pull from his flask and puffed another breath, then allowed his mind to relax. His irises brightened with a purple glow and his silver scales emerged to take their place beneath his eyes.

The cityscape came to life with veins of golden fate. They were weaker than he'd ever seen them though, thin strands of nearly imperceptible light. The world was shutting itself down, closing itself off. Soon, he suspected, very soon it would have no fate at all. It was just as well.

A streak of lightning and a burst of thunder exploded overhead. It latched onto the southwest tower and twitched atop its peak like a frustrated hand trying to solve a puzzle box. Electricity fed into the spire and for a moment it surged with a mix of crackling light, blue and gold.

Malehk narrowed his eyes against the brilliant sight and, as it slowly began to fade, his curious mind wandered backward. He was reminded again of the beasts inside the tower and the gemstone hearts from which they were grown. He remembered the man in the hospital and the horror of watching Caul steal and imprison his soul. He remembered the screams as they faded away and how the whole room withered and died, even... the ferns.

His face went slack and turned toward the outskirt slums of Six, to the patch of shadow at the foot of the wall. "No," he uttered to himself. His mind moved swiftly to another night, the night that Marianne had died, to the wilted rose in her room. Amidst the chaos, between the bullet trails, the plaster dust, and the raging light of fate, had he seen Marianne's soul being pulled from her body? Had he seen a face made of smoke above her bed? The more he thought back on it, the more certain he became. No. He'd seen two.

His gaze snapped back to human, and he blinked hard against the dryness in the air. Then his eyes went wide and turned back to the southwest tower, the cradle of monsters and abducted souls. He muttered a mouthful of tsesh curses while bobbing his head and uncapping his flask. "He was there. That slimy, soul-sucking, son-of-a... He was there." Malehk poured a large mouthful of whiskey down his throat then bunched up his face and licked his teeth. "All right, you raspy bastard," he said, smacking his lips. He stuffed the flask into his pocket and retrieved the pistol from its holster. "Let's do this."

#

The storm was a thick, black ink over the city. Even the bursts of lightning inside its churning plumes seemed muffled and muted. They were dull throbs of light within the heavy canopy. In the southwest corner of Mallis Two, outside the bright lights of the city's core, the world was even darker, and in a barren patch of dirt at the base of the southwest tower, cooling in its shadow, it was darker still. There were no people, no cars, no holograms. It was still, black, and unnaturally quiet.

In the dark and in the silence, the smallest light and the faintest sound can be worlds unto themselves. They become a beacon that tells the deepest stories and guards the most sordid secrets. On that night, that beacon was a small wristband comm that was flickering blue in the dirt. It sputtered in the night with a single drop of blood forming a black spot on its bright screen. Its speaker was crackling over a woman's voice on the other end. '-report. Agents have been dispatched to your location. Maintain your position.'

No one would hear the order. The two men in the guardhouse were dead, each with a perfectly placed bullet hole between their eyes. The gate that they were protecting swung lazily and creaked on its hinges. Opposite the guardhouse and across the barren field, the black tower rose to meet the storm, snatching bolts of lightning from the clouds, drinking them in, and swelling with light for long, sluggish heartbeats at a time.

The tower was a monument and a tomb, a museum of souls that had been stolen by Caul Cerrone and reshaped into monsters. Malehk had ascended past dozens of the gurgling cylinders inside, each housing a different beast, each at varying stages of growth. Some were hulking creatures born of nightmares, others were half-formed bodies of tangled limbs and pointed teeth. Some of them almost looked human, sleeping toddlers with barely a hint of pointed ears or spined tails. All of them had names, forgotten titles that blinked across the quiet monitor of their tomb. Malehk couldn't help but read them as he climbed the stairs. 'Hughes', 'Owen', 'Woodward'.

He scanned them all with violet eyes until he found what he was looking for. A lonely cylinder ten stories up. Inside the tank, through the orange light and slow-rising bubbles, the small silhouette of an unremarkable shape floated in the gel.

Malehk didn't have to read the monitor to know what was growing inside, but part of him wanted to be wrong. Part of him wanted it to be impossible. He turned the glow of his eyes from the sleeping silhouette to the digital screen anyway and read the name: 'Price-Krosse'.

# # #

The black steel door at the tower's base burst open. It flipped wildly and smashed against the wall with a violent bang of metal on metal. From inside the orange-lit interior, Malehk rushed out to the chill of the nighttime air. His face was masked, and his eyes were blazing with purple light. He was clutching a glowing pistol in one hand and cradling a baby-sized bundle of gray blanket in the other. He scanned the scene, immediately seeing the flicker of the comm and the flash of red police lights that were filling up 81st Avenue and growing closer by the second.

The nearest route to Old Mallis was more than a mile away. The speeding cars were less than half that distance and more than twice as fast. Malehk's heart thumped rhythmically in his chest, each beat firing another dose of adrenaline into his limbs. He would have to be fast, not just his feet, but his mind and his trigger as well.

Fate had all but vanished from the city. Through his serpentine eyes, Malehk had watched it fade away and the world slip into darkness. But standing there in that field, he saw its golden light return. It swirled up in a blaze around him, flaring outward then arcing back to plunge into his heart. It radiated like fire from the bundle in his arm and danced across the ground at his feet. A single beam thrust forward, carving a strip of light down the road and between the approaching cars.

Malehk looked down at the gray blanket then back up to the glowing path. He hadn't planned for a fight. He had only six shots left in his gun. He rolled his shoulder to loosen the muscles, then nodded and whispered through his mask, "If you say so."

Tucking the bundle into his chest, he leaned forward then broke into a sprint toward the street. His breathing huffed inside the steel mask and his violet eyes pierced through the storm of soldiers ahead. The gap was closing fast and neither side was slowing down.

With his arm pumping at his side, Malehk primed his gun then snapped his hand up and fired a single shot. The bullet pierced the front tire of the lead car. The vehicle's weight shifted and sunk. The rubber tore away, and the steel rim jerked sideways, digging deep into the pavement with a burst of sparks. The patrol car twisted and was flung, trunk over hood into the air by its own momentum.

Malehk dropped to one knee and craned his head backwards as the tumbling car sailed over him. It smashed through the brick and glass of a building at his back. Using his own speed Malehk skipped back up to his feet and jumped to the hood of another car. The metal rippled loud beneath his feet as he ran up to the roof and jumped again. He cleared a third car and slid across the top of a fourth, finally tumbling back to the street.

As the patrol cars squealed and spun behind him, Malehk took a breath to shake the bite of pain from his hand and check on the bundle in his arms. It was safe inside the blanket. "Good job," he groaned.

His strained grunt came muffled through the vented mask as he pushed himself with a bloody hand back onto his feet. The sirens blared through the street and the tangle of squad cars were beginning to regroup. Malehk looked further down the road and saw another car. It was a Runcourte, the Legacy.

He snarled at his bad luck then dashed sideways between two buildings. The route was too narrow for a vehicle, but he heard car doors slam and the drumroll of boots giving chase as he rushed through the alley. Ahead of him, fate was shaking like a mesh of static across the opening to the next street. It was a warning. They were waiting for him.

Tucking the blanket in close, he jumped and planted a foot on a windowsill then repelled to the opposite wall. Each leap gained more height until he sprung from the alley a dozen feet in the air. There were ten officers crouched and waiting in a line around each corner. Malehk turned his pistol and fired, dropping two of them in a burst of red before he landed. Three bullets left.

The officers swarmed around him, joined by others now pouring from the alley. Malehk ducked their attacks and maneuvered the blanket away as best he could. He slammed back against a parked car then slid aside as a trooper's fist punched through the window where his head had been. Malehk fired another shot. It blasted up through the man's head. He dodged another attack and fired again, this time tearing through one of the officer's chests. One shot left.

Malehk slowed his breath. A heavy fist hammered against his jaw. The frame of his mask bit into the skin of his face. A steel baton slammed against the small of his back. Pain burned up his ribcage and he slid forward onto one knee. Another baton cracked against his shoulder, and he felt something break beneath the muscle.

The tsesh drank in each blow. The concussion and the pain poured through his body until his serpentine eyes were blazing with light. One more attack landed, a boot that cracked his mask in half and twisted his head to the side. Malehk used the momentum to spiral himself toward the car. He hopped up to the hood and launched himself into the air. Pouring the power and rage of their attacks into his last bullet. The weapon trembled in his grip. The blue lines along its barrel surged with light. He pulled the trigger.

The shot exploded from the gun with a hundred times the force of any other and punched a crater, three feet wide into the ground. Shards of pavement erupted into the air. The parked car rocked sideways from the blast and its remaining windows shattered inward. It was as if a bomb had detonated in the street and all the remaining cops were pitched backward from the explosion. They were flung in every direction, sailing over the car, and crashing into the building. Dead or disabled, all of them crumpled to the ground.

Malehk's shattered pistol rattled to the ground just before he landed, a mass of heaving blood and leather. He landed on his feet, but quickly dropped to his knees. He spit a mouthful of blood at the pavement and sucked in a painful breath. His eyes were dark again and the guidance of fate was gone. Instead, he looked to the bundle beneath his arm. After a long and aching groan, he dropped his weight against the banged-up car and bounced the precious heap of blankets on his knee.

"Don't try that at home," he said as if he were squeezing the words from his chest. "I am no role model." Malehk released a deep sigh and rolled his head along the metal frame of the car. The cold surface dulled the pain inside his skull to an aching throb. He glanced at the broken gun near his feet then back to the precious package in his arms. "C'mon," he finally managed, grunting as he struggled to stand. "They'll be back."

He never heard the gunshot, and he cursed himself a fool for not expecting it. The bullet punched through the back of Malehk's skull. It tore a path inside before bursting from his left eye. He stumbled forward, blinded by pain and darkness, spun around by shock and confusion. It took a moment for him to understand what had happened. It was a moment he didn't have.

He was reaching for his sword when another shot rang out. This one pierced his shoulder, shattering the joint and ripping away the tattered muscle. The force was enough to twist his body and attention around to see the Runcourte a half-block away. There was a young agent beside it, with a smoking gun in hand. The grinning brat had pointy blond hair and a jagged black tattoo across his eye. Another man was exiting the driver's side, an old and skinny man with thin silver hair glossing the top of his head. It was Valen Kirsch, Daemon Pramoore's right-hand man.

The world turned upside-down. Malehk didn't even realize he was falling until his tailbone cracked against the road. Blood poured from his shattered face and bubbled from his lips. He was spitting his breath and sucking in fresh air through his nose. It smelled like smoke and metal. He tried forming words with his mouth, desperate words, angry words, but they were all drowned out by blood and broken bone.

An irritated growl rolled out instead. He kicked as best he could at the road and shoved himself and the bundle to the front of the car, putting it between him and his attackers. He laid the wad of blanket as gently as he could on the road and managed to cough out a word. "Ahh... shen." He looked around the scene, hoping to find some route to salvation. There was nothing, just blood and empty shadows. Malehk hissed through his nostrils and fumbled his good hand through the depths of his pocket, finally touching the smooth surface of his flask.

"Are you still alive?" Valen called out. He was getting closer. His voice echoed loud and dominant through the hollow street.

Malehk coughed and hacked more tissue onto the road and twisted the cap from his flask. "Never better," he grunted back. His voice sounded strange and foreign inside his broken skull. It was low, airy, and full of rocks. "Your guy's a lousy shot." He tipped back a large gulp, then another, spitting out the second in a crimson mix of whiskey and blood.

"You have something that doesn't belong to you," Valen continued. He was at the back end of the car.

A hoarse chuckle ripped through Malehk's chest like sandpaper. "I didn't see your name on it."

"Here you are." Valen's voice was clear and close.

Malehk looked up to see the slender, well-dressed man looming over him.

Valen tugged his pant legs up and crouched at Malehk's feet. "I'm glad that you survived."

"Your concern is very touching."

"I wouldn't want this to be over too quickly." Valen reached out with his thin and gnarled fingers and gripped Malehk's knee.

Black energy poured out from the old man's hand and burrowed like a thousand worms into Malehk's flesh. A wet scream howled from his lips as the muscles in his legs withered and dissolved. The pain tugged at his spine and squeezed breath and blood from his lungs. When it finally ended, he was left puffing angry air through his teeth.

"Tell me," Valen continued, "why did you come up here? You had to know that this would happen."

Malehk hummed to mask the pain that was crawling up his body. When he caught his breath enough to speak, he said, "I had a promise to keep."

Valen tilted his head and narrowed his eyes. "That was probably a mistake."

The tsesh grinned wide and laughed as best he could. "Yeah," he said with a nod, "and that's not even my worst idea tonight." Then his face went calm. Silver scales prickled to life beneath his one good eye, and he turned to stare the old man down. His iris flashed with purple light and sliced back into its serpentine form.

Realizing what was about to happen, Valen toppled backwards, his lanky arms scrambling for the pistol tucked beneath his expensive suit. The snake eye staring back at him gleamed with burning fury until it filled Malehk's body. His skin became translucent, and his veins glimmered a deep magenta against the darkness of the night.

By the time Valen drew his gun it was too late. Malehk purged his power. The energy tore outward from his body in a violent and sweeping eruption. The initial blast launched the parked car into the air. It smashed through the distant Runcourte, sending both vehicles tumbling through the street in pieces. Valen was consumed immediately, his eyes still gaping as he was swallowed up in a blast of purple flame. The shockwave pulverized the old man and reduced his broken pieces to ash. He died more quickly than his victims ever had.

The explosion crashed through walls, toppling buildings in a hailstorm of brick and ragged steel. The ground split open, rending apartments wide open and plunging them into the depths beneath the world. The jagged gash ripped through the street. It spread and split the dirt field beneath the southwest tower and slammed into its black base. Lightning struck its peak and chased the tower downward as it cracked and fell. It's buckling metal howled out to the night. Girders twisted out of shape and the stone foundation burst into orange light and black clouds that spat heavy chunks into the streets.

Another whip of lightning raked across the top of the wall where the tower once stood. The surge bowed upward in a line of electric spikes that crackled and grinned along the rim of the city. Black smoke mushroomed into the air and spread, blotting out every neon glimmer for blocks.

Every building around them was razed into ash and debris, leaving behind ruptured walls and naked framework. Car alarms began ringing out as the echoing blast began to fade. People were screaming and calling out for help and sirens were howling in from the distance. Smaller explosions burst from inside the collapsing remains as gas lines were shredded and electrical cables were torn apart. A ring of purple-tinted smoke billowed outward from the blast, leaving only a bare patch of scorched concrete in the epicenter of destruction, with Malehk's twisted and broken body lying in the middle beside a gray, bundled up blanket.

CHAPTER 26

Akara watched the news feed with cold and amber eyes, sitting in the dark room that was once his father's throne. He studied Daemon's false humility in front of the cameras and the ravenous reporters who ate it up as if they were starving. He'd practiced and perfected his transitions from somber empathy and iron resolve then back again. He spoke with closed-fist gestures and spoke of hard work and determination. He warned the city of the serpentine terrorists and their army of monsters that lurked beneath the city.

It was all very moving and believable for those who knew no better. Every other line of the speech was spoken over dramatic, panning shots of the city in ruins. Construction vehicles, each marked by Pramoore's corporate logo, were clearing away the rubble that was once the southwest tower. Thick steel plates had been bolted across the hole in the wall, and the entire operation was being overseen by uniformed Legacy agents armed with heavy rifles. Huddled families, each painted in soot and tattered clothes were being wrapped in blankets and ushered into vans by masked officers. Emergency vehicles were treating the wounded and putting out fires.

As Daemon continued to speak, the words beaded up and rolled across Akara's hardened thoughts. They were noted and filed away in the shadowy back of his mind, left to dwell beside countless memories that wouldn't be missed should he forget them. They were lies to lead lost souls. Akara wasn't lost. He was tsesh. His path had been laid out for him before he was even born. He was a king.

"Lord Akara," Kade's deep voice drew his attention across the room to the open door. Dim light was creeping inside from the dank tunnel running past outside. They had relit some of their lights and restored a bit of power. Not enough to draw attention or signal false hope, but enough to filter air, preserve food, and navigate the labyrinth of their new kingdom.

"Yes, Kade."

"There's someone here to see you."

No sooner had the face appeared in the door than Akara jerked his gun from its holster. It wound up with light as he leveled it on her. It was Thisa Rosewood, Master Agent of the Legacy. She flinched back, half outside the door and half tucked against Kade's large chest.

"Akara, wait!" Kade shouted with an outstretched hand.

"You brought a Legacy agent to our door?"

"Ex-Legacy agent," Thisa corrected with a meek finger.

"I don't recognize the difference."

Kade took a slow and cautious step into the room, making sure to keep himself between Thisa and the gun. "You're going to want to hear her out," he said, gesturing for the king to lower his gun.

Akara studied his expression, keeping the weapon trained on the door while he considered the words. Kade was a looming shadow in the dark room, backlit not only by the soft light of the halls, but by a swirl of fate as well. Akara switched off the gun and lowered it to the desk. He tilted his head to the side, seeing only a shoulder and half of a face peering around the corner. "Enter."

Thisa hesitated long enough for Kade to wave her in. As she crossed the threshold, Akara switched on the lamp at his desk to get a better view. She was old, but younger than he'd expected. Her hair was a mess of brown curls in desperate need of a shower, and her eyes deep chocolate, wise and kind. As with all Master Agents, Akara had heard her name before, but she wasn't dressed as an agent. She was wearing a tan tunic with an olive skirt swishing beneath it. She wasn't armed. Instead, she was cradling a gray blanket, wrapped up in a bundle in her arms.

"Lord Akara is it?" she asked, more curious of the title than the name.

"Why are you here?" he asked curtly. "How did you find this place?"

"Your friend, Malehk," she answered in her deceptively soft tone.

Akara's fingertips slid across the lip of his desk and waited near the hilt of his gun. "Your information is old, and that's a lie," he said. "Malehk Knight is dead."

"He's not," she responded quickly with a defensive hand toward the gun. "He's alive." When the tsesh made no move for the weapon, she repeated more calmly. "Malehk is alive."

Akara was a statue with fierce, topaz eyes. A foolish piece of him wanted to believe her, and he resisted the urge to look back at the devastation playing out across the news feed on his desk.

"He survived his purge," Thisa continued. "We managed to find him before the Legacy. We brought him back to our compound."

"I need to see him." Akara's statement was locked somewhere between a concession and a command.

"You can't," she said as if he should have already known it. "Not yet. He barely survived the attack. He died three times on the table while we were operating on him."

"Then you have yet to answer my question, Ms. Rosewood, and you're running short on time." He openly rested his hand on the gun and locked eyes with her. "Why are you here?"

"Yes, of course." Thisa offered a subtle nod and walked in slow steps toward the king. "When we found him, Malehk was holding this." She shrugged up the bundled blanket. "He said that it's something you've been searching for for a long time."

Akara's black scales hunched up beneath his narrowed eyes. "Searching? What is it?"

She smiled and presented him with the package, pulling back a corner to reveal the baby inside. She was pale, and her fists were clenched into tight balls. Her eyes were squeezed shut over patches of tiny black scales. The child opened its eyes and looked up to the king through serpentine slits that shone with the deep and familiar blue of sapphires.

Thisa looked to the silent king and answered. "Hope."